MALONE'S PRIDE

LAYLAH ROBERTS

LET'S KEEP IN TOUCH!

Don't miss a new release by signing up to my newsletter. You'll get sneak peeks, deleted scenes, and giveaways: https://landing.-mailerlite.com/webforms/landing/p7l6go

You can also join my Facebook readers' group here:
https://www.facebook.com/groups/386830425069911/

BOOKS BY LAYLAH ROBERTS

Doms of Decadence

Just for You, Sir

Forever Yours, Sir

For the Love of Sir

Sinfully Yours, Sir

Make me, Sir

A Taste of Sir

To Save Sir

Sir's Redemption

Reveal Me, Sir

Montana Daddies

Daddy Bear

Daddy's Little Darling

Daddy's Naughty Darling Novella

Daddy's Sweet Girl

Daddy's Lost Love

A Montana Daddies Christmas

Daring Daddy

Warrior Daddy

Daddy's Angel

Heal Me, Daddy

Daddy in Cowboy Boots

Haven, Texas Series

Lila's Loves

Laken's Surrender

Saving Savannah

Molly's Man

Saxon's Soul

Mastered by Malone

How West was Won

Cole's Mistake

Jardin's Gamble

Romanced by the Malones

Twice the Malone

Mending a Malone

Malone's Heart

Malone's Pride

New Orleans Malones

Damaged Princess

Vengeful Commander

Wicked Prince

Men of Orion

Worlds Apart

Cavan Gang

Rectify

Redemption

Redemption Valley

Audra's Awakening

Old-Fashioned Series

An Old-Fashioned Man

Two Old-Fashioned Men

Her Old-Fashioned Husband

Her Old-Fashioned Boss

His Old-Fashioned Love

An Old-Fashioned Christmas

Bad Boys of Wildeside

Wilde

Sinclair

Luke

Rawhide Ranch Holiday

A Cozy Little Christmas

A Little Easter Escapade

Standalones

Their Christmas Baby

Haley Chronicles

Ally and Jake

TRIGGER WARNING

This book contains the following things that might be triggering for some people. Physical, sexual, and emotional abuse of the heroine in the past.

This book also contains spanking and BDSM.

PROLOGUE

Blood poured down his arm.

Hannah's heart skipped as panic held her frozen.

Shit. Shit. Shit.

He was bleeding.

Raid was standing there, bleeding. Right in front of her.

"Hannah? Hey, Hannah! You okay?"

She stared up into his hazel-green eyes. "Sure, I'm all right. A bit tired today, but good. I . . . oh shit! You're bleeding!"

"Yeah, darlin', sliced myself while fixing a darn fence. You think the Doc could see me for a minute?"

"See you for a minute? You're bleeding!"

Way to state the obvious, Hannah.

He had a shirt pressed to his arm. Not his shirt. Which was too bad, really.

She wouldn't mind seeing his bare chest.

She bet his bare chest would be mighty fine.

"Hey, can one of the doc's see you?"

Glancing over, she saw Tanner, Raid's younger brother, walk in. He was in the process of pulling on a T-shirt.

And wow . . . he might not be built as big as Raid, but his chest was definitely very nice.

"Hannah, yo, darlin'? You mind looking at me?" Raid sounded annoyed for some strange reason as he ran his hand through the air in front of her face.

Maybe he's annoyed because he's bleeding and you're standing there like an idiot ogling his brother.

"Oh my God! You're bleeding!"

"What's wrong with Hannah?" Tanner asked. "She's gone all pale and looks like she's gonna puke. Shit, she's not scared of the blood, is she?"

"I'm not scared of blood," she replied, offended.

"That's good, honey, because I'd have to tell you that you're in the wrong job if you are," Tanner replied. "Now, you think you can get one of the docs to see my idiot brother? I told him I'd take him to the emergency room, but he insisted on coming here."

Crap! She needed to get a doctor out here now!

"I've got to get a doctor!" She stood and turned to run off, only she somehow tripped over the foot of her chair, falling onto her hands and knees with a thump.

Ouch. Shit. That hurt.

But what hurt more was the blow to her pride. She'd just fallen over . . . right in front of Tanner and Raid Malone.

Raid Malone.

The man she'd had a crush on for years yet had never had the courage to do anything about. The guy that featured in her dirtiest dreams.

That Raid Malone.

"Hannah!" he called out.

Tears filled her eyes. Could this get any more humiliating? It was too much.

"Are you all right? Hannah?"

She glanced up to see he'd rounded the counter.

"You're not supposed to be back here."

"You okay, darlin'?"

Shit. She loved it when he called her darlin'. She didn't know why. It wasn't special. He called lots of people that.

You don't mean anything to him, Hannah. Remember that.

"Hannah?"

"I'm fine. Guess I'm just falling for you."

Shoot. Why'd she say that? Because this was what they did. They flirted. For Raid, it was a fun game.

For Hannah, it was like a form of torture.

Raid smiled wickedly. "Well, you're only human, darlin', so don't beat yourself up. It's hard to resist this much handsome."

Right. Good. She had herself under control now.

"I'll just go get the doctor." She started crawling along the floor.

"Hannah!" he barked. "You want to get off the fucking floor first?"

Why did he sound so irritated? She had no idea what she'd done.

Was he mad at her? It wasn't her fault she was super clumsy.

She was only ever clumsy around him. For some reason, her brain and her body would disconnect from one another and she'd end up either running away to avoid him, or doing something stupid like what she'd done right now.

"Hannah," Raid said in a low, commanding voice. Whoa. That was a tone she'd never heard from him before. He sounded so dominant.

Now she knew she was dreaming. That was another reason they'd never work. Even if she could get past tripping up over her own feet and actually manage to have a normal conversation with him, and even if he genuinely liked her in return, there was still the issue of her being a submissive.

And Raid wasn't a Dom.

His brother, Alec, was. In fact, a couple of the Malone brothers might also be. But as far as she was aware, Raid wasn't.

And Hannah wasn't sure that she could be with someone who wasn't a Dom.

Crap. She was still on her knees.

Get up.

"Is everything all right out here?" a feminine voice asked.

She closed her eyes. Great, now Jenna, her close friend and boss, was here to witness her humiliation. Along with everyone else in the waiting room.

"Hannah? What's wrong? Did you fall? Oh, Raid. What did you do?" Jenna asked. She was a petite, curvy brunette. She and her husband, Curt, had moved to Haven a few years ago. Both of them were busy between Curt's security company, Jenna's job, and the two children they'd adopted.

Rats!

"I just cut myself. Hannah fell. She might need you to check her over. Hannah, can you get up?"

A large hand appeared in front of her.

A big, tanned hand with dried blood on it.

"Fuck." The hand disappeared. "Tanner."

Tanner moved in front of her, and grabbing her under the arms, he lifted her onto her feet.

Did Raid not want to touch her? Was that why he pulled away?

Or it could be because he's bleeding to death.

"You're bleeding," she said, staring up at him.

Raid studied her in confusion. "Did you hit your head this morning, Hannah? Doc, can you check her for a concussion? And while you're back there, make sure she didn't hurt herself when she fell."

Was he serious?

"Hannah?" Jenna asked quietly. "Are you all right? Did you hurt yourself badly?"

She shook her head, at a loss for words. "I'm fine. I'm good. Really. You need to take Raid back. He's *bleeding.*" She wasn't sure why it was hitting her so hard.

Probably because it was Raid. And she was always an idiot when Raid was around.

"Right. Raid, you come back with me. We'll clean you up and see what we're dealing with. Hannah, why don't you take a moment? Get a drink of water. Rest."

She didn't need to rest. What she needed to do was die of embarrassment.

"I think you should see to Hannah first," Raid insisted. "She's not acting right."

Lord. What was he doing? He'd never shown this much concern for her health before. There was no reason for her to be seen by Jenna. She was fine.

And the longer they stood here, talking about her, the more embarrassed she grew.

Tanner sent her a strange look that she couldn't decipher.

"All I did was trip and fall. I haven't hurt my head. I just . . . I need to go to the bathroom. Excuse me." She rushed off, not looking at any of them, before hiding in the break room's bathroom.

Looking in the mirror, she grimaced at herself.

"You're a giant dork, Hannah. The dorkiest of the dorks." What was she thinking? Why did she do that? She took a deep breath and then slowly let it out. "You've got to learn to be cool."

It was all Raid's fault. He brought out this dorkiness in her. She'd worked as a medical receptionist for years and was always calm in a crisis.

Always.

But the sight of Raid bleeding had muddled her brain.

Unfortunately, she had to get back out there. "Okay, Hannah, he's just a man. Not a god. He has his flaws like everyone else. Just think about him getting pimples on his butt and having smelly feet."

Pimples on his butt.

Smelly feet.

Got it.

Taking a fortifying breath, she walked out the door and came to a sudden stop as she saw Tanner waiting in the break room. He was sitting on a chair, reading a gossip magazine.

"Um, what are you doing back here?" she asked.

He glanced up. "Oh, hey, Hannah. The big idiot insisted that I come check you're all right. Something about brain damage, bruised knees . . . blah, blah, I stopped listening after he said that." He stood.

Lord, he was beautiful.

All the Malone men were in their own way. Some of them were downright intimidating. Others were crazy–like Raid and Tanner. They ran wild through the entire county. She didn't think there was a bar or nightclub in a hundred-mile radius that didn't batten down the hatches when one of them walked in.

They weren't the settling-down types.

Although all the rest of their brothers had found their significant others. Even grumpy West had sweet Flick, who was about to pop out their first baby.

So perhaps there was hope for Raid and Tanner and the masses of women who likely had crushes on them.

But not for her. They weren't for her.

She was too dull. Too ordinary.

Raid needed someone with as much life and energy as he had. Not the forgettable medical receptionist. The only thing interesting about her was that she was a sub. But so was half the population of Haven.

And that wasn't something that would likely attract Raid.

"I'm fine. He shouldn't have wasted your time by sending you to check on me."

Tanner ran his gaze over her. "Yeah, you look fine to me too, honey. But it wasn't a waste of my time. Any time I can spend with you over that big, ugly idiot is not a waste. Not only do you smell better, but you sure are prettier."

"Good Lord, you are such a flirt." She rolled her eyes at him. "Do women really fall for cheesy lines like that?"

He put a hand on his chest and pretended to stumble back. "You wound me."

She gave him a skeptical look. Yeah, right. She wasn't buying that for a second. "You'll survive. It's not fatal."

He grinned. "That your expert opinion?"

"Yep."

"Come on, I'll walk you back out. His Lord and Master has me under strict instructions to 'keep an eye on you'."

"You should be with him. He's the one who is actually injured."

The only thing she was suffering from was acute embarrassment.

"Eh, I spend way too much time with him as it is. Wasn't lying when I said you smell better."

"Thanks," she said dryly. "Glad I smell better than a man who works outside with animals all day."

Tanner slipped an arm around her neck and led her back to reception.

"Tell me this, honey. How come you can give me as good as you get and put me in my place, but the second you spot my brother, you can't remember how to walk?"

Shit.

She really didn't know how to answer him. Because she

couldn't tell him the truth. That she became a bumbling idiot because she liked his brother.

Nope. Not happening.

"I don't know what you're talking about. Excuse me, I need to get to work."

Internally, she groaned. Like that hadn't made it obvious she had something to hide.

Tanner shot her a knowing look but stepped away. "Sure thing, darlin'. You get back to work. I'll just wait over here."

She did her best to ignore him as other patients came in and she took a few phone calls.

Then she heard his voice.

She wasn't going to look. She was not. But she couldn't help but glance up, and that's when she saw Tanner watching her closely.

Shoot. Now, if she didn't look at Raid, it would be obvious that she was purposefully not looking.

This was so ridiculous.

But when she turned, she really wished she hadn't. Because Simone, a gorgeous tall woman with dark blonde hair, was pressing against him, smiling.

Simone had been working as the clinic's nurse for the last month. Hannah didn't dislike the other woman, but she was pretty sure they weren't going to become best buds. Simone lived in Freestown and traveled to Haven each day. Hannah knew that Doc Harper and Jenna would have preferred to hire someone local, but there hadn't been anyone qualified.

That left them with Simone. Who flirted with anyone with a dick under the age of sixty.

So Hannah really shouldn't get jealous that she was flirting with Raid. Or that he was staring down at her with a grin on his face.

Nope. Not. Jealous.

"Raid, brother, you ready or what?" Tanner asked, sounding surprisingly grouchy.

She glanced over at him in surprise.

"Yeah, I'm coming." Raid's gaze turned to Hannah.

She tried her best to act normal. Well, what she thought was normal. She also wasn't going to risk getting out of this chair. No way did she want a repeat of earlier.

Concern filled Raid's face. "Hannah, are you all right?"

"What is it? Did something happen?" Simone asked, eyes wide.

Hannah narrowed her gaze. Did she really think anyone was buying that fake concern?

Or maybe you're just being a bit sensitive because you don't like the way she's pressed up against Raid.

"She fell over," Raid explained, taking a step toward her.

"Oh, she's just clumsy." Simone ran her hand through the air dismissively.

What? She was not! Well, only when Raid was around.

"Yeah, I've noticed that." Raid smiled at her.

But Hannah was too embarrassed to smile back.

"She seems fine now." Simone sent her a strange look. "Aren't you, Hannah?"

"Yep. All good. So, did Jenna patch you up?"

Raid gave her a thorough look, but then a smile crossed his face. "Yep. She said I'm in prime condition." He flexed his good arm.

Hannah pretended to feel faint, waving her hand in front of her face. "Oh my. I feel faint."

"Because of my greatness?"

"Because your ego is stealing all the air in the room."

He barked out a laugh, and she smiled, feeling something inside her ease at the sound. Then Simone moved closer to him.

"Raid, you should really go home and rest. Hannah can get you all sorted. Then I'm sure she has work to do."

Wow. Those were some sharp daggers she was sending Hannah's way.

"Sure, don't want to hold Hannah up. You got everything you need, darlin'?" he asked.

"Considering you're in here so often, I basically have your details memorized," she said dryly. "I'm beginning to think you're hurting yourself on purpose just so you get to come see me."

Lord, she wished.

But Raid just burst into laughter.

Ouch. That hurt.

"Right, darlin'. Hurting myself just to see you. That would be a kind of stalker-level obsession, wouldn't it?"

That's what she wanted.

Stalker-level obsession.

Too bad no one was ever going to be into her that much. Let alone gorgeous, sexy Raid Malone.

"Do you need a follow-up appointment?" she asked stiffly.

He gave her a surprised look. Crap. Had she revealed too much?

"Just to get the stitches out, darlin'," he replied, watching her closely.

Shit. Shit.

She could never let him see how much she wanted him.

"That appointment will be with me," Simone said. "I'll take good care of you, Raid."

Gag.

But Raid just stared down at the other woman with a smile. "I'm sure you will, darlin'."

Stab. Stab. Stab.

See? She wasn't special at all.

"We'll send you a text reminder," she said as she made the appointment.

"Bye, Raid. See you Thursday night," Simone said in a sultry voice.

Hannah's stomach tightened into a knot. This was nuts. She needed to get over this stupid crush. He was out of her league. Anyway, he saw her as a friend or a sister.

She was positive she did not feature in his dirty dreams.

Raid Malone was not for her.

"She likes you, you know."

Raid frowned as he glanced over at Tanner. Fuck, Alec was going to be pissed about the twelve stitches in his arm. He was supposed to rest it for two weeks. At least he'd already planned on taking some time off to go to New Orleans to see his cousins. So Alec couldn't get that angry about him being off work. Not that he'd actually be angry about his inability to work. No, any anger would be over the fact that he'd gotten hurt.

Alec had BBS.

Big Brother Syndrome.

He tried to smother them all in his protection, particularly Raid and Tanner, since they were the youngest. Even when their father had been around, he'd been nothing to write home about. Alec was the one who'd always protected and taken care of them. He and West.

"Who? Simone? Yeah, man, she wasn't exactly hiding her interest."

She was pretty. And had made it clear she was interested. But for some reason, he wasn't really attracted to her. And he wasn't sure why.

Weird.

"I wasn't talking about Simone," Tanner said as they drove out of Haven.

"Jenna? Shit, Curt will have a fucking heart attack," he said, talking about Jenna's husband.

"Not Jenna, dipshit. Hannah."

Raid stilled. *Hannah?*

He played their interaction over in his mind. She was interested in him? Nah, that couldn't be right. He'd known her for years and never once gotten that vibe from her.

Sure, they flirted a bit. But that was just for fun. She usually sassed him about his giant ego while he tried to stop her from hurting herself as she tripped up.

Hannah was cute and clumsy.

Adorable.

"That's ridiculous. I've known Hannah for ages. We all have. She's never once indicated that she likes me."

"Fuck, you're blind."

"You're seeing shit that isn't there."

"Look, if you're not into her, that's fine. But maybe you should be a bit more aware of her feelings when you're making dates with another woman right in front of her."

He stared at his brother in shock. Why did he sound so pissed off?

"What the fuck are you talking about? Hannah doesn't have feelings for me. And I wasn't making a date with another woman in front of her."

"Um, Simone?"

"Oh, that? She just said she was going to be at Dirty Delights Thursday night and hoped to see me there. It wasn't a date."

"That wasn't what it sounded like," Tanner told him. "And you don't think it strange she made it sound like a date in front of Hannah?"

"What? Are you saying she was trying to hurt Hannah?" His protective instincts stirred.

No one hurt Hannah.

No one.

Fuck. Was he into her? He hadn't thought of her like that . . . had he?

Although she was pretty. And sweet. And funny.

Plus, she didn't take herself or him too seriously.

"You're seeing shit that's not there."

"When Simone said that she'd see you Thursday, Hannah looked like she might cry. She works in a doctor's office, yet she got so flustered by seeing you bleeding that she tripped over her own feet."

He hadn't liked that. She could have hurt herself.

"She's always tripping up around me." Sometimes, he swore that she was actually trying to run away from him.

Which was silly, right?

"Yeah, she doesn't do that around anyone else," Tanner told him.

"What? Really?"

"Really," Tanner said.

Raid swallowed heavily, thinking about all of their interactions. Did she like him? Was she clumsy around him because she was nervous?

"The flirting is just for fun."

"Maybe for you," Tanner pointed out.

"Fuck. Why didn't you tell me?"

"I'd been planning to, but I hoped you might pull your head out of your ass and notice. And maybe I was hoping you might feel the same."

For Hannah?

He tried to think about it . . . he cared about her. Worried about her. There were more than a few times that he'd thought about her.

Fuck.

Then he thought about not being around her . . .

"I like her. I just hadn't thought about her like that."

"Which is fine, man. You don't have to want her back. Maybe it's best that you don't. Hannah's the sweet girl next door, and you and me . . . well, we don't mix well with sweet. Right?"

"Are you thinking about Lilac? Dude, she wasn't the girl for you."

Tanner had fallen hard for a girl he'd met in Hopesville when they'd been there at a rodeo one night. They'd spent a week together before she'd just disappeared. Without a word. Raid hadn't told any of his other brothers about her. Sometimes, they could be interfering bastards.

Tanner just grunted, clearly not agreeing.

Fuck.

"I didn't realize you were still hung up on her."

"I'm not. And we're not talking about me. We're talking about Hannah. You just see her as a friend, which is fine. But maybe just be aware that it hurts her if you're flirting with someone around her."

He really didn't like the idea of hurting Hannah.

At. All.

"Your reaction to her falling over was interesting, though."

"What do you mean? She could have hurt herself."

Tanner shot him a look. "She tripped. You were bleeding. You don't think your reaction to her falling over was a bit of an overreaction?"

Had he overreacted? "I would have reacted that way if any of our girls had hurt themselves."

"Hannah's not one of us."

Immediately, he wanted to reject that. Which made him think ... fuck.

"Maybe I'm attracted to Hannah."

What the hell?

She was beautiful with a gorgeous smile.

"Since when did you become Hannah's protector, anyway?" Raid asked.

"She doesn't have anyone looking out for her. Except Jake."

Raid snorted at the mention of the sheriff. He wasn't their biggest fan. And he didn't like that she only had Jake looking out for her.

And Tanner, apparently.

"I've known Hannah a long time," Tanner said. "She's sweet and kind, and she doesn't deserve to have her heart hurt."

"Not gonna hurt her." Raid really didn't want to do that. Maybe he should ask her out.

Fuck. He couldn't.

"I need to think about this."

"You do that," Tanner replied.

"Now isn't the time to ask her out, anyway. I'm leaving for New Orleans next week. Regent has been practically begging me to come. It's getting embarrassing. For him, obviously."

"Obviously," Tanner agreed.

Yeah. He needed some time to think about this.

"Spill."

"Spill what?" Hannah asked, picking up her glass of sparkling wine to take a sip. Mostly so she could avoid looking at her friends.

But that didn't mean they would let her get away with avoiding them.

"Tell us what happened to put that kicked-dog look on your face," Melody added to her original demand to spill.

Her other friends, Josie and Carlie, nodded in agreement.

She sighed. There was no way they'd let her get away with not answering.

"Raid came in today."

"Ahh." They all said it together, and she wrinkled her nose at them.

"What happened?" Josie asked. She'd dyed her hair purple this week and it looked fabulous.

"Did you stumble over your words? Freeze up? Run the other way?" Carlie asked, tucking her blonde hair behind her ear. They were valid questions since they were all things she'd done in the past when faced with the gorgeousness that was Raid Malone.

"I fell over."

They all sucked in a breath. They understood the enormity of that situation.

"Oh, honey," Josie said with empathy.

"It was so embarrassing," she said.

"How did he react?" Melody demanded. "He wasn't mean to you, was he?"

Lord, she could just imagine how Melody would react if she told her that Raid had been cruel to her. Melody was loyal and protective, and she wasn't afraid of anyone. She'd wade in to protect her friends against anyone. Then Brye, her boyfriend, would wade in after her.

Followed by all of them. So she was glad she could tell her the truth.

"No, of course not. He acted really concerned about me. Even though he was the one bleeding, he wanted Jenna to check me over first."

"Oh, that's so sweet." Josie smiled dreamily. "See? Maybe he does like you."

Hannah shook her head. "He doesn't. He would be that way with any of you if you hurt yourself."

"How do you know that?" Melody asked.

"Because that's just the way he is," she said lamely. "And he's never once shown he's interested in me."

He did send Tanner to check on you.

But again, he'd likely do that for anyone.

"And when he came back out the front after being stitched up, Simone was all over him. And she said that she'd see him Thursday night."

They all gave her devastated looks.

"Oh, honey, I'm so sorry," Josie told her, taking her hand.

Shoot. She didn't want anyone to feel sorry for her. She just wanted them to stop trying to keep this dream alive.

There was nothing between her and Raid, and there never would be.

"That doesn't mean that something couldn't happen between you two," Carlie said. "Don't give up hope."

She shook her head. "I want to find that someone special. I want to get married. To have children. I just . . . that's all I want. To have someone look at me the way Brye looks at you, Mel." She glanced over at Brye, who was sitting at the bar, pretending that he wasn't keeping an eye on them.

"He's so overprotective," Melody muttered. Her ponytail flicked back and forth as she shook her head. "Won't even let me go for a drink with the girls without coming to watch over me."

"And you love it," she said. Because they all knew she secretly did.

Melody huffed out a breath but didn't deny it.

"And that's what I want," Hannah said. "That's why I love this community. I love how its people take care of each other. But especially how the men watch out for the women and children. I want to feel protected, safe, loved."

"And you don't think Raid will ever give you that?" Carlie asked.

"Raid is gorgeous, wild, fun, crazy, kind, and completely out of my league."

"Do you want a spanking?" Melody asked.

"Uhh . . ." Was she really asking her that? Because she kind of did. Just not from Melody. "No."

"Then stop saying stupid shit like that," Melody told her. "You're fucking unbelievably gorgeous. And smart. And the kindest person I know. Whenever one of us needs something, you're the first person to offer to help. And I'm so thankful that you're in my life."

"Wow. That's really nice."

"Any man would be lucky to have you, Hannah," Josie added.

"Thanks, guys." She knew they meant every word. But they were also her best friends and kind of biased. "I just . . . I don't think he's 'the one', you know?"

They all gave her looks filled with scepticism.

"I've been thinking that I do need to date, though," she added quickly, hoping to distract them.

"Yeah?" Melody asked.

"Yeah, I was thinking about joining that BDSM dating website that Josie's cousin used."

Josie sat up straighter. "Oh yeah, Abbie met her new boyfriend on there."

"Online dating for those into BDSM?" Carlie asked, looking worried.

"Yep," she said cheerfully. "Maybe I'll load my profile up and find my dream Dom."

She hoped.

"I don't know about this," Melody said.

"Look, I've lived here for years. I've dated a few men, but nothing has ever worked out. I need to try something new. I don't want to spend the rest of my life alone. So I think this is worth a try."

"Just be safe, okay?" Carlie said, looking worried.

"I will. I'll be fine. Really, what could go wrong?"

HANNAH GLANCED down at her phone, noticing with some trepidation that she had several notifications from the BDSM dating site.

She'd only signed up last night.

Oh God. She really wasn't sure about this. Maybe she'd made a mistake.

Turning into the next aisle, she came to a sudden stop.

There he was! What was he doing here?

Get out of here, Hannah.

She quickly dove backward, her feet nearly tangling each other up as she moved around the end of the aisle, then stopped to breathe.

Oh God!

Why the hell did she do that? She was an idiot! Instead of running away from him, she should have casually approached him and said hi. Been all cool.

Only problem is you aren't cool, Hannah. You're a giant dork.

God, she totally was.

Taking a deep breath, she shook off her nerves and peeked around the corner. He was gone.

Whew.

Dork status check: Yep, still intact.

Hopefully, he'd left the store.

Hannah walked down the cookie aisle, searching for Nutter Butters.

Urgh. She stopped and glanced up.

Way up.

She really, really wanted a packet of Nutter Butters. But they were right at the top and several inches back.

Shoot. She glanced up and down but didn't see anyone who could help.

Ahh, well. There was only one thing to do, right?

Grabbing hold of a shelf above her, she put her foot on another shelf and heaved herself up. Then she reached up with her other hand.

Nearly there. Nearly there.

Suddenly, someone grabbed her around the waist and lifted her down.

"Hey! I was close!"

"Close to falling," a gruff, disapproving voice said as she was placed on the ground.

She closed her eyes. Shit. Shit. Shit.

Why hadn't she left? Why hadn't she just walked out? Did she really need Nutter Butters that much?

The answer to that was yes. Yes, she did.

He turned her around to face him.

"I wasn't going to fall. I've done that before." She opened her eyes to glare up at him. Then she remembered something. "Shit! You shouldn't be lifting anything. You've got stitches."

"My stitches are fine, darlin'. *You* shouldn't be climbing shelves that weren't made for climbing. You could have fallen and cracked your head open."

Whoa. Okay, he really didn't look happy right now.

"But I needed some Nutter Butters," she said quietly, pointing up at the aforementioned cookies. As if that would help explain what she'd done.

"And you couldn't have found someone to ask to help you?" He placed his hands on the shelves on either side of her head.

Holy crap.

He was so close that she could feel the heat of him.

"Um, no. I was in a rush."

He frowned. "Hannah, you shouldn't–"

"Hey, Raid. Hi, Hannah." They both glanced over to see Addy walking toward them.

Addy had moved to Haven recently after her husband died. She was lovely. However, she often had a sad, lonely look in her eyes. She could use someone to make her smile again.

Like Raid.

"Sorry, am I interrupting?" Addy bit her lip and took a step back.

That was Hannah's cue to go. She slipped under Raid's arm. "You're not interrupting. I was just leaving."

"Wait, Hannah." Raid reached for her.

"I've got to go. I have to, uh, be somewhere." She turned away and walked off. She wanted to run, but she held herself back.

"Hannah!" Raid called out again. "Wait!"

That wasn't happening. She thought she might just lock herself in her apartment from now until eternity.

She ran home, locked herself in her apartment, and poured herself some wine.

Then she started looking at the notifications from the dating site.

One month later . . .

Raid Malone walked into Dirty Delights and immediately searched the bar to see if she was there.

He'd spent the last four weeks unable to do much but think

about her. His brief trip to New Orleans had turned into a longer stay. Jeez, his cousins were a mess. Especially Regent.

Raid wasn't sure that Regent would survive without Raid's help. But Raid was needed back on the ranch. Alec had been desperate for him to return.

And he'd been eager to come back and see her.

He'd been unable to stop thinking about her. And he'd come to the conclusion that there was only one way to cure that.

He was going to ask Hannah McLeod out.

There she was. She was smiling widely, her face flushed with happiness. Dark brown curls lay in a mess down her back and she was wearing a cute, bright yellow sundress with a lacy white cardigan over it.

At least he hoped they were those colors. Sometimes he had trouble with colors. But that was usually red and green.

Sweet and classy.

Totally Hannah.

He moved to the bar, needing to get a drink before he headed over to ask her out.

"Hey, Raid." Brye nodded to him.

"Hey, you waiting on Mel?" he asked.

"Yep." Brye winced as the girls at the table with Hannah all let out shrieks. "Jesus, my eardrums are never gonna be the same."

Raid grinned. "They look like they're having fun."

"Yeah, they're all excited about Hannah's new boyfriend."

What. The. Fuck.

He turned to Brye. "Her what?"

"New boyfriend." Brye shook his head. "Some sort of hotshot entrepreneur. Loaded. Gorgeous. Smart. Those're Mel's words, not mine."

"Hannah has a boyfriend?"

Brye zeroed in on his face. "Yeah. She does. And she's happy. I mean, I was always hoping that she'd get with you."

"You were?"

"Yeah. You must've known about her crush on you. Guess it's a good thing she's over that."

Over that?

A good thing?

How was it a fucking good thing?

"Although I'm not sure how I feel about some guy I haven't met yet. Like I said, I would've preferred it to be you. But you and Hannah probably would have been a disaster, huh?" Brye grinned at him.

"Yeah. A disaster."

He felt ill.

He'd waited too long.

Fuck.

1

hree months later . . .

"SON OF A BITCH!"

Raid dropped what he was doing and took off toward the roar of pain his brother let out. They were fixing some old farm equipment.

He saw Tanner holding his hand and ran toward him.

"What the hell? What happened?"

"Nothing major. Just caught my fingers in the machinery. Shit. I think one of them might be broken."

Raid studied his brother's fingers. Yeah. His little finger was swollen and red.

"What were you thinking?" Raid snapped.

"Guess I wasn't watching what I was doing."

"Alec is going to fucking kill you. Come on, I'll take you to the emergency room."

"Nah, I'll just ice it," Tanner replied.

"Are you trying to give Alec a heart attack? Because you know Mia will worry if you don't go get checked out. And we both know how Alec reacts when Mia worries."

Alec would murder them both if they upset Mia.

"Fine," Tanner grumbled. "But we're just going to the clinic."

Raid stared at him. "The clinic? Your finger looks broken."

"Yeah, which they can basically do nothing about. So I don't need to see someone."

"You're seeing someone," Raid said.

"Then it will be Doc or Jenna. They can x-ray my hand, do whatever is needed. I'm not going to the emergency room."

"Fuck. Fine. Let's go." It didn't make a difference to him, anyway.

After pulling up in front of the clinic, he turned off the truck. "I'll drop you off while I go get some food."

"You're not coming in?"

"You don't need me to hold your hand."

"I came and held yours last time you were here," Tanner pointed out.

"You serious?"

Tanner shrugged. "Yeah, why? Is there some reason that you don't want to go in?"

His gut clenched. Hannah.

She didn't work there anymore. She'd moved away to be with that dipshit boyfriend of hers.

Not that he knew whether the guy was a dipshit. He was just assuming.

Who moved that quick in a relationship? Not that he cared. It wasn't like they had been together or anything. He'd moved on from his brief thought about dating her.

Brief, right. She was all you could think about while you were in New Orleans.

"Fine. I'll come in."

He climbed out of his truck and followed Tanner into the clinic, where he was already smiling down at the new receptionist.

Raid didn't even know her name. He hadn't been in recently. Which was surprising for him.

He was leaning against the wall, waiting for Tanner to finish with the smiling receptionist when he saw her walk into reception.

He tensed. She was back? When did she get back? And why the hell had no one told him?

Raid waited for her to look over at him. To see him. Would she get all flustered and trip up? Or would she crack out some joke? Maybe try to flirt badly with him.

Except . . . maybe she'd come back with the guy she was seeing. Fuck. He deflated at that thought.

Shit. Did he still feel something for her?

Not good.

"Ariel, do you know where this file is?"

He frowned as he glanced over at her. Why did her voice sound so flat? So lifeless? That wasn't Hannah at all. And she hadn't once looked up from the piece of paper in her hand.

Then his gaze moved over her and he noticed that her hair was covering half her face. But that wasn't as strange as what she was dressed in. She was wearing this oversized black shirt that went down to mid-thigh. Loose and shapeless. It almost looked like a man's shirt.

Did it belong to her new man?

Raid had to hold on to the jealousy that threatened to take hold as he studied her. She was also wearing some wide-leg, black pants. Maybe that was fashion now. He didn't know and didn't care. Raid was a man with simple fashion needs. Jeans and a T-shirt in summer. Jeans and a long-sleeved shirt in winter. A jacket if it got really cold. Sometimes a Henley too.

Boots and a hat.

All he needed. All he cared about.

If this was the latest fashion, then he didn't think much of it. But none of that mattered. What he was concerned about was this wasn't what Hannah wore.

In summer, she always wore dresses and skirts. Happy clothes. Bright colors with lacy cardigans. In winter, she'd wear trousers but always with a cute blouse. Modest clothing that still looked sweet and feminine.

And she always wore color. Always. She was like a ray of sunshine on a cloudy day. Well, when he wasn't getting the colors messed up.

And yeah, he realized he'd just thought of her as a ray of sunshine. He was getting fucking poetic. That made him feel a bit queasy. But it didn't mean it wasn't true.

He was also just realizing that he'd actually paid attention to what she wore. How had he not clued in earlier that he was into her? He couldn't even tell you what Mia was wearing when he saw her this morning.

Shit.

Was this because of her new guy? Was he forcing her to dress like this?

Okay. Shit. He needed to stop thinking about Hannah. And her man.

"Hannah?" Tanner asked, and she glanced up at his brother.

Raid nearly flinched as he took her in. She was pale, with dark rings under her eyes. And her face looked gaunt.

What. The. Fuck.

He took a step forward before he even realized he was going to do it, and her gaze shifted to him.

In her eyes, he saw something flash. Something that looked like raw, unadulterated pain.

Fuck.

Fucking hell.

He sucked in a pained breath. What the hell?

Then, a shutter came over her face, and without even acknowledging him, she turned her gaze away from him.

What was going on?

Why wasn't she looking at him? Was she upset with him? But why would she be? And she was barely looking at Tanner. Hannah would typically have been full of empathy, worrying and fussing. They'd both been into the clinic a lot over the years and she'd never been anything but caring and sympathetic.

Well, other than when she was trying to run from him, banging into things, or hurting herself.

Right now . . . she looked almost cold. And that wasn't something he'd ever thought he'd associate with Hannah.

"Hannah," he called out.

She didn't even turn to look at him.

What. The. Fuck.

Okay, perhaps he'd gotten used to the way she reacted around him. To the sweet way she would blush, stare at him, or trip her her own feet.

How she'd stare at him with this look of adoration. Yeah, he might have taken that for granted slightly. And maybe he'd been a dumb asshole for not realizing that all of that meant that she liked him. At least not until it was too late. He'd cursed himself for that. But he hadn't expected that in the month he was away, she'd find someone else.

That knot in his stomach tightened again.

"I apologize for interrupting, Tanner," she said in that same monotone voice. "I'll come back, Ariel."

"Sure thing," the cheerful receptionist replied and turned back to Tanner. "One of the doctors will be with you soon."

"Uh, thanks," Tanner said.

"How long has Hannah been back?" Raid demanded.

The receptionist gave him a startled look. "Oh, she's been working here a week now. Just part-time. Do you know her well?"

Raid frowned. "Yeah."

Ariel bit her lip, looking slightly confused and worried. Probably wondering why if he knew her so well that he hadn't known she was back.

"We've been busy on the ranch," Tanner said. "Haven't had a chance to get into town. So we haven't heard the latest news."

"Oh, right."

Raid ignored them both and walked over to the back office. Where she'd disappeared to.

"Oh, I don't think you should just–" Ariel started to say before she was interrupted by Tanner.

Raid knew his brother would keep her occupied for a minute while he spoke to Hannah.

"Hannah," he said in a firm voice.

She startled and stared up at him, her face growing even paler, her breathing erratic.

Was she shaking? What the fuck?

But then she pulled herself together, giving him a cold look. "Yes? Can I help you?" She moved her gaze to her screen once more.

"You can look at me," he said demandingly. Yeah, maybe he was being a bit of a jerk. But he couldn't handle this Hannah.

She was worrying him. And Raid wasn't a man who usually worried about anything.

She turned her head toward him, but her eyes only hit his chin.

What was going on with her?

"Yes?"

"Can I help you, Raid?" she asked. "I'm working and I'm kind of busy. Plus, I don't think you're meant to be back here."

Why was she being so cold? Such a . . . well, kind of a rude bitch. He didn't get it. This wasn't his Hannah.

Urgh, she'd never been his, though, had she?

Maybe this was because of the man she was dating? Perhaps he didn't like her talking to other men? Could that be it?

He studied her face. She looked even more exhausted and pale close up.

Wasn't she sleeping? Eating properly?

Why wasn't her man taking care of her?

"Hannah. You can talk to me."

Her eyes flicked to his briefly in surprise before moving away. "I'm not sure what you're talking about. If there's anything I can get for you, please let me know."

It was a dismissal. And he wanted to press her further.

But she wasn't his. And he didn't actually have that right.

Then again, when had that ever stopped him from doing anything?

"Raid! Hi!"

He turned to see Simone standing in the doorway, smiling at him.

"Um, hi."

He wanted to keep questioning Hannah, but she'd already returned to her work, dismissing him.

He walked out of the office, ignoring the way his stomach screamed at him to stay. To make sure she was all right.

Fuck.

2

T *wo weeks later...*

HER PHONE BEEPED.

Instantly, she wanted to vomit. She didn't want to look at the message. Didn't want to see what it said.

It won't be him.

But still . . . it was like her body was now trained to react this way to the sound of a text message or call.

With dread.

Taking a deep breath in . . . she let it out slowly. Then, with a hand that shook, she picked it up to check the message.

MELODY: *We're going to Dirty Delights tonight. Eight. You're going.*

. . .

HER HAND TREMBLED as she lowered the phone to the coffee table. She knew she needed to reply because she didn't want to go to Dirty Delights tonight, and Hannah didn't want to go anywhere. But, she also didn't want Melody turning up on her doorstep, ready to force her. Which was something her friend would do if Hannah didn't reply.

HANNAH: *I have a headache. Sorry.*

SHE KNEW it was a lame excuse. And one she'd been using the last three weeks, ever since she'd returned to Haven.

Why had she left? She'd been so stupid. She'd left her friends. The place where she was safe. All her memories of her grandma were tied to this place.

Including the house that she'd left to Hannah.

The house she no longer lived in . . . because she was so fucking stupid.

Clenching her hands into fists, she tried to calm her breathing as the room swam around her.

This wasn't good. She couldn't pass out.

She managed one breath. Then another. She knew her friends hadn't liked it when she'd left. They had liked it even less when she'd taken more and more time to answer their texts. When she'd stopped taking their calls.

They hadn't cared for it, but there hadn't been much they could do when she'd been two states away.

But now . . . Steven was gone. He was out of her life. And she was back here. However, she wasn't the Hannah who left. And, understandably, her friends wanted to know why. They wanted to know what had happened to their Hannah.

What they needed to understand, though, was that their Hannah no longer existed.

She was a shell of herself. Withdrawn and cold.

It wasn't like she could just come out and tell them what had happened. So she'd been full of excuses for the last three weeks about why she couldn't go out with them.

That she was unpacking . . . they'd offered to help, and she'd declined.

That she wasn't feeling well . . . that excuse was getting old.

Her phone buzzed again, making her jump.

Fuck. What was wrong with her?

It wasn't him. He wasn't texting to berate her. Or to tell her what to wear or how to act.

Or that he was coming over and to prepare herself.

At the time, she'd liked those sorts of texts. The other ones, not so much, although she'd never made that clear. But she'd enjoyed preparing herself for him. Getting naked and waiting.

Now the memory made her want to vomit.

You are not going to be sick. You are not.

She took a deep breath and let it out slowly. This was ridiculous.

She had to stop this.

Besides, she knew it had to be Mel. There was nothing to fear from her.

MELODY: *Nope. You've used that excuse too many times. You're coming even if I have to drag you out.*

FUCK. For the last three weeks, she'd hidden away as much as she could. She had to go to work, of course. She desperately needed the money. So she was thankful that Doc

Harper and Jenna had given her a job, this time as the practice manager

They'd filled her position when she'd left and they'd been under no obligation to hire her again. She thought they might have created the job for her out of pity since their clinic was kind of too small to need a manager. But she'd taken their charity. She'd barely had the money to get herself back to Haven, so she couldn't be picky.

Thankfully, this tiny apartment above the florist's shop had been empty and was owned by the town council. They'd let her rent it without a bond.

It had been a lifesaver. Otherwise, she'd be couch surfing. Or worse, living on the streets. Although that was something that would never happen in Haven. The men of the town would be in an uproar at the idea of a woman living on the streets.

She could never let them know what had happened. They'd all rally around. They'd give her everything she needed and more.

But rather than make her feel less foolish and . . . and weak, it would make it all worse.

Stupid Hannah. Taken in by a man.

Stupid Hannah. Couldn't see that she was being used.

Stupid Hannah. Now, she's dirty and won't ever be clean.

"Shit. Fuck," she whispered, digging her fingernails into the palms of her hands. She couldn't deal with this.

It was too much.

Breathe. Just breathe.

She couldn't even leave the house unless she'd pulled on a layer of protection on. She dressed and acted in a way to keep people at bay, to shut everything and everyone out. All she could do was concentrate on one moment at a time. Just getting through the day until she could go home and hide again.

Now it seemed her friends had had enough. She knew they

just wanted answers.

But she was ashamed, upset, and mad at herself.

Such a fool. She'd been such a fool.

All your fault.

Urgh! Stop it!

HER PHONE BUZZED AGAIN.

MELODY: *Tick. Tock. Five minutes to decide.*

FUCK. She didn't want them here. So that only left her one choice. Unless she wanted to leave town and never see or speak to anyone again.

It was tempting.

She closed her eyes. This wasn't fair. She loved this town. Adored the people who lived here.

She had good friends. She'd had an awesome life.

And she didn't want to let him ruin that for her.

HANNAH: *I'll meet you there.*

Melody: *Good. Don't even think about not turning up.*

FOR THE LAST THREE WEEKS, Melody had gone from tough love to tiptoeing around her. Now, it seemed like she'd swung back to tough love.

Too bad none of it would work.

Nothing was going to break through the shell Hannah had erected around herself.

Nothing.

RAID SPOTTED her the moment she walked into Dirty Delights. His gaze moved over her with a frown. She was wearing a pair of loose-fitting jeans with an oversized black sweater. Her hair was loose and acted like a curtain for her to hide behind.

Her shoulders were slumped as she moved her way into the bar.

He wanted to storm over there and take her into his arms. To ask her what was wrong.

And demand that she let him fix it.

"Word is she broke up with him."

"What? Who?" He turned to Tanner, who was also staring at Hannah, worry in his gaze.

"Hannah. She broke up with the guy she'd been seeing."

"Word is?" he repeated his brother's words. "What? Are you listening to gossip now? You on the phone tree or something?"

"Phone tree? What the fuck is a phone tree?" Tanner asked.

"You'd know since you seem to know all the town fucking gossip."

"Fine. Next time I hear something about her, I won't tell you what's going on."

"Why are you telling me this? Hannah is just an old friend. Not really even that."

"Don't be an asshole. I know you were going to ask her out, remember?"

Fuck. Telling Tanner that had been a mistake.

"Do not tell anyone that."

Tanner's face softened slightly. "You know I wouldn't do that to you, brother."

He wouldn't either. Tanner had always kept his secrets. The

two of them had always been fighting as kids. But the minute someone outside their family went for one of them, the other one would come to their defense.

"You could ask her out now."

"Are you trying to get a second job as a matchmaker?" Raid asked him.

A strange look came over Tanner's face. "I just want you to be happy."

"Look, yeah, I was going to ask her out. But I've had time to think. We're not suited. She has 'white picket fence and kids' written all over her. That's not for me."

Yeah. Right.

Tanner just shook his head and got up to get another round.

Raid tapped his fingers on his thigh thoughtfully as he watched Hannah reach her friends. They each hugged her, but he noted she didn't hug them back.

That wasn't normal either. He'd seen her in here several times with the other girls. And they were always touching each other. They were always laughing. Teasing each other. They were a close-knit group.

But there was something wrong. He frowned as he watched. What was it?

Then it came to him.

Hannah wasn't smiling. She didn't look upset or uncomfortable or as though she was in pain.

She appeared indifferent. Cold.

Just what the fuck was going on with her?

HANNAH FELT TERRIBLE.

She wasn't comfortable. Her stomach and head hurt. And she felt like she was going to break into tears at any moment.

But she didn't let any of that show.

Because if she showed any cracks in her armor, then her friends would take advantage. They'd press any button they could find, digging their way in deep until they figured out what she'd been hiding from them.

But she couldn't let them see what was going on. She knew the way she was acting confused and hurt them. And she hated that. But she couldn't let herself crack.

"Okay, spill," Melody demanded.

Whoa. Déjà vu. Only the last time that Mel had said those words, they'd been demanding information about Raid.

God, that seemed so long ago. She'd give anything to go back to when her only worry had been how she was going to embarrass herself in front of Raid.

That night had been the turning point in her life, though. From now on, there was going to be a pre-Steven and an after-Steven.

And the after-Steven Hannah . . . well, that wasn't something she really knew how to deal with.

Hence, the reason she was trying to hide from everyone until she figured out this new-Hannah.

The one who grew scared when her phone beeped.

Who didn't know how to act around people she'd known for years. How to pretend to be happy and normal. It was so hard. She didn't know how old-Hannah did it.

But then again, old-Hannah hadn't had to do anything. Because she'd been happy. She'd had friends she loved and a job she adored.

Old-Hannah had thought that she was safe, living in a town where people watched out for her.

Stupid, naive, old-Hannah hadn't realized the dangers that lurked just outside Haven's borders. Where people didn't care about her. Wouldn't look out for her.

Why hadn't she been content with what she'd had? Why had she gone looking for more?

So damn stupid.

"Hannah? What's going on?" Josie asked.

"What do you mean?" She tried to smile. It was difficult. It took so much damn effort. Energy that she really didn't have.

"This isn't you. Why are you wearing those clothes? Why have you been avoiding us? What the fuck did Steven do to you?"

She winced as Melody spoke loudly, drawing attention from those around them. Brye was at the bar, watching them.

Watching her. And there was concern on his face.

"Nothing. You're imagining things."

Melody's head snapped back as though Hannah had slapped her.

Inwardly, Hannah winced.

Old-Hannah wanted to reach out and take Melody's hand. To apologize, beg for forgiveness, then lay everything at her feet. But she just couldn't . . . she didn't want them to know what happened to her.

It wasn't fair to them . . . she knew they'd blame themselves even though it wasn't their fault. The only person at fault was Steven.

And her.

New-Hannah couldn't tell them what had happened. Because she was ashamed and embarrassed. And because she was trying to hold herself together.

"I'm fine," she finally said. "There's nothing wrong with me."

"No?" Carlie asked.

"No," she said firmly.

Suddenly, Josie reached over to touch her hand and Hannah snatched her hand back, her breath catching in her throat. Her head began spinning as the air was trapped in her lungs.

Shit. Shit.

She knew as soon as she did it that it was a mistake. If she hadn't reacted like that, maybe she'd have some chance of making them believe everything was fine.

Maybe.

"Nothing's wrong, huh?" Melody said. "Don't bullshit us, Hannah."

Fuck. Shit.

"Whatever is going on, you can tell us, honey," Josie added, chewing on her lip. Today, her hair was bubblegum pink. It looked crazy, but it suited her.

"I need to go to the bathroom."

"Hannah! Stop running away from us." Melody reached out, but she managed to avoid her as she moved toward the bathroom.

"I'll be back. Everything is fine. Promise."

Her legs were shaky, her vision tunneled as she attempted to make her way to the bathroom. There was a bunch of rowdy guys by the door that led out the back, and she paused, unable to see how to get past them without having to push her way through.

Which she really didn't want to do.

Her breathing grew choppy.

Fuck. Fuck.

She could not lose it here. There was no way. But her skin was growing flushed, and she was sweating. If she waited too long, one of her friends would spot her and come to her rescue.

And that was the last thing she needed.

"Hey! Move out of the way. You're blocking the way to the bathroom," a deep voice said demandingly.

She jumped, turning.

There he was.

Why? Why did *he* have to be here? She swallowed heavily.

He was the last person she wanted to see.

Because while new-Hannah knew that she'd never be in a relationship again, that it wasn't something she could risk, old-Hannah looked at Raid Malone and wanted to swoon. Or fall at his feet and beg him to wrap her up in those thick, muscular arms.

To have him promise her that he'd keep her safe and love her always.

Which was just stupid. Not only because Raid had never shown her any sort of interest, but also because she knew that no one could keep her safe.

She couldn't risk letting anyone close.

Not even Raid Malone.

Some of the guys turned to look at them, one of them stepping forward. He was huge. Steven hadn't been a big guy, but he'd still hurt her. This guy could crush her.

Though Raid was even bigger than this guy, she still didn't hesitate to take a step closer to Raid. Whether it was because she was scared and wanted his protection or because she wanted to protect him, she wasn't sure.

Either way, her brain hadn't really been in control of the movement. She stilled, waiting to see what the other guy would do. But her movement had drawn his attention, and his body softened as he took her in.

"Sure," the big guy called out. "Get out of the way, assholes. Let Hannah through."

Did she know him? She peered closer. Wait, he was one of their newly enrolled patients at the clinic.

"Thanks, Rusty," she said to him quietly. Thankfully, her voice didn't shake. Much.

Rusty had moved here with his three brothers and one sister, although none of them looked alike. She glanced around for their sister, Peony, but couldn't see her anywhere.

Rusty nodded to her, and his brothers did the same. She slid past them and walked toward the toilets.

"Wait for me if you get out first," a deep voice said behind her. "I'll walk you back."

She jumped, turning. She hadn't realized that Raid had followed her into the hallway.

"Oh. Thank you for your help, but I'm fine now. You don't need to escort me back."

His head tilted to the side as though he was trying to comprehend her words. He studied her intently. She moved her hands behind her back, pressing her nails into the palms of her hands to hide her stress.

What was he thinking? Did he see that she'd changed?

Well, of course he sees that, idiot. It's as clear as the nose on his face.

But would he guess why?

No. Even her friends didn't know for sure. They figured it had something to do with Steven. They just didn't know exactly what.

And they wouldn't find out from her.

"Wait out here for me if I take longer than you do," he said firmly.

She frowned slightly. Why did he care? Well, she guessed he was an overprotective guy. She'd seen that many times over the years with his sisters-in-law, but especially when that day when she'd fallen over in the clinic.

Old-Hannah wanted to cringe in embarrassment.

But new-Hannah? Well, she simply didn't care that much.

At least that's what she tried to tell herself, anyway. She wasn't going to let herself feel anything for Raid. That would be stupid.

Because she couldn't have that in her life anymore. She couldn't have anyone as beautiful and pure as Raid.

Not when she was . . . when she wasn't herself.

So she wouldn't wait around for him to take her back to her friends like he'd asked. She could imagine the way they'd react.

"Those guys won't bother me. I know them."

"Then why didn't you ask them to move?"

Because she hadn't taken a good look at them, so she hadn't registered who they were. It seemed like she spent half her life in a haze, not taking much in. She'd been too worried about getting past without touching them.

But she didn't say any of that. Instead, she just shrugged, unsure what to say.

"Hannah, is something wrong?" He stepped forward.

Oh no. She didn't want him to touch her. He shouldn't touch her.

She stepped back.

His eyes flared open.

Shit.

Raid Malone might be crazy and wild. It might seem like all he wanted was a good time. But she knew that he was smart and could be very observant.

So it wouldn't be a good idea to spend too much time around him.

Or to show too much of herself.

"Thank you. Bye," she blurted.

Thank you, bye?

She ducked into the bathroom, barely holding back a groan. She was such an idiot.

Thank you, bye?

What happened to Miss Cool, Calm and Collected?

Yeah. That seemed to fly out the window every time she was faced with all the hot deliciousness that was Raid Malone.

She entered a stall, determined to be quick and get out before he did.

3

As she left the bathroom, she found Raid waiting in the same spot. She barely bit back a sigh of exasperation. She should have known it would be impossible to get rid of him that easily.

Put your armor on.

Don't let him get to you.

"You waited."

You waited?

Lord, she was just full of witty conversation tonight, wasn't she?

He nodded, still eyeing her. There was something in his face she didn't like.

He looked contemplative.

Not good. Really, really not good.

"I have to get back to my friends," she told him.

"You've changed," he said abruptly.

She straightened her shoulders. "Everyone changes."

"Not this much. Not over such a short period of time. When I was in the clinic getting stitches, you weren't like this."

Right, because that was before Steven.

"Like what?" she asked.

What was she? A glutton for punishment? Why did she ask that? She didn't want to know what he thought of her now.

Was she trying to make him say something that would hurt her?

Hannah took him in hungrily. Raid had the most gorgeous eyes. They were hazel-green. He had eyelashes that she would kill for. Long and lush. He obviously hadn't shaved in several days, but that only added to his appeal. He was built thick and wide. Powerful.

She wondered what it would be like to have Raid at her back. Protecting her, backing her up. She bet no one would mess with her if she was with him.

That would be amazing.

But he deserved far better than her.

"Removed, cold, as though you've detached yourself from the world. You're acting like you don't care anymore."

Nothing was further from the truth. None of this was because she didn't care.

It was almost like she felt too much. She was too scared to do anything, to go anywhere.

Too scared people would figure out what had happened. That they'd look at her differently.

That they'd see how dirty she was.

"I don't know what you're talking about. And, considering we never knew each other well, I don't think you have much of a right to talk to me like this."

"Is that so?" There was a heated note in his voice that made her insides quiver.

She didn't like that he might be angry with her. Hannah was a people pleaser. She enjoyed doing things for other people. It filled her bucket.

And she hated that anyone would be upset with her. She especially hated the idea of Raid being angry at her.

Wait, no. That wasn't her anymore. New-Hannah wasn't a sub. She no longer went out of her way to make others happy . . . even at the expense of her own happiness.

That's what had gotten her into this mess to begin with.

So rather than cave and apologize for her attitude, she threw her shoulders back. It was better this way.

For him.

Raid needed to stay away from her. That would keep him safer.

"It is so. Now, if you'll excuse me, my friends are waiting."

Not that she was in a big hurry to get back to the inquisition.

As she strode past, he reached out to grab her arm. Hannah jumped with a gasp. She couldn't help it. So she tugged her arm free from his hold, aware that the only reason she could do that was because he let her.

Her breath shuddered in and out of her lungs.

"Fuck, Hannah. What's going on?"

"Nothing." She practically spat the word at him.

Chill. Calm.

Even though she knew it was dumb to show any weakness, she couldn't stop herself from taking a step back.

It wasn't like he'd missed the way she'd jumped a mile as soon as he'd touched her.

"Nothing? Stop fucking lying to me. It's very obvious that something has happened. Was it that guy you were dating? Did he do something to you?"

Shit. Fuck.

Calm. It's only natural he'd think that, but he doesn't know anything. You're safe.

"I don't think that's any of your business. Good evening."

This time, he didn't try to grab her.

And she told herself it was a good thing, even as her heart ached.

Why couldn't he have wanted her?

But that wasn't fair. This wasn't Raid's fault. This was all on her.

When Hannah got back to the table, she realized that Mel, Carlie, and Josie were gearing up for round two of 'interrogate Hannah'. But she just couldn't do it. She was feeling too raw. Too vulnerable.

She had to shore up her defenses again.

"I'm sorry, I have to go," she said.

"You can't go," Melody said, standing up. "We still need to talk to you."

She shook her head and winced. "I know you'll think I'm lying, but I really do have a headache."

And this time, it wasn't a lie. Her head was thumping, her stomach churning.

"I have to go." She'd only drunk water, so she didn't have a tab to pay.

That was the only thing she could afford to drink. Making rent and buying food were priority number one. And she needed some more clothes and shoes. She'd donated most of her old clothes.

Swallowing heavily, she headed outside into the dark and started walking back toward her apartment, which wasn't too far from Dirty Delights.

She wouldn't have dreamed of walking home in the dark two months ago. She wasn't any fonder of the dark now. But she didn't have money for a taxi.

While on her way, a vehicle drove up beside her, and she stiffened.

It's not him. It's not him.

She forced herself to turn to look, relief filling her as she saw it was a deputy sheriff's vehicle. The truck came to a stop and Duncan Jones climbed out. Duncan was a good man she'd known for years. He was now married to Laken, and they were expecting their first child.

"Duncan, hi," she called out.

"Hey, Hannah. How you doing?"

"Good."

"Yeah? What are you doing walking around in the dark, sweetheart?" he asked in a concerned voice.

This was something she'd missed about living in Haven . . . and which also now worked against her.

She'd always appreciated how the men who lived here watched out for all the women. She'd never minded having rules to follow. Those rules had kept her safe. Every woman was supposed to have a guardian who watched out for her. Whether that be her husband, boyfriend, dad, or brother. Or Jake, the sheriff, who looked after all the women who didn't have an official guardian.

To some people, it would seem sexist. She knew that most people who didn't live here often didn't understand.

But she'd liked it. All she'd ever felt was safe. And sure, if you broke the rules, then there were consequences. For a lot of women, those consequences could be a trip over their man's knee, getting their butt reddened.

That hadn't worried her either.

And not because Jake would spank her, that wasn't the way he took care of them. But because she'd understood it. Break the rules, get punished.

Hannah had never been a rule-breaker. She was a good girl. The only spankings she'd ever gotten were reward spankings that were quickly followed by orgasms. And those had always taken place at Saxon's, the local BDSM club.

But, right then she was breaking the rules. The women of

Haven weren't supposed to walk around in the dark on their own.

So . . . did that make her a bad girl?

Oh God. She was about to be sick. But she had to pull it together. So she threw her shoulders back.

"I'm walking home."

"Walking home?" he repeated, as though it was a foreign concept.

"Yes. I've just been at Dirty Delights with Mel, Josie, and Carlie."

Duncan frowned, seeming even more upset. "And they just let you walk home on your own?"

Hmm. What to tell him? She didn't want to get her friends in trouble. Better that she was than them.

"They didn't know I was walking home," she confessed.

Duncan made a thoughtful noise. "Did they check?"

Well, fuck.

"The reason they didn't walk her home is because they knew I was following her," a voice said from the shadows.

She cried out, turning to see Raid step out of the darkness.

What. The. Heck.

She put her hand to her chest. "Are you trying to give me a freaking heart attack?"

The light from Duncan's cruiser meant she could see Raid's eyebrows rise and the stern look on his face.

Uh-oh.

"You're just lucky I wasn't someone bent on doing something worse than giving you a small fright," he growled. "I've been following you all the way from the bar and you didn't even know I was behind you. What were you thinking, Hannah? Anything could have happened to you! You have no business walking around on your own at night."

What?

Oh God.

He'd been behind her the whole time, and she hadn't realized? She thought she would have sensed him.

Anyone could follow you at any time.

Without meaning to, she let out a small squeak of fear.

"Hannah?" Duncan queried in a concerned voice as she took a step back. "Hey, are you all right?"

Shit.

Get it together, Hannah.

"Yes, of course." Crap. Even she could hear the way her voice shook.

"Hannah, come here," Raid said in a low voice.

What? Was he nuts? She wasn't going near him. He'd just given her a fright, pointed out how vulnerable and unsafe she was, and scolded her.

No way did she want to go anywhere near him.

"Hannah, baby. Come here."

Baby? Why was he calling her baby? What was happening right now?

"Hannah?"

She glanced over at Duncan as he spoke. Somehow, she'd ended up pressed against his cruiser with her back to it. How had that happened? She didn't even remember moving.

"W-what?"

"Sweetheart, you need to talk to me," Duncan urged. "Why were you walking home in the dark? Why didn't you take a taxi or tell your friends that you needed a ride?"

"They were all drinking."

Both men shot her looks. Right.

"You're telling me that Brye wasn't there watching over Melody? Or that you couldn't have asked Devon to call you a taxi or arrange a ride?" Duncan asked skeptically. "Sweetheart, you've lived here for years. You know the rules of the town. Putting yourself in danger like this . . . breaking the rules. This isn't you, Hannah. You're not acting yourself."

"I'm fine." Her voice sounded faint and wrong, but she knew neither of them would believe her. "I want to go home."

"Hannah." Raid took a few steps toward her and she stiffened.

There was a strange gasping noise. Shit. Was that her?

She needed to get herself under control.

Suddenly, Duncan moved closer to her. "Raid, maybe you should give her some space. She doesn't seem to want you near."

Shit.

So much for hiding her fear.

"Hannah, you're not scared of me. Are you?" Raid asked in a low voice.

Crap. There was genuine concern in his voice. And she felt so awful. She wanted to hug him tight and tell him she was sorry. But she couldn't do it. Not only because she couldn't bring herself to touch him. But because she was scared to touch him. Worried it would bring down all the emotional armor she'd carefully erected.

Armor that was slowly crumbling.

But even though Hannah should say she feared him, do whatever she could to push him away . . . she just couldn't. That would only make her feel even worse, and she already had enough regrets. And those regrets kept her awake at night. They ate away at her insides.

So, the last thing she needed was more.

"No."

"No?" Duncan repeated skeptically. "That's not the way you're acting, Hannah."

Crap. Crap. Crap.

She forced herself to stand tall, to push her emotions down. Far, far down. Taking a calming breath, she let it out.

"I'm good. Honestly, I'm not scared of Raid. I just don't want to be touched."

"You've never had a problem with people touching you before," Duncan said.

Shit. She was a hugger. She'd always been touchy-feely.

Now, that was biting her on the butt, wasn't it?

"And I've never known you to break the rules," Duncan added.

She hugged herself tight. What would he say if she told him that she didn't take a taxi because she had less than thirty dollars to her name and didn't get paid for another week?

And that most of that pay would need to go to overdue bills.

All because she was so freaking stupid.

"I know," she said. "It won't happen again."

Mostly because she didn't intend to go out again.

"All right, sweetheart," Duncan said. "We're only upset because we care about you. You know that, right?"

She willed the tears to stay away. Icy. She needed to be an ice queen. When she thought she had herself under control, she nodded.

"I k-know."

"She's getting cold," Raid said in a low voice. "I need to get her home."

"You're planning on taking her home?" Duncan asked.

"Yep. There a problem with that?" Raid straightened his shoulders as though he was preparing for an argument from the other man.

"Not from me," Duncan replied calmly. "But Hannah has to agree."

"Hannah is freezing and not making great decisions about her own safety," Raid countered.

Wait . . . what? She took one walk home in the dark and suddenly she couldn't make good decisions about her own safety?

You make crap decisions about your own safety.

Yeah. Right. She did.

But it still didn't mean that Raid was taking her home.

"Hannah, you all right with Raid taking you home?" Duncan asked.

She opened her mouth to say that no, she was not when Duncan's phone went off.

"Shit, I have to take this. It's Laken," Duncan explained.

He stepped away from them both, his voice lowering to a soft croon as he spoke to his pregnant wife on the phone.

Once, she would have been filled with want and jealousy over that. She'd wanted nothing more than a big, tough man who turned to dough for her.

"You're shivering, baby." Raid grew closer and pulled off his jacket. "Come here."

"I . . . I . . . why do you keep calling me baby?" she asked.

"I'm not sure you're ready for me to answer that right now." He held out his jacket. "Let me put this around you."

"But then you'll be cold."

"I'm not worried about me right now. I'm worried about you. Step forward," he ordered.

Her body was moved and he put the coat around her shoulders before her brain caught up. Instant warmth surrounded her as well as his scent, which was so delicious. But she couldn't let herself show how any of that affected her.

"Hannah, I'm sorry that I scared you," he said in a soft voice that made her shiver for an entirely different reason. "But you had me worried. You were walking along without a clue I was behind you. So fucking dangerous." By the last sentence, his voice had hardened and she could hear the displeasure in it.

She swallowed against the need to apologize again.

This was her life. He wasn't her man or her guardian.

He wasn't responsible for her.

"Hey, I've got to get back to Laken. She's not feeling well," Duncan said, walking swiftly toward them. "I'll drop you off on the way, Hannah."

Except her place wasn't on his way. It was in the opposite direction. But before she could open her mouth to argue, Raid spoke up.

"As I said, I'm taking Hannah home. You get back to Laken."

Duncan paused, then stared down at Hannah. "That okay with you?"

"Yes, of course. You go." What else could she say?

So much for the ice queen, who was trying to look out for herself.

Still, he hesitated. Duncan was a good man. But he needed to put Laken first. She definitely came before Hannah, who wasn't really worth his time. "Go, Duncan. I hope Laken is all right."

"You're taking responsibility for her?" he said to Raid.

Responsibility for her? No. Nope. She shook her head, but neither of them was looking at her.

Drat.

"Yep, I am. I have her." Raid gently held her arm as though he thought she might run away.

She tried not to flinch, but she couldn't stop herself.

He glanced down at her as Duncan left with a wave.

"Can you let go of me?" she asked as calmly as she could.

"Promise me you're not going to try and take off," he countered.

"As if I could outrun you," she scoffed.

"Hannah," he said warningly.

"I'm not going to run off." Sheesh.

Old-Hannah hadn't been a runner. New-Hannah was, but not literally. She was just running from her problems.

So far . . . that wasn't working out that well for her. Her problems just seemed to follow her around.

Probably because you are the problem.

"Come on, let's get you home."

He was a steady presence beside her. He didn't talk, which was surprising. There was no joking around or craziness. Just Raid walking beside her.

Seeing her home safely.

Under other circumstances, she would have given her right leg for this right here. For Raid Malone to walk her home, to care enough about her comfort to provide her with his jacket.

For him to be here with her like this.

But these weren't other circumstances. And she was too busy worrying about how to get rid of him when they got to her apartment to really enjoy the moment.

He'd been following her. A shiver ran down her spine.

What if Steven came back? He knew that she lived in Haven, which wasn't a big place. He could easily find her if he came looking.

Perhaps it really was time to move. Her sense of safety had been severely compromised, and she wasn't sure if it would ever return.

You feel safe with Raid, though.

Yeah, she did. But it wasn't like she could hire him to be her bodyguard.

What would she pay him in? Cuddles and kisses?

Yeah, right.

She took a deep breath and tried to calm herself. Steven

wasn't going to come looking for her. He had what he wanted from her.

There was no way she'd ever see him again. She was safe.

Sure, she might be broke, dirty, and scared of her own shadow.

But she was safe from Steven.

She hoped.

4

They reached the bottom of the stairs to her apartment. Hannah turned to look up at him. She had to get rid of him as soon as possible. "Thanks for walking me home."

"Don't even start with me, Hannah," he grumbled.

Huh? What the heck did that mean?

Raid took off up the stairs. She stood, staring after him. Shoot. She should have known it wouldn't be that easy.

Also . . . she was damn glad for security lights. Because the sight of his ass in those jeans as he strode up the stairs . . . truly epic.

"Hannah, get your butt up here."

She sighed grouchily. "Hold your horses. Sheesh, when did you get so bossy?"

"Oh, so that gets a real reaction, huh? I'll have to remember that," he muttered as she climbed the stairs toward him.

Shoot. She shouldn't have reacted. But it was hard to hold on to her calm around him.

Ice queen.

"If my being bossy gets to the real you, then prepare yourself, darlin'," he murmured to her.

Rats.

Yep. She'd messed up.

"I don't know what you're talking about," she replied stiffly.

"Unlock your door, Hannah."

Calm. Chill.

You cannot knee him in the balls. Do not react.

"I was planning on doing that."

As she unlocked the door, he moved in behind her. The heat of his body made her head spin slightly. Or maybe that was the lack of food she'd had today.

It was hard to eat when you felt constantly nauseous.

"You're not fooling me, baby."

She was going to ignore that whispered remark. She was also going to do her best to ignore the way his warm breath brushed across the cool skin of her neck.

This wasn't good.

The thing she really didn't understand was *why* he was there. Why was he pretending like he cared about her? It wasn't like he ever had before.

Okay, that was a bit unfair. He'd cared about her wellbeing when he saw her hurt herself, like when she'd fallen over like a giant klutz at the clinic. But when she wasn't in front of him, she was pretty sure he hadn't even known she was alive.

So why is he here?

Hannah had to bite back that question since she wasn't certain she wanted to know the answer.

Unlocking the door, she stepped inside. Only to have him grab her arm gently.

Again, she flinched.

And cursed herself. Fuck. She needed to stop that.

"I really want to know why you keep flinching when I touch you," he grumbled.

No, he didn't.

Cool and calm.

"I don't know what you're talking about. Again, thank you for walking me home. As you can see, I'm here and I'm safe. Have a good night."

"Nice try, darlin'. Not happening. Wait here."

"What?" she asked as he switched on a light.

He turned back to her. "Wait here. Do not move."

"Where are you going?"

"Walk-through."

And then he was gone.

Walk-through? He was checking to make sure that there was no one there? An almost giddy sense of euphoria filled her.

How much would she love someone to do that for her every time she came home? Coming home alone, especially when it was dark, almost always gave her anxiety. She hated it, which was another reason she avoided leaving her apartment unless she really had to.

Tears filled her eyes, and she had to quickly blink them back.

She would not give in to them.

She. Would. Not.

What the heck was happening right now? And how did she get it to stop? How did she get him to go?

Dumb ass. Why would you want him to go? To stop protecting you?

Because he was a reminder of the time before Steven.

Before she lost who she was.

Maybe Raid was one of those guys who was only attracted to the chase, to wanting people who didn't want him.

Well, more fool him. Because she still wanted him. She'd just never let herself have him.

Raid returned to where she was standing by the door. A pleased expression filled his face.

Shoot. She should have moved, Hannah realized, but she'd been too busy thinking. And her apartment was small, so it hadn't taken him long to walk around it.

But now he thought she was obeying him. Or something like that.

"Good girl."

Shit. Crap.

That flayed her. However she couldn't let him see.

Those words had once been her crack. Hearing them from him would have sent her soaring. She'd been a praise whore. Well, that wasn't an official term or anything. Just something she'd called herself.

But she'd loved being praised. Being called a good girl.

Not anymore, though.

And she had to dig her fingernails into her palms to stop herself from reacting.

Do not show him. Do not.

She forced herself to let out a grumbling noise, turning away from him. "Do not flatter yourself."

It hurt acting this way. Old-Hannah wept inside. She wanted to offer him a drink. To thank him for being a gentleman. For watching over her.

Old-Hannah would bask in that praise for days.

But she couldn't let her out.

"You can leave now." She made sure her voice was indifferent.

It was for the best. Better for both of them that he thought her a bitch.

He moved closer, getting into her space. She couldn't help but take several steps back until she hit a wall.

His eyes were narrowed. And she knew that she'd given herself away once again.

Rats.

"I don't know what's going on, darlin'. But I will find out. Now, I'm going to leave you so you can regroup those defenses you're determined to put up. Not sure that's the best idea, but I have a feeling that if I stay longer, you'll say something we'll both regret. I'm going to stay on the other side of the door until I hear it lock, though. And this might be a retreat, but a Malone never surrenders."

What the heck?

Then he shocked her by leaning forward and kissing her forehead before he walked out the door.

Holy. Crap. What was that? And why now?

Why couldn't he have done that months ago? Back when she wasn't broken. When she was whole?

A sharp knock on the door made her jump and cry out.

"Fuck, sorry, baby. I didn't mean to scare you," he said through the door.

Great. She put her hand on her chest. Now, after everything that happened, she was going to die of a freaking heart attack. It definitely felt like her heart was trying to pound its way out of her chest.

"What is it?" she asked after she gave herself a few seconds to calm down.

"Lock the door."

Shit. Why hadn't she remembered to do that? She always locked her door now. Even during the day, when she never used to do that in Haven.

"Right." She turned the lock and leaned back against the door before sliding to the floor.

Deep breath.

You have this.

"Sweet dreams, darlin'," came through the door.

There was no way he could know that none of her dreams were sweet anymore. That once all of her fantasies had been filled with him and the gorgeous babies they'd have made together.

And now . . . now all that filled her mind were sour thoughts. Dark, depressing ones.

Memories of Steven.

Drawing her legs up to her chest, she wrapped her arms around them and pressed her face to her knees.

That's when the tears started. Hannah promised herself she wasn't going to cry anymore. But this time, it wasn't over the loss of the life she'd had. It was the loss of her dreams, of the life she could have had.

RAID SLID BACK into the seat next to his brother at Dirty Delights.

Tanner gazed over at him. "That was quick. You walk her home?"

"Yeah, she wasn't very impressed, though. She didn't want me around, that was clear."

Tanner let out a snicker.

"You think this is funny?"

"Asshole, every woman you've ever crooked a finger at falls over their feet to try and get to you. Stuff has always come easy to you."

"What are you talking about? We're so similar we could be fucking twins. The two musketeers."

Tanner's lips twitched. "More like Pinky and the Brain." He was referring to a cartoon about two mice they'd watched when they were younger.

"I'm no smarter than you."

"I know that. You're Pinky."

"What?" Raid snapped, insulted.

"The character everyone loved."

Raid shook his head. "You can't tell me that women don't throw themselves at you. I've seen it."

Tanner gave him a cocky grin. "I get my fair share of attention." That smile dropped. "But I'm not interested in that scene anymore. I want what our brothers have. Someone special."

Yeah, Raid understood that. "She's so different now. She's colder, or she's trying to be."

"Hmm. Seems like she's trying to push everyone away." Tanner nodded over at her friends, who all looked sad. "Why would Hannah push everyone away who cares about her?"

Fuck. He didn't want to think about that reason. "She's not all right."

"What are you going to do?"

Raid frowned. "I don't know."

"Malone men don't give up when they want something."

Raid snorted. "Damn straight."

The longer he'd followed her in the dark tonight without her noticing that he was behind her, the angrier he'd grown.

She needed a keeper. Someone to make certain that she took care of herself.

Raid Malone thought he was just the man to take on that task.

5

It was Sunday morning.

Raid had spent all day yesterday thinking about Hannah, wondering what was going on with her.

If pushing her was the best thing to do or not.

What he should probably do is go tell Jake that he was worried about her. He was the sheriff, after all. Plus, his wife, Molly, was a psychologist. She could use all her crazy psychic abilities on Hannah.

Molly was pretty good at that stuff.

She'd come out to the ranch a few times to chat with them. Beau thought she was trying to fix them . . . but Raid knew the truth.

There was nothing to fix. The Malones were as good as it got. There was no fixing perfection.

He'd told Molly that and she'd agreed.

Well, she'd gone a bit red in the face before bursting into laughter. But that was basically the same as agreeing, though, right?

And then she'd written a paper or something on them. He

was vague on those details. But if other people wanted to read about how amazing they were . . . then so be it. He'd even told her that she could use his name, but she'd said she'd keep that part out so he wasn't bothered by a whole lot of doctors wanting to question him.

Molly was definitely good people. At one stage, he'd thought about kidnapping her and keeping her for himself. But she'd told him how much she loved Jake and he'd never come between a man and his woman.

After two sleepless nights and a day where he couldn't even concentrate on rewiring West's truck so that the horn wouldn't blast every time he put his indicator on, Raid decided he needed to do something.

Which was why he was there, standing on her stoop with coffees, Danishes, and plenty of Malone determination.

He held everything in one hand while he knocked firmly on the door.

Nothing.

He frowned. Maybe she was grocery shopping or something.

Or perhaps she's hiding from you.

Well . . . if she wanted to get rid of him, then this was the wrong way to go about it. Because there wasn't a lot that Raid Malone needed or wanted. A belly full of food, a roof over his head, some cold beer, and his family to be safe and happy.

But when he decided he wanted something . . . then he was like a dog with a bone. He didn't give up or let go.

"Hannah, open up."

Still nothing.

"Guess I'll just wait out here until she gets up or shows up," he said loudly, sitting down and sipping his coffee.

He ate his Danish and stared out at the parking lot. Not the best view. He wasn't sure how he felt about her living here. At least there were security lights. Even so, it was a back entrance. At night, someone could hide back here and jump her.

Yeah, he wasn't liking this at all.

Fuck. Where was she?

With a sigh, he got to his feet. He had a feeling he knew exactly where she was . . . hiding from him.

"Guess I'll get my jacket back another day, darlin'."

With a frown, he turned away.

Even though every part of him wanted to go back, he couldn't force her to open the door.

But this didn't mean that he was giving up. Just that he needed to regroup.

CRAP!

She was out of painkillers. The last thing Hannah felt like doing was going to the pharmacy. But she had a killer headache that just wasn't going away.

Moving to the dining table of her tiny apartment, she ignored the wave of dizziness that washed over her as she picked up her handbag.

She really needed a good night's sleep. And she should probably eat something. The trouble was she didn't really feel hungry. And when she tried to eat, she just felt nauseous.

Stepping out of her apartment, she walked carefully down the outside stairs. The last thing she needed was to trip and hurt herself. Walking out of the alley onto the street, she headed down the block to the pharmacy. She was grateful it was within walking distance since she barely had any gas left in her car.

Glancing up as she heard laughter, she saw Savannah Ferguson and Lila Richards walking along the footpath. Both were pushing strollers. Savannah's was a double, as she'd had twin girls not long ago. Lila's stroller held her daughter, Meggie. While her son, Bronson walked beside her.

They looked so happy. A stab of loneliness hit her. She'd never have that. Before they could notice her, she quickly crossed the road.

Cowardly?

You bet.

But she just couldn't handle people right now. Her head was thumping, and it was making her feel even more nauseous.

As she stepped into the pharmacy, she saw him.

Crap!

How did this keep happening? Sure, Haven was a small place, but not that small.

Deep breaths. He didn't see you. Just leave.

But she really needed some painkillers. She could go to the grocery store, but she didn't feel up to walking that far.

Moving down the aisle with the painkillers, she grabbed a packet and headed to the cashier. She kept her head down, hoping like hell no one noticed her. After paying for her painkillers, she put them in her handbag and then moved toward the door.

"Hannah?"

Rats.

Before she looked up, she pushed all of her emotions down. So far down, she was convinced they wouldn't surface. Then she glanced up at him.

"Hi, Raid."

He raised his eyebrows. "Hi, Raid? That's all you've got to say to me?"

"Was there something more you wanted?"

Every word made her die a bit more in side. She didn't want to be like this. To push him away.

But she had to.

Raid folded his arms over his chest as he glared down at her. "I've come to your apartment several times, darlin'. Are you avoiding me?"

"Why would I avoid you?"

"I'm not sure. I was hoping you'd tell me."

"I like my privacy. And I don't need anything from you. Now, if you'll excuse me. I need to go."

To her shock, he let her go.

She told herself it was for the best. That it was what she wanted.

So why did she feel so sad?

"Raid?"

He glanced up in surprise to find Melody and Brye standing beside the booth he and Tanner were sitting in at the diner.

It was Friday morning. He'd been into Haven twice during the week to try to see Hannah, but each time she'd either been out or ignored his knocking.

Short of breaking in, there wasn't much he could do.

And then when he'd seen her at the pharmacy, she'd been so cold to him. He wasn't going to force himself on her.

Hannah had given Mia his jacket to return it to him. Mia had given him an interested look, but hadn't said anything.

Which was a freaking miracle.

Tanner glanced up from his food and looked from him to them with interest.

"Hey. You guys want to sit?" Tanner asked.

"Um, no, we just spotted you as we were walking past," Melody said with uncharacteristic hesitancy. "I just . . . was Hannah all right with you walking her home last weekend? Was she . . . did she seem okay?"

He saw the worry etched into Melody's face. Brye's, as well. Brye ran the local gym, of which Raid was a member but didn't make it there that often. Still, he knew they were both good people.

"No," he said. "She didn't seem okay. Do you have some insight into what's going on with her?"

They both shared a look, and Brye sighed. "Tell him, Mel."

"I don't know. I don't know where her head is. She might not forgive me for saying anything to you about this."

"If you have some idea of what is going on with Hannah, you need to tell me," he demanded, unused to not getting his way.

Melody straightened her shoulders. "Not if you're not really into her."

"I followed her home the other night. Kept her safe."

"Which a lot of guys around here would do. And you haven't exactly shown an interest in her before now. She had a crush on you for so long and you barely knew she was alive."

Fuck.

It took all he had not to flinch at the accusation.

"Hannah needs someone who cares about her wellbeing. Who's invested in her enough to keep pushing even when she pushes them away."

Raid narrowed his gaze at Melody. Brye wrapped an arm around her and drew her close, sending Raid a warning look. He obviously didn't like the look on Raid's face.

"I was going to ask her out months ago," Raid admitted.

He knew she was shocked when she jolted, staring at him wide-eyed. "What? You were?"

"Yes."

"Then why didn't you?" A look of such anguish crossed Melody's face that it took his breath away. The hurt and pain in there . . . fuck.

What had happened to Hannah to make Melody feel like this?

And did he really want to know?

"Because by the time I got back from New Orleans, she was already seeing someone else."

Melody glanced away for a moment. "And now? How do you feel about her?"

"Not sure that's really your business."

"Maybe it wasn't before. But Hannah is different now. And she needs us to look out for her since we didn't before." Melody chewed her lip, looking unsure.

"Look, Hannah doesn't seem interested in talking to me. I've tried knocking on her door a few times this week and she never answers. The one other time I did see her, she totally brushed me off."

"She's avoiding all of us," Melody told him. "We're scared for her. Really worried. She's not herself. She's pulling away from us and we don't . . . we don't know what to do." Her voice cracked and all three men leaned toward her.

Brye drew her into his chest. "Hush, sweetheart. It will be all right."

"But what if it's not? We've all tried to help her and she keeps putting up this wall."

What the hell had happened to her? Worry churned in his gut.

"You know that Hannah started dating this guy, Steven," Brye told them. "She met him on a dating site."

"What?" Raid snapped. A dating site?

"Yeah." Brye ran his hand over his face. "I didn't find out until after she'd started talking to him that she'd signed up for the site." He sent Melody another stern look.

She started shifting from foot to foot, but she started talking.

"It was a site that specialized in helping submissives find a Dominant."

"Jesus fucking Christ, are you kidding me?" Raid shot out.

Around him, people stopped and stared. He took a deep breath and let it out slowly before leaning forward. "You let her fucking do that? What were you thinking?"

"Hey! Watch your tone!" Brye glared at Raid.

"The two of you better sit," Tanner said, moving out and sitting next to him so they could sit across from them.

Brye continued to glare at Raid.

"Brye, honey, it's okay," Melody said. "Raid's right. We shouldn't have let her use that site, let alone encourage her. But Josie's cousin used it and found this amazing guy. And on the website they said that they vetted people and they gave her a number to call if she thought anything felt wrong during her first date. They even offer a chaperoning service and advise people to have their first date somewhere public, like in the bar area of their club."

Fuck. Just, fuck.

This guy could be anyone. Could have done anything to her.

"What happened?"

"I don't know," Melody whispered. "I really don't. She started talking online to him and he said all the right things. And that he didn't want her to meet with him until she was comfortable. He even said that she could bring a friend with her. They talked for two weeks until she was begging him to meet up."

Christ. So he'd lulled her into feeling secure around him. But then what?

"I said I wanted to go with her. But she told me they were meeting somewhere public. Hannah told me that if she was going to do this, then she needed to trust him. What I didn't learn until later is that they met at a restaurant in Lafayette where he lived. That she had a great time. But slowly, she started changing. She grew more distant. We thought it was normal. You know how you get when you're first dating someone and want to spend all your time with them."

"Don't recall you ever wanting to spend all your time with me, sugar," Brye said with raised eyebrows.

Melody waved her hand through the air. "Ugh, that's because I already knew you. It wasn't new love. We went straight into the old married couple kind of love."

Brye frowned. It was clear he didn't like her describing their relationship like that. It was also clear he heard the note of longing in her voice.

"Did you want that new love feeling?"

"What? No, of course not!"

"Are you lying to me?" Brye asked in a surprisingly firm voice.

Melody stiffened and looked at him.

Hmm.

"Someone's heading toward a spanking," Tanner sang, winking at her when Melody glared at him.

"I am not!"

"Yeah, you are, sugar," Brye told her in a low voice.

She gulped and looked up at her man nervously. "Crap."

"Mel, Hannah?" Raid asked impatiently.

"Right. Um. When she told us she was moving to live with him, we were concerned, but what could we do? But then, she stopped answering our texts and even put her house up for sale. We were so worried, but she wouldn't talk to us."

"And then she came back here?" Tanner asked.

"Yes, and she won't tell us what happened. But she's different. It's not just the way she dresses, but the way she acts. Hannah was always a hugger. She was always so happy and animated. Now, she hates being touched, she doesn't smile. She wears a lot of black baggy clothing, when she always wore color.

She was happiness and now she's so sad. And I think she's lost weight."

"I don't think she's sleeping, either," Brye added. "Every time I see her, it's like the bags under her eyes have gotten bigger."

"And she's really jumpy," Melody added. "We're all worried that he did something to her."

Fuck. Fucking motherfucker.

His hands clenched into fists. If there was something he hated, it was people who abused those who were smaller than they were. Kids and women. People who couldn't fight back.

Those sorts of people were scum.

"You think he hurt her?" Tanner asked in a low voice. "Wouldn't she tell someone? Jake? Or you guys?"

Melody licked her lips. "I thought she would . . . but she's not our Hannah. She's acting so quiet and secretive. Hannah was always so social. Now, she goes to work or stays home. I had to threaten her to get her out the other night. That's not normal for Hannah. She loves being around people. That's what she does. She looks after people. I guess . . . we're not used to looking after her and I feel like we're doing a terrible job."

"It's not your fault, Mel," Brye told her, tightening his hold on her.

But Raid saw the guilt on her face. He knew that she thought it was.

"I think we should have protected her better. She hasn't even been to Saxon's recently. And that's something she needs."

That was something that had made him hesitate more than once. But if Hannah was in his life, if she was 'the one', then he'd do whatever was necessary to keep her happy.

Hell. More than once, he'd thought about spanking that round ass of hers. Especially the other night when she'd started walking home in the dark. Yep, several times he'd thought of spanking her.

If she needed him to take some BDSM classes on tying her up, he'd do that too. He liked being in control. He just didn't like following rules. So having to follow the rules at Saxon's didn't sit right with him.

"I'm just . . . I'm really frightened." Melody looked up at Brye, who ran his finger down her cheek. "It worries me that she never smiles anymore. That she dresses differently and acts so strange. That she's trying to push us away. She's hiding something and . . . and I don't know what to do. I usually know what to do."

He understood what she was saying.

"And I guess I came over here to talk to you because she's had a crush on you for the longest time. You used to be our favorite topic of conversation. She was always moaning about how she'd acted in front of you, embarrassing herself. God, I'd give anything to watch her get all flustered around you. I didn't think you felt the same . . . until you rushed off after her the other night." Melody bit her lip. "What I'm trying to say is that if you're not interested in her, then maybe it would be better to stay away. But if you are, and God, Raid, I hope you are. Then please, don't give up on her. Don't let her push you away. And I know it's utterly ridiculous of me to ask that of you when all you did was walk her home. But I am that desperate. You might need a moment to think about that, and I get it. I just . . . I want my Hannah back, and I'm willing to beg, borrow, or steal to help her."

Empathy had him leaning forward and taking hold of her hand. "She's lucky to have you as her friend, Melody. And whatever happened to her wasn't your fault. It was all on this asshole. Understand?"

Relief filled her face for a moment. "I don't know what this guy did to her. But if you can help her . . . if you can bring her back to us, then I'll make you my world-famous pavlova every birthday and Christmas."

"What the hell is pavlova?" Tanner asked.

"It's beaten egg whites and sugar, baked, then served cold with whipped cream."

"That sounds . . . interesting," he drawled. Was that meant to be a good thing or a threat?

"It's really good. My grandma was from New Zealand. They had it every Christmas."

"It actually is good," Brye said. "I thought it sounded weird at first, too."

"I'll do what I can, Melody," he told her. Although how the hell he was going to get Hannah to talk to him when she wouldn't even open her door, he had no idea.

Melody opened her mouth as if to argue, but Brye shot her a look, and she nodded. "Thanks. Anything you can do, we'll be grateful for. Hannah is worth fighting for."

They headed off, and Tanner turned to him. "Fuck."

Fuck was right.

"Might need to fake an injury just to get her to see me."

Or better yet, he could actually injure one of his brothers so he could take them in. Maddox would be a good idea. That bastard was growing bossy as hell now that he was a dad. Even Beau was ready to murder him.

Raid didn't know how Scarlett put up with him.

Yeah, that was a much better plan.

"Sounds like if you're interested in her, you better make sure you're serious. Because if something has happened to Hannah, she's too fragile to be messed around with."

"I wouldn't do that."

Tanner shrugged. "And Jake would kick your ass."

"Like he could manage that. He's an old man now." He sat back with a sigh. "What the fuck do you think happened to her?"

"Nothing good, brother. Nothing good."

Yeah. And that thought fucking terrified him.

6

Raid was just getting out of the cab of his truck the next day when his phone rang.

He glanced down at the name of the caller.

Wet Blanket.

Hmm, why would the Haven's sheriff be calling him? He hadn't done anything lately to warrant a call from Jake. And if he had, the asshole usually went to Alec first.

Raid was kind of sick of that. He was a fucking grown man. He could deal with any fallout he'd caused. Fact was, he hadn't instigated much havoc since Beau and Maddox found Scarlett.

Since then, he and Tanner had tamed right down.

So, in other words, all of their wildness had been because of Beau. And a bit due to Butch.

They were the troublemakers. Not him.

The phone stopped ringing, and he climbed out of the truck, looking over to where Tanner was taking off his boots before heading into the house for lunch. Hopefully, Mia had baked them some goodies. "What did you do?"

Tanner turned back. "What?"

"Wet Blanket is calling."

Tanner narrowed his gaze. "Why would Jake call? Shit, do you think Beau has gotten himself arrested?"

Fuck. That hadn't occurred to him.

"Wait," he said. Then he shook his head. "Nah, he'd call Maddox first, then Alec or Jaret."

Tanner nodded. "Yeah, we'd be last on the list. Well, still ahead of West since he'd probably leave him in jail to rot."

His phone started ringing again.

Okay, he was getting a bad feeling about this.

"Yeah?"

"Raid, it's Jake."

"What can I do for you?"

There were a few seconds of silence before Jake spoke. "Duncan told me he saw you last weekend with Hannah McLeod."

Raid straightened. Shit. Was this about Hannah?

He hadn't stopped thinking about what Melody and Brye had told him yesterday. In fact, he'd barely slept last night. Every possible scenario he could think of had rolled around in his brain.

But he'd yet to decide what to do about it. How he could break through to her.

"That's right. I saw him. Is something wrong with Hannah?"

Another pause. "Before I tell you that, I need to talk to you about your intentions with her."

"My intentions with her? What does that mean, exactly?"

"That's what I want to know. Duncan said that you told him you would take responsibility for her. But since you haven't spoken to me about that, and since Hannah hasn't said anything, I'm thinking he meant for that evening and nothing more. Am I right?"

Raid ground his teeth together.

Fuck. He had a really bad feeling.

"Something has happened to Hannah, hasn't it? What?"

"I can't tell you–"

"You rang me!" he said in a sharp voice. "What's happened to Hannah?" He was aware of Tanner growing closer to him, but Raid didn't look up from his boots.

This feeling of panic . . . it wasn't something he'd felt before. And it gave him that last push he needed.

He cared about Hannah.

A lot.

He'd come to the conclusion that he'd need to start off by being her friend. That he'd need to show her that she could trust him so he could coax her into talking.

Slow and gentle.

Even if he knew nothing about going slow and gentle, he figured he could learn for her.

Right?

Maybe.

"You sound worried about her."

"Jake, don't fucking mess with me." Fuck. He knew what he had to do. "I'm taking responsibility for her. I'm her guardian, so you need to tell me."

"You get that you can't just declare that and it's suddenly so. Hannah has to agree."

"She will," he vowed.

Jake grunted. "I wouldn't normally do this, but Hannah isn't herself at the moment."

"I know," he said. "I know she isn't and I know why."

"You know all of it?"

No. But he didn't want to tell Jake that.

"I know enough."

"Both Molly and I have been trying to get her to talk. So have her friends. She's not talking. Fuck, if you can get her to open up

. . . then I'm going to take this chance. Raid, Hannah fainted today."

Fuck. Fuck.

Had he waited too long? Should he have gone straight to her apartment after talking with Melody and Brye?

Had she done something to herself? What was going on?

"Where is she? At the hospital in Freestown? Is she okay?"

"She's not in the hospital. She fainted at work this morning. Jenna wanted to admit her to the hospital for further tests, but Hannah refused."

"What the hell? And you let her?"

"Let her? I can't force her to go to the hospital."

"You're the sheriff. It's your job to take care of the women of this town."

"I thought you were taking responsibility for her?" Jake drawled.

Fuck. Yeah. He was.

"Where is she now?" He'd go to her and drag her to the hospital. "And you should have fucking well led with this."

"I wanted to know if you really cared or if this was just some sort of temporary interest."

"I'm going to ignore you fucking insulting me like that," he said through gritted teeth. "Where is she?"

"She might not welcome you either. She's not letting anyone help her. She's locked herself in her apartment and ignoring everyone. If you weren't interested in what happened to her, I was going to get Molly over here with me and do a welfare check."

He sucked in a breath. A welfare check happened when Jake had cause to believe that someone in town might be close to harming themselves or in danger and unwilling or unable to reach out to their guardian or Jake for help.

It didn't happen often. In fact, he couldn't think of another instance. But that meant Jake was seriously worried.

"I'll get through to her. Did Jenna tell you anything?"

"Not much, just that there was no visible sign of injury or illness and it could be low blood pressure as Hannah had just stood up when she keeled over."

Fuck!

Fuck this going soft shit.

That was clearly not the right path to take. Hannah needed him in her life keeping her safe and healthy.

Which was exactly what he was going to do.

RAID RACED UP THE STAIRS.

He hadn't wasted any time in getting to her apartment, only stopping to briefly fill Tanner in. His brother had looked concerned, before telling him to go. That he'd explain to Alec and Mia what was going on.

Jake was sitting at the top of the stairs. He stood when Raid reached him.

"She hasn't spoken to you? Let you in?" Raid asked.

"Nope. I was gonna give you another ten minutes, then I was going in by force. Out of everyone in this town, Hannah has never given me cause to worry. I've never had to warn her about following the rules. She doesn't speed, doesn't even jaywalk. She's always been sweet and kind to everyone, so I don't need to tell you how much this worries me."

Yeah, he didn't need to say it because it was worrying Raid, too.

He took another step up, and Jake got in his way.

Anger flooded Raid, though he tried to hold it back. He was generally pretty easygoing.

Until someone threatened someone who mattered to him.

But he held himself in check because he knew Jake wasn't trying to hurt Hannah.

"Get out of the way, Jake."

"I've known Hannah for years. She's one of my citizens, but she's also a woman on her own. And it doesn't make me happy that I don't know what's going on. It has Molly worried, which I like even less. So sometime in the next forty-eight hours, I want to know what it is that you know."

Shit.

"Look, what I know is that she was dating a guy."

Jake nodded.

"And she moved away to be with him too quickly. She stopped talking to her friends, sold her house. When she came back, she was different. Jumpy, remote."

"Right. And you don't know the reasons for any of that?"

"No. But I will."

Jake eyed him skeptically. Raid braced himself. Knowing what was likely to come.

"I've seen all your brothers find their women and settle down . . . sort of. I was starting to wonder if that would ever happen to you and Tanner. I just hope you know better than to toy with her."

"Again, I'll forgive you for insulting me because you care about her. But don't do it again, Sheriff. Hannah is mine. I take care of what belongs to me."

And those words completely cemented it.

Hannah would be his.

Now that he'd fully made the decision, he could breathe easier.

It felt right.

To his surprise, Jake just nodded calmly. "That's what I was hoping you'd say. Don't look so shocked. Most of you Malones are a pain in my fucking ass. But I know that when you find someone you care about, you protect them. Just take care of Hannah. I'm going back to the office, but call me if she won't let you in. We'll have to go in by force."

Raid nodded. But he wouldn't be making that call. If anyone went in by force, it would be him.

Hannah stared at the news playing on the TV.

Con man arrested in Alabama.

Was it him? Had he finally been caught?

Con man tries to steal thousands of dollars from a woman in Montgomery, Alabama.

She trembled, her stomach rolling.

Is it him?

She felt faint. Like she was going to pass out.

Yeah, you already did that, remember?

God. That had been humiliating. Every second Saturday, she worked mornings at the clinic in reception. When she'd seen the news report come on and had stood suddenly—she hadn't been sure whether to hide or run and be sick. The next thing she knew, she'd woken up with Jenna leaning over her, looking concerned.

Please, let it be him.

Deep down, she knew she should have told Jake what had happened from the beginning. But Steven had scared her into not even confiding in Haven's sheriff. Plus, she didn't want him to know what an idiot she'd been. How she'd been duped.

It had all been so frightening and embarrassing. And with the way things tended to happen in a small town, if she said anything, then everyone would soon know.

What if it is him?

Her breath came in sharper pants and she moved to the sofa and sat, unable to stand anymore.

A knock on the door made her jump. She rubbed at her chest as her heart went into overdrive.

Fuck.

She'd thought Jake had left. She felt awful for leaving him out there, but Jake had a way of getting people to talk to him. Hannah guessed it was a good talent for a sheriff to have.

She was too vulnerable and scared right now. She couldn't shore up her defenses enough to deal with him.

If it was him, was her nightmare partly over?

Her phone kept buzzing with more texts coming through. She quickly gathered her courage and turned it over, glancing down. They were all from her friends, including Jenna. Even Doc.

Everyone was worried about her. She was surprised that she didn't have more of them turning up on her doorstep.

Maybe they're finally sick of you. Perhaps they've had enough of you treating them how you have been and they're giving up.

Stop it.

She needed to stop this. She was working herself up when there was no need to.

Her friends loved her. They'd been trying to get through to her and she kept shutting them out.

You only need me, sweet Hannah. Those friends of yours just use you. How often do they expect you to do everything for them while giving you nothing in return?

They take, take, take.

All you need, sweetness, is me.

Lord, she was going to vomit.

Hannah rushed to the bathroom as another knock sounded

at the door. She ignored it. She heard someone talking, but her hearing was muffled.

Leaning over the toilet, she started dry-retching. There wasn't anything in her stomach to come up.

When it finally stopped, she sat on the bathroom floor, trying to calm her breathing.

Her friends loved her.

She wasn't a burden.

He was a psychopath who had manipulated her. Hurt her. But she didn't have to let him win.

If only he'd get the fuck out of her head and leave her alone.

She dragged herself off the floor and brushed her teeth, staring at her gaunt, pale appearance.

Fuck. She looked like hell.

She was letting him win.

And she felt so fucking angry at herself.

After she'd woken up from her faint, she'd just wanted to run. To come back to her apartment and hide.

So many people had been calling and texting since then and she'd ignored them all.

Because all she could hear was him. All she could feel was him touching her.

Shame and fear clung to her, making it hard to breathe as she stumbled out of the bathroom. She had to get to her safe space.

There was more knocking on the front door, but she ignored it and made her way to the side of the bed. There was about two feet between the edge of the mattress and the bed. That's where she wedged herself.

She'd put the blankets and some pillows down here for when she tried to sleep. She couldn't lie in the bed, she felt too vulnerable.

Tell Jake what happened.

She closed her eyes and leaned her forehead against her knees.

But what if it wasn't Steven who'd been arrested?

One shuddering breath, then another.

Open the door to Jake. Tell him.

Getting to her feet, she stumbled to the door.

She could do this.

Jake wouldn't judge her. He might scold her for not telling him. For not being more careful with her own safety.

Old-Hannah shriveled at the thought of letting Jake down. What if . . . what if he was disappointed in her?

Then you just suck it up.

Another knock and she made up her mind. She forgot to check how she looked or that she might want to see who it was first. She just opened the door.

Well. Hell.

She definitely should have checked first.

7

F uck.

He tried to hide his reaction to her. But Raid couldn't help the slight flinch.

How did she look this much worse in just a few days?

"R-raid?" She stared up at him in shock.

He frowned. Why was she surprised? Then he realized she hadn't looked through the peephole to check who it was. "You should always look first before you open the door."

It was her turn to flinch. And he was surprised at her reaction. He had kept his voice soft but firm.

Still, not so firm that she should physically flinch away from him. Like she thought he might hurt her.

"Baby, what's going on?" he asked quietly.

"I, um, I thought you were Jake. He was here earlier."

He quelled any hurt that she might want Jake and not him. Because this wasn't about his feelings. This was about her.

And right in that moment, he would do anything for her.

"Yeah, he was here, but he called me because you weren't opening the door and he was getting worried about you. He was going to get Molly to come over so they could do a welfare check."

"W-what? He was?" Her eyes were wide with shock.

Did she not realize how much the people in this town cared about her? And how worried and concerned they were?

"Yeah, baby. Everyone is worried about you."

"Because I got a bit dizzy?"

He frowned. A bit dizzy?

"You fainted, darlin'." And right now, she looked like she was close to passing out again. "You weren't just dizzy. And I think everyone's concern goes beyond that."

A grimace this time. "I don't want to cause anyone to worry."

"I know you don't." Christ, she looked so fragile. This wasn't happy, sweet Hannah. And it wasn't frosty, stay-away-from-me Hannah.

This Hannah was so delicate, she was almost brittle. And he was scared that one wrong touch or move would break her.

Which meant he had to tread carefully. It was going to be a tough balancing act. Being firm yet gentle.

But he'd figure it out because the last thing he wanted was to harm her.

"You got something to eat, darlin'?"

She gave him a startled look. "W-what?"

He put his hand over his stomach. "I missed lunch and now I'm starving. Pretty sure I'm in danger of fading away."

She blinked. Then she glanced down at her watch. "It's five to one."

"Yep. And lunch is at twelve on the ranch."

"So you're fifty-five minutes late to eat, and you're starving?"

"I'm always starving. Doesn't matter what time it is. So you got any food, or do we need to go get some?"

"Go get some?" she repeated, looking like she wasn't following at all.

His poor baby.

"Yeah, baby. Food. For a man who is starving." He leaned against the doorway. Sure, he could force his way inside her apartment. But this was about far more than low blood sugar. Even if she hadn't been acting oddly leading up to this, it was clear to see something more had happened. "What do you say?"

"I, um . . . now isn't a good time."

"There's never a time when it isn't a good time to eat."

She stared at him for a moment.

"Well, maybe when you're using the toilet," he mused. "That doesn't seem a great time to eat."

More staring.

"Or in church. I imagine the pastor wouldn't appreciate that."

"Or a funeral," she whispered. "Or while swimming."

"Good points, darlin'. But you know when is a good time to eat?"

"When?"

"Right now. So, are you going to take pity on me and make me a sandwich?" He gave her his best puppy dog look.

Something like amusement filled her face. And he couldn't lie, his legs went a bit noodle-like with relief. Because he'd been afraid that his Hannah had completely disappeared.

That she wasn't just hiding. That she was truly gone and not coming back. However, that twitch of her lips gave him hope.

"So, I not only have to supply the fixings, but I have to make you the sandwich as well?"

He let his lower lip droop. "I can make it myself. I might keel over while doing it, but I'm willing to take that risk."

"Well, I should be grateful that you're willing to keel over while making yourself a sandwich because you're starving from missing lunch fifty-five minutes ago," she said dryly.

Thank fuck.

He didn't know what had happened today. And from what he was guessing, it wasn't going to be good . . . and it was going to make him mad. But whatever had happened had helped her drop her icy cold shield. And let the real Hannah shine through.

His challenge was going to be getting that Hannah to stay here with him.

While also keeping his shit together when learning what had happened to her.

"I'm glad you understand where I'm coming from, darlin'. Now, in order for me to make this sandwich, am I coming in or are we going to the store to get the fixings?"

She stared from him to behind him. Then, back over her shoulder at the kitchen. He tried his best to hide that he'd grown tense. If she tried to make him leave, he knew he was going to get forceful.

And then she'd likely clam up again.

"Darlin'?" he murmured. "What are we going to do?"

"I don't . . . I don't know, Raid. I just . . . I don't know."

He got it then. Or, at least, he thought he did. Hannah was struggling. He could see it in her face. It might be because she was exhausted, perhaps overwhelmed, but it could also be part of who Hannah was. He knew she liked to submit when she went to Saxon's. Maybe it was about more than just play or sex.

But Hannah needed to not be making decisions right now.

These were things that he needed to know about her. He had to do some research so he could give her whatever she required. But his priorities right now were to ensure she was all right physically.

Then, emotionally.

There was a lot to unravel here. Yet what mattered most was that he was here, and she was talking to him.

"Darlin', I'm hungry, and I've been out here a while. Let me in, yeah?" He worded it as a question, but put some sternness into his voice.

Even though she still looked worried, the tension left her, and she nodded.

Her shields were down enough that her need to please came through. As well as her desire not to have to make the decision about what to do. Because he'd taken it out of her hands.

That's what she needed from him. Someone to take over, even if it was just for a short while. To give her some respite.

He knew Alec thrived on being in control. That he was a better man for having people to look after.

Sometimes, that meant he was a bossy, interfering bastard.

They'd all been ecstatic when he found Mia, figuring he'd focus his control-freak behavior on her. And that the rest of them would be able to breathe without him trying to smother them.

He also knew that while Alec felt better when he had a woman to take care of, Mia thrived from having him look after her. Not take over her life completely, but someone she could go to if she needed help. Someone who would help her, cheer her on, be there when she fell. Someone who had no problem standing between her and the world when she needed a bit of added protection.

For the first time in his life, Raid felt that need to be that for someone else.

But not just anyone. Hannah.

Yep, maybe it was time he had an awkward, but necessary, talk with his brother.

Hannah didn't give him any more problems as she let him in and shut the door behind him. More proof that her shields were seriously shaken.

Tomorrow, she might wake up with them firmly in place

again, so he knew he had to prepare himself for that. But today, he'd push his advantage.

Raid glanced around the small apartment as he'd barely paid attention the other night. He'd been expecting neat and tidy. Something warm and inviting.

It looked to be basically three rooms. A combined lounge and kitchen with two doors off it, which he guessed led to her bathroom and bedroom.

There were clothes on the pale pink velvet sofa. Unopened mail across the kitchen island. A white fluffy rug on the floor that looked like it needed a good vacuum.

Okay, he'd been very worried before.

Now, he was really, really worried.

Why the hell hadn't he done more earlier? He shouldn't have let her turn him away.

"I, um . . . my place is a bit of a mess." She stared around the room as though unsure how her apartment had gotten into such a state. "I, uh, um . . . I'll just pick up a few things."

As she turned away, she managed to trip over a pair of boots. Thankfully, this time, before she could hit the floor, Raid was there to grab her. He picked her up, holding her against his chest as she let out a shocked gasp.

"Fuck, baby, you feel so good in my arms, but you also feel way too light."

"W-what?"

Crap. That probably wasn't something he should say to her. But it had just popped out. And his concern increased. Was this why she'd fainted? Because she wasn't eating enough?

"When was the last time you ate?" he demanded. He tried to ignore the way she was shaking.

Because if he thought about the reason for her fear, he might lose his legendary temper. And that wasn't what she needed.

But he also didn't want to let her go. Because he thought she needed to feel someone touch her. Someone who wasn't intent on hurting her.

He sensed rather than saw her clam up. She was rebuilding those walls, but that wasn't something that he could let her do.

"Did you have breakfast? Because when I make a sandwich, I make a *sandwich*."

Confusion filled her face. But he was glad to see she no longer had that frosty expression that he was growing to hate.

"Am I supposed to know what that means?"

"You will, baby."

"Um." She chewed her lip. "Are you going to put me down?"

"Hmm. I like the way you feel in my arms, so I'm thinking no."

She raised her eyebrows. "No? You don't think that it might be a bit hard to make a sandwich while holding onto me?"

"I think I can manage. Plus, if you're in my arms, I know you're safe."

She stiffened.

Fuck.

He didn't like that. He liked it even less than when the frosty ice queen tried to make an appearance, all expression on her face disappearing.

Did that mean she didn't believe she was safe? Or was it an indication that at some time she hadn't been safe?

Yep.

He fucking hated that.

"Baby," he whispered.

She shut her eyes and had a pained look on her face. "Please put me down."

"No." He made his voice firm. He didn't want to frighten her. Didn't want her to shatter on him.

But he also had to make a few things clear.

"I don't want to put you down because I like the way you feel in my arms. I think I should have led with that. But sometimes, I don't say the right thing. Some of my brothers know what to say and when. Some of them are blunt as hell. Well, perhaps just West. Me, I guess I'm a bit of both. So when I picked you up and said how light you were, it wasn't because I was criticizing you. And it wasn't because I don't like the way you feel in my arms. I love the way you feel against me. I could carry you like this all day. Okay?"

She stared up at him, her mouth slightly open. "What is happening right now?"

"What's happening is me telling you that you're important to me. I like you. I want to get to know you better. And, baby, I'm worried about you. A lot."

She bit her lip, looking scared and confused.

"Everyone is worried about you."

"I don't want people to worry about me. I don't want to be a problem."

He squeezed her while letting out a small growl. "What's your middle name?"

"What?"

"Middle name, darlin'? What is yours?"

"Um, Megan."

"Hannah Megan McLeod, you are not, nor could you ever be, a problem. Do you understand me?"

"Um, well, I—"

"And if you hadn't fainted today, you'd be over my knee right now for even suggesting that."

He felt her stiffen, but he needed to keep going.

"And I know that there's probably supposed to be communication and an agreement and a safeword. But since I'm not spanking you right now, we'll let that part slide until I am spanking you."

"You . . . what . . . you're going to spank me?"

"I'm your guardian." He moved so he could settle on the couch with her on his lap.

He didn't know why she wasn't eating. But it was evident that she really wasn't taking care of herself.

He needed to step in.

Both as her guardian and her soon-to-be man.

She didn't know it yet, but everything for Hannah was about to change.

8

Hannah wasn't sure what was happening right now.

She didn't really know why Raid was here . . . he was acting odd. Since she'd been back, she'd barely seen him. Of course, that could be because she hardly went anywhere. To the clinic for her part-time job. To the grocery store or the pharmacy.

Well, there was one night when her friends had guilted her into going to Dirty Delights.

Which had been a mistake. Unfortunately, she couldn't go back and change it. Only now, for some weird reason, Raid seemed to think he was in charge of her.

Her guardian.

She'd never had one. Jake had always looked out for her. But she'd never given him cause for concern.

Until she'd learned that it didn't matter how good you were, how much you tried to be good and do what you were told.

Someone could still screw you over.

There will always be bad people who could hurt you.

Lord, she was stupid.

"Hey, darlin'. Where did your mind just go?" he asked gently.

She was kind of surprised. She hadn't realized Raid could be gentle. Funny, yes. Sexy, of course. And the other night, she'd learned he could be stern and commanding.

But this was something new. And she was learning that she might have been a bit short-sighted when it came to him.

"I, um . . . Raid, you're not my guardian."

I like you.

He didn't mean that like she hoped he did. There was no way he could.

And even if he did . . . would he want her when he knew what had happened to her?

"I am. I claimed you the other night in front of Duncan. And I just told Jake earlier that I'm now your guardian after he called me because he was concerned about you."

"He shouldn't have done that." She hadn't agreed to anything.

"Of course he should have. Because I need to know if something happens to you. Like you fainting. Now I want to know why you didn't go to the hospital for some more tests. And also why you left the clinic and hid yourself in your apartment."

"I wasn't hiding."

She'd totally been hiding.

"Don't lie to me, baby. I get that something happened to you. I know that it wasn't good. I'm guessing your bastard ex had something to do with what happened, and that makes me furious. But whatever you want to tell me, whatever else happens, just do not lie to me. Understand? You can refuse to answer, but no lies between us."

She tried to calm her breathing. Looking up at him, she gave a short nod. "No lies."

"That's my good girl."

She had to close her eyes against the pain of those words.

Words she would have once loved to hear from his lips. Months ago.

Words which now flayed her.

"Can you not call me that?"

He stiffened. "A good girl?"

"Yeah. That." She cleared her throat. "Please." Her voice broke on the last word and he held her tight.

"I won't say it to you again. At least until I know what the fuck is going on."

There was a note of frustration in his voice. And she got it. She'd be frustrated with her if she were him, too. Which meant he wouldn't stick around for long.

So maybe you should take what you can get while you can get it.

Because this might be the only time Raid Malone held her like this. And even though she didn't want to melt into his arms, to feel a sense of safety, that's what was happening.

And perhaps, for a little while, she could forget that she was messed up. That she couldn't have normal.

That she couldn't have someone as beautiful as Raid Malone.

"I can't ever tell you," she whispered.

"You will." There was a note of steel in his voice.

"You won't . . . you really would be better just leaving, Raid. I'm not worth the hassle. I promise."

"That's the last time I want to hear you say that, too. Unless you want me to start keeping track. Then, when you're feeling better, we can have ourselves a reckoning."

"A reckoning?" she asked.

"Yeah, where you learn the error of your ways. And when I say 'your ways,' I mean this bullshit you have going on where you try to tell me that you're a hassle or a problem or not worth it. Damn it, Hannah."

She winced at his tone more than his words.

He'd see.

The more time he spent with her, the more he'd see.

"You should leave."

"Nope. That's the last thing I should do. See, I thought maybe you needed time. That you only needed soft and gentle. And you do need that. But you also need someone to be stern with you, too. Who won't let you get away with shit. I'm a new age kind of guy, so I can admit when I'm wrong."

She gaped up at him.

A new age kind of guy? Was he kidding her? He had to be joking.

"Are you trying to make me laugh?"

A soft look came over his face. "I would love nothing more than to see you laugh."

Christ.

Why? Why couldn't he have done any of this before? With old-Hannah? She would have lapped it up like someone who was starved being led to a buffet.

And now she knew she had to send him away—for his sake and hers.

Because hope is a terrible thing. It leads you to do stupid things.

And she couldn't let herself believe that she could have him. It would be far too painful when he left.

"But I'm not joking. And from now on, I will give you what you need."

"What does that mean?" she asked, concern filling her.

Because she could kind of guess what it meant.

"It means that as your guardian, your health, well-being, safety, and happiness is all my concern. So it's up to me to ensure that you're well looked after. Beginning with taking you to get checked out so we can find out why you fainted today."

"But I already know."

Don't tell him.

"Yeah? So tell me."

"It's none of your business since you aren't my guardian."

"I declared it with Jake and Duncan."

"You forget that I've lived in this town for years. I know that's not all it takes. I get a say."

"Unless the sheriff is seriously worried about your health and safety. Enough to do a welfare check. Then he can ask someone to watch over you until he's satisfied you're well."

"That's never done." Not that she knew of, anyway.

"Baby, you fainted. You've tried to shut everyone out, push them away. I don't know why you think you have to face whatever demons you have alone when the whole fucking town wants to grab their pitchforks and rifles and fight them for you. You have more people in your corner than you can possibly know, Hannah. But even more importantly, you have me."

"Oh, that's more important?" she asked faintly. Lord, he had a big ego.

But she couldn't say that it was unattractive.

"Yep, because I will do whatever is necessary to make you laugh again, fight those demons back, and get back the Hannah we used to know."

"She's gone, Raid. She's never coming back. And if you think you can bring her back, then you're going to be disappointed."

"Then a new Hannah. One who doesn't push people away. One who knows her own self-worth. One who has a reason to smile."

She shook her head, tears filling her eyes until he became blurry.

"I don't think that's possible."

"No crying," he ordered. "And yeah, it is. If you accept some fucking help."

"You can't just order me not to cry," she informed him as tears dripped down her cheeks.

"Sure, I can. Do. Not. Cry. Do as you're told."

"Do as I'm told?" she asked, feeling those tears start to dry.

"Sure, that's the way this works, right? I tell you what to do, you do it."

"The way what works?"

"This guardianship stuff. And the fact that you're a sub."

Her temper stirred. "Just because I'm a sub does not mean you get to tell me what to do all the time. That's not the way it works."

"It's not?" he asked.

"No. That sort of thing requires consent and going through limits. And not all subs are the same, you know."

"They're not?"

"No. Some subs might want a 24/7 power exchange, while others might like to submit only when they play. Or for pleasure. We all have different needs and desires. So you can't just boss me around and expect I'll obey you."

"Well, I wasn't expecting you to always obey me."

She stared up at him suspiciously.

"Figured sometimes you might disobey me and then I'd get to spank you."

"I was never a brat," she said. "I liked doing what people wanted because I liked to please. I cared about other people's feelings and desires, and I liked meeting them. It made me feel needed."

Crap. What was she doing?

She tried to get off his lap, but he held her against him.

"Keep going," he ordered quietly.

She shook her head. She'd already said too much. Revealed more than she should have.

"You said 'was', baby. Do you not still have those same needs? Wants?"

"No."

"You're sure?"

"I'm sure." Because that's what had got her into this trouble. She'd been stupid and naive and a pushover. So now all she wanted out of life was to be left alone.

"You need to leave," she told him.

"No."

"Go!"

"Not happening."

"Damn it, Raid! Just go! I need you to leave. Let. Me. Go!"

He let her go, and she stood up, but he stayed where he was on her sofa. It was a ridiculous sofa. Feminine and delicate, and he looked wrong on it.

But he didn't seem to care.

She clenched her hands into fists. Crap. She needed to find her calm. Needed to bring the ice queen back.

But it was so hard with him. He just seemed to push all of her buttons.

"And I told you I'm done giving you space, darlin'. That it was the wrong thing to do. Because leaving you on your own gave you the opportunity to hurt yourself. And I can't allow that to happen."

"I didn't hurt myself." That had never really occurred to her.

"You hurt yourself when you don't take care of yourself. When you neglect your health to the point that you faint. And I'm not just talking about your physical health."

"My health isn't your business. I'm not your business. I don't want to be your business." She said it as nastily as she could. Because she needed him out of there.

"You can bullshit me all you like, baby. But I'm here and I'm not going anywhere."

"Damn it! You're the most stubborn man I've ever met!"

"Nice of you to notice."

"That wasn't a compliment."

"Wasn't it?"

"Urgh. You're also infuriating." She stomped her foot. Wow. Hannah didn't think she'd ever stomped her foot before. She wasn't the temper tantrum sort of person.

"So kind."

"Raid Malone. I know you know that those aren't compliments. Just like I'm pretty sure you know, you can't just boss me around and expect me to obey. Or barge in here and try to take over my life. I'm a grown woman. Yes, I was once a sub. And I . . . I once had a crush on you. I once wanted a relationship, marriage, the picket fence, and kids. But I'm not that girl anymore. And you need to go. Because I no longer want you."

9

Raid stared at her for a long moment.

She expected him to storm out of there. Raid wasn't known for his even temper. He'd never harm her, but he might get grumpy. She had to prepare herself for that.

As if she hadn't had enough stress today, this was just adding to it.

"Nice try, sweetness. But I know what you're doing. You're trying to do whatever you can to push me away. Do your worst. I'm not going anywhere."

She winced. "Can you not call me that either?"

Surprise filled his face, followed by anger. This was Raid.

He won't hurt me.

"Sweetness?" he asked.

She nodded woodenly.

"Is that what he called you? Sweetness? Good girl?"

"Sort of," she whispered. She knew she was revealing too much. But honestly, the stubborn ass wasn't leaving.

And she needed him to go.

Because the longer he was here, the more she worried she'd lose all of her shields. And she needed them.

"What did he do to you, Hannah?" he asked.

She shook her head. Part of her wanted to tell him. But she didn't want him to look at her differently.

What if he doesn't? What if he still wants you?

He deserves better than me.

"You need to go, Raid."

"No, Hannah. You're mine to take care of."

"I'm not! I'm not your responsibility."

"Like I told you, I've decided differently."

"You've decided differently?" she said in a low, quiet voice.

"Yep. And you know once you say it, there are no takesies-backsies."

"Takesies-backsies?"

"Yeah, you've heard of takesies-backsies, right? Well, this is the opposite. Now, I was serious. I really am hungry. Are you going to let me starve to death?"

She had to check the urge to immediately go and make him something to eat. She squelched that part of herself that wanted to take care of him.

"If you're hungry, the diner isn't far. Leave."

"Hannah, baby, you're just not getting this. I'm not leaving. I am here to stay until I'm sure that you're all right. Maybe even beyond that. This is what is going to happen. I'm going to quickly make us both a sandwich. You're going to get your handbag and whatever else you need for a trip to the hospital. And then, we're heading off."

She shook her head, then had to close her eyes for a moment as the world spun.

Shit.

She probably needed to eat. Or at least sit down. Coffee.

Maybe she just needed coffee. But she worried that as soon as something hit her stomach, it would come back up.

When she opened her eyes, she let out a startled gasp as she saw that Raid was now standing in front of her.

"How do you move so quietly?" she snapped.

Then she felt bad.

Then she felt angry because she felt bad.

Honestly, it was a vicious freaking cycle.

"When you grow up with seven brothers, you learn how to sneak around quietly. Some of those assholes are freaking psychopaths."

"What?" She gave him a startled look.

"West used to wake us up for school by pouring cold water on our heads. Psychopath."

Oh, yeah. She could see West doing that. He was a bit scary. So was Alec, but in a different way. The only time West seemed softer and happier was around Flick.

"Why did he do that?" she asked.

"Because we wouldn't get up otherwise." Raid sent her a wicked grin. But that quickly faded into a look of concern.

Lord, Hannah was so tired of people staring at her like that. Or, even worse, with pity.

"I don't want you here."

"Tough."

"I'm not going to the hospital, Raid. I'm not having any tests done."

His eyes narrowed, and she had to shore up her defenses. It was hard for her not to give in. To give him what he wanted.

Where was her icy resolve?

Damn it. She had to do better than this.

The trouble was that this was Raid . . . the man she'd always dreamed about, always wanted.

Her resolve was waning in the face of his stubbornness.

"No?" he murmured.

"No."

"I could force you."

She tensed. "You can't do that."

"Do I need to remind you that I'm your guardian?"

"That's not happening, Raid."

"Baby, I'm done arguing about this. It's done. But okay, if you don't want to go to the hospital, that's fine."

Her head spun at his about-face. "What?"

"I want you to sit down. You're too pale and I don't want you fainting again." Instead of guiding her to the sofa, he pressed a hand to the small of her back to push her toward the small dining set.

She flinched and tried to jump away, but he either didn't notice or was ignoring her reaction.

Thankfully, the apartment had come furnished, even if it was a bit worn and older. Especially the dining set. Raid drew out a chair for her, glancing down at it with a frown as it wobbled.

"This doesn't seem safe."

"Raid–"

"Come here." He took hold of her wrist and led her to the kitchen.

This time, surprisingly, she didn't flinch. Was she getting used to him touching her? She didn't think that was really possible.

Then, so suddenly that he didn't even give her a chance to tense or protest, he turned and lifted her onto the counter.

"Raid!" she cried breathlessly.

The only problem was that she didn't know if she was breathless from fear or because Raid Malone had just lifted her.

Again.

Like she weighed nothing.

"Yeah?"

"I'm not a doll that you can just carry around or put where you want me to go."

He raised his eyebrows, looking amused. What did he think was so funny? She wasn't being funny. She was actually quite serious.

"I mean it."

"I know you do, darlin'. But, the thing is, I like picking you up. I like putting you places. So I think I'm gonna keep doing it."

"You can't keep doing things just because you like to do them," she told him as he searched through her cupboards and fridge.

Embarrassment hit her as he saw how much food she had . . . which wasn't a lot.

She attempted to slide off the counter, but he turned back to her, trapping her on the countertop.

Her breath caught in her throat.

Not Steven. He wasn't Steven.

A large, warm hand rested on her chest. "Breathe, baby. Sorry, I scared you. Just remember that I won't ever hurt you."

"You need to stop touching me."

"Bossy, aren't you? Luckily, I think your bossiness is cute."

He . . . she . . . what?

"My bossiness is not cute. And I'm not the bossy one. You are."

"You're the one throwing around orders, darlin'."

"And you're not listening to any of them."

"Nah, because you don't really mean them."

Was it possible for her head to explode?

"Raid . . ." she trailed off, completely unsure what she wanted to say. "What's going on here?"

"You know what's going on," he told her gently. "I told you that I care about you. I want to make sure you're all right. And if you're not going to go to the hospital, then I'm going to feed you, make sure you rest, and look after you. What I'm not going to do is leave you. What if you faint again? You could fall and hit your head. What if you're ill?"

"I'm not sick." Icy calm. Chill. "I just got dizzy because I stood up too fast. And you need to give me space before I decide to call Jake and let him know that you are harassing me."

She lightly pushed at him, and he took two steps back.

Finally, she could breathe a bit easier. And she was going to ignore that ache she felt in her stomach as he stepped away from her.

She did not like him touching her.

Right. You can tell yourself that until you're blue in the face. It doesn't change things.

Not only did she like his touch, but she feared after this that no one else's touch would ever feel as good as his.

Although that shouldn't be a problem, since she was done with men.

"You're not going to do that."

"I will." She worked on pulling her shields together.

He shrugged. "All right, darlin'. I can't stop you. But that means that Jake will be doing a welfare check on you. And if he thinks you need it, he'll move you in with him and Molly. Or in with Melody and Brye. That what you want?"

God, no.

She couldn't do that.

Shit.

"You're better with me. I might be bossy. But I only want to make sure that you're all right."

"You don't . . . you don't really like me. This is just . . . it's the chase. You think I'm a damsel in distress and you have a hero complex."

She made sure to keep her voice cold and emotionless.

Even if, on the inside, she was losing her mind.

Old-Hannah wanted to take the words back because she knew that he'd leave now, and she'd never have an opportunity like this again.

Sure enough, anger filled his face. Raid was an easygoing guy most of the time. But he had a temper. And it usually came out when someone he cared about was threatened.

Or, apparently, when you told him that he had a hero complex.

"Excuse me?" He stepped forward. And even though she'd braced herself, she couldn't help but flinch back.

Her head banged into the wall behind her. The pain wasn't that bad, but it was enough to make her whimper as she closed her eyes.

"Fuck. Fuck!"

She opened her eyes to find him pacing the room, his head down, his shoulders slumped.

He looked dejected.

Oh God. Is this what she was doing to him? She was making him feel sad and disheartened. Lord . . . she was destroying him.

This right here was another reason to keep pushing him away.

But she just couldn't do it. What the hell was wrong with her?

Tears dripped down her face. "I'm sorry. Raid, I'm so sorry. I'm so very s-sorry." Trembles rocked her slight body as she sat there, hugging herself, trying to calm herself down.

She struggled to breathe as she lost it.

Then, suddenly, she was in his arms. And she didn't have the energy to fight him. Or to fear him.

He gathered her against him. Holding her so tight that it made it harder to breathe. But she needed that.

She felt like she was falling apart, and needed him to hold her together.

He moved with her, and she ended up in his lap on the floor. But she didn't care. More. She needed more.

"Tighter," she urged. "Hold me tighter."

"Baby," he whispered.

"Please hold me tighter. I'm going to lose it if you don't."

"Maybe you should let it all go, baby. Just let it all out."

A sob broke free. Then another one. Tears fell down her cheeks as she shuddered in his hold.

"I can't ... I can't ..."

"You can," he told her. "You can let go because I'm here, Hannah. And you know I'm going to keep you safe. Can you feel how strong I am? I have you surrounded. I'm not letting go. I'm not letting you push me away. I'm here."

"You shouldn't be! You should just let me go."

"Why?"

"Because I'm not worth it!" The words slammed through the room, bringing instant silence. "I'm not worth it, Raid. You deserve better than me. You deserve beauty and sweetness and sunshine. I'm not any of those things anymore. Before ... before all of this, then we might have worked. But not now. I'm ... I'm dirty."

"Fuck. Fuck!" She jumped and he then hushed her gently. "Shh. Shh. Shh. You don't need to fear me. I'm sorry. I know I need to control it. But, fuck, baby girl, don't ever fear me. Okay? I'm not him. I'm not going to hurt you."

She didn't even try to deny what had happened. It would be pointless. It was obvious she was a mess. And that Steven had something to do with that.

Even if Raid didn't know the details, he had the big picture in his mind.

"I k-know you're not. But I c-can't help it."

He rocked her back and forth. "Let it out. Let the poison out. Give it to me."

"I can't!"

"Baby," his voice broke.

"I just can't. I don't want you to have it. It's mine. It's my cross to bear." She pressed her face into that spot where his neck and shoulder met.

He was so warm. So strong.

And yeah, she felt safe in his arms. She felt safe for the first time in months.

"I'm sorry I didn't make it clear to you earlier that I want you," he whispered. "I didn't realize until it was too late, and by the time I was ready to ask you out, you were already seeing him."

She jolted at that information. "What?"

"After I got back from New Orleans, I came into town to find you. Wanted to ask you on a date. But Brye told me that you'd met someone."

Oh God.

This was so much worse. She could have had him. Then, none of this would have happened.

But more importantly . . . she would have had him.

What would she have done if he'd come up and asked her out? Would she have broken things off with Steven?

Lord, she didn't know.

And it didn't matter.

Because what was done was done. And there was no erasing it or taking it back.

"You can give it to me, baby. I have big shoulders. And I promise that if I'm going to lose it, then I'll walk away and lose it on my own. I usually have good control of my temper, but women or children being harmed . . . that can set me off. But I will control it around you. I promise. And no matter what. I will never harm you. Not ever."

"I know," she whispered. Those tears just wouldn't stop. She was a complete mess. "I k-know. I do know you w-won't hurt me. It's just . . . it's instinctive."

"Fucking bastard," he muttered, and she could hear the banked anger in his voice. He was trying to keep calm.

For her.

"I fucking hate that he taught you to fear people."

Because she hadn't been like that before. She'd been open and loving and trusting.

"I was a fool. A stupid, naive fool. That's why this is all on me, R-raid. It's not for you to shoulder. It's not your nightmare to l-live."

"Anything to do with you is my business. And a nightmare shared is a nightmare halved."

"I don't think that's how the saying goes."

"I don't think I care much how the saying goes."

To her shock, she felt the urge to smile at that. He wouldn't. Raid made his own rules.

But she stifled the smile.

"However, I get the feeling you're not ready to share what happened."

"Really? You have that feeling?"

It felt bizarre that she could joke like this. She was drained, completely done in. There was nothing she had left to give to anyone. But letting out those tears also felt a bit cathartic. She'd cried since everything happened, of course. But those tears had never released the knot inside her. They'd never made her feel better.

So even though her head was thumping, and she was more tired than she could ever remember, she felt lighter. As though her burdens were lifted.

Maybe he was right in a way. Perhaps she had given him some of her worries. She hadn't told him anything. But she'd shared her tears, her pain.

And he'd taken them on without even flinching.

"I'm very intuitive."

"You are?" she asked.

"Yep. Ask anyone. They all say it. That Raid Malone, he's fucking intuitive."

"What else do they say?" Her words were almost slurred with how tired she was.

"They say that Raid Malone, he's very good-looking. Far better looking than all his brothers. And he's smart. Far smarter than all his brothers. Oh, and he's charming."

"Let me guess? Far more charming than his brothers?" she said dryly.

"Why, darlin', thanks for the compliment. I mean, it is the truth, but I appreciate you saying it."

"You're terrible."

"I know you're having a bad day, so that's why you're getting your words all jumbled. See, the word you're looking for is gorgeous or amazing or sexiest man you've ever seen in your life."

"That's not one word."

"It's hard to describe me in one word."

"Well, modest definitely wouldn't be the word I would use," she said dryly.

He squeezed her tight. "Finished crying?"

"Yeah. I think so."

"Good. Don't do that again." There was a chiding note in his voice.

She tensed. "What? Lose it like that? Get scared of you? I can't really help doing that . . ." She wished she could stop. She really did.

How amazing would it be if she could simply forget? Move on with her life? If she could touch people again and have them touch her without flinching or panicking.

Yeah, she needed a memory erasing pill.

"No, I don't mean that. Of course I would prefer you didn't flinch when I touched you. But I know that's going to take time. What I meant was, don't cry again."

Wait . . . was he joking?

He had to be right?

Forgetting that she likely looked terrible, she leaned back to stare up at him. "Are you joking?"

He frowned and stared back down at her. "Why would I be joking?"

"Um, because you can't order me not to cry."

"Sure I can. I just did."

"Raid!" she cried. "I have to cry."

"Why?"

"I don't know . . . it's a way of releasing stress and worry, I guess. It's natural."

He frowned. "It's not natural. And if you need to get rid of your stress and worry, I have a better way for you to do it."

All right, now this she had to hear.

"I'm all ears."

"You give it to me."

"Huh?"

"You give it to me and you let me take care of it for you."

"So if I have a worry . . . say someone at work was causing problems for me. I'd just tell you and then the worry would magically disappear?"

"Nothing magic about it, darlin'. I'd make the worry disappear."

"And how would you do that?"

"By taking care of it for you."

She waited.

But he didn't grin or wink or laugh.

He was . . . he was serious. How could he seriously think that was an option?

"I can't tell you my problems and have you take care of them for me."

"Why not?"

"Because I . . . that's not how things work."

"That's not how what things work?"

"It's not how anything works! And don't you think you'd get sick of taking care of all my concerns and worries?"

"Hmm."

Okay, now she had him. She waited for him to tell her that she was right.

"Do you have that many, darlin'?"

"Currently, it seems like I'm drowning in them," she muttered.

Shit. What the hell was wrong with her? Had she entered some alternate universe where she just blurted stuff out?

He drew her even closer. "Fuck, baby. I don't like that."

"Yeah, try being me, then." It was an attempt at a joke. But it fell epically flat.

"Baby, if I could take it all away from you, put it all on me, then I would."

She shook her head, sadness filling her. "Why couldn't this have happened before . . . why now?"

"Maybe the universe had a different plan in mind for us," he said.

"Do you really believe that?" Did the universe really think she had to go through everything she had in order to find Raid at the end?

If so, the universe sucked.

"No," he said in a tight voice. "I think this is my fault for not seeing what was right in front of my nose."

"It's not your fault, Raid."

"Maybe not fully," he admitted. "Most of it is your ex's fault. But for not making a move on you earlier, yeah, that's mine. And what I've learned from that is that when you want something you don't waste time, you don't fuck around, you go after it and you take it."

"And I'm the thing you want?" she asked faintly.

"Baby, you're everything I've ever wanted. And more."

10

R aid knew she was exhausted.

He knew this because she looked it, she sounded it, and because she had stopped fighting him. She'd dropped all her shields; no doubt she had no energy left to keep them up.

He needed to get her to rest and eat.

And he really wanted to have her checked out.

He stood with her cradled in his arms.

"Whoa, you're strong."

He was, but she was also too light. However, he didn't tell her that. Raid was a man who could learn from his mistakes.

Luckily, he made very few. Probably like one or two a year.

He set her back on the counter and placed his hands on either side of her, grabbing hold. "Right. This is what's going to happen."

She eyed him with surprise.

"I won't take you to the hospital on two, no, three conditions."

"Just three?"

"Let me think about that for a moment. I could make it four, but that seems overkill."

"No. You think?"

"Hmm. We'll start with three, you brat."

She bit her lip. "I'm not a brat."

"No, you're a . . ." Fuck. He couldn't call her a good girl. But that's what she was. He hated that those words were lost to her. "You're my precious girl."

Relief filled her face, then it flooded with anger. "I hate that he took those words from me. They were once mine. Once, they made me happy. I was a . . ." Her nose screwed up as though she'd tasted something bad.

He fought back his temper. That was the last thing she needed. Taking a deep breath, he let it out slowly.

"Then we'll take them back."

"What?" she asked.

"We'll take them back. You and me. I might not know what he did to you, but I will one day. He doesn't get to keep those words. He doesn't get to continue to use them to hurt you. If you want to be a good girl again, then that's what you will be. Understand?"

"I don't think that's possible."

"Did you think it'd be possible for me to be here like this in your apartment?"

She shook her head.

That's what he'd thought.

"And did you think it'd ever be possible that I'd get to hold you in my arms as you cried without you having a panic attack?"

She bit her lip. "I had a small one. Deep inside."

He just raised his eyebrows at her.

"No, I didn't."

"And did you think it would be possible for me to do this?" Reaching up, he cupped the side of her face with his hand. He knew it was risky. It could make her go back into her shell. Bring up the ice queen. But he had to try. To show her that she didn't need to fear him.

And that the things she thought were gone forever actually weren't.

She flinched but didn't move away. And even though he hated the flinch, he knew they were making progress.

It might be a matter of two steps forward, one step back. But as long as they were going forward, he could deal.

"We're not going to let him win, Hannah."

"I think he already has."

"No, baby. But it's okay if you're having doubts. I'm sure enough for the two of us."

"Why are you really here, Raid? I'm nothing special. I'm not worth all the bother I'm going to give you. It's amazing that you want to help me. You keep saying the right things, well, mostly, but I just don't get it. Before, I was just Hannah. Kind of quiet and boring. Now, it's worse. I'm broken-Hannah."

"I'm going to kill that motherfucker." He kept his voice soft, even though that was extremely hard when he wanted to yell the words.

She still gasped, her eyes wide. But at least she didn't pull away.

"You are not broken, Hannah."

The look she gave him was full of pity. So was the pat on his arm. It was the first time she voluntarily touched him since she returned home to Haven, and it was a pity touch.

Eh, what the hell, he'd take it.

She was touching him. And he was touching her.

That was far more than he'd thought they would have today. His phone buzzed but he ignored it.

No way was anyone interrupting this conversation. It was too important.

"I am. I'm so broken, I don't even know where all the pieces are. I'm just trying to patch them together with duct tape and a bit of prayer. Don't you see it, Raid?"

He raised his other hand to cup her face. "What I see is a seriously beautiful girl who's been through something traumatic. I see someone who is kind and caring and sweet. She might be trying to hide herself behind an icy mask, but there're cracks in that mask. And while parts of her might have changed, the core of her is the same. And there's no telling who this new Hannah might be."

"She's nothing good. You deserve better."

Oh, hell no.

"And you just earned yourself a spanking."

She tensed. "Raid."

"Not now. Obviously, you're not ready for that." He dropped his hands to the counter. "But when you are, you'll be getting one for ever suggesting shit like that. I'm the one who doesn't deserve you. I'm not going to let that stop me from having you, though."

"I can't give you me."

"Baby, you already are. You cried in my arms. That's the start of it."

"You're impossible. This can't happen."

"Nothing has ever been impossible for a Malone."

"Lord help me. You're not even joking, are you?"

"Nope. This is happening. But I can be generous. I'll give you some time to get your head around it."

"Right," she said. "How much time?"

"I don't know. A day or two."

"So generous."

"I thought so."

She narrowed her gaze at him, but he just smiled. "You might not be ready to talk about what happened, and I can be patient. But that patience will only go so far. I'm going to convince you to tell me. To give me that burden, those fears. Otherwise, it's going to stand between us. And I won't allow anything to do that. Not even you."

"I feel like yesterday I went to sleep in one universe and this morning I woke up in another."

"Welcome to the universe of Raid Malone. It can be a bit rocky at times, so you might want to find someone strong to hold on to. And in case you don't pick up what I'm putting down, I mean me."

"Does anyone say that anymore?"

"I just did. Now, there's nothing in your cupboards. Not even enough to feed a mouse. Which, don't freak out, I think you might have one."

"Oh yeah, I definitely do."

"Ah, you didn't think to put down some mousetraps, darlin'?"

"Well, no."

"Because . . ."

"That might hurt him."

"They're meant to kill the mouse, that's the idea. To get rid of it." His phone buzzed again, and he sighed.

She chewed her lip. "I know. It just seems mean."

"Baby, you can't live in an apartment with mice. I'm gonna get you some traps."

"But what if the traps catch the mouse?"

He just stared at her, not sure what she was asking.

"What do I do with the . . . with the body?"

Oh, now he understood what she was asking. "I'll take care of it, baby."

She bit her lip, looking worried. But then she nodded. She seemed to sag, obviously completely done in. Raid wasn't sure whether to first feed her or put her down for a nap.

"Baby, are you sure you won't reconsider going to the hospital for tests?"

"It was just a bit of low blood pressure. You said you wouldn't take me."

"On three conditions."

She eyed him coolly.

"One condition is that you eat something. I might have to order something in, but you will eat."

She huffed out a breath. "I'm not that hungry."

He just folded his arms over his chest and looked down at her.

"But I guess I could eat something small."

He grunted. "Second condition is that you take a nap."

"I don't sleep well."

"Which is why you're taking a nap, darlin'." He thought that part was obvious.

But there was a strange look of dread on her face. Suddenly, it occurred to him why she didn't sleep well.

"Nightmares?"

"Yeah," she whispered.

Mother. Fucker.

His hands clenched into fists, but he pushed the anger down. Way down. It would come up later. That was something he knew for sure. But he'd make sure it was when she wasn't around.

"You won't have a nightmare while you're napping."

"How do you know?"

"Because I'm going to order you not to."

Her mouth dropped open, then she shook her head. "You're nuts."

"Maybe. But you're not gonna have a nightmare." He'd sleep beside her to keep her fear at bay if he had to.

Fuck. He was going to make such a good Dom.

"Reckon I'm a natural at this."

"At what?" she asked.

He waved his hand through the air dismissively. She had enough going on right now. He'd explain his newly resolved mission to be a Dom.

"Third condition. You let Jenna check you over."

Yeah, he'd thought that might be the condition she'd balk at. But it was also the one he wasn't going to give on. He really was worried about her.

"Jenna already checked me over. She said it was low blood pressure."

"She said that for sure? Or did she say it was a possibility?"

Hannah chewed at her lip. "Pretty sure she said that's what it was."

"I'm not willing to bet your health on 'pretty sure', darlin'. This condition is non-negotiable. Jenna or the hospital."

"I'm not going to the clinic."

"No problem. She'll come here."

Her eyes widened. "Here?"

"Yep. I'll call her. And I'll get some food delivered. A lot of food. Her number is in your phone?"

"Ah, yes. I don't know where it is, though."

He helped her off the counter, and she glanced around as though lost. They eventually found her phone on the coffee table and she gave him Jenna's number.

"Sit on the couch, baby. Find something to watch. I'll make a few calls and be back."

He called Jenna, who assured him that she'd be there soon. Then, before he could phone the diner to send up some food, there was a knock on the door.

"Are you expecting anyone, baby?" he asked.

Jenna can't have gotten there that quickly.

"No, but it could be one of the girls." She held up her phone. "There're several messages."

"Stay there. I'll handle it."

He opened the door. And to his shock, it wasn't any of her friends that stood on the other side.

"Well?" Renard said as he stood there, balancing trays in his arms as well as a cooler bag off one wrist. "Are you just going to stand there, or are you going to let me in? I've got hot food in my arms and just had to walk up all those stairs carrying it."

"What are you doing here?" Raid asked as he reached out to take two of the foil-covered trays.

"Trick or treating." Renard blasted past him and into the apartment. He glanced around. "Shit. What kind of couch is that?"

"Um, it's pink velvet," Hannah said, standing and gaping at the loud, blunt man.

"Hannah, sit back down," Raid ordered. He didn't want her moving up and down too much in case it was her blood pressure that had caused her to faint.

And he wanted her resting.

"Pink velvet? Fuck, who's heard of such a thing. Looks uncomfortable." Setting the trays he was holding on the dining table, he walked over and sat down on the sofa. "Shit. This is even worse than it looks. It could've been used as a torture device in eighteenth-century Britain."

"It's not that bad!" Hannah protested.

"Doll, it's definitely that bad."

"Hannah, sit. Renard, get up and explain what you're doing here," Raid ordered as he set the stuff he was holding down as well.

But Renard didn't move as Hannah sat. Instead, he turned to study her. "You look like shit."

"Jeez, thanks. Give it to me straight," Hannah said dryly.

That was his girl.

"That was giving it to you straight. Heard you lost weight.

Can see it now with my own eyes. Of course, I would have seen it earlier if you'd come into the restaurant."

Renard worked for Saxon in the upscale restaurant he'd opened. People traveled for miles to go there. Although it seemed that half of them came for the food, the other half came hoping that Renard would come out from the kitchen to entertain them.

"Um, oh. I'm sorry?" Hannah said.

"Well, make sure you don't do it again. I don't got time to spend chasing down women who aren't taking care of themselves to tell them to smarten up and take care of themselves."

"Right. Um, sorry."

Renard stood as Raid started peeking under the foil. His eyebrows rose as he saw a whole lasagna in one pan.

"Hey, those are for Hannah!" Renard stormed over to him. "Hands off, Malone."

"All of this food is for Hannah?" Raid asked.

There was enough food to feed twenty people. And there would still be leftovers.

"Yep. It is."

"For me?" Hannah got up and walked over to them.

"Hannah, sit back down. You're supposed to be resting," he said warningly.

"Hey! Watch how you talk to her, boy," Renard snapped.

What the hell?

Then the other man turned to Hannah. "And you . . . sit back down. You fainted. You need to rest."

"Isn't that what I just said?" Raid asked.

"You're a Malone. I don't listen to what you say. Not unless your name starts with A and you can add it to the word smart."

Dear God.

"Renard, you really made all this food for me?" Hannah asked, staring down at the food in shock.

"You fainted, girl."

"Does everyone know?" she whispered.

Renard shot her a look. "Everyone knows. You know how Haven works, girl. You grew up here. Nothing is a secret and everyone is worried about you. What the hell is going on with you?"

Raid watched the shutter go over her face at Renard's words. "You can tell everyone not to worry. I'm fine."

Renard just snorted. "You can't fool me, doll. And you're not fooling anyone else with this act, either."

She shot him a look. "It's not an act. This is who I am now. And while it was nice of you to make all this food, you really shouldn't have. I can't accept it."

"Holy crap, is that an entire tray of mac and cheese?" Raid gaped at Renard.

"Hannah loves Italian. There's also some potatoes au gratin. Guess that's French, not Italian, but she likes that too. You got some steak, put them on the grill. Steak goes great with potato au gratin. And a mushroom risotto. And there's tiramisu in the cooler bag."

"Tiramisu?" she asked.

"Yep. That's her favorite," Renard informed Raid.

Raid didn't care if she wanted to eat the whole tray herself. Or that Renard knew her favorite food when he didn't.

If she ate it, he would be fucking ecstatic.

"You should take it all back," she said.

Renard snorted. "Didn't spend hours making all this food just to take it all back. Don't be stupid, girl."

"Don't call her stupid," Raid growled at him. There was no way he was going to stand by and allow Renard to talk like that about his girl.

"What?" Renard snapped. "Of course I can. I can call her stupid if she's being stupid. I do it all the time."

"He does," Hannah confirmed.

"Not anymore," Raid said firmly.

Both of them gave him surprised looks. To his surprise, rather than get angry, Renard smiled. "Is that so?"

"Yes."

"About fucking time. I'm going now. Girl, you eat this food, understand? I hear you've fainted again, I won't be happy. You taking her to the hospital, Malone?"

Raid scowled but decided it would be easier to answer. "Jenna's coming to check her over."

"I guess that's acceptable. I've got to go. Got more important things to do than stand around and chit-chat with the two of you. Stop taking up all my time." He stormed out of the apartment, slamming the door behind him.

Raid looked from Hannah to the door. "Did that just happen?"

"I think we were just Renard'd."

"What?" Raid asked.

"It's what some people are calling it after you're, um, given a taste of Renard's brand of showing he cares. I can't believe he made all of this for me."

There was such shock in her voice it made him frown. "Well, of course he'd make all this for you. Why wouldn't he?"

"I didn't realize he cared."

"Enough food to feed the San Antonio Spurs says otherwise, darlin'."

"I guess it does, doesn't it?"

It was stupid, but he wanted to be the one to put that look of wonder on her face. Not grouchy, eccentric Renard.

"Fucking Renard."

She shot him a look. "You sound almost jealous."

He just grunted.

But out of the corner of his eye, he saw her face lighten for a moment.

Did she find him acting like a jealous idiot funny?

Well, he could do that with his eyes closed.

"Right, what do you want to eat?" he asked.

"Tiramisu."

"Good choice." He didn't care what she ate.

As long as she damn well ate.

"Back on the sofa, though."

"I shouldn't eat on the sofa. I might spill something."

"Would you even notice a mark on that monstrosity?"

"It's not that bad." She made her way back to the sofa as the doorbell went again. "I can get it."

"You'll sit," he ordered. "I will get it."

"Bossy," she muttered.

But she sat. Satisfaction filled him.

Yep. He definitely liked being in charge.

11

Hannah tried to avoid Jenna's gaze.

She knew that her friend just wanted to know she was all right. But she was feeling far too vulnerable to let anyone in.

If she did, then everything might spill out.

And she wasn't ready for that yet.

Jenna took off the blood pressure cuff.

"How is her blood pressure?" Raid asked, leaning against the wall.

Jenna had tried to make him leave while she looked Hannah over. But both Hannah and Raid had refused. When Hannah said she wanted him to stay, his face had gone all soft, his eyes melting into pools of affection.

She liked that.

God, this was so hard. Raid was all she'd ever wanted. If she was smart, she'd keep pushing him away until he gave up.

Hannah guessed that she wasn't that smart.

The problem was, she knew he'd leave when he realized he

couldn't fix her. That she couldn't be a proper girlfriend to him. When he found out she wasn't worth it.

Stop it.

You cannot let him win.

That was what she was doing, wasn't it? She was letting Steven win.

Jenna shot her a concerned look. Shoot. That was part of the reason she tried not to look at anyone too much. She hated seeing pity. "Hannah, are you sure you want to talk about your health in front of Raid?"

"I'm her guardian." Raid narrowed his gaze at Jenna, looking slightly irritated.

She swallowed heavily. "I want Raid here."

"All right." Jenna nodded, standing up straight. "Well, your blood pressure is low. When was the last time you ate? Have you been drinking plenty of water? What about any headaches? Any other dizzy spells?"

"I'm fine." She was aware that it wasn't an answer to either question.

Jenna frowned.

"Hannah," Raid said in a warning tone. "Don't lie. Jenna needs to know the truth."

Jenna whirled on Raid. "Don't use that tone with her."

Hannah looked up at Jenna in shock. She'd never heard the other woman talk like that.

Raid just stared at her calmly.

Jenna ran her hand over her face. "Sorry. I'm just feeling . . . protective."

Of Hannah? Because she was losing it? Because she'd fainted? Because it was clear that she'd been hurt? Jenna was her friend as well as her boss. Jenna had a busy life with her family, so she didn't come out with them that often, but Hannah loved her.

"I didn't mean to snap," Jenna added.

Raid's face softened. "It's all right, darlin'."

She sucked in a breath as he called Jenna darlin'. She fought to contain her upset at him using the term of endearment that she wished he'd use just for her.

It wasn't like he was going around calling anyone else baby.

So she had no right to complain about him using the nickname darlin'.

Right?

She glanced up to find them both looking at her assessingly. Raid opened his mouth and she tensed, waiting for him to point out her reaction.

"Answer Jenna's questions, baby."

She looked away, chewing her lip. She really didn't want to answer.

Then she felt him come over and crouch in front of her. "Hannah. You need to tell us so we can make sure you're safe and healthy. Okay? Nothing you say goes beyond this room. Right, Jenna?"

"Of course not."

"I really am all right. I'm not ill."

"How about you answer Jenna's questions and let her make the diagnosis, huh?" Raid said with amusement.

She huffed out an annoyed breath. "Um, I eat when I'm hungry. I could probably drink more water, I guess. I've felt dizzy a couple of other times, but I've never fainted. Yeah, I guess I've had a few headaches. But I often get headaches when I'm . . . when I'm stressed."

"Right," Jenna said with a nod. "I want to take some blood and make sure there's nothing else going on. All right?"

Raid was nodding as he stood.

"No way," Hannah said firmly.

Both of them stared down at her.

"Shoot. I forgot you don't like needles." Jenna gave her a sympathetic look. "I'm so sorry, Hannah. But I think it's important to run these tests."

"And I think it's important that all my blood remains in my body," she countered. "You know what? I'm feeling kind of tired now."

"You're scared of needles?" Raid asked.

Crap.

She wasn't supposed to be showing any weakness.

Yeah, she was doing really well with that.

"I wouldn't say scared," she said.

Right.

She risked a glance at him, wondering if he was running out of patience with her. But he just gave her one of his soft looks.

Shoot.

"I'm going to help you," he said.

"You don't need to help me."

He leaned closer to speak quietly. "No lying, remember?"

She glared at him but didn't object as he sat beside her.

"Lean into me, baby. I'll keep you safe."

"I don't want to do this." And she didn't. She was sick of being made to do things she had no desire to do.

"Trust me?"

Shit. That was a tough question, and she glanced at him, then over at Jenna, who was getting things ready. Looking back at him, she swallowed heavily. "I don't know."

Would he get angry at that? She grew tense and her breathing started to come in sharp pants.

But he just nodded. "That's fair."

"It . . . it is?"

"Yeah, baby. But I'm hoping you trust me enough to know I'm not going to hurt you. And I won't let anyone else hurt you, either. However, I'm worried about you. So, will you let Jenna take some blood? And let me help?"

What else could she do but nod?

"That's my girl."

His girl. She waited for it to feel wrong, but to her shock, her stomach grew warm with pleasure. Okay, she didn't mind being called his girl.

"I'm ready when you are," Jenna said quietly.

She gulped in a breath. She was going to be sick.

Then Raid suddenly picked her up and put her in his lap. And now she had a new set of problems to contend with. Because when she'd been in his lap before, she'd been too upset to truly notice his body. Or how it felt against hers.

His thighs were hard and muscular under her bottom and thighs. His firm chest was against her side. His scent was utterly delicious, like leather and a bit of spice.

So. Yummy.

Steven had always smelled sweet. Like vanilla. And she'd always loved that scent.

But then she'd grown to hate it.

Now, taking in Raid's scent, she could appreciate the rough masculinity of his scent. He smelled real. Not artificial.

"Raid," she whispered. Her stomach had dropped slightly.

This is Raid.

"It's me," he whispered. "Remember, I'm not him. I'm not going to hurt you."

She heard Jenna take in a sharp breath. Crap. She must have heard him.

"Don't think about anyone else but me. Just me. Put your face against my neck."

She buried herself into him as she felt him pull her arm out. A whimper escaped her.

Damn it.

She sucked in a breath.

The sleeve of her oversized shirt was rolled up.

"Gonna need you to breathe, baby," Raid told her.

She shook her head, determined to hold in her whimper as Jenna tightened the strap around her arm.

Crap. Crap. Crap.

"Baby, breathe," Raid urged.

She felt the prick of the needle.

"You can relax, Hannah," Jenna told her.

She shook her head as her lungs burned.

"Hannah. Breathe." The command was impossible to ignore, as was the way he squeezed her stomach with his arm. Her breath whooshed out of her, then back in.

Shit.

She felt light-headed. She might have held her breath a bit too long.

"You're being so good," he murmured to her.

Shit.

She waited for the nausea to hit her at hearing that word. But it only came in a small wave. She tensed, then relaxed.

"So good."

Right. She got it now. First, calling her 'my girl' and then 'good'.

"I know what you're doing," she said as she felt Jenna place something on her inner elbow.

"What's that?"

"You're trying to desensitize me to those words."

"No flies on you."

She snorted.

"All done," Jenna said. "You can relax now."

Hannah turned to look at Jenna, who shot her a quick wink. She felt her cheeks growing warm.

Crap. How had she forgotten that she was sitting on Raid's

lap? She wriggled, trying to get off, but Raid grabbed hold of her hips, holding her still with a grunt.

"Let me up."

"Nope," Raid replied. "Need you to stay where you are for the moment."

"Don't worry, I'll let myself out," Jenna said, her lips twitching as she grabbed her bag. "I'll let you know the results as soon as I have them. But in the meantime, rest, drink lots of water, and eat. Okay, Hannah? You're due at work next on Tuesday?"

"Ah, yeah."

Why wouldn't Raid let her up? She moved her hips and he let out a small grunt. She froze. Shit. Was she hurting him?

Or something else?

Crap.

"If you're not feeling up to it, then don't force yourself to come in, understand?" Jenna said.

"All right."

"I'll let myself out." Jenna's face turned stern. "Raid, don't hurt my friend or I will hurt you. Get me?"

"I wouldn't dream of it."

Then Jenna was gone. And whoa, had she just warned Raid away from harming her?

That had been intense.

"Let me up," she said in a breathless voice.

Yeah? Do you want up? Or do you want to grind against the hard-on you can feel pressed against you?

Raid gave her another squeeze and kissed the side of her face. "Relax, baby. I might be turned on, but that doesn't mean anything has to happen."

"Aren't you in pain? Wouldn't it be better if I got off you?" Part of her couldn't believe she was having this conversation.

At one stage in her life, she'd have been ecstatic to know that

Raid Malone was turned on by her. Now, she wasn't quite sure what to do with it.

"In pain? A little bit. But it's not anything I can't handle. I spent most of my teenage years with a hard-on. Fucking pain in the ass when you get a boner in the middle of Stats class. Well, not a pain in the ass, as such."

To her shock, she let out a giggle.

"What? The teacher was hot."

"You aren't supposed to notice if your teacher is hot."

"You're not? It's the only good thing about school, in my opinion."

"Raid," she groaned.

"Relax, baby. I'm fine. It's my body. I can deal with a hard-on. Been getting them for a long time. It's not something for you to worry about. Okay?"

She wasn't so sure, but she nodded.

"Time to eat. Then a nap."

She sighed. "So very bossy."

12

Hannah sat back with her hand over her stomach.

"More?"

"God, no."

Raid stared down at her bowl of dessert. "You only ate a third of it."

"You gave me enough to feed three people!"

"I did not. I gave you a Malone serving."

"A Malone serving?"

"Yeah. See, us Malone men, well, we're worth two of any other man. So we have to eat twice as much." He grinned at her.

She just shook her head. Lord, he was too much.

"Sure you can't eat anymore?" he asked.

"Nope. I'm done."

He grabbed the bowl, and to her shock, considering he'd already eaten a huge bowl on top of a large serving of lasagna, he ate the rest of hers too.

"You're like a bottomless pit," she said in awe.

"You should have seen the amount of money Alec spent on groceries when we all lived at home."

"Enough to run a small country, I'm guessing."

He grinned. "You'd be right, darlin'."

She tried not to show any reaction when he called her that. But despite his doesn't-have-a-care-in-the-world persona, Raid was smart. Intuitive.

"You didn't like when I called Jenna darlin', did you?"

"It's nothing to do with me," she told him stiffly.

"Hannah, look at me." His tone was firm.

She was screwed. Even though she tried to resist, it was futile.

She stared up at him.

"Hannah, in this town, the only people I truly care about, whose opinion and feelings I would take into consideration, are my brothers, their women, and you."

She blinked.

"You don't want me calling anyone but you, darlin', then you say the word and it's done."

"That simple?" she asked

"That simple, darlin'."

She sucked in a deep breath. He didn't really mean it. He wasn't going to change that habit just because she wanted to be his one and only darlin'. And didn't want anyone else to be. Because she was acting kind of jealous.

But his face was sincere.

That simple.

He leaned into her. "Hannah, breathe."

The air went out of her lungs.

"You with me, darlin'?"

"I . . . I think I'm about twenty steps behind you. And quite possibly heading in the wrong direction."

He just grinned. "You're with me. And trust me, you head off in the wrong direction, I'll turn you around."

She just bet he would. "Pretty sure you're already

making my head spin. I don't know which direction is up or down."

"Just trust that I'll catch you if you ever stumble and fall. All right?"

Shit. Fuck.

"I'll try."

"Good g–that's good," he added quickly.

She closed her eyes tight. She hated being messed up like this. Raid couldn't even call her by the two words like he wanted to.

Good girl.

"Hannah."

Opening her eyes, she looked over at the TV, which had a basketball game playing.

"You don't have to stay with me, you know. Jenna said I'm fine. You probably have other things you need to do."

"Hannah, Jenna didn't say you were fine. She said you need to take it easy. And if I had other things to do that were more important than taking care of you, then I'd go do them. But since nothing is more important than looking after you, I don't need to leave to do them."

"Raid . . ." Lord, that was so unexpectedly sweet that she wasn't even sure what to say.

"I know you feel you have to keep trying to push me away to see if I'll give up and leave. You do what you need to do, darlin'. Test me. Push me. You'll see. I'm here to stay. I'm going to go get you some more water. You stay there."

As he got up, he grabbed the dirty plates and took them to the kitchen.

A man who cleaned up after himself.

Who put her needs first.

Who stuck around even when she was doing her best to convince him to leave.

A man who knew what he wanted and wasn't afraid to say or show it.

A man who was loyal and kind and protective.

That was the sort of man she'd always wanted.

He returned with a glass of water. "Drink that down, darlin'."

She slowly sipped the water, wondering how she was going to survive when he left. Glancing over, she watched him watch the game.

Shoot. She was being a terrible hostess.

"You need chips," she said suddenly. "And beer. It's a crime to watch a game without chips and beer."

"A crime, huh?"

"Yes. I think so."

He nodded with a sigh. "Pretty sure you're right. But there's no one around to arrest us, so we'll just have to go on committing a crime since you haven't got any. I checked."

"I'll go buy you some." Shoot. Did her budget stretch to beer? Well, with all the food that Renard brought over, then she guessed she could manage it.

"Yeah, I don't think so." He moved so he was crouching in front of her. "Only place you're going, baby, is to bed."

Holy. Crap.

Her heart might have just stopped for a moment.

"For a nap." His eyes went slightly lazy with arousal. "Although I like where your mind was going."

Yikes.

"Come on." Standing, he held out his hand to her. "Let's get you into bed. For your nap."

"B-bed?"

"Yeah, you can't nap on this couch. This thing is torturous." He stretched out his back.

"Sorry." She winced. It was pretty uncomfortable. "Like everything else, it came with the apartment."

"It needs to go to the dump."

When she didn't put her hand in his, he simply reached down and picked her up, putting his hands under her armpits. Then he took her hand to lead her to the bedroom.

"Um, wait, Raid!" she said, trying to dig in her heels.

But it was pointless. He was a man on a mission.

Shit. Shit. Shit.

"I can take myself to bed!"

"I want to tuck you in."

He . . . he what?

Then he opened the door, and it was too late to stop him.

He walked into the room, seemingly oblivious to her discomfort. Although she figured that he'd noticed and was just ignoring it.

He paused, glancing down at her bed. "Are you a restless sleeper, darlin'?"

"What do you mean?"

"All your blankets are on the floor." He let go of her hand and moved to the side of the bed, staring down at the mess, then over at her. "And so are the pillows. Darlin' . . ."

She swallowed heavily and wrapped her arms around herself. "I don't, um . . . I don't like to sleep in the bed."

"Is it uncomfortable too?" Then he did something she hadn't seen coming . . . he lay on his back on her bed.

Raid Malone was in her bed.

Holy. Crap.

"Not too bad, considering," he said. "A bit small. Mine is a Californian king."

"I thought you lived in the bunkhouse at the ranch?"

"Oh yeah, but I bought myself a big-ass bed and set it up in my room there. Takes up most of the room. But it's totally worth it. Raid needs space."

"I feel like referring to yourself in the third person might be a sign that you need to have a few chats with Molly."

"Been there, done that, got the T-shirt. Seriously, Beau had T-shirts made for us all. Only Tanner and I wear them, though. Sometimes Butch."

She gaped at him.

"What's with sleeping on the floor, baby?" he asked, sitting at the end of her bed.

Hannah chewed her lip. What to tell him?

"The truth." It was said in a low, firm voice. One she was coming to recognize meant that he expected to be obeyed.

"So bossy."

"Hannah."

"And stubborn."

"Hannah," he said warningly.

"What if I want some privacy? What if I don't want to tell you?" She held herself tighter.

"Come here, darlin'." He pointed at the floor between his feet.

She shook her head.

"Come here."

Without thinking about it, she found herself moving. Crap.

"Are you sure you're not a Dom?" She didn't know why she said it. She didn't mean to say it. But it just popped out.

Fuck.

"I didn't mean to, uh, I mean . . ."

"I've never been to a BDSM club. But I might have some interest in it. Definitely not against it. Not if it would mean giving you what you need."

"You can't . . . I mean, you shouldn't change yourself for me."

"I wasn't intending to change myself. I'm being me right now."

"Are you saying you're always this bossy?" She gaped at him.

"With you, I am." He grinned. "And I like it. I like the way you react to me. I like the idea of getting you to a place where I can take full control and give you pleasure. Besides, I've always liked to be in control in the bedroom. Not a huge stretch to think I might enjoy being a Dominant."

Uh, well, it might be.

"You . . . I mean, you don't just wake up one morning and decide to be a Dominant."

"You don't? How does it happen then?"

"You think about it, agonize over it, read about it, experience it, and then you decide."

"Good. That's what I'll do then."

"Are you sure that you earned that T-shirt?" she asked.

"What?"

"The one that Beau printed you after your sessions with Molly."

He threw back his head and laughed. And it felt like her entire body warmed. She couldn't remember the last time she'd felt this warm. And it had nothing to do with the temperature or weather. And everything to do with him.

With the way that Raid made her feel.

"You leave that for me to worry about, all right? I don't think that you're planning to go to Saxon's anytime soon to play. Am I right?" His voice was so gentle that it made her blink back tears.

"I never want to go again." She said it with complete certainty. She meant every word.

There was no way she was ever going to submit to anyone again.

Raid watched her steadily. No sign of shock or disagreement.

"I mean it. That isn't me exaggerating or being dramatic. It's not something I want you to fix. I never want to go back."

"Then you won't," he said simply.

"What if . . . what if people try to make me?"

"And who do you think is going to do that?"

She shrugged.

"If anyone tries to make you do something that you don't want to do, then you tell me."

"And what will you do?" she asked.

"Take care of it."

"All right. Raid, Raid is trying to make me take a nap, and I don't want to."

He gaped at her. Then his lips twitched.

"Well, hello, little smart-ass," he murmured.

Uh-oh. Was that too much?

Before worry could really take hold, he reached up and slowly flicked her nose.

"Did you . . . did you just flick my nose?" she asked.

"Yep, smart-asses get their noses flicked."

"That seems rude."

"Gonna add an addendum to my 'no one gets to tell you what to do' rule."

"A what?"

"An addendum. You know, additional material that is added to clarify or add to something."

"I . . . I know what an addendum is. Just didn't know that you'd know."

"When we were younger, we had a lot of family meetings. I figured if I researched how a meeting was supposed to be run, I might have more chance of winning an argument."

"Did it help?" she asked.

"It did not."

She couldn't hold back her lip twitch. "Do I want to know what you were arguing for?"

"I think the question is, what didn't I ask for, darlin'." He winked at her before his face grew serious. "Why are you sleeping on the floor?"

She glanced over his shoulder. "Never imagined that Raid Malone would be in my bedroom."

"You didn't? I dream about you in my bed all the time."

Her gaze shot to his. "You do not."

"Baby, you are delusional if you don't think I've dreamed about you. About going to sleep with you in my arms, waking up with you, and all the things in between."

A slight tendril of panic unfurled. "Raid–"

"Why are you sleeping on the floor, darlin'?" he asked.

"Because it feels safer," she blurted out.

"You don't feel safe sleeping in here?"

"Not . . . not really."

"Where is your suitcase?" he asked suddenly.

"What?" she asked in confusion. Why would he want to know that?

"Your suitcase. We'll pack up some of your stuff and move you out to the ranch."

She took two stumbling steps back. "No."

"No? Why not? You don't feel safe here. I can make you safe there. So we'll move you now."

Wow. He made it sound so simple.

"Because I'm not ready for anything like that."

He eyed her for a long moment. "I don't like that you don't feel safe enough to sleep."

"It's just . . . it's just in the bed. I guess I like feeling hidden. That's why I've been sleeping between the bed and the wall."

It was stupid. It wasn't like it would actually give her any protection if Steven or anyone were to break in.

Steven isn't going to come looking for you.

"You can't be getting a very good sleep on the floor."

That was true.

"If you want to stay here and you want to sleep on the floor, then we're going to get you a stretcher or a blow-up mattress."

That sounded amazing. There was just one problem.

But how to tell him?

"I'll look into it."

She expected him to protest or take over. But he shocked her by nodding. Then he gently pushed her back before standing. He lifted the blankets off the floor and put them on the bed.

"Hey! What are you doing?" she asked.

"You're napping in the bed."

"But I–"

"I'm going to be in the apartment, so you'll know you're safe, therefore you'll sleep."

"Therefore?"

"Therefore." He nodded as he made the bed.

Raid Malone was making her bed.

Holy. Heck.

He even pulled down the blankets on one side for her.

"Raid. You don't need to stay while I nap."

"Where else would I be?" he asked.

"At your house?"

"To do what? Think about you? Worry that you're not sleeping, or that you've fainted again and hit your head and are bleeding out on your bathroom floor? Think I'm better here."

"I'm not going to faint again."

He shot her a quelling look. "I think you should get ready for your nap and stop arguing. It can't be good for your blood pressure."

"It might raise it."

"I need to talk to Jenna. Maybe no arguing could be added to the list of things she wants you to do."

"An addendum?"

He shook his head at her while waving his finger in the air. "So sassy. Get into bed. I'm going to be on the other side of your door, keeping you safe. Only time I might go out is to make a phone call, but I'll be right by the door. No one is getting to you. No one will hurt you. I promise."

She stared at him. She knew she should tell him to go again. It wasn't that simple though. There was no way she could just go to sleep because he was here.

But the truth is, she was tired. Every part of her wanted to curl up in that bed and sleep.

Raid's face softened as he took her in. Almost as though he could read her mind. "You're exhausted, darlin'. You need some sleep or you will end up in the hospital. Get ready, climb into bed, and I'll be back in ten minutes to tuck you in."

Seriously.

What the heck was happening to her life?

13

Raid peered through the open door to check on Hannah. Just as he'd thought, she was asleep within minutes. Hannah might believe that she didn't trust him, but the proof was there. She knew he'd keep her safe, so she was able to rest.

And fuck . . . if he didn't feel damn good about that. He liked the fact that he gave her that.

That he could help her.

What he didn't like was not knowing the reason that she felt unsafe in the first place.

Patience.

It wasn't his strongest attribute. But he'd try.

For her.

Moving to the front door, he opened it and stepped out, leaving it open so he could hear her if she woke up. He was going to call the brother he knew would be the most help.

The one who'd always been there for him. Who was more like a dad than an older brother. Although he fucking hated when Raid said that.

Said it made him feel old.

Before he could call Alec, though, he saw a dark-haired man walk up the stairs. Joel Saxon paused, looked up at him, then over to the open door.

"Hannah's taking a nap," he told him.

Saxon's eyebrows rose. "Good. How is she doing?"

Raid eyed him for a moment. He knew Saxon was protective. Especially of the subs who belonged to his club. Like Hannah. So this wasn't an unexpected visit.

"Jenna's been by. She's going to run some tests. At the moment, it seems that it could have been her blood pressure."

Saxon frowned. "She's not herself."

"No."

"Did she tell you what happened? With that guy?" he asked.

"Not yet. But she will."

Saxon looked him up and down with a nod. "When I heard you'd taken responsibility for her, I was surprised."

"Yeah?" Raid said warningly.

"You and your brothers are a bit wild. But one by one and sometimes by two, I've watched you all settle down. Nothing like a good woman to put things into perspective."

Raid remained quiet, sensing Saxon had more to say on the matter.

"I wanted to check on her myself. However, the fact that she hasn't once been by the club since she got back, plus the fact that she runs whenever she sees me, tells me that she might not actually be ready to see me."

That wasn't what he'd expected the other man to say. He'd been anticipating Saxon warning him to treat Hannah right.

"I don't know exactly what happened, but whatever it was, it was enough for Hannah to try to keep everyone at a distance. Mostly through avoiding them. She might have outwardly changed, but I know the real Hannah is still in there. She needs to feel safe. That's what will help break down those shields she has up."

Saxon stared at him for a long moment. "And you think she feels safe with you?"

"I know she does."

"I suspect you're right since you're the only one she's let close." He paused for a moment. "Hannah's a sub. Perhaps she doesn't feel like playing at the moment, but in the future . . ."

"I'm prepared to give Hannah whatever she needs."

"She'll know if it's faked," Saxon warned. "And that will make her feel bad. If the scene isn't for you, then you would be better off allowing her to play with another Dominant who has no sexual interest in her. We have a number of married Dominants who help with our single subs."

"Yeah, that won't be happening," he said coldly. "Hannah is mine."

Saxon's mouth curved into a satisfied grin. "Interesting."

Was it?

"Once she tells you what happened, I want to know. I want to help find this fucker who hurt her."

"You'll need to get in line."

Instead of getting angry, Saxon just smiled again.

So weird.

"Aspen and I will have to have the two of you around for dinner one night."

What the fuck was happening right now?

The other man turned and started walking away while Raid stared after him. Saxon paused at the bottom of the stairs and looked up at him. "It's rather cliché, but you need to know that if you hurt her, I will make your life a living hell."

Ahh. Good. There it was. He was actually relieved. It might be predictable, but that's what he'd been expecting Saxon to say.

All of that other shit he'd been spouting about dinner just weirded Raid out.

Once he was alone, he drew out his phone and called Alec.

"How is Hannah?" Alec asked without saying hello.

Raid didn't take offense. He knew Alec was worried about his girl.

"She's all right. She's sleeping right now."

"Good. Probably the best thing for her. She's letting you stay with her?"

"For the moment. She keeps trying to push me away."

"I haven't seen her since she's gotten home, but both Mia and Flick have, and they're quite worried. She's not the same."

"No. She's not."

"You're serious about her. Really serious?"

If anyone else asked him that, then he would likely have taken offense. But he knew that Alec wasn't trying to insult him.

"I am."

"Good. Then you'll be just what she needs. Be her rock. She can try to push you away, but Malone men are stubborn. We don't do anything we don't want to do."

"I know. I'm letting her push because that's what she feels has to do. But I'm not going anywhere. I'm not sure when I'll get back to the ranch. Maybe when she's well enough to go to work."

"Don't worry about work. Just remember, go with your gut. Sometimes she might need you to push back, other times she might need some space."

"Space?" He didn't like that idea.

"You've got to give her time to miss you."

He wasn't so sure. Although he could kind of see the wisdom in that.

"I don't want to leave her, Alec."

"Good. I like this."

So did he. A lot. Which is why, no matter if they went backward. Or if she tried to close him out or keep him at a distance, he wouldn't let her.

She was 'the one'.

"Alec, she's been sleeping on the floor. And there was no food in her house. And the furniture in her apartment is shit."

"Want me to rally the troops?" By troops, he meant the women in their family.

"I got her to nap in her bed. I'm going to stay the night. So I should be able to get her to sleep in her bed. But I'm not going to push her into letting me sleep with her, and her couch is shit."

"I'll get onto it. And Mia will start cooking."

He didn't bother saying thanks. Alec would know that he felt it. "Renard bought her over some meals. But some of Mia's baking would be appreciated."

"Renard cooked for her?"

"Yep. And Saxon was just here. I wouldn't be surprised if her friends turn up soon."

"People care about her. Hannah is a good person. What did Saxon say?"

"Not a lot. He's worried about her. He suggested that when she's ready to play again that I let her play with one of the married Doms."

"Like fuck," Alec spat out. "You're not letting another man touch her."

Raid nodded. He damn well wasn't. "Course not."

"Fucking Saxon. I'll have words with him."

"I can fight my own battles, brother."

Alec grunted. "Like you can't give her what she needs."

"You think I can?" It wasn't a doubt he'd admit to anyone else. In fact, he'd argue to the death that he could.

But this was Alec.

"Look, there are no hard and fast rules for this sort of stuff. You are who you are. You work out what she needs and what you're happy to give her. If there're gaps, you negotiate to figure that stuff out. If she needs to go to Saxon's and play, then you work out what you can give her to make her happy there and not change who you are. But, bottom line, if she's the one, she was made for you and all this stuff will work itself out. You'll always do what is best for her."

"Yeah. I will. And it's not like I can't tie her up and give her whatever else she needs." Easy-peasy.

"Saxon will make you do courses," Alec warned.

"Fucking courses. I'll ace that shit."

"Damn right. We all like various levels of control. And I can help you if you need it. The main thing is to talk to her. Ask her what she needs and wants. She might need a supporter, a cheerleader, a protector, someone to provide boundaries. Someone to take control. It might just be about sex. It might go beyond that."

"I'd give her all that anyway," he said arrogantly.

"Of course you would. You're a Malone. Malone men always give their women what they need."

Damn straight, they did.

A frightened noise from inside the apartment had him turning. "Gotta go. Hannah's having a bad dream."

"Later."

He ended the call and raced inside, only pausing to shut the door behind him. He didn't want any surprise visitors walking in.

Moving swiftly to the bedroom, he kneeled beside the bed and reached out to run his hand down her face.

"No, no, please. No!"

Fuck. This was killing him. He was going to fucking murder the motherfucker who hurt her. Who made her have bad dreams. Who made her pull back from all of her friends and flinch when they tried to touch her.

Yeah. Raid was going to murder that bastard.

"Baby, stop," he whispered as she whimpered and thrashed around. "You're safe. I'm here. You're safe, baby. I'm here."

"Raid," she whispered.

"Yeah, that's right. Raid."

"Can't have him . . . dirty . . ."

He was dirty? What did that . . . Shit, no. She wasn't talking about him.

Hannah was talking about herself. She thought she was dirty? And that's why she couldn't have him?

Oh yeah. He was going to kill that motherfucker.

14

"You can't stay the night."

Hannah carefully sat at the dining table. The chair creaked under her weight. So, she was somewhat worried about what was going to happen when Raid attempted to sit.

He was heavy. All of him was pure muscle.

And damn . . . part of her really wanted the chance to examine every inch of his skin.

The other part knew that was never going to happen.

"It's all right. Alec had a blow-up bed delivered," he replied as he set the tray of lasagna down in the middle of the table. It landed with a bang. She gave the table a worried look. "So I don't have to twist my back into a pretzel trying to sleep on that torture device." He nodded his head over to the sofa as he spooned up massive servings of lasagna onto both plates.

He put one in front of her. "Eat up. There's tiramisu afterward or, if you'd rather, Mia sent some brownies."

"Brownie?"

"Yep. We need ice cream, though. Everything tastes better with ice cream."

"Are Mia's brownies not that good?" she asked.

"Shit." He gave her wide eyes. "Don't say that. Alec will kill you."

Alarm filled her. The last thing she wanted was for Alec to be mad at her.

"And anyway, Mia's brownies are the shit. But they're even better with ice cream. I'll go out and get it if you want the brownies."

"I don't need the brownies."

"Tiramisu it is." He sat without a care that the chair might crack under him.

She sucked in a breath, but the chair held.

"I don't need any dessert."

"Everyone needs dessert, darlin'."

"Not me. I just got rid of my ass and thighs. I don't need them to come back."

She was staring down at the lasagna as she said that, so she didn't see his expression change. But she felt the atmosphere in the room change.

Hannah looked up at Raid.

"What did you say?" he asked in a low voice.

"Um . . . that I don't need my butt and thighs back. They were enormous." That's what Steven had always made clear, anyway. He'd encouraged her to stop eating sweets and take up exercise to get rid of what he'd called her bubble butt and jelly thighs.

Now that she thought about it . . . what a jerk!

"Bubble butt and jelly thighs," she murmured.

"Excuse me?" he asked in a low, warning voice.

"That's what he told me that my ass and thighs were. He said it with a smile on his face, as though he was joking. Like it was an inside joke we had together. Look at Hannah's fat ass and thighs."

What an idiot she'd been. The signs had been there all along.

Hannah had never worried about her body until him. She'd been happy with the way she looked. She'd always gotten admiring looks at the club. No one there had ever told her that she had a bubble butt and jelly thighs.

"Well, fuck him!" Raid snapped.

She jumped and stared at him, startled. "What?"

"Fuck him and his Tootsie roll!"

Okay . . . she really didn't expect, after what she'd just been thinking, that she'd feel like giggling. "Tootsie roll?"

"Yep. Guy like that can only have a micropenis. That's why he was trying to make you feel bad about your body. If he got in first, made shit up to make you feel bad, then he was obviously hoping you'd be so worried about your body that you wouldn't notice that he had areas he found concerning. Like his widdle diddle."

"Widdle diddle, really?"

"Well, what would you call it?" he asked

She shook her head.

"Tell me. What would you call his dinkie winkie?"

Oh, dear Lord. "I call it disappointing."

He stared at her a moment, then he threw his head back and roared with laughter.

"And it doesn't matter the size," she told him primly. "It's what someone can do with it. Unfortunately, he was a three-pump chump who didn't care if I came or not."

"Fucking asshole. Fuck him and fuck his opinion. Did you like your body before him?"

"Yes," she answered quietly.

"Then fuck him. Say it after me. Fuck that disappointing dinkie winkie."

"Raid."

"Say it."

Screw it. What would it hurt? "Fuck that disappointing dinkie winkie."

"Well done. Now, are you going to have dessert? Bring back that gorgeous ass of yours and those scrumptious thighs?"

"Yes. I am."

His face was filled with approval.

She liked that look.

"But you still aren't staying the night," she told him.

"Did you sleep this afternoon?"

She had. And that had shocked her. She'd dropped off far easier than she'd expected, and if she'd had a nightmare, she couldn't remember it.

Only issue was, instead of waking up refreshed, she'd woken all dazed and kind of nauseous.

Raid had told her it was because her body didn't want to wake up. That it wanted more sleep.

She guessed over a month of sleep deprivation would do that.

"Yes. You know I did."

"And do you usually sleep that well?"

"No."

"So you sleep better when I'm here because you know I'll keep you safe. I'm staying the night."

"Raid, you have things to do."

"Yeah, like what?"

"Like . . . like whatever it is that you do."

"Well, my plan tonight was to watch the game and think up something to do to annoy West. Maybe Maddox, he's a fucking stick-in-the-mud now that he's a dad. Those are things I can do here."

"But you don't have anything with you."

"Alec dropped me off a bag of stuff."

"He did?"

"Yep. I called him while you were napping."

"Wow. He works fast." She tensed. "He came in here while I was asleep?"

Not that she thought Alec Malone would hurt her or anything, but she didn't like that she hadn't woken up when someone had come into her apartment.

"Of course not. I wouldn't let anyone in your apartment while you were sleeping."

Holy heck.

That made her tummy all warm, but she tried to hide her reaction by dropping her gaze to her plate of food.

"Saxon came by too."

"Really?" Her head shot up again in surprise, although she should have expected it. In fact, she would have expected him to come check on her earlier.

But she guessed the fact she kept running away from him had put him off.

God, she hated what she was doing. Why couldn't she just get over what had happened? Move on. Go back to old-Hannah.

Because she's gone. And you have no idea how to get her back.

"He and Aspen want to have us over for dinner one night," Raid went on. He ate some more lasagna.

"What?" she asked in a strangled voice.

"Yeah. For dinner. Weird, right?"

"Very." She chewed at her lip. She didn't know what to do with that right now. Obviously, Saxon thought she and Raid were an actual couple. "You won't get very good sleep on a blow-up bed."

"Darlin', if you want me to sleep in bed with you, you only have to ask."

Her mouth dropped open. "That's not what I meant!"

His gaze turned to her again, his face serious. "I know what you meant. Darlin', I will stay on the bed out here. I am not going to press you for anything you're not ready for. I know you think I'm being a pushy bastard and I'm moving too fast. But nothing happens that you don't say yes to. Understand?"

Her breath was choppy, her pulse racing. "Right."

"And it might seem fast, but I've wanted you for a long time, Hannah. Do you know what that means, though?"

"What?" she asked.

"That I've got patience. Because I've already been waiting for a long time and I can wait some more. I can wait for you. Because you're worth it."

Dear. Lord.

"Now, are you going to eat some food, or do you need me to feed you?"

"I can feed myself!" Sheesh.

"Too bad. I do a killer choo-choo train. Total hit with Seb, Liam, and Lucas."

His nephews.

She'd love to have some nieces and nephews. She'd make a great aunt.

But that wasn't in the cards for her. She didn't have any siblings. Or even any cousins. All she'd ever had was her grandma, and she'd died years ago.

God, Grandma would be so ashamed of her. She'd sold the family house.

For Steven.

Fuck. Him.

15

R aid got his way.
It felt like Raid got his way a lot. In fact, she was
willing to bet that he didn't often hear the word no.
He was spoiled.

"Darlin', I can hear you tossing and turning. You need me to come in there and sing you a lullaby?"

She froze as she lay in bed.

Holy. Crap.

He'd do it too.

When he'd decided that she wasn't eating enough dinner, he'd picked up her fork and started doing the choo-choo train. It was ridiculous. It wasn't just train noises, but a whole performance with the conductor (the fork) and a tunnel (her mouth).

No wonder his nephews loved it.

Loved him.

Just like she . . . whoa, nope! She was not going there. Because there was no way that she was in love with Raid Malone.

That was ridiculous.

She barely knew him.

Liar. You've known him for years. Had a crush on him for over a year.

She wasn't in a place to love anyone.

It was hard to love someone else when you loathed yourself.

"Hannah?"

She glanced over to find him standing in the doorway. He'd insisted that she keep the door open to help her feel safer.

She'd tried to protest.

But Raid hadn't given in.

So spoiled.

"What are you doing?" She tugged the covers up even higher. Right up to her chin.

He leaned against the doorway, arms crossed over his firm chest. She had her nightlight on. And her bat was under the blankets next to her. There was no way he could see that, though.

However, she had to admit that it did make her feel safer knowing that he was sleeping just outside the bedroom door.

"Checking on you. You were tossing and turning. Do you need some help getting to sleep?"

"Someone made me take a nap and now I'm not tired."

Liar.

"You're exhausted, baby. Probably overtired. You need a nap every day to catch up."

"I can't nap every day."

"Why not?"

"Um, because I have to work."

"You're not working full time, are you?"

"No." It was a bit of a hit to her struggling bank account. She was thinking about getting another job to help. "Just Tuesday and Wednesday mornings and all day Thursday and Fridays. Then I work every other Saturday."

What other job could she get to work around those hours?

"So that leaves plenty of time for naps."

"Do you have an answer for everything?" she snapped.

"Let me think. Yep, I think I do."

"Has anyone ever told you that's annoying?"

"All the time. I don't care."

"You're infuriating," she told him.

"Yep, heard that too."

"Frustrating."

"Keep going, let it all out, baby girl." He grinned.

Urgh!

"Stubborn."

"Uh-huh."

"Manipulative."

"That's one of my best."

"Arrogant."

"I'm a Malone. We're just honest. We know we're the shit and we're not afraid to tell others."

Dear. Lord. "And modest too."

"Now that one I can't agree with. Never been modest. I know I'm hot."

"Urgh! It's impossible to win an argument with you. I don't think I ever will. You're too spoiled."

"Spoiled."

"Uh-huh. I bet no one ever argues with you, do they?"

He stepped forward and sat on the bed, facing her. Hannah drew herself up, so she was leaning against the headboard. She had on an oversized T-shirt she'd gotten from Goodwill, but she kind of wished she'd worn something nicer.

Crap. What was she doing? Why hadn't she just told him that she was fine and then pretended to go to sleep?

Now, he was sitting on her bed.

She didn't know whether to panic or throw a party.

"Have you met my brothers, darlin'? All they do is argue. And since I got here all you've done is argue with me."

"I have not!"

"Yeah, baby. You totally have."

"Not true."

"You're arguing with me right now."

"Rats."

He grinned. "You're so adorable. Now, you going to tell me what's on your mind?"

"I was just thinking that you get your way a lot. Are you sure you don't want the bed? I would fit on the blow-up bed better."

"Baby, no way in hell are you sleeping on the floor while I'm in a bed."

"I'm used to it, though."

"Hannah, no." His voice was firm, and it didn't invite any more argument.

She wisely decided to shut up.

"Now, lie down on your side, facing away from me."

"What?"

"Do as you're told."

She lay down, giving him her back. "You won't always get your way."

"You didn't even hesitate."

"What?" What did he mean?

"You didn't hesitate to give me your back. You might not be ready to admit it, but you trust me."

Shoot.

He was right. She hadn't hesitated. "It doesn't mean anything."

"Of course it does, baby. But if you need to tell yourself it doesn't, you can do that."

"Urgh, why do you have to be so agreeable?"

He burst into laughter, and she glanced over her shoulder at him.

"You might want to make up your mind, darlin'. Am I argumentative or agreeable?"

"Both. You're an anomaly."

"Yep. Heard that one too. Lie back around. I'm going to give you a back rub."

She tensed.

"Shh. Don't get all tense. Just relax." He carefully tugged the blanket down.

She was still fully covered, but . . . what if her T-shirt rode up?

And then his hands were on her back, massaging and rubbing. With a groan, she moved onto her front and turned her head to the side. Another moan escaped her and he paused.

"Don't stop, please."

"Holy shit. This is my penance, isn't it?" he muttered.

"What?" She glanced over her shoulder at him in confusion.

"Nothing. Just lie back down, baby. You're too tense. Let me help you."

"Maybe we should stop." She'd gotten carried away. She couldn't believe she was letting him touch her like this.

He's always touching you.

He was. She was managing to keep everyone else away, at a distance. But not Raid.

"What's wrong?" he asked.

"You keep touching me."

"Yep."

"Why?"

"Because the more I touch you, the more you get used to it. You might not have noticed, but you've stopped flinching."

Rats. She had.

And it had barely taken him any time at all.

"I think you need to go back to your bed," she told him coldly.

"No, baby. What you need to do is stop thinking and just let everything happen. It's when you get in your head and start overthinking shit that everything starts to go bad."

He wasn't wrong.

But it didn't make her worry any less. That was until he started massaging her back again. Another groan escaped. He found a really tense spot, and she gasped, then moaned.

"You're so good with your hands," she told him.

"Definitely my penance."

16

"What is that?"

Hannah stared at the item in her living room. It hadn't been there when she'd gone down for her nap. She rubbed at her eyes, wondering if she was imagining things.

"It's still there."

"Isn't it beautiful?" Raid said with a sigh.

"Seriously? Beautiful?" It was a huge, black monstrosity. Beautiful, it was not.

"Yep."

"Where is my sofa?"

"On its way to the dump, hopefully."

"Raid! That wasn't mine! Oh my God! I'm going to have to pay for that." She started panicking, rubbing at her chest.

"Whoa, easy, baby. It's not on its way to the dump. I had Tanner and Beau take it to the ranch to store it."

Oh, that was good.

Wait a minute . . .

"Tanner and Beau were here too? While I was sleeping?"

Panic gripped her once again. She couldn't believe that she hadn't even realized that they were here. That she'd slept through them bringing a huge freaking sofa into her apartment.

Oh God.

"Easy, baby. I didn't let them in the apartment. They carried it up the stairs and then I got it into place. They carried the other one down. That's it. No one else was in your apartment."

"No one else?" she asked faintly.

"I promise."

It was Sunday. She'd woken up this morning, determined to get rid of him. He had a life. He didn't want to spend all his time babysitting the crazy lady.

So she'd decided to give him the ice queen treatment.

He'd laughed in her face.

Such a jerk.

He'd ended up staying here all day. Even insisting on her taking another nap this afternoon. Which is how he'd managed to sneak this ugly sofa in.

There was no shaking him. It was utterly aggravating. And yet . . . minute by minute, she could feel herself believing in him more and more.

Wanting, hoping that he wouldn't give up.

That he could break through and help her fully trust him. He was getting there. Which is why he was still in her apartment.

And why she now had a black, monstrous sofa in her living room.

"Where did this come from?"

"Beau bought it. Scarlett hated it and banned it from her house. Beau didn't want to get rid of it because this is the comfiest couch you've ever laid on. Swear to God, an hour on this couch, and you won't want to get off it. So Beau had to pretend to get rid of it, but he put it in Jaret and Clem's barn. And now, it's here." He looked so pleased with himself.

However, she was totally with Scarlett on this one.

"It's huge. And ugly."

"But comfortable. Come sit on it with me." He sat and patted the spot next to him.

"You should have asked me." She glared at him.

"Come sit." Pat. Pat.

She put her hands on her hips. "This is my apartment. You can't just make decisions like this."

"Come. Sit." More patting.

What was she? A dog?

"You should have asked."

"If you don't like it, I promise I'll change it back."

"And you won't let anyone in here when you do."

"Never, baby. That's something I wouldn't do without your permission. I promise. But if I have to watch another game on your sofa, I was going to need to visit the chiropractor."

She sighed. Okay, that was fair. Only . . .

"You could just go home, you know. Then you wouldn't have to worry about my sofa."

Her stomach tightened at the thought of him leaving.

"Nope. You need me to look after you."

"So you're planning on staying tonight too?"

"Yep. Now, come . . . sit . . . please?" He gave her a begging look.

Rats.

She was a sucker for that look. Stomping over, she sat on the sofa.

"Oh, dear Lord."

"Well?" He gave her an expectant look.

"It's like sitting on a cloud."

He just gave her a smug look and turned on the TV.

Darn it.

Looks like this monstrosity was staying.

And so was Raid.

It was kind of scary how used she was getting to him. And in such a short amount of time.

He looked after her. Made sure she ate, drank water, and napped. Several times already, people had turned up at her door, but he'd sent them away before she even had to decide what to do.

Perhaps under other circumstances, she might be upset with his high-handedness. But she appreciated that protection.

Right now, she needed it. She hadn't had a chance to rest and recover. And he was giving her a safe space to do that.

So she could let him get away with being bossy and a bit heavy-handed. She could even put up with him moving a monstrous, ugly sofa into her space.

Yeah, she could forgive him for a lot.

"You mind if I watch the game, darlin'?" He switched the channel over.

"Is there always a game on?" she asked curiously.

"Yep." He grinned and stood. "Beer?"

"I don't have any beer."

"Sure you do. It arrived with the sofa." He moved into her small kitchen and returned with three bags of chips and two beers.

"It's like magical fairies keep visiting," she muttered as he put the chips down on the coffee table. He opened one beer and handed it to her.

She took a sip before he sat and opened a packet of chips. She ate a salty chip.

Yum.

They watched the game. Then heated some of the food that Renard had brought over before settling in for a movie.

She didn't know how it happened. But the power of the sofa was too much for her and she grew sleepy.

Really. It was ridiculous how much she was sleeping. But she guessed her body was playing catch-up.

She blamed her tiredness for the fact that she kept letting Raid do what he liked, including staying here. As soon as she had more energy, she was going to kick him out.

It wasn't until she felt herself moving in the air that she partially woke up.

"Raid?" she whispered.

"It's all right, baby. I have you."

She was placed in the bed and covers pulled over her. Just as she was drifting off again, she felt his lips against her forehead.

"I won't ever let anyone hurt you again."

17

"Hannah?"

She gaped at Raid on Monday morning as he walked into the apartment.

"Uh, Hannah?"

She couldn't stop looking. Holy. Heck.

A grin crossed his face as he moved toward her. Reaching out slowly, he pressed on her chin to close her mouth. "Gonna catch flies with your mouth open like that."

"Huh?"

"Can you get me a glass of water, darlin'? I need to take off my shoes."

"Huh?"

His grin widened. "Gotta admit, I like this."

"Huh?"

With a chuckle, he turned her around and lightly patted her ass to get her moving. "Please get me a glass of water."

This time, it was said with definite command, and she stumbled her way into the kitchen to get him a glass of water. Then her entire face grew hot.

He'd patted her ass. Without her freaking out! Which, admittedly, she hadn't been doing much in the last two days.

But this had taken him touching her to a whole other level.

She quickly got him his glass of water and turned.

Keep your gaze down.

Don't look at his delicious, wide, tattooed, muscular chest.

Don't look. Don't look.

If she didn't look at his bare chest, then she couldn't act like a crazy person.

Well, hopefully.

Then she banged into something. Water splashed over the sides of the glass onto the floor.

"Oh rats! Sorry!"

"You're all right, darlin'." He took the glass from her and gulped the water down.

She couldn't help but watch. It was like there was a force-field drawing her to him. When he put the glass down, she looked him over.

"I didn't know cowboys went jogging." But boy, was it a nice sight. Shorts that ended mid-thigh. The T-shirt that he'd started out wearing was now tucked into the back of those shorts. And the rest of his skin was on display.

Yum.

"Did you just say yum?" His eyes twinkled as he stared down at her.

"Nope."

"I think you did."

"And I think you're delusional. I mean, I already knew you were. You have these delusions of grandeur."

"Delusions of grandeur? Me? Darlin', I'm a cowboy. I don't have any delusions that I'm grand."

But he was. He was more than grand. He was amazing, wonderful, fantastic.

"And cowboys need to keep up their cardio, too. For work and any extra-special curricular activities." He winked at her.

Holy heck.

Her body went hot, then cold.

Then she realized how close he was . . . how big he was. She closed her eyes, and when she opened them, it wasn't Raid who was standing there, staring down at her.

It was Steven.

She let out a startled scream and scrambled backward, right onto the counter behind her. She flinched in pain, holding her hands out.

"No, no, no!"

"Hannah! Baby, it's me. It's Raid!"

She closed her eyes, and when she opened them again, Raid was crouched over her, staring down at her in shock.

"Hannah? Are you all right?"

She was trembling, her breath coming in sharp pants as she attempted to figure out what the hell happened.

"He was here . . . standing right here. He was here."

Raid's face tightened. His anger was clear. But she wasn't scared because she knew he wasn't angry at her.

"Flashback. Baby, you need to tell me what that bastard did to you."

"I can't . . . not right now." She wasn't sure if she wanted to throw up, scream, or punch something.

"But you will."

It wasn't a question. She was thinking that she would. However, part of her was still worried that Raid would think badly of her.

"It might change how you see me," she warned, staring at her feet.

"Come here, Hannah." His tone was so soft. So sweet that tears entered her eyes.

She couldn't. If she did, she was going to collapse.

"No." It took everything in her to deny him.

"Hannah–"

"I didn't think it would ever be possible for me to hate someone," she said. "But I hate him. I hate him so much." She was still shaking as she said it, her stomach rolling nauseously.

"Whatever he did to you . . . whatever happened . . . it wasn't your fault."

Wasn't it? She wasn't so sure. She thought it was very much her fault for being an idiot.

"Baby, come here."

"I can't." She wanted to. So much.

But he must have had enough because he slowly moved toward her.

"Raid," she said in a low voice. "Please don't."

"Why not? Because you fear me? My touch?"

"Yes."

He froze, and a stricken look crossed his face before he backed up considerably.

Shit.

She'd just messed up.

"But not because you'll hurt me physically. I just . . . the more you touch me, the more I want you, and I can't ever give you normal, Raid. Not anymore."

Understanding filled his gaze. "Baby, have you met me before?"

Huh?

"I'm not normal. My whole family is nuts. What makes you think I want normal?"

"I was normal before." And he didn't want her then. Did he consider her more interesting now?

"No, you weren't."

"What?" Her gaze shot to his. "Yes, I was."

"Nope."

She glared up at him. "I was normal."

"Baby, first, no one in this town is normal. They're all freaking nuts. It's what makes Haven so great."

Shoot. She couldn't argue with that.

"I was the most normal of them all."

"Nope. And anyway, as I told you, I made the decision to ask you out when I was in New Orleans. Remember?"

He was right. He'd wanted her back then . . . before she'd been broken.

"What sort of normal do you think I want?" he asked.

"Oh, I don't know. A girlfriend who doesn't freak out and have weird flashbacks. Steven hasn't even been in this apartment, so why would I see him here? What about a girlfriend who doesn't have to sleep on the floor or with a baseball bat close at hand? Who doesn't feel the need to protect herself by bringing out the ice queen and dressing in an armor of baggy clothes?"

She was heaving for breath by the time she was finished. She stared up at him.

To her shock, a smile was on his lips.

"What?" she snapped.

"You called yourself my girlfriend."

She shook her head. "No. No, I meant . . . that's what you want. That sort of girlfriend. Not me. I'm not your girlfriend."

"We'll see."

Dear. Lord.

She was in trouble here.

"There's something I need to know."

"What is it?"

"Is he still out there? Are you in danger? Is there a possibility that he might turn up here?"

Shit. Fuck.

She shook her head. She didn't want to answer. Because she didn't want to think about it.

"Hannah, I need to know. If you are in any sort of danger, then I need to make moves to protect you. And Jake needs to know what is going on."

"I'm not in danger," she told him.

"Are you sure? You wouldn't lie to me?"

She might have. But this time she wasn't. Because he'd been caught. Or at least she thought he had.

"He . . . he's not going to search me out. He's not interested in finding me. I was a mark for him. Someone to target, use, then move on."

"What?" He gave her a confused look.

"He never cared about me. It was all a ruse. A con."

"To con you out of what?"

"I don't want to talk about it right now. I'm feeling quite tired. Perhaps you should go home. Don't you have to go to work?"

"Don't change the subject, darlin'. You should know that I'm keeping a tally of your transgressions, and once Jenna gives the all-clear, it might just be time for a reckoning."

"A reckoning? What sort of reckoning?"

"Well, it could be doing lines." He eyed her.

Lines? Really? That was a deterrent?

"Perhaps a spanking."

A spanking? She'd only ever had spankings for pleasure.

"Or perhaps not. Did he do that?"

"What? No, he didn't. I'm not scared of being spanked." And that was the truth. Steven hadn't ever spanked her.

Not once.

In fact, after she'd moved away to be with him . . . he'd barely slept with her.

Just enough to string her along, she guessed.

"Yeah?" Interest filled Raid's face.

"But that doesn't mean you get to spank me," she said hastily.

"Of course I do. I'm your guardian."

She gave him an exasperated look. But he reached out and gently cupped the side of her face. "You're certain you're safe?"

"He won't come looking for me. I promise."

His look was filled with doubt. "Did he hurt you, baby? Hit you?"

She shuddered, and suddenly, she was drawn into a warm chest. She didn't care that he was sweaty from his run. That he needed a shower.

She needed that warmth.

"I'm going to kill that bastard. When I find out what he did and who he is, I'm going to murder him."

Thank God he was never likely to run into Steven.

Because she knew that he meant every word. And that kind of scared her to death.

18

Hannah ran the vacuum up and down the carpet. This carpet really had seen better days. She didn't even want to know what half of these stains were.

Raid had headed out to the shop. Apparently, he wanted some snacks. Like there wasn't enough food in the house. The man was a bottomless pit. She guessed that run this morning made him hungry.

While he was out, Hannah had decided to make herself useful. She was getting tired of feeling like she was going nowhere. A hamster stuck on a wheel.

Running and running, but never reaching a destination.

She was due back at work tomorrow, so she might as well get some cleaning down now.

Suddenly, the vacuum stopped. She spun around to see Raid glowering at her, holding the plug up with one hand.

"Hey! I was using that! What do you think you are doing? And how come you're back so quick? Where are your snacks?"

"I forgot my wallet. What the hell do you think you're doing?" he demanded, giving her an angry look.

Huh? Why would he be mad about her vacuuming?

"Vacuuming. The apartment needs cleaning."

"If the apartment needs cleaning, then I'll do it."

What was happening right now?

"Why would you clean my apartment?"

"Because you recently fainted. And we still don't know why. You're exhausted, so you should be resting."

Her entire body softened. "Raid, I'm not ill."

"You don't know what's wrong. And you won't until the blood tests come back. So, until then, you'll do as you're told and take it easy."

"Do as I'm told? Are you for real right now? Raid Malone, you can't tell me to do what I'm told."

"I'm your guardian, remember?"

"I still haven't officially agreed to that." She gave him a cool look. He was taking this guardian stuff far too seriously. "I might need to call Jake and tell him that you're not my guardian."

"You do that, darlin'. Doesn't change anything."

"He could arrest you," she threatened.

"Nah, he won't."

"Why? Because the two of you are friends?"

He threw back his head and laughed. "No, darlin'. We're not really friends. Jake's arrested me at least five times."

"He's done what?" she asked, gaping at him.

"Uh-huh. He loves arresting me. Then he gets to call Alec to tattle. Once, he called West. That asshole left me in jail all night."

"What?" West left him in jail all night? Jake arrested him? Anger filled her. "How dare they!"

Raid gave her a surprised look. "Are you angry with them, baby?"

"I am! I'm going to give them both a piece of mind when I see them next." Then she realized what she'd said and how ridiculous she sounded. She shot Raid a look, prepared to see him laughing at her.

But his face had gone all soft. His eyes were warm pools as he watched her. "You care about me."

Rats. Shit.

"Even if I have to wait for you to admit it, it will be worth it. Because you do care about me, don't you, Hannah?"

"I can't have you!" she cried.

"Why? I told you that I don't need normal. Or is it because you think you're dirty?"

She gaped at him. Then she stumbled back, dropping the vacuum. She moved so suddenly that the room spun.

She was going to be sick.

Suddenly, she was picked up and held against a warm, broad chest.

"Let me go." Her voice was strangled. Filled with anger, horror, and fear.

He knew.

How did he know?

Panic grasped hold of her chest. She couldn't breathe.

"Breathe, baby."

Yeah, she'd like to do that. But it wasn't happening. Her lungs had seized and she couldn't get a breath in.

He knew.

Oh fuck. He. Knew.

"Shit. Fuck. Shit. Fuck. I shouldn't have said that. I didn't mean to just blurt that out. Fuck, breathe, Hannah."

She was aware of him sitting on the sofa with her on his lap. He placed his hand over her chest.

"Please, baby, please. You're going to pass out if you don't breathe. Please. Just take a breath in for me. Do it for me."

She couldn't. She couldn't do it.

"Fuck!" The word snapped through the room, a bolt of fury

pushing it. Then he turned her to face him, her legs straddling his thighs as he cupped her face between his hands. "Listen to me, Hannah Megan McLeod. You're going to breathe right now."

Then he pressed his lips against hers.

It shocked her. At first, she thought he was trying to give her a form of mouth-to-mouth. But his lips moved against hers, and her mouth dropped open with a groan.

Lord, that felt good. She gasped in some air as she fell into the kiss. He shifted her, so she was lying sideways across his lap, her back cradled by his arm as he kissed her long and deep.

Then he drew back.

She stared up at him, her heart racing, her breath coming in quick pants. But not because of panic.

Nope. Her body was reacting to that kiss. And it wanted more.

She wanted more.

But . . . she shouldn't have more.

He knew.

"How do you know?" A tear slid down her cheek. "How?"

"First, I want to make one thing really clear. You are not dirty. You could never be dirty. No matter what that bastard did to you . . . you, baby, are pure. You are clean. You are and always will be my beautiful, sweet Hannah."

A sob broke out of her. She could tell he was speaking the truth. Or what he saw as the truth.

But he didn't know . . .

"I'm n-not."

"You are." It was said with such ferocity.

"I went with him," she whispered. "I let him do things . . . if you're dating someone, if they're your boyfriend, isn't it . . . I mean, the line . . . isn't it blurred?"

His eyes widened. "If you're asking me what I think you're asking me, then there is no blurred line. There is consent and there is no consent. Now, some people might give consent to their partner to take over, to be in a 24/7 power exchange relationship. They might want to be forced. Or to be hurt. There are all sorts of kinks, and I never yuck on someone's yum. But there is always fucking consent. You don't give that . . . I don't care who that person is to you or you to them. It's not right."

She sobbed, trying to wipe away tears.

"Did he . . . did he rape you, baby?"

She shook her head.

"You're not lying to me, are you?" His face was pale, and she swore she could see tears in his eyes. But maybe that was her imagination. Or perhaps she was seeing things because her own eyes were blurred.

"No." She wiped at her cheeks.

He brushed her hands away and took over wiping the tears away.

"You can tell me anything. It will not make me see you differently."

She took a low, shaky breath in. "He didn't rape me. There was . . . he did other things."

"Motherfucker."

"I thought I loved him. And all along, I was just a target. I think that's maybe what hurts the most. That he never cared about me or wanted me. He used my body to get to me. He used my needs against me, and that's why I can't ever . . . I can't ever submit to anyone again. Because when I think about doing that, I think about him."

"Baby," he murmured.

"He's ruined so many things for me. All because he wanted to use me and take from me. He's taken it all."

Raid cupped her face. "Then it's time to start taking it all back."

"I can't. How can I get my life back?"

"One step at a time."

"It's too big. There's nothing left. I'm drowning." She couldn't even breathe.

"Then you hold on to me. I'll be your anchor. I'll be your life-raft. Whatever fucking metaphor you want to use, all you need to do is hold on to me."

"Aren't you scared?"

"Of what? Of him?"

"No. Of me drowning you as well . . . pulling you down . . . of the stench he's left on me shifting to you."

"There is no fucking stench on you. Do you hear me?" he said fiercely. "That's added to your tally."

"I have the feeling I'm not going to sit properly for a week."

"Make it a month."

Wow. She didn't know whether to be scared or turned on.

Perhaps a bit of both.

"You are not going to pull me down. You do not smell. Wait a minute." He started sniffing her.

"Hey! What are you doing?" She tried to wriggle away, shocked as he pushed his face into her throat to sniff. "Raid! Stop sniffing me like you're a dog."

"If I were a dog, I'd be sniffing you somewhere else. Hmm . . . I could try that." He gave her a wicked look.

She groaned. "That should disgust me."

"It doesn't? Good to know." He grinned.

"Raid . . . I'm not . . . I'm not ready for anything like that yet. A kiss is one thing . . . sex is something else."

"Baby, I am not going to push you for more than you're ready to give. This is going at your pace, understand me?"

"He didn't rape me." She thought it bore repeating. "But I thought he was going to. And I'm not sure how I . . . how I'm going to react. Or if I can get aroused anymore."

"Now, you're lying," he whispered. "I saw the way you looked at my bare chest."

Holy. Crap.

Yep. She was a total liar. She'd taken one look at his naked chest and she'd wanted to lick him all over.

"He ever have you sit on his face?" he asked in a conversational voice.

"What? No." What the heck? Why was he asking her that? She could feel her face growing red. "I've never done that."

"Never?"

"And I'm never going to do that." It sounded far too insane.

"Did no one ever tell you?"

"Tell me what?"

"That you never say never to a Malone, darlin'. We just take that as a challenge."

Holy crap.

"I'm in trouble, aren't I?"

He just grinned. Yeah, she was. But the delicious kind. Still . . . as much as she wanted to do all sorts of things with Raid Malone, she couldn't imagine it ever happening at this point in time.

"Don't worry about that now," he told her, gathering her close. "Everything will be all right."

Would it?

She really wished she could just stop worrying and believe him.

"I'm going to get a blanket and we can snuggle on the couch."

"Snuggle?" she asked.

"Snuggle. What's wrong with snuggling?" he demanded.

"Nothing's wrong with snuggling. I just didn't realize you did it."

"Baby, I'm the King of the Snuggle."

"That's a big call."

"Not really. I'm just that good." He grinned.

Dear. Lord.

"Just one thing I want to ask about him . . . then we won't talk about him for the rest of the day."

"What is it?" she asked.

"You said you were a target, and he was a con man?" he asked.

"Yes."

"What did he con you out of?"

She sucked in a breath, growing tense in his arms.

"Hannah?"

"What do most con people go for?"

"Money." He was silent for a moment. "You sold your grandma's house."

Definitely no flies on him. "Yes."

"Baby." It was all he said. But it was enough. Tears filled her eyes again.

Rats. She hated this. Feeling so helpless. So out of control.

"Did you report him?" he asked.

"No. I couldn't. And you can't either! Please, don't tell anyone about this." She'd planned to tell Jake the other day . . . but now, she just couldn't.

"Fuck, baby."

"Please."

"I won't talk to anyone until I have the full details. But if you tell me and I decide it's worth reporting, then that's what we'll do. Understand?"

She sniffled, the tears rolling down her cheeks. "All right."

"Uh-uh. No more tears." He wiped them away with his thumb, then tilted her head back so she was looking up at him. "No. More. Tears."

"I don't like them either. But it doesn't mean I c-can just stop."

"You can. You will."

She rolled her eyes at him.

"None of that cheek, missy." His face turned tender. "You're exhausted, aren't you?"

"I don't want a nap." She couldn't take any more sleeping.

"No nap. Last thing you need is to be alone right now."

Well . . . she wasn't so sure about that. Maybe she needed to be alone so she could shore up her defenses. He kept surprising her, shaking up her world.

"How bad are things?" he asked.

Pretty bad. Then she realized Raid meant her finances.

"I have a place to live and food in my fridge. Things could be worse."

He frowned, looking like he didn't like that.

"Don't you need to get some snacks?" she asked hastily. "I don't want you to fade away."

"I don't need to go anywhere. I'm right where I need to be."

Shoot. She was in definite trouble here.

"I don't think I can take you being sweet to me right now. Not if you don't want me to cry anymore." She leaned against him tiredly.

"What do you need right now?" He ran his hand up and down her back, rubbing at the tight muscles.

She let out a small moan. "More, please."

"Baby, tell me what you need. I'd give you anything."

"I wish I didn't have to think for a while. I'm just tired." Tired of it all.

"I can do that, baby."

"What?"

"Take over for a while."

"I don't know." In theory, it sounded good. In reality, it might not be. Sure, she enjoyed submitting. But that was always at Saxon's. Where she felt safe and protected. Where her boundaries were known and respected.

"Nothing scary. I won't do anything except make the decisions, so you don't have to."

"I feel like you do that anyway."

"So what do you have to worry about?"

Hmm.

"Do you have a safeword?" he asked.

"Um, yeah."

"What is it?"

"Peach."

"All right, baby. You say peach and we go back to our usual dynamic."

"You being bossy all the time?"

"Exactly."

19

Hannah ended up lying on the couch with a blanket over her.

"Do you want something to eat, baby? A drink?" Raid called out.

"I want a coffee. But I'll get it." She sat up and turned to stare at him.

He shot her a firm look and pointed a finger. "Stay where you are. I can get your drink and I'm already up. Plus, you're resting."

"I don't need to rest."

"The bags under your eyes and those blood test results say otherwise."

"The blood tests didn't say I needed to rest."

He shot her another look, and she bit her lip. Jenna had just called ten minutes ago to tell her that her blood test results were all good, except they showed that she was low in iron and several other vitamins.

More rest. Eating lots of vegetables and fruit. And she was sending over some vitamins.

That had just made Raid even bossier. Now she'd been

ordered to stay on the couch and do nothing for the afternoon while he did everything.

That wasn't easy for her. She was a person who liked to take care of others.

But Raid is in charge.

"Jenna said you need more rest. I say you need more rest. So guess what you're getting?"

"A Maserati? I always wanted one of those."

"Smart-ass. And you're not drinking just coffee, either." He walked over with a cup of coffee and a glass of water. "Drink your water first."

She let out a long sigh.

He just eyed her. "I'm adding to the tally."

She gulped, knowing he meant the tally of how many spanks she was getting when he deemed her well enough.

"Where am I at?" she asked.

"Not sitting down for at least a month. Heading into two."

"Yikes. That's a lot of spanks. I don't think your hand can handle it."

"Good thought. What's on your acceptable list? Paddle? Belt? Cane? Whip?"

"You are not using a cane or whip on me!"

"So paddle and belt are acceptable. Good to know."

She was definitely in trouble here.

"Have you ever spanked someone?" she asked as she sat up to drink some coffee.

Yum. Coffee.

Who wanted water when coffee was available?

"Yep." He came back with some cut-up apple and banana in a bowl. "You haven't got much fruit or veggies in the house. I need to go do some shopping."

"You don't need to do any shopping for me." She didn't want him spending his money on her.

He just shot her a look before he sat on the coffee table. It creaked under his weight.

"This apartment is not Raid-proof," she muttered.

"We could move to the bunkhouse."

"Um, no. I think I'd rather stay here."

"I'd kick out Tanner so you didn't have to put up with his smelly feet."

"He has smelly feet?" This was alarming. Tanner was as gorgeous as the rest. Perhaps slightly crazier, as he was known to shoot at unwanted visitors at the ranch. But charming. To know that he had smelly feet was like learning that Santa Claus wasn't real.

Of course, Santa was totally real. So that wasn't a worry.

"Nah, he doesn't. But don't tell him that. Got to have a way of keeping him humble."

"That's terrible," she told him. But her lips were twitching. "How does he keep you humble?"

"No need for that. I'm totally humble."

Uh-huh. And she had a magical money-growing tree.

Lord, she could really use one of those.

"I'm going to go get some food for dinner. I'm gonna cook steak."

"You can cook?"

"I can cook steak. Every man can cook steaks. I think you'd get your man card taken from you if you couldn't."

"Man card?" she asked.

"Yep. Man card."

"Sounds serious."

"It is very serious. As is cooking steak."

She bit her lip.

"Uh-oh," he said.

"What? What's uh-oh."

"You're biting your lip. That means you're thinking. When

you're thinking, stupid shit comes out of your mouth."

"It does not!" She gaped at him.

"Darlin', it totally does. So hit me with it, so I can add to the tally. I'm thinking one-third with my hand, one-third the paddle, and one-third the belt."

"You're joking, right?" Sometimes it was hard to tell.

"Am I?" He looked thoughtful. Like he wasn't sure.

"Jenna said that I'm all right. I can go back to work tomorrow. I'm just a bit run-down."

"She said to only return to work if you felt up to it. I think you need another day off to get some more rest."

"But there's nothing seriously wrong with me. And I know you're meant to be working right now. So if we're talking about tallies, we should probably discuss what I owe you–"

He moved quickly, placing his hand over her mouth. It was so sudden that her body reacted instinctively, freezing with fear.

It's Raid. It's Raid. It's Raid.

He removed his hand just as quickly. "Fuck. Sorry. Fuck!" He stood, and she shied back with a small gasp.

Self-loathing filled his face, and she hated it. Lord, she fucking hated it.

"Screw him!"

"What?" He gave her a startled look.

"I said, screw him! Screw Steven! I hate his guts."

"Okay, baby. You might want to calm down–"

"Why? So I can be a good girl? I hate those words now. I used to love them and he took them too. But perhaps I don't want to be a good girl and do what I'm told. Maybe I want to be naughty. What do you think of that, Raid Malone?"

She straightened her shoulders and gave him a challenging look.

To her shock, he grinned. "I think, hell yes, baby girl. You can be whatever the fuck you want and I'm here for it. You want to be *my* good girl. *My. Good. Girl.* Those words are yours and you're taking them back from him. Then that's what you'll be. Sweet and obedient. I will fucking pick you up, carry you around, keep you safe, protect you. You want to be naughty? My bad girl. You can do that too. Give me the sass, break the rules, push your boundaries. I will give you everything I just said. But I will also be here to make sure you know who is in charge, who takes care of you, who punishes you when you're naughty."

Good. Lord.

Had she awakened some sort of beast? This was not what she'd expected.

Yet, it was everything she'd ever wanted.

"Rules?" she asked.

"Yes, rules."

"What are these rules?" she asked suspiciously.

"No putting yourself in danger. No lying. No talking badly about yourself, including calling yourself names."

Crap.

"No putting your health at risk. If something happens, like your car breaks down, or you hurt yourself, you have another dizzy spell, then you call me immediately."

"Is that it?" she asked sarcastically.

"For now."

Darn it.

"But I will warn you, my good, naughty, sassy, sweet, sexy girl, that if you put your health and safety in jeopardy, we'll be on a whole other level. Understand me?" There was a serious look on his face.

She nodded. "I think so."

He grinned.

Seriously. She was worried about these mood swings of his.

"Right. To go back to what started this. Your supposed tally.

You don't owe me anything. And that's an instant five if you mention owing me or paying me back again, understand?"

"Don't you need to get back to work?"

"I'll go back when you do. The ranch isn't going to collapse without me there. I mean, sure, the others rely on me since I'm the best there is. I know the ranch better than any of them. But still . . . it will survive."

"Raid," she whispered. "I don't want to take advantage of you."

"It's not taking advantage if I'm willingly giving to you. If I want to give to you. If it makes me feel good to do things, to look after you. Is it?"

"I guess not."

"You guess? I think there's something you're not getting, baby."

"What's that?"

He leaned toward her, but didn't touch her. He was probably worried she was going to freak out like before. "That perhaps all of my life has been leading to this point. That I was put on this earth precisely for this. To take care of you."

She gaped at him.

What the heck did you say after something like that?

"I need to get some things from the store, but I don't want to leave you alone. When I leave you alone, you start to think. Or you try to clean."

"I won't . . . I'll be fine."

"I think you should come with me."

She shook her head. "I want to stay here."

He frowned down at her.

"I promise I won't do any thinking. Or cleaning."

He grunted. Then he pointed a finger at her. "You'll stay on the couch, eat your fruit, drink your water, and you will not think."

"Right."

"Good. I'll be back soon. I'm locking the door and taking a key. You stay here." Leaning down, he brushed his lips over hers, leaving them tingling.

Then he was gone. And she was still sitting there in shock.

What the heck had just happened?

And since when did he have a key?

WHEN RAID WALKED into the apartment twenty minutes later, he came to a stop. Then he slammed the door shut and carried the box of groceries to the kitchen bench. He put it down and then stood with his hands on his hips, staring at his girl.

Who was not lying on the couch like he'd ordered when he'd left.

"What do you think you're doing?" he asked.

"I thought I'd make my smashed potatoes," she explained, turning from where she had a large pot boiling on the stovetop. "To go with the steaks. They take a bit of cooking because you boil them first before you roast them. And um, they, um, they're delicious." She stumbled over her words as he moved toward her. Grabbing her hand, he led her back to the sofa.

"What did I say before I left the apartment?" he asked as they stood in front of the sofa.

"Uh, well, you told me to sit and eat and drink. But the potatoes needed to go on."

"They could have waited until I got back and you know it. You're testing me."

Her eyes went wide, and she looked worried. He needed to reassure her quick.

"Which is a good thing."

"It is?" she asked.

"Yep. Means you're starting to trust me. You know I won't harm you. Might heat your butt a bit, but I don't think that worries you."

"Uh, I wouldn't go that far."

Turning her to the couch, he pointed. "Sit!" Then he landed two smacks to her ass before moving away. He didn't want to crowd her.

She stood there, gaping at him. "You spanked me."

"I popped your butt. Probably didn't hurt more than when you ride over something bumpy on a bike."

"Really?"

"Really. Now, sit your butt down before I come over there and pop it again."

She sat without argument.

Huh. Seemed those pops on her butt worked perfectly.

Shit, he was good.

20

L ater that evening, she heard a soft snore.

She was lying in front of Raid on the sofa, which is where he'd positioned them both. He wasn't a fan of personal space, that was for sure. She'd tried to convince him to let her sit down on the other end, but he wasn't having it.

Nope, after a dinner of smashed potatoes, steak and corn on the cob, he'd ordered her back to lying on the couch.

After wrapping a blanket around her, he'd laid down between her and the back of the couch, his arm over her waist. Eventually, she'd relaxed and lost the blanket since the man was like a furnace.

Only problem was, he'd now succumbed to the power of the sofa and fallen asleep.

And she needed to pee.

She tried to squeeze out from under his heavy arm, but he just tightened his hold on her.

Shoot. She rolled onto her back, just managing not to fall off the sofa, then attempted to slide again.

He grabbed hold of her arm. He didn't hold her hard, but there was no getting free.

"Rats," she whispered.

Even when he was asleep, he was basically bossing her around. Telling her where he wanted her.

Which was apparently here on the couch with him.

If only her bladder agreed. She was close to peeing herself.

She shuffled toward the edge of the couch.

"Where do you think you're going?"

"Shh, go back to sleep. I just need the bathroom."

"I don't want you to go. You're my snuggle buddy."

She'd like to be more than just a snuggle buddy.

Hannah sucked in a breath. What was she going to do when he went back to the ranch? She was so used to him in the apartment now. Letting him stay with her had probably been a stupid idea. Because she was attached to him now . . . and she was going to be lonely without him.

It's for the best, though.

You need to get back to reality. Life with Raid Malone looking after you isn't real.

Nope, it was definitely her fantasy come to life.

"I need to use the bathroom, though."

"Too much coffee."

"Too much water," she countered. "Someone keeps shoving it down my throat."

"You don't like things shoved down your throat?"

"No."

"Too bad."

There was a beat of silence. Then she felt her cheeks growing hot as she realized what he was saying.

Jeez Louise.

Was he trying to kill her?

"Raid, let me go before I pee myself."

All of a sudden, he sat up and brought her with him. A squeal escaped her at the movement before she could stop herself. He stared down at her. "Not going to hurt you."

"I know." And she did. But some things were instinctive. "You just moved so quickly. I wasn't expecting it."

He grunted. He still looked half asleep. "The power of the sofa got me, didn't it?"

"Um, yep."

"Thought so. It's a powerful thing. I'm gonna pick you up now."

"What?" she gasped as he stood with her in his arms and started walking. "What are you doing?"

"Taking you to pee."

"I don't . . . I don't need you to carry me."

"But I want to." He set her down in the bathroom.

"You can't always do what you want," she informed him.

"Can't I?" He turned her toward the toilet and swatted her ass.

"Hey! You can't smack my butt whenever you like, either."

"Guardian!" he sang before he shut the door behind him.

Darn it. If he wasn't so cute, she would want to wipe that smug look off his face.

"You peeing in there, darlin'? Or just plotting ways to murder me?"

Urgh.

Yep. Lucky he was so cute.

21

"Right, you ready to go?" Raid asked as he looked her up and down on Wednesday morning. She'd wanted to go back to work yesterday, but he'd insisted she wait another day.

Bossy bastard.

She waited for him to say something about her outfit, but he simply held out his hand to her.

Instead of wearing all black or gray today, she'd put on one of her old skirts. Sure, it was still long, but she'd often worn long skirts. And it was a light blue with white daisies on it.

Maybe it didn't exactly go with the black shirt she had on, but it had made her feel happy when she put it on.

And she hadn't had that in a long time.

"Uh, yes. You didn't have to wait for me. I know you start early on the ranch."

"Baby, you've lived with me for several days now. What do you know about me?"

"Well, let's see, you're arrogant, you're bossy, you sometimes snore, you don't like hearing the word no, and you really like watching sport on TV, drinking beer, and eating steak."

He stared down at her for a long moment.

"Oh, and you eat a lot. Seriously. A lot." She was pleased with herself.

"You're lucky you're cute," he muttered.

"Funny, that's what I've always thought about you." She felt smug about that.

But instead of looking disgruntled, he appeared amused. "You think I'm cute?"

"What . . . that's not . . . I was trying to point out what a pain in the butt you are."

"All I heard was that you think I'm cute." He grinned. "Now, hand over your bag."

She glanced from the bag she was holding, then over at his hand. The bag only had a book, her lunch, and a jumper. Why would she need him to carry it?

"It's not heavy."

"Give me the bag." The words were stern. Firm.

She handed the bag over without thought. Drat.

"That's better. I don't care how heavy or light it is. I carry the bags. I open the doors. And I pay when we're out. Got me?"

Not really.

"Sure," she said.

He eyed her, then he took her free hand and led her outside. The door locked automatically behind her and he started down the stairs. His hand was warm and firm around hers. She should probably protest.

But the truth is, she didn't want to.

They reached his truck, and he unlocked it before opening the passenger side door.

"How high is this?" Shit. She only had short legs. And she was wearing a long skirt.

"I'll help you in." Before she could attempt to get in, his hands were around her waist and he lifted her inside.

Heck.

She was in before she had time to think about it. And then Raid put her stuff in the back before rounding the front of the truck to climb in.

"I'll drop you at the clinic. Go to work. Then I'll be back to pick you up."

"What?" She gave him a surprised look. "You don't have to pick me up."

"Yeah, I do."

"Raid, that's nuts. I only work until one-thirty today. You won't get any work in."

"I don't want you walking home."

She gave him a look. "I'll be fine. You don't even need to come back tonight."

The words hung in the cab of the truck. And she instantly felt awful. As though she didn't appreciate him dropping everything to take care of her.

"I'm sorry," she said hastily, feeling tears fill her eyes. Great. Now she was crying.

Why was she always crying?

"What?"

"I didn't mean to sound like a bitch. Sorry."

He pulled up outside the clinic. "Baby, I didn't think you sounded like a bitch."

"I did, though! It's not that I don't appreciate you taking care of me. You cooked for me, bought my food, you kept everyone away from me when I didn't want anyone close, and I basically just told you to go away."

"Whoa, Hannah, look at me."

She glanced up at him, wiping away her tears.

"Stop crying."

"I'm trying."

"Stop. Crying." It was said firmly. But tears didn't listen to firm. Tears didn't listen to anyone. Tears did what they were going to do.

And right now, those tears wanted to drip down her cheeks.

Those tears were assholes.

He wiped at her cheeks. "You need to stop crying. I hate when you cry."

"I know. I'm sorry."

"Hate when you say sorry, too. And when you think bad things about yourself."

"Is there anything you like about me?" she asked, starting to feel insulted.

His face grew soft, and he reached out slowly to brush more tears off her cheeks. "Only everything."

"Shoot. Don't be kind to me when I'm crying."

"Why not? Won't that stop the crying?"

"Nothing seems to stop the crying. I just go from sad tears to happy."

He shook his head and unbuckled her seatbelt. "I'm going to hold you now."

"Okay." She wasn't sure how he was going to do that when she was sitting across the console from him.

But like most things, Raid easily solved that issue by lifting her over the middle console and onto his lap. Where he hugged her against him. "Are you sure you want to go back to work, darlin'?"

"I need to get some sort of normalcy back into my life." And she also needed money.

He kissed the side of her head. "Okay. But I'm coming back tonight at least, all right?"

"Are you . . . I mean, I'm not sure . . . what is happening here?"

"You know what's happening."

Did she?

"And is this really the conversation you want to have right now?"

"I take your point," she said. It wasn't the time or place. "But I also don't want you running yourself ragged taking care of me. You need to work as well. And you should be sleeping in your bed."

What are you doing? That's not what you really want!

"You don't want me to stay? To spend time with you? Check in with you?"

She opened her mouth to agree. But she couldn't. "Crap. I want those things."

"You do?"

"Of course I do! I want you. I want us. It's just . . . things are going fast. I know we've only kissed, but I didn't even think that was going to be possible. I just need things to go slow."

"I can do slow."

She shot him a skeptical look. "You can?"

"Yep."

"How slow?"

"How about this? I'll pick you up at six tonight."

"Pick me up?"

"Yep. I'll pick you up. We're going for dinner."

"Dinner?" she repeated.

He tilted her face back with a finger under her chin. "You feeling all right, baby?"

"I'm not sure. I might be a bit dizzy."

"Right. You're going to the hospital. Jenna must have missed something."

"No, wait! Stop! Jenna didn't miss anything."

He eyed her suspiciously.

"I didn't mean I was actually dizzy. Just my brain was spinning from you wanting to take me on a date."

"Why wouldn't I want to take the prettiest, sweetest, sassiest girl in town on a date?"

Lord. He said the loveliest things. And every time he said something like that or gave her one of those soft looks, she felt herself growing stronger.

She wasn't going back to old-Hannah. She didn't think she could ever be her again.

But new-Hannah wasn't who she wanted. She just wanted to be Hannah.

And maybe, with some time and help, she could figure out who that was.

"I dunno. Maybe because she cries all the time."

He sighed dramatically. "That is certainly an issue."

"Hey!" She whacked him on the chest. "Rude!"

He grinned down at her. "Six tonight?"

"Six tonight."

"That's my gorgeous girl."

He kissed the tip of her nose and then lifted her back over to her seat.

"Wait there while I come around and open your door."

She waited, and he opened the door before lifting her down.

"Thanks." He grabbed her bag and handed it to her. "Does it look like I've been crying?" She wiped at her cheeks.

"Yep."

Awesome.

"Hey! What's going on? Why are you crying?"

Turning, she saw Melody rushing toward them, looking furious. Behind her were Carlie and Josie, looking equally upset.

What was happening?

22

M elody stepped between her and Raid, pushing at his chest. "You stay away from her, you big bully! You were supposed to make her feel better, not make her cry!"

"Mel!" She stared at her friend in shock as the tiny woman glared up at Raid, her hands on her hips.

She looked to Carlie and Josie, waiting for one of them to step in and try to settle Melody down. Except they were both frowning up at Raid, looking like they'd like nothing more than to kick him in the balls.

Wait. Crap.

She'd just remembered. She was the peacemaker of the group. It was up to her to calm them all down.

"You guys are overreacting," she started to say.

"Overreacting?" Melody cried. "You're crying! He made you cry."

"Raid didn't make me cry."

"You don't have to protect him, Hannah," Carlie told her,

pushing up her sleeves. "We have your back. We're not going to let him hurt you."

She put her fists up.

As though she was seriously about to fight Raid.

Hannah gaped at her.

"Yeah, big boy. We're going to make you hurt for hurting our friend," Josie told him, raising her chin.

"You guys, Raid didn't make me cry!" she yelled.

What the heck? This was ridiculous.

"Get behind Carlie, Hannah. We got this." Melody pushed Raid again.

Right. This was getting out of control. She had to do something before Raid got hurt. She risked a glance up at him, expecting that he'd look angry.

Steven would have been furious. Steven would have walked away, and then lost it at her later.

But Raid just gave Mel, Carlie, and Josie a calm look. "It's good you're looking out for your friend, but to do that, you actually have to listen to her."

She sucked in a breath and waited for the others to react.

"What do you mean? Of course, we listen to her," Melody said. "We always listen."

"You're not right now," Raid pointed out gently. "She's trying to talk to you and you're all ignoring her."

The three of them turned to look at her, and Hannah swallowed heavily. "Guys, I love that you're trying to look out for me. But Raid didn't cause my tears. Well, he sort of did, but not like you're thinking. They were sad tears, then happy tears. Promise."

Uh-oh. They didn't look at all that convinced at her words.

"Darlin', I can get them to listen, but you have got to do some better talking," Raid drawled. Now he looked amused.

Damn him.

She glared at him. He winked at her.

"You're lucky you're cute," she muttered. "Because you have a really annoying personality."

He threw back his head and laughed. "You love my personality."

"I think you lied when you said you'd spoken to Molly. And that those T-shirts might be fake."

"Damn, you're funny." Leaning forward, he placed his hand around the back of her neck and drew her into him. And then he kissed her forehead. "Tonight, at six."

"I'm not sure. I feel like I might be busy."

"Doing what?"

"Emptying the dishwasher."

"I did that while you were in the shower."

"Vacuuming."

"I did that yesterday."

Rats. Wait. She had one for him.

"Declogging my shower."

"Tonight at six. You'll be there."

It wasn't a question, but a command.

"Fine," she muttered grudgingly. It was all an act. She wanted to go out with him. Although, the idea of a date was kind of terrifying.

"Later, ladies. Thanks for looking out for my girl. I'll put your bag inside, baby." He ran it into the clinic. Which was kind of silly when it barely weighed anything.

But still so sweet.

My girl.

Holy. Crap.

She was his girl. And she had a date with Raid Malone.

Oh God.

Oh. God.

Raid ran back out and took off. Melody looked up at her. She reached for Hannah's hand, then seemed to think better of it and snatched her hand back.

Hannah winced inwardly. She hated that she'd done this to her friends. Once they wouldn't have hesitated to take her hand, to hug her. In fact, most of the time she initiated the contact, so they wouldn't have even had to think about it.

Now, they stared at her like she was fragile. Like they didn't know her.

Yep. She hated it.

So she reached out and took Mel's hand. Her strong friend. The one that didn't take any shit. That same friend gasped in shock and then glanced away, blinking rapidly.

"Mel," she said in a broken voice. "I'm . . . I'm so sorry."

She'd done this to them. She'd hurt them and their friendship. And she hated that.

"Why are you saying sorry?" Melody asked, looking bewildered. "What do you have to be sorry about?"

"Because I've pushed you guys away. I've been acting so cold. It's not because I don't love you guys. I do. It's just . . . I just . . . I guess I thought I was better off on my own. And I didn't want to tell anyone what happened, and I knew if I spent any time with you all, that you'd get it out of me."

"Oh, Hannah," Carlie said. "All we want is to make sure you're all right."

"We just want our friend. You don't have to tell us everything," Josie told her.

"Well, I want to know," Melody added fiercely.

Both Carlie and Josie frowned at her.

"So I can kick her asshole-ex's ass!" Melody scowled. "Whatever that dick did, he deserves to be castrated. I'd cut off his dick and shove it down his throat, make him choke on it while I played tennis with his balls."

Hannah stared at Melody in shock. So did Josie and Carlie.

"Oh my God," she said, as Josie and Carlie started giggling.

"I wasn't trying to be funny," Melody said with clear disgruntlement.

"Sorry. I just . . . I wish you could do that to him. I wish I could tell you it all. It's just . . . I feel so dumb."

"Oh, Hannah." Carlie leaned into her, wrapping an arm around her. And for the first time since she'd gotten back, she didn't step away from her friend's touch.

Carlie sighed happily.

"No matter whether you tell us or not, we're here for you," Josie told her.

"We're besties. Remember?" Melody said. "Us against the world. Screw everyone else."

"What about Brye?" Josie asked.

"I suppose he's all right," Melody said grudgingly. "I don't want to rip his dick off at least."

"Lucky Brye," Hannah said dryly. "Wait, what are you guys all doing here? Shouldn't you be at work?"

"We took the day off," Josie told her.

"All of you? Together?" she asked.

You cannot feel upset about that. Of course they didn't invite you. They thought you would say no.

"Yep," Melody said. "We were going to do an intervention."

"An intervention? For whom? Oh my God, is Brye eating too many corn puffs again?"

"God, no!" Melody said. "He hasn't had a corn puff in six months. Thank God. Once, he went to the store and came out with a whole shopping cart of them. A whole cart!"

They all nodded. They remembered.

"Then for who?" she asked.

Then she realized they were all staring at her.

"Wait. For me? But I don't need an intervention."

"We've been so worried, Hannah," Josie said quietly. "You aren't yourself. And you wouldn't let us in. And then you fainted . . . we tried to visit and call but you don't answer your phone and then Jake said to give you and Raid some time . . . we just . . . we . . ."

"We were gonna kidnap you," Melody told her. "Take you somewhere and ply you with mimosas until you spilled."

"Really?"

They all nodded.

"What were you going to do if I fought back?" she asked.

"I have a stun gun." Josie brought it out of her handbag.

Hannah took a big step back.

"Isn't it pretty? It's pink. My cousin got it for me."

"Josie, we talked about this," Carlie warned. "Friends don't stun gun other friends."

Josie pouted. "I've never gotten to use it."

Hannah patted her arm. "I think that's a good thing, sweetie."

With a sigh, Josie put the stun gun away. "I guess so. Not sure why I even bought it."

"I could always take it," Melody said. "I could threaten Brye with it if he ever looked at another corn puff again."

"Brye would spank your ass if you did that," Hannah said.

"Yeah. Can I borrow it?" Melody asked.

Josie grinned. "Haven't been spanked in a while, huh?"

"No." Melody took it from her. "He's been so busy at the gym that he hasn't even noticed all the naughty things I've done lately."

"Raid is keeping a tally," she blurted out.

They all turned to look at her.

"He's keeping a tally so he can spank me when I . . . when I'm more comfortable with him. Like that." Although part of her thought she was ready now.

And the other part of her thought that part was nuts.

Hmm.

"He's going to spank you?" Carlie asked.

"Yes."

Josie clapped her hands. "That's so awesome! I'm so happy for you."

They all stared at her.

"What?" she asked. "Hannah likes being spanked. Right?"

"I liked being spanked for fun. At the club. Before everything happened."

"And now?" Melody asked.

"I'm not sure how I'll react," she admitted. "What if I get scared? What if I don't like it? What if Steven took that from me, too?"

She rubbed at her chest, feeling it tighten.

"You can't let him win," Melody told her. She grabbed Hannah's hands in hers, pulling them away from her chest. "You have to show that fucker that he can't win. That he hasn't beaten you. That you're strong. And if anyone can help you get through any fears you have, I bet it's Raid."

"You're right. And I know he won't hurt me. He'd never harm me."

"Of course he wouldn't," Josie said. "And if he ever did, I also have Mace." She dug around in her handbag and brought out a bright-pink canister.

The three of them took a big step back from her.

"It's all right, the lid is on. See?" She pulled the lid off.

"You guys, I need help. He's taking me on a date. Raid Malone is taking me on a date. What am I going to do? What should I wear?"

"Right, we've all got the day off," Carlie said. "We're all going back to our houses to find things you might wear or need. We'll meet you at your place after work with food and booze."

"Right." She stared around at them. "You guys are the best friends I could ever wish for."

"Even though one of us wanted to stun gun you?" Melody asked dryly.

"Yep. Even then."

23

Hannah stood in front of the mirror in her bedroom, staring at herself.

It was her. And yet it wasn't.

It was a melding of old-Hannah and new-Hannah. No more baggy, dark clothing. She was wearing a pale pink dress that suited her coloring far better. It was long and puffy at the bottom, then cinched in at the waist. It had three-quarter sleeves with a V-neck.

A bit big for her, but it would have fit her perfectly before she'd lost so much weight.

There was one thing she knew for certain, though. This dress didn't belong in any of her friends' wardrobes. They'd turned up this afternoon with champagne, orange juice, cheese, and crackers.

And dresses and shoes and accessories.

It had been overwhelming and shocking.

But she also knew that they'd gone out and bought all this stuff. For her. Even if they were trying to pretend it was stuff they'd just had lying around.

She swirled around.

"Well? What do you think?" Melody asked, impatient as always.

"I think she rocks it," Carlie said.

"You're going to make him cream his pants," Josie added.

"Ew, Josie!" Carlie cried.

"What?" Josie asked.

"You totally are," Melody agreed.

"Thanks? I think." She tugged at the dress. "I feel a little . . . exposed."

The last thing she wanted was to draw any attention to herself.

Melody walked up behind her and put her arms slowly around Hannah's waist. She knew that the other woman was being careful not to scare her. That she might even be worried about Hannah rejecting her.

"You look beautiful, Hannah. You always have. You always will. You're the best person we know. Our best friend. You're kind and caring and funny. We love you so much."

It was almost too much coming from Mel, who would generally rather poke a finger in her eye than admit to feeling something soft and mushy.

Hannah sniffled.

"Uh-uh, don't muck up my make-up," Josie warned. "No crying."

"That's what Raid would say. He doesn't like me crying."

"Aww," Carlie said. "That's so sweet."

"Why were you crying around him? Have you cried more than once? What did he do?" Melody asked fiercely.

She turned and took Melody's hands in hers. "Nothing. I'm just . . . I'm a bit of a mess."

"You're not a mess," Josie told her. "Something bad

happened and you don't have to tell us. But you're allowed to react the way you want."

"But I pushed you guys away. I can't lie, I might do it again. I just . . . I feel so stupid. I feel so exposed and used. And it hurts. Right here." She placed her hand on her chest and they all moved in to hold her as she sobbed. "I really am sorry. I never want to lose you guys."

"And you never will," Melody told her, stepping back.

Josie and Carlie nodded.

"Thanks guys. And not just for the dress and shoes which I know you all bought for me, but for all of it."

None of them appeared phased that she'd worked out that they'd bought all of this for her.

"Enough of this mushy crap," Melody said, clapping her hands. "You look amazing and you have a sexy-as-fuck man picking you up soon. We need to fix your makeup and get out of here before your cowboy turns up."

They packed up everything while Carlie fixed her make-up for her. Then Josie and Carlie took off with waves goodbye. Melody hung back and took hold of her hand, squeezing it. "You feel safe with Raid?"

"Yeah. I do." She swallowed heavily. "I have moments, but I'm coming to trust him. I want to believe in him . . . in us."

Lord, she still couldn't believe there was a them.

"Then believe it."

She gave Melody a worried look. "I'm so much work, though. What if he decides I'm not worth it?"

"You listen to me, Hannah McLeod. You're acting like he's doing you a favor. He should get down on his knees and thank God that you're interested in him. He was blind as a bat before, then he woke up. Thank fuck. But you aren't some charity case. You aren't less than him. You're a fucking queen and he should bow down."

"I don't want him to do any of that. I just want him to care about me, to want me, to love me."

"You're worthy of love, Hannah. And unless I'm wrong about him, Raid knows all of this. Sometimes, you just have to take a chance and leap. Then pray like fuck that someone will catch you."

There was a knock on the door.

"I've stayed too long," Melody said. She moved to the door and opened it. "Hey, Raid."

"Hi, Melody. You good?"

"Yep, just leaving." She turned to look back at Hannah. "Remember, leap and believe. And if he doesn't catch you, I have a very sharp knife and I'm not afraid to use it."

Raid stepped in so Melody could leave, and the door shut behind her.

"Do I want to know what that was about?"

Hannah shook her head. "You really don't."

Then his gaze moved over her, taking her in. Her heart raced, waiting to hear what he thought.

"Jesus, Hannah. You are so fucking beautiful."

She blushed. "I am? The girls bought me this dress."

"Then I owe them thanks because you look gorgeous in it. But the dress is just the icing on the cake, baby. Because you would be beautiful wearing a sack. Or better yet, nothing at all."

She could feel her face growing even hotter as he said that, and she choked on her words. "Raid!"

"Come on, we need to get going. Do you have a jacket?"

"Uh, it's not that cold out, is it?"

"It will get cold later. You need a jacket."

She shrugged and grabbed one from her bedroom. She didn't think it would get that cold to really bother with one, but if it made him feel better, then she'd take one.

He held out his hand, and she gave him the jacket. Then he held it for her to get into.

Wow.

No one had ever done that for her before. Then he took her hand and walked her to the door, shutting it behind them. He kept hold of her hand as he led her down the stairs.

"I don't like you coming up and down these stairs in the dark," he grumbled.

"Uh, I don't, really. I mean, I never really go anywhere at night."

"The days get shorter in winter. It will be dark when you get home from work on those days. You need more security lights."

It was only the end of summer. Ages until winter hit. And he was worrying over nothing.

"I'm sure the security lights here are good enough."

"Good enough isn't enough," he told her, pausing and pressing her back against the building wall. She waited for the panic to hit. But all she got was a wave of arousal.

"What?" she asked faintly.

"When it comes to your safety, good enough isn't enough," he told her, cupping the side of her face. "I want to know that you have the best."

Her knees weakened. "You're a smooth talker, cowboy."

He grinned. "That's nice you think so. But it's just the truth."

Such a smooth talker.

Was he going to kiss her? Please let him kiss her.

"I'm going to keep you safe, baby. From everyone who might hurt you."

"What if . . . what if the person I'm most worried about hurting me is you?" she whispered.

He took a step back, his face shutting down. "I'm sorry. I didn't mean to make you afraid."

"You didn't! Shit, I didn't say that right." She looked around, but there wasn't anyone around. And she had to be brave. This wasn't all on him.

There were two people in a relationship. They both had to make it work.

And she had to fix what she'd just broken.

So she pushed down her nerves and stepped into his space, pressing her breasts against his chest.

"I'm falling for you, Raid Malone. A little bit more every time I'm with you. And that makes me so scared. Because the more time I spend with you, the harder it will be for me to ever say goodbye if you decide to walk away." She pressed her face into his chest after that admission.

"Look at me, Hannah."

She shook her head.

"Do as you're told." His voice was so firm. So stern.

God, it was delicious. A shiver ran through her as she glanced up at him.

He cupped her face between his hands. "You're being so good for me, aren't you?"

She tensed.

"Uh-uh, you're being so brave. You can keep being brave a bit longer. We're taking those words back, remember? And you are so good. Thank you for telling me how you are feeling."

She took in a deep breath.

"But you need to stop worrying. Because, baby, I'm not ever walking away. And I wouldn't ever let you walk away either. You know I want you. I've made that clear. I care about you and I just want to protect you. What you might not realize is that I intend to possess you. Not tell you what you should do, or what to wear. Although I can do that sometimes if you need or want it. I have no problem with taking control. In fact, I like it. I'm thinking I might need it."

What? Really?

"I can give you time, I can go slow, I can wait for you to feel safe enough to tell me what happened to you. As long as you promise that you're safe."

She nodded.

"As I said, I will not ever walk away or allow you to."

Maybe part of her should have protested that. She should be allowed to walk away if she wanted to, right? But there was some safety in knowing he wouldn't allow it.

"No matter what?"

"No. Matter. What. You. Are. Mine."

Then he slowly dropped his mouth to hers and slid his hand behind her head to hold her to him as he kissed her.

And he showed her exactly how little issue he had with taking command.

His lips moved softly against hers, before his tongue slid along them, pushing into her mouth. She moaned as pleasure flooded her and she pressed against him, wanting more.

But he drew back, staring down at her. A noise of disapproval and longing escaped her.

"More."

He shook his head. "It's time for dinner. And I'm not standing and kissing you in a dirty alley all night."

She pouted, and he tapped her lower lip. "Put that away."

"You could make me."

24

He stared down at her for a moment, then he let out a loud laugh. "I could, darlin'. But not in the way you're hoping."

Drat.

"Come on, dinner will be getting cold."

He led her to his truck and lifted her inside. Then he ran around to the driver's side and climbed in.

She was sitting there, her lips tingling, her body alight with arousal.

"Baby? You okay?"

"I don't know. Is it possible to go into shock from a kiss?"

He let out another bark of laughter. "Are you saying that was good?"

"Sooo. Good. I've never been kissed like that. With passion and control. Hunger and fire."

He glanced over at her. "I like that."

Yeah. So did she.

"Now, buckle your seatbelt," he ordered as he started the truck.

"Did you take an extra dose of bossy medicine before you came out tonight?" she asked as he drove away from the curb.

"Nope." He grinned over at her. "This is just me, darlin'."

Hmm.

"Where are we going for dinner?" She hadn't let herself think about it, because there were only a few places to eat in Haven.

At Dirty Delights. The diner. Or Fet.

Fet would be the place of choice for a first date. But she couldn't help but feel nervous about going there. What if Saxon was there?

She wasn't scared of Saxon. At the club, he was always there, watching over and protecting the subs. He and Aspen were now married, and Aspen was one of her favorite people.

But still . . . was she ready for that?

"Hannah? You okay?"

"Sure!" No way did she want to ruin their first date.

"I think I've made it clear that I don't like when you lie, darlin'. So I suggest you stop."

Her eyes widened, and she glanced over at him. "What? I wasn't lying."

"You're still doing it. Perhaps it's time we start seriously talking about punishment."

"You're going to punish me?" she asked in a high-pitched voice as they left the outskirts of Haven. Where were they going?

Shoot. They were heading in the direction of the ranch the Malones owned. Was he taking her to dinner at his place?

"I don't know. You ready for that?"

She thought it over. She trusted him and she didn't want him to think she didn't. But there were some things she couldn't imagine doing right now.

Like being tied down.

Or even held down.

Yet . . . the idea of being spanked again . . . and by Raid . . . yeah, that held some appeal.

"I'm going with not yet," he said in a low, soothing voice.

"What?"

"If you have to think about it that hard, then I don't think you're ready."

Shoot. He was right.

"Maybe I'll never be ready," she muttered.

"Hmm. I think you will. But if you're not, as I've said before, we can come up with something else."

"Or perhaps I won't need to be punished at all. Because I'm a good girl."

She froze and waited for that sick feeling to hit. For the panic. But it didn't come. Maybe because she'd said the words herself? Or perhaps it was like he'd said and she was taking those words back from that asshole.

"You are a good girl. My good girl."

Her breathing grew harsher, but she worked on keeping herself calm as her hands clenched into fists.

"I think I'm going to be sick."

"You're not," he told her. "You're not going to be sick." He drew down a gravel driveway and then parked just below a hill.

Getting out, he ran around his truck, opening her door. Then he unbuckled her seatbelt, lifting her down.

"You are not going to be sick. Look at me. At me, Hannah."

She'd heard him sound stern, sound firm.

She'd never quite heard this tone before.

"At. Me. Hannah."

Her gaze went up to his. His gaze was fierce, encompassing, and there was no looking away.

"You're my good girl."

She shook her head, and he cupped her face with his hands.

"My. Good. Girl."

"Raid," she whispered. She couldn't do this, and she couldn't believe he was pushing her.

What happened to going slow?

"Whose good girl are you, Hannah?" he asked in a low voice.

"You said you'd go slow!"

"There's a time to back off, baby. And there's a time to give a push. Whose good girl are you?"

"Yours!" she cried.

He drew her against him, holding her tight as she shook. "That's right. Mine. My good girl. My Hannah. Not his. You're not his. Understand?"

She sagged against him, feeling exhausted. And the night had only just begun. Her head was thumping. It felt like she'd been through a detox. And she just wanted to sleep.

Actually, she figured that was a good way of thinking about it. That she was detoxing Steven from her body, her head, her life.

"My poor baby. I didn't intend to do that tonight, but it needed to be done."

He kissed the top of her head. She let the feel of him surround her. That sense of safety chased away the lingering sense of illness and self-loathing.

"You're exhausted, aren't you? Do you want me to take you home?"

She stiffened and tried to pull back, away from him. "No! Please."

"I don't want you to push yourself too far." He stared down at her in concern.

"I know my limits."

He raised his eyebrows. "I'm not so sure about that. But we need to talk about those limits. And rules. Including the one about not lying to me."

Uh-oh.

"Do we have to talk about that now?"

"No. I think we've had enough serious stuff for tonight. Although, you're still in trouble for lying before. That's going on the tally."

"Rats."

"Rats?" His lips twitched. "Fuck, you're adorable." He lifted her into his arms and started walking up the hill.

"Raid! Let me down!"

"Why?"

"Why? Because I'm too heavy to carry around like this. What if you hurt yourself? Or trip and fall?"

"I'm not going to hurt myself. And I'm definitely not going to trip and fall while I'm carrying precious cargo."

Oh, dear Lord.

He just kept getting sweeter and sweeter.

"How did you know I was lying earlier?"

"You bit your lip."

"Rats."

His chest moved as they reached the top of the incline. Then she gasped as she saw what lay on the other side. There was a small stream working its way through the land. Lush trees and rolling hills lay beyond the stream.

But it wasn't any of that which had captured her attention, what had her mouth dropping open as awe filled her.

It was the fairy lights draped around a large tree that went across to another big tree. Both of them framed a small table set with a white tablecloth and brushed brass tableware. There were white napkins and white chairs. And in the middle of the table was a vase filled with white peonies.

"I love white peonies."

"I know," he said.

"How?" she asked, turning her head toward him.

"I was in the clinic once when you got a delivery of white peonies for your birthday. You told me they were your favorite."

"I did?" she asked, not remembering that. Which was nuts when she usually remembered every encounter with him. "And you remembered after all this time?"

"Yeah. I did. Come on, dinner will be getting cold." He set her down, then took her hand and led her down to the table. There was another table set off to the side, with several covered trays.

"Did you do all this?" she asked.

Hannah couldn't understand any of it. This was like a scene from a movie. She'd never expected this.

"I had some help," he admitted. "Mia did the cooking, and I think Lara sort of helped. While Clem and Scarlett helped me decorate. Flick just moaned about the fact that West was being an overprotective ass who won't even let her pee on her own."

"Seriously?"

"She's likely exaggerating." He thought about that for a moment. "Maybe."

"Where are we?" she asked.

"This is Malone land. But the ranch's main house is still a ten minute drive from here."

They stepped up to the table and Hannah couldn't wait for the sun to go down so she could see the fairy lights in the dark. No wonder he'd wanted her to wear a jacket.

"This is so beautiful. I can't believe you did this for me."

"Why wouldn't I do this for you?"

Because I'm not worth all this fuss.

Stop it. She wasn't about to let that stupid voice derail this for her. Take away something so beautiful.

Raid held out a chair, and she sat. "There're even cloth napkins."

"Clem said we needed them. That kind of surprised me,

since I'm pretty sure Clem doesn't own any napkins. Half the time, she doesn't even use glasses to drink."

She didn't know Clem well, but from the few times she'd met her, she'd seemed hilarious.

Then Raid picked up her plate before moving to the other table.

"Oh, I can get my food." She stood and took the plate from him, then waited for him to grab his plate before moving to the table. He lifted the lids of the trays.

Whoa. That was a lot of food.

"Are people joining us for dinner?" she joked.

"They better damn well not," he replied. "Although with my family, you can never be too sure. If they show up, don't get alarmed if I pick you up and run for it."

"Why would we run?"

"Because those bastards will devour everything in sight. They're interfering and nosy. And I am not ready to share you."

"Is that why we're here tonight and not at Fet or Dirty Delights?"

He turned to her. "Why would I take you to Dirty Delights for our first date?"

"I don't . . . I don't know. There aren't many options in town."

He stared down at her for a long moment. "Was that what you were worried about?"

"What?" she asked, even though she knew what he was asking.

"In the truck on the way here, you looked worried, and I asked if you were all right. Was that what was concerning you?"

"I guess I thought you might take me to Fet, and I didn't feel ready for that."

"You should learn to trust me."

She sucked in a breath. "I mostly do. And I think . . . I think I'm getting there, Raid."

"Good." He filled his plate and carried it to the table. She gave herself far smaller portions of the beef cheek casserole, mashed potatoes, and mixed greens.

"This looks so good."

"It does?"

"Um, yep. You don't think it does?" she asked.

"I think you gave yourself enough to feed a rabbit."

"I, um, this is as much as I need."

Mumbling to himself, he grabbed her plate and returned to the table. With a far larger portion of everything.

"Raid! I can't eat this much."

"You can try."

Dear. Lord.

He was out of control. She glared up at him until he drew her chair out for her. And then she melted again.

25

"That didn't happen." She gaped at Raid as he took a sip of his beer.

Oh, did she mention there was a portable cooler filled with drinks? He'd really thought of everything.

"It did."

"But that's terrible!"

"It was his own fault. He shouldn't be so uptight. I mean, we shouldn't have had to go to school every day."

"Everyone has to go to school every weekday."

"Really? Seems barbaric. Still, West needed to learn a lesson."

"So you filled his car with balloons that were filled glitter!"

"Every time one popped, more glitter filled his car. He got it detailed and still years later, he'd find some glitter. Best prank ever."

"Poor West. I'm beginning to see why he is the way he is."

Raid grinned at her. "And what way is that, darlin'?"

Uh-oh. Hannah squirmed in her seat. They'd finished their meal and were now talking while the sun was beginning to go down, and the fairy lights were flickering on. Soon, it was going to be utterly magical.

"I'd rather not say," she replied primly.

He roared with laughter. "Right. Only I can see it on your face. You're thinking what we've all thought a time or two."

"What's that?"

"How the hell does Flick put up with him?"

"Raid Malone! I was not thinking that!"

She totally had been.

"Are you going to eat some more?" he asked.

"Oh no, I'm finished."

He gave her plate a look of disapproval. Then he folded his arms over his chest. "Did you eat lunch?"

"Yes, I ate lunch."

"Got to keep an eye on you."

"You do not! No one has ever had to keep an eye on me. I've never filled someone's car with glitter balloons."

He grinned down at her as he stood and took hold of her hand. Then he led her closer to the river. Letting go of her hand, he bent, picked up a flat stone and flicked it, sending it skimming across the water.

"Oh, I've never been able to do that."

"No?"

She shook her head. "I'm not co-ordinated enough."

"You used to trip up all the time over nothing. It was cute."

"It wasn't cute!" she protested. "It was embarrassing. And I only really did that around you."

"Yeah." He reached out and grabbed hold of her hand, tugging her toward him. "And why did you only do that around me, darlin'?"

"Because I got all flustered."

"Did you?" He used his finger under her chin to tilt her face back. "You got all flustered around me? Because you liked me?"

"You know I did."

"You used to imagine me kissing you?"

"Yes," she said, staring at his lips.

"Yeah? And was it anything like reality?" he asked.

"Hmm. I don't know. I can't really remember our last kiss."

His eyes widened before he wrapped his hand around the back of her head. "Excuse me? You can't remember our last kiss? Are you saying it wasn't memorable?"

"I'm saying maybe you can remind me how it felt . . ." Part of her couldn't believe she was doing this. Flirting with him like this. Practically goading him into kissing her.

Then his mouth dropped to hers, and he kissed her. And holy heck! There was no forgetting this kiss. He went deep. And he went hard.

One hand stayed around the back of her head, holding her steady for his mouth to take ownership of her, while his other hand dropped to her ass.

She moaned into his mouth as he squeezed her bottom.

Shit. That felt so good.

He drew the skirt of her dress up so his hand was underneath it. And the only thing between him and her ass was a pair of lacy panties.

She tensed for a moment, but he just kept his hand there, squeezing as his tongue teased and tormented her.

It was too much.

It wasn't enough.

She wanted more, yet knew she probably wasn't ready for it.

And when he drew back, she chased his lips with hers. A whimper escaped her.

"Now, did you ever imagine me kissing you like that?"

"No," she whispered. "That was magical."

"Yeah, it fucking was. And memorable." He gave her a stern look.

Oops. Seemed he hadn't liked her joking about forgetting what their last kiss had felt like.

"Definitely memorable. Although I do have a pretty terrible memory. So you might have to remind me. A lot."

He grinned down at her, the intensity fading slightly while a warmth took its place. "I think I can do that."

"I like that."

"Me too," he replied. "Now, let's teach you to skip stones."

Huh?

Weren't they going to kiss anymore? She wanted to go back to the kissing part of the evening.

But then he stood behind her, his body pressed to hers as he drew her arm back to show her what to do.

This might just be the best night of her life.

And definitely memorable.

26

Raid was prepared for a fight.

Luckily, he had a secret weapon. This morning, he'd left all his stuff here. Sure, it wasn't much. A toothbrush, a pair of pajama pants, and some clothes. Just things that Tanner had brought for him after he'd decided that he wasn't leaving her apartment.

But hopefully it was enough to convince her to let him inside.

When they reached her door, he held out his hand. "Key, baby."

"Are you sure we shouldn't have stayed to clean up?" she asked for the third time.

"Darlin', it's under control." He was going to owe all of his brothers' women big time. But totally worth it to see the look on her face when she'd seen where they were having dinner.

He hadn't wanted their first dinner to turn into a damn spectacle. Which is what he thought might have happened if they'd gone out to Fet or Dirty Delights. They could have driven to Freestown, but he was glad he'd decided to go for privacy.

It meant he could make out with Hannah without anyone watching.

"Okay." She handed over her key without argument.

Hmm. This was weird. What was she thinking? Things tended to go wrong when Hannah started overthinking.

Opening the door, he let her step inside and turned on the light before he grabbed her hand. "Wait here while I check the place over."

She gave him a shocked look but nodded.

It didn't take him long to check the apartment, and when he returned, she was still standing there.

"My good girl, aren't you?"

She bit her lip, but otherwise didn't show any negative reaction to his words. They were getting somewhere.

Moving closer, he took hold of her hand and led her into her apartment to the sofa.

But when they got there, she refused to sit.

"Baby? Is something wrong?"

If she asked him to leave, what would he do? He didn't want to upset her. But he also didn't want to go.

You'll do what she needs.

"I need to . . . to tell you about Steven. And I'm . . . nervous. Scared you'll see me differently."

Fuck. Finally. He didn't know what had brought this about, but he was grateful for it. "Come here, baby."

"I can't." She shook her head. "I don't think I can touch you while I tell you."

Raid didn't like that. He wanted to cuddle her while she did this. He knew it wasn't going to be easy for her. And if he hadn't known it before, he could see it in the way she was trembling.

"Baby, if you're not ready to tell me, I can wait."

"No, I want . . . I want to show you that I trust you. I might still have moments where I get . . . where I forget that it's you, and forget to be brave, and I forget that you'll catch me if I fall. Shoot. I'm not making any sense."

She wasn't. Yet, at the same time, he thought he understood.

"I'm always going to catch you, Hannah."

"I know." She let out a deep breath. "All you do is give to me, and I have to, no, I need to show you that I want this. Us. I want to try. If you do?"

He didn't know how she could still have doubts . . . but he would reassure her as much as she needed.

"Hannah, I do. I want this. I want us."

She nodded so fast that he worried she was going to hurt her neck.

"Baby, I want you to sit with me."

"Soon. I have to get this out."

"Nothing you tell me will change how I see or feel about you."

She shot a pained look at him. "No? What if it was my fault?"

"Your fault? How the fuck would him conning you be your fault?"

"I fell for it," she cried. There was so much pain in her voice that it made him flinch back. "How could I be so stupid! I sold my grandma's house for him. Do you know how long that house has been in my family? Over eighty years. And I sold it. I sold it because a man told me that he wanted me and that he wanted us to build a life together. But to do that, we needed to find a house of our own. One that could be for our family. He said that he wouldn't be comfortable moving to this town and living in my house. It had to be our house. Which meant we both had to contribute. Which I thought sounded fair. I wanted to help build our life together. To feel like we were equal. But to do that, I had to sell Grandma's house."

"Baby," he murmured. He hated this for her.

She paced back and forth, clearly unable to stay still. "I can't believe I fell for his lies. I met him on an online dating site. Did I tell you that? I can't remember if I did. It was a site for Dominants looking for subs and vice versa. They recommended that you met in a public place for the first few dates. To tell a friend where you were going. To send details of your date to a friend. And to not meet at club for the first time unless you had someone with you to watch out for you."

"You didn't do those things?" he asked in a soft voice. He didn't want her to think he was in any way blaming her.

"No. I was an idiot. I . . . I knew that Melody wouldn't approve of me meeting with a stranger without having someone with me. And I figured she'd tell Brye. Then Brye would tell Jake. So I didn't tell them that I was going to meet him. But I insisted we meet at a restaurant. We just hit it off. It was like he liked all the same things as me. I spent the weekend in Lafayette with him. We went to the movies. We ate out. We did tourist things. He told me that his family didn't know about his kinks. That they wouldn't understand. And that his employers would likely fire him if they found out."

"What did he say he did?"

"He said he was part of a tech start-up and had to travel a lot. Which meant I couldn't see him as much as I might like. But he still made time to call me. And he messaged me. He said all the right things. When we . . . when we finally started taking things further, it didn't feel as good as I thought it would. But I thought it was me. That's when he started getting in my head."

"How did he do that?"

She bit her lip.

"Hannah. What did he do?"

"It happened after the first time we went to a club in Lafayette. It wasn't what I was used to. There were no monitors. No one even asked me to fill in any paperwork or go over rules or anything! I didn't even realize there were clubs like that. I'm always safe at Saxon's. No matter what, someone is always watching. If I say my safeword, someone will stop everything. But there . . . it was like flying without a parachute. But I thought I could trust Steven. Things went . . . they went further than I thought they would."

"What did he do?"

"Nothing too bad. It's just I didn't want to be . . . I didn't want to be completely naked in front of others. Not that first time in a strange club. And so . . . when he ordered me to strip off, I said no because we'd negotiated differently. He threatened to punish me, but I said my safeword. I'd never seen him angry before, but this look of fury filled his face. He told me to get dressed, that the scene was over, and we left."

That motherfucker. Raid might never have been to a club, but he knew that consent was everything.

And that boundaries should always be respected.

"Come here, baby." He kept the anger out of his voice. "Come, let me hold you."

"If you hold me, I won't be brave enough to get this out."

"Hannah . . ." Fuck. He wanted to bring her to him. To reassure her that she didn't have to tell him any of it. Not for his sake.

For hers.

Because she was trembling so hard that it was hurting him.

"I have to get this out," she told him. "My way. I have to tell you how stupid I was."

"You are not stupid."

"I am. Because there were signs. Big fat red flags that said, hey, Hannah, you should run away from this guy. You should go back home and tell someone about this asshole." She ran her hand over her face. "It's not like I didn't have people I could've turned to. I could have told Jake or Saxon or Brye. But I didn't. I stayed with him. Because I felt so guilty."

"Why did you feel guilty?"

"I didn't do what he wanted me to do."

"Fuck, Hannah. No. He didn't take care of you. He didn't respect your boundaries. That was all on him. Not you."

"I know that now," she whispered. "But he . . . he stopped talking to me. He said he needed time to think about where we were going. That I embarrassed him. That I wasn't a good girl for him."

He was rethinking taking those words back.

How fucking arrogant had he been? Thinking that he could help her. That whatever it was, he could just erase what had happened with that guy? That he could suddenly become her Dom and give her what she needed.

"Fuck, Hannah, I'm sorry."

She wiped at her cheeks. "Why? It wasn't your fault."

"Yeah, but I'm the one who arrogantly said that we'd take those words back for you. I've been using them, pushing you. I should have waited until I knew what was going on. What actually happened."

She shook her head. "Raid, you wanted to help me. And that is never a bad thing. I appreciate that more than you can know. The fact that you can say those words and I don't feel like vomiting is more progress than I ever thought I would make."

He still didn't like it.

"I want to be your good girl, Raid."

"You always are," he told her. "And if we ever get to the point where you want to play, and you say your safeword, I will always honor it. As well as your boundaries. Fuck, if you need to say it at any time, I will listen."

She moved forward and kneeled in front of him, placing her hands on his knees. "I know you will. I'm not . . . I trust you, Raid."

He understood now how big that was. Placing his hands over hers, he frowned at how cold they were.

"Baby, you're freezing."

"I need to keep going. Please?"

He nodded, even though that took everything he had. She took in a shuddering gasp.

"I should have told him we were done. But he had my head spinning, and I started to think I was the bad guy. I embarrassed him. I didn't do what he wanted. I've always liked to please people. I used to get social anxiety when I was younger because I'd worry about saying the wrong thing and upsetting people. It probably started after Mom dumped me at Grandma's. Her new husband didn't like me and I took that on as my issue. That I'd said or done things that he didn't like."

"What? She just dumped you?" How did he not know that?

"My grandma didn't want anyone to know. She told everyone that my mom had taken a job overseas in a country that she didn't want to take me to for my own protection. I think Grandma was ashamed of what Mom did."

Which wouldn't have helped the way Hannah felt about what had happened with her mother. What a bitch for dumping her daughter for a man.

"My grandma was amazing. She really did love me. But I guess a part of me always thought that I could have been better, you know? Then Mom's new husband would have liked me. Then I could have stayed with them. But as an adult, I realized I'd been better off with Grandma than having a mom who could do that."

She was.

But still . . . it had to hurt. Even now.

"My father used to go through different women," he told her. "Most of us have different mothers. He got in deep with some bad guys. Alec got us out of some hot water and moved us here. He's always been more of a father to us than our real father.

Who is likely still out there. I just hope to fuck he's not still procreating."

"I'm so sorry," she told him.

"My point is that shitty parents don't define us and we shouldn't take their actions on. What your mom did was awful. But it wasn't your fault. Just like my father taking off on us wasn't our fault. In fact, we were a lot better off without him."

"You had Alec."

"And you had your grandma," he said.

"Right. And I sold her house, something she left to me so I would have stability, so I would be safe, and I sold it. To give the money to him," she said bitterly. "I should have walked away from him after that fuck-up at the club. Instead, I went grovelling to him, promising to do better, to be a better sub and girlfriend. He said he would have to punish me." She gulped. "It . . . it wasn't good. He, uh, he tied me up and started touching me. For a start, I was into it. I got aroused and stuff . . . but his touch just didn't feel right. It was just slightly too painful. It was almost like he wanted to make me respond against my will. When I came, I felt like crying. And then he fucked me and it was so . . . so robotic. After he came, I expected him to untie me, to cuddle me. That everything would be okay. Instead, he left me tied up for over an hour on my own. I didn't even . . . I didn't even know if he was still in the house. Don't you think I should have clued in then? But no, I was grateful he came back and untied me. Grateful! What was wrong with me?"

"Nothing was wrong with you and everything was wrong with him. Fucker."

"The strange thing was, the next day, it was like none of that had happened. Everything was amazing. That's when he told me he wanted things to go further. That he could see himself waking up beside me every day and going to sleep next to me every night."

He squeezed her hands as she paused.

"I just wanted to please him. I didn't want him to be mad and stop talking to me. So I ignored my friends and all those warning signs, and I said yes. He convinced me that I'd feel better if I was on an equal footing with him, if we bought a house together. So I sold Grandma's house, and we went house shopping. We found this gorgeous house. By then, I getting cold feet, but Steven had this way . . ."

"This way of what?"

"Making me feel like I owed him, I guess. Or that I should be super grateful that he wanted me. He, uh, he had this way of saying things . . ."

"What sort of things?" he demanded.

"I never really had issues about my body. I was pretty used to not wearing much at Saxon's and people only ever stared at me with admiration. But for some reason, I didn't like the idea of being naked at a club with Steven. And it wasn't until later that I worked it out. It was because of him. Those little comments he'd make about what I ate or how I needed to work out. If I just did some squats, my ass would be phenomenal. Or how I needed to swap to skinny lattes rather than full-fat ones, Things like that . . . I started feeling self-conscious. To eat less."

"That fucking bastard."

"Yeah. I know. Anyway, by the time we found a house, I was kind of a mess. I deposited the money in the account he gave me without much thought. And when he asked for money to pay for movers and cleaners and the lawyers' fees, I just . . . I emptied my account and gave it to him. How could I be so stupid?"

His poor girl. She'd already had issues from being abandoned by her mother. Then this asshole preyed on her . . . he made her feel indebted and even grateful to him for wanting her.

Then he took everything from her.

"After that . . . he, uh, he disappeared. He said he had to go away for work and I was to wait for him to get back to help him pack up his stuff. It should have been a sign that he didn't want me to stay with him at his house. But he said it was because it would be nicer for me at a motel."

"He disappeared?"

"Yeah. When I tried to call him, it didn't go through. I thought something had happened to him and was frantic. I started calling hospitals. I called the police. They said he had to be missing twenty-four hours. I didn't know anyone who he worked with. So I decided to drive by his house. I thought perhaps it might have a clue. Imagine my shock when I saw two older people there."

"What?"

"Yeah. Turns out it wasn't Steven's house at all. They'd been on an extended holiday in Florida. I still wasn't getting it. I went to the police station and filed a missing person's report. And they couldn't find the man I described. There was nothing about him. They were giving me these strange looks and asking if there was anything else I wanted to tell them." She ran a shaky hand over her face.

"You didn't tell them about the house?"

"Not then. I didn't want them to think badly of him. I, um, I went back to the motel and I had to pay for another week. That's when my credit card declined. It was a Saturday, so I couldn't contact the bank."

Fuck. That fucker.

"I had some cash on me, so I paid for the next night and I figured I'd talk to my bank on Monday. Imagine my surprise when I went to the bank and found that my credit card was maxed out. I was down to my last forty dollars. I was so confused. I went to the house we'd bought. Surely I owned part of that, right? When I called the real estate agent, she had no idea what I was talking about."

"He took the money from your grandma's house."

"I lost everything. There was nothing left. And I just . . . I got so mad. I figured there would have to be some way for the cops to trace him. Maybe they could use my phone or I don't know. I don't understand techy stuff. I called the police station and told them he was no longer a missing person and that I wanted to report a con man."

"Did they send someone out to you?"

"No. They said to come in. So I grabbed my stuff because I knew I wasn't coming back to this motel. As I was coming out of the bathroom . . . that's . . . that's when he attacked me."

27

"What?" Raid asked.

"I don't know how he knew what I was going to do. . . was he listening to my call? Did he have the room bugged? I honestly thought he'd be long gone." She leaned forward and rested her face in his lap. "I can't talk about it. I can't."

What? What the fuck else happened?

"Baby? Hannah, I'm going to pull you onto my lap now." She didn't protest as he lifted her, holding her tight against him as she shook. "You can tell me all of it, baby. There's nothing that you can't ever tell me."

"I know. It's just so hard." She buried her face in his chest.

"What happened?"

"He . . . he slammed me against the wall, and before I could scream or anything, he had his arm across my throat. I couldn't breathe. I tried to claw at his arm, but he grabbed my hands in a crushing grip."

"Fuck. That motherfucker."

"I didn't even get a chance to ask him anything. To ask him

why. I was just trying to survive. He told me that he knew I was going to go to the cops and that I'd better not. Because if I did, he'd have to hurt me."

What the fuck?

Why the hell had she told him that she was safe? She should have gone to Jake with this straight away.

"I was struggling for air, barely conscious. But I'm sure he said he'd like to have a reason to come back and play with me. Which didn't make a lot of sense to me. He let go of my hands, but I was too weak to fight back as he . . . as he tore off my clothes. He didn't . . . he didn't rape me. But he . . . he touched me. And then he . . . he touched himself. He got off on hurting me."

Raid could barely hold back his furious howl.

That bastard had touched his girl. His baby. That was completely unacceptable.

He was shocked that Steven would've stuck around to ensure that she didn't go to the police. Surely, there was more risk in doing that?

He'd fully intended to kill this motherfucker before.

Now, he wanted to do it slowly and painfully. He wanted to take his time so that this guy experienced every bit of pain and fear that his girl had. Only he wanted that multiplied by a hundred.

"I woke up on the floor of the motel. I was so scared."

He didn't know if he was strong enough for this. But he had to be. If she was strong enough to tell him, he had to be strong enough to hear it. To be here for her.

"I managed to get up and move to the bathroom, where I could already see the bruising around my throat. I was shaking like a leaf and I just wanted to get out of there. My stuff was already packed up, so I threw it in my car and I drove until I was several hours away. By then, I was losing it. I was shaking and crying. I could barely see."

"You didn't go to the cops?"

"No. I didn't even call them. I couldn't risk them figuring out what had happened. I just wanted to get out of there and get to the one place where I felt safe."

"Fuck, baby. What did you do? Did you get another motel?"

"I didn't want to use the rest of my cash on a motel when I needed it for gas and food. Not that I felt like eating. So I . . . I slept in my car."

Slowly, he rocked her back and forth. Shit. He hated that. How unsafe she'd been.

"You should have called your friends, Jake. Any of us would have come for you."

"And then you would have wanted to know who hurt me. I couldn't risk it. Even if I didn't call Jake, someone would have told him. I was safe as long as I didn't tell the police what happened. And to do that, I figured I was better not to tell anyone what happened."

Fuck. Did she really think she was safe from that maniac?

"Baby girl," he said carefully. "You told me you were safe."

"I am. I'm home in Haven. And I haven't told the police. I did what he said."

"I'm glad you feel safe in Haven, but this guy conned you and strangled you until you passed out. Just because you didn't talk to the police doesn't mean you're safe."

All these weeks, and she hadn't told anyone because she thought that would keep her safe?

Fuck. Shit.

What did he do? He didn't want her to be scared, but he needed her to know that she couldn't trust what this asshole said.

"Hannah, you're a threat to him. At any time, he could come here and find you. You need to report him."

"No, that's just it. He can't come back and get me."

"Hannah . . . he can. I don't know why he let you go free. But at any moment, he can come for you. It would be easy for him to find out where you live. To come here and grab you."

Fuck. He'd let her go to work on her own today. And then there was all that time she'd spent here in her apartment alone.

She was a sitting duck!

That was all going to have to change. From now on, he was on her like glue. No one was going to hurt his girl.

"No, he can't. Because he's in jail."

"What?"

"I saw it on the news the other day at the clinic. Right before I . . . before I fainted. That a con man in Alabama had been arrested. The news said that he'd found his target using a dating website. It has to be him!"

Fuck. Could it be him? Or someone else?

"Luckily, his latest target must have been smarter than me. It didn't give the details about how she figured things out, but the guy's name was Michael Atwater."

"Does that mean something to you?" he asked, confused.

"Michael was Steven's middle name. It has to be him. The circumstances were too similar. I tried to see if there was any description of what he looked like. But I couldn't find any more information. I thought about calling the police . . . but I just know that it's him. So, you see, I am safe."

Yeah, he didn't quite share her belief.

"And that was before you fainted?"

"Yeah, I think I stood up too suddenly, all excited, and then the next thing I knew, I woke up on the floor."

He ran his hand up and down her back. His thoughts were a jumbled mess. Perhaps he should be relieved that this guy had likely been arrested. But he needed to make sure it actually was the same person.

And he was rethinking some of his actions with her, cursing himself for doing things like pressing her up against the wall earlier. For being so fucking pushy.

It was a wonder she wanted anything to do with him.

"You still need to report this."

She tensed in his arms. "Why?"

"Because what if this con man that was arrested isn't Steven? We need to find out."

"But he has to be." Her voice broke. "He has to be!"

He tightened his hold on her as she started shaking.

"Baby, hey, baby. Nothing bad is going to happen to you. I'm here. I won't let any harm come to you. Just hold on to me. I'll protect you."

He could hear how she fought to breathe, to calm herself, and he tightened his hold on her.

Shit. What if that was making things worse? What if touching her was making her more upset?

He set her off his lap, then next to him on the sofa.

HANNAH STARED UP AT RAID.

How had she gone from being cuddled on his lap to sitting on the sofa? And why? Oh God, was it because of what she'd just told him? Had he decided he no longer wanted her? Because she'd let herself be fooled by that asshole?

Because she was dirty?

She tugged at her hair. Hard.

"Whoa, don't do that, baby." He gently extracted her hands from her hair and held them in his hands.

Okay. That was nice. Maybe he wasn't disgusted by her.

"Listen to me. I want you safe. And I have to be certain that you are. That means making sure that this guy is behind bars. Part of me will be upset if he is."

"What? Why?"

"Because I wanted to make him hurt for what he did to you."

She stared up into his eyes. With someone else, it might have been an empty threat. But she could see how serious he was.

He really meant it.

"Then I'm glad he is."

"You are?"

"Because I don't want you to get in trouble for me."

She wasn't worth it.

"Baby, you only get into trouble if you get caught. And us Malones never get caught."

"You guys are always in trouble. You always get caught."

"Do we? Not in the things that really matter, I promise you that. And if I need help getting rid of a body, I have some cousins in New Orleans who will be happy to help."

"I don't think I want to meet these cousins."

"You don't. They're such bores. All stiff and formal. Well, sometimes Maxim can be okay. But yeah . . . you're better with the Texan Malones. We know how to have fun."

"Well, I'm certain this guy is Steven. And that he's in jail. So I guess I don't have to worry about how to dig a tunnel through to your jail cell."

His eyes twinkled for a moment. "You'd do that for me?"

Her face dropped, her gaze going to where he held her hands. "Yeah."

"Thanks, darlin'. That means a lot. Now, look at me." His words were bossy, but his tone was soft. Which was kind of surprising. But she raised her eyes to his.

He slowly moved his hand to cup the side of her face. She thought they'd gotten past him having to move slowly. But she guessed he was being careful with her after what she'd just told him.

She was feeling kind of fragile, so maybe she needed that care.

"Darlin', thank you for telling me all of that. I know how hard that was."

That piece inside her that was worried telling him would change his view of her started to ease.

"But I'm going to have to ask you to do something else that's not gonna be easy."

Shoot. She thought she knew where this was going.

"I need you to tell Jake."

"No way. Not happening." It was a reflex. But also, she meant it. She wasn't going to tell Jake. If she did that, then Steven might find her.

But Steven is locked up. He can't get to you.

"Baby, you have to. Or if you won't, I can. But I know that he'll still want to talk to you to get the details."

"You said you wouldn't tell him." A feeling of betrayal filled her.

"I said that I wouldn't tell him if you weren't in danger."

"But I'm not."

"We don't know that for sure. Jake can help us find out. And he can help keep you safe."

She shook her head. "If I . . . if I tell him and it's not Steven, he'll come back! He'll hurt me!"

"Nobody is hurting you," he said fiercely. "No. One. Understand me? I will never allow it."

She breathed in deep, letting it out slowly. "Raid, I'm scared."

"I know, precious girl. I understand that. The con man that was arrested might be Steven, in which case you have nothing to worry about. But if he isn't, I still won't allow him to harm you. I will protect you."

"I can't ask you to do that. Steven might hurt you. I couldn't live with myself if that happened. I'm thinking I shouldn't have told you."

"You definitely should have told me. And I'm so proud of you for being brave."

Whoa. Those words were as heady as hearing she was a good girl. She felt a rush go through her.

He was proud of her.

"No one is going to hurt me or you. Do you trust me to take care of you?"

"Yes." There was nothing else she could say to that. She trusted him or she wouldn't have told him what happened to her. "But–"

"No buts. Let's just stick with yes," he said firmly.

"Jake's going to be upset with me for not telling him."

"Jake is going to be upset that something bad happened to you. That he couldn't protect you. And that you were too scared to go to him and tell him what happened. But even if he is upset with you, he will not show it."

"How do you know?"

"Because I won't allow him to."

"You know that you're not in charge of everyone, right?"

"I'm in charge of you. And no one is allowed to upset you." He winced for some reason. Did he have a headache or something? "I mean, I want to help keep you safe from everything."

"You can't keep me safe from everything," she pointed out.

"I can."

Whoa. He really was crazy.

And she was loving it. Loving him.

No. Nope. Hannah wasn't ready for that.

"The more people that know what's going on, the better we can keep you safe."

"I don't . . . I don't want everyone to know." More panic worked its way into her throat, tightening her airways.

"Whoa, baby. I wasn't talking about telling everyone. But starting with Jake would be a good idea. Then we can find out if this guy who was arrested is the same one."

"And if he isn't?" How could she have been so stupid? She'd been so happy when she'd thought he'd been caught. She'd hoped that it might be a turning point for her. That she might start sleeping at night and stop looking over her shoulder all the time.

All right . . . so things hadn't magically changed. But a weight had lifted off her shoulders.

But now . . . now that weight was coming back. And she wasn't sure she could breathe.

He grasped hold of her chin. His touch was light. But the look in his eyes was intense. "Remember, you use me as an anchor. Hold on to me in the storm. I will always hold you up. I am here for you and I'm going nowhere."

She sucked in a breath, nodding shakily.

"Tell me you believe me."

"I believe you. I was . . . I was scared that you might see me differently."

"I do."

She veered back in shock, losing his touch. What?

"I can see now that you're even stronger and braver than I thought you were."

She shook her head. Was he nuts? Her? Brave? Not even a little bit.

"You are," he insisted. "Hannah, you could have given up, but you didn't. You kept going. You went back to work, found a place to live, and opened yourself up to me."

"I've been hiding, though. I haven't wanted anyone to know

what happened, so I've been pushing them all away. Hiding in plain sight behind baggy clothes and my ice queen persona."

"You didn't want them to know because Steven might find out," he guessed.

"That was part of it. You know, I don't want to talk anymore."

"Hannah." He didn't say anything else. He just waited.

Urgh, she'd always been a sucker for silence. She wanted to fill it.

"Because I was ashamed."

He sucked in a sharp breath. "You know you have nothing to be ashamed of."

"I had misgivings about him. There were huge red flags, and I still let him manipulate me. Let him . . . let him hurt me. Touch me. I was so stupid!"

"No," he said fiercely. "You were manipulated by someone who is obviously a master at it. How many people before you do you think were fooled? He knew how to read you. How to keep you compliant. But that is all on him, not you. Do not call yourself stupid again or you're going to be in trouble. Understand me?"

28

F uck.

What was he doing? He was supposed to be soothing her. Keeping her calm. Treating her gently.

Not bossing her around and telling her that she'd get into trouble. The last thing she needed was him trying to dominate her.

But he'd had enough of her speaking badly about herself though. He was getting to the point of wanting to gag her every time she said something like that.

Maybe you should. You could kiss her.

And force something else on her? No way. He wouldn't do that. From now on . . . kid gloves. He was going to show her that he could be gentle and sweet.

That was the best thing he could do for her.

"You really don't think that it's my fault?"

"Fuck, no, baby. And no one else will either."

"I'm still not ready for people to know," she admitted. "I'll . . . I'll tell Jake, but only if he promises to be careful about how he looks into Steven. And to not tell anyone else in Haven."

"I'm sure he will do that. But baby, you need to know that no one will see you differently. To them, you'll always be Hannah. The person they admire and love."

She sniffled and rubbed at her eyes.

"No crying," he said sternly.

"I'm not."

"Are you sure about that?" He hated the idea of her crying. The thought that she might ever be sad enough to cry made his stomach ache.

His girl should never be that sad. And she wouldn't be if he had his way.

"Yep," she replied.

"Good."

She let out a shuddering sigh. "I feel exhausted, yet like a big weight has been lifted from me."

Yeah, he felt exhausted too. And like a huge weight had been placed on his shoulders. But he welcomed that weight. Relished it. If it meant that she could live freely without fear or worry, he'd take everything she could throw his way.

She yawned, and he stood. "Let's get you to bed, baby. You've had a big day. First day back at work after fainting, then the best first date imaginable, followed by telling me all of that."

"The best first date imaginable?" she asked as he held out his hand.

He'd had to quell his initial thought. Which had been to pick her up in his arms and carry her to bed.

He had to take more care with her.

"Yep. I know you were calling it that in your head."

"It's like you're a mind reader," she said dryly.

"What can I say? It's a gift."

"Yeah? What am I thinking right now?" she asked as she followed him into the bedroom.

"You're thinking, damn, that Raid Malone has one fine ass."

"Wow. You're good."

He sighed. "I know. Now, do you want to get ready for bed? I'll sleep on the couch tonight. It's comfier than the blow-up bed." He'd get rid of the blow-up bed tomorrow.

"You don't need to sleep on the sofa."

Fuck. Did she not want him here? He wanted to give her whatever she needed. But he didn't want to leave her.

He also had to find a way to protect her and be less controlling. The last thing she needed was him trying to take over her life. That asshole had manipulated and undermined her.

Raid didn't want her to ever compare the two of them.

"I want to give you what you need, baby. But I can't leave you alone. Not until I make sure that this bastard isn't going to get to you."

Her eyes grew wide. "Um, Raid. You can't spend all your time with me."

He frowned. "I'll work it out. When you're at work, you should be safe. The rest of the time, I want you with me. The ranch is safe, so you can come there with me."

"I, uh. You can't do that."

"Darlin', I get that it feels like I'm smothering you, but I have to know you're safe."

"No, it's not that. I just . . . it sounds like a lot of hassle."

He cupped her face between his hands. "You are never a hassle. And I want to stay here with you. I couldn't sleep if I left you here alone."

"I want . . . I want you to sleep here, too." She gave him a shy look. "But won't the sofa hurt your back?"

"It will be fine. Go get ready for bed."

Was that a flash of disappointment on her face? He couldn't figure out why, so he shrugged it off and got to work making sure the apartment was secure.

HANNAH CLIMBED into bed and lay staring at the ceiling.

Tonight had been . . . a lot.

She was utterly exhausted, and yet her mind wouldn't quieten.

You should have just asked him.

She'd tried to hint that she wanted him in bed with her . . . but she couldn't bring herself to out and out ask him.

Because what if he rejected her?

Hannah knew herself well enough to know that would devastate her.

So instead of asking for what she really wanted . . . she was in here alone and he was out there.

A tremble rocked her body.

"Raid?" she called out.

"Yeah, darlin'? You okay? You want a glass of water? Painkillers? Milk?"

Lord, he was so nice. And attentive. Protective.

Ask him.

"No, I'm good. Just wanted to say good night."

"You were really brave telling me all that, darlin'. Don't forget that I'm proud of you."

Those words warmed her from the inside out. Then she rolled over, curling up into a ball.

It took a while for sleep to come.

SHE COULDN'T BREATHE.

She clawed at the hands wrapped around her neck, but she was too weak.

This was it. She was going to die . . .

"Tell anyone what happened, and I'll come for you . . . I'd like to play more with this pretty body. I could make you beg so prettily."

"HANNAH! Fuck! You need to breathe! Hannah, wake up!"

Someone shook her, and she opened her eyes. She couldn't breathe. Oh God. Shit. Shit.

She clawed at her neck, ignoring the pain of her fingernails scoring her skin.

"Stop. Shit, Hannah. Stop, you're tearing up your skin." Raid grabbed her hands, drawing them above her head and pressing them there.

He placed a hand on her chest. "Breathe, Hannah."

She shook her head. She couldn't! Already, she could feel herself slipping into unconsciousness.

"Hannah, please, breathe."

Lord, she wished she could. Panic held her in its grip. Why couldn't she breathe?

A change came over his face. It was filled with fierce determination. "Hannah, fucking breathe. Right. The. Fuck. Now."

Shit. There was pure command in his voice, and she managed to take a small breath.

"You can breathe. You can do it. Take another one in. Let it out. That's better. Do it again. Understand me? I am not going to let you pass out."

She needed this. That utter intensity. The confidence. He wasn't going to let her fall.

"Now again. In. Out."

She managed to take a deeper breath.

"That's it. Follow my breaths. In. Hold. Out." He let go of her hands and took one, placing it on his chest. "In. Hold. Out. That's it. That's my good girl." Then he winced. "Fuck, I didn't mean to say that."

He didn't?

Why? Because he didn't think she was a good girl?

More like he doesn't want you to freak out at those words.

Considering that she'd just had a huge freak out, she couldn't blame him for that.

"Let's sit you up." He switched on the bedside lamp by her bed, and she winced at its sharp light. "Sorry, baby. But I want to check the scratches on your neck."

"Shit. I hate when I scratch up my neck," she muttered, not thinking.

Then she realized that he'd frozen, and glanced over at him.

"That's happened before?" he whispered.

"Um, yeah. A few times after it happened."

"Motherfucker." His jaw was tight. Fury radiated from him.

"But not in ages." Ever since she'd learned that he'd been arrested. Or she hoped he had.

She started shaking. Crap. Shit.

"Baby, I'm going to hold you now, okay?"

She nodded, wondering why the heck he was even telling her.

Hold me. Please.

Then she was in his lap with his arms around her. But they weren't tight enough. She needed to feel more secure.

"Tighter," she urged.

"I don't want to hurt you."

"You won't. I know you won't. And I know if I tell you to ease up, you will. Please. Please. Please."

"Shh. You don't have to beg. I'm here." He held her until the shaking stopped. "Will you be all right while I go get the First-Aid kit?"

A whimper escaped her and she held on to him, shaking her head. "No. I don't need the First-Aid kit."

"Yes, you do. But you can come with me." He stood with her cradled against his chest. Whoa.

"So strong."

"Baby, you barely weigh anything at all. Is your kit in the bathroom?"

"Yes." She directed him where to find it, and he grabbed it before setting her on the counter.

She wanted to protest, to grab hold of him, but she was trying to be brave.

Even though she didn't feel brave at all.

He opened the kit. "Shit, darlin'. Where's the rest of it?"

"What?"

"We have a First-Aid kit in nearly every room at the ranch and they're all about twice the size of this one."

"Really?"

"We hurt ourselves a lot."

She bet. She knew how much they came into the clinic with injuries.

He cleaned up the scratches and put disinfectant on them. That was more than she would have done herself.

"You need to pee, darlin'?"

She shook her head, feeling her face grow warm.

"All right, then. Let's get you back to bed." He lifted her down, but her legs started buckling. "Whoa, darlin'."

"Seems I'm falling for you again," she joked.

Well, it was sort of a joke. Since she'd already fallen for him. In fact, she was all the way there.

Raid was it for her. He always had been. Always would be.

He carried her back to the bed and went to lay her down, but Hannah latched onto him without thought, wrapping herself around him.

"Uh, baby?"

"Yes?" she asked.

"You want to let go of me so I can put you back to bed?"

"No."

"No?" he repeated.

"I don't want to sleep alone," she confessed.

He froze and then lifted her so they were face-to-face. "Are you sure?"

"Yes. Please. I can't . . . I can't sleep alone."

"It won't scare you more?"

She gave him a shocked look. "Raid, you only ever make me feel safe."

There was a conflicted look on his face that she didn't really understand. Then he nodded and put her down. This time, she let go.

"Scoot over."

"Oh, but this is my side."

"Not while I'm in the bed. I'm on the side closest to the door."

Wow, that was old-fashioned and over-protective. And she kind of loved it.

So she gave up her side of the bed and lay there as he took care of turning off the light and climbed in. They both lay there.

She was on her back, staring at the ceiling. Why wasn't he touching her?

Maybe because you forced him to sleep in the same bed as you.

Shit. Shit.

A tremble ran through her that she couldn't suppress.

Rats.

She tried to stop them, but she couldn't. Another one ran through her. It was so hard that there was no way he couldn't have felt the bed shake.

"Are you cold, baby?"

"No."

There was a beat of silence.

"Scared? You want me to get out?" He rolled to the side of the bed, but she reached out and grabbed him without thought.

"No! Please!"

"Okay. It's all right. I'm here. How about instead of me trying to guess, you tell me what you need?"

You can do this, Hannah.

"Will you . . . if it's not too much trouble . . . could you, maybe, hold me?"

Far out. That took a bit to get out.

"Course I will, darlin'. Come snuggle into me."

She rolled into him so fast that she hit her nose on his bicep.

"Ouch." What an idiot.

"Are you all right?" he asked.

"Yeah, just clumsy." She thought she'd gotten over being clumsy around him . . . it seemed not.

"Darlin'," he murmured with amusement in his voice.

She sighed, and he moved his arm, wrapping it around her as she rested her face on his chest.

This was safety. This was perfect.

29

"I don't think I can do this." She put her hand on her stomach as it jumbled with nerves.

Raid had just called Jake, who said he'd meet them at his office in forty minutes. Hannah had already called the clinic to let them know she'd be late for work.

"I'll be with you the whole time," he told her. "Unless you'd rather be on your own?"

She shook her head frantically. Why would he even think that? He was still acting kind of odd, but she didn't have the capacity to think about Raid right now.

She was too busy freaking out.

"I want you there. I can't do it without you."

His face softened as he dished up some scrambled eggs onto two plates. Shoot. That looked good, but she felt too ill to eat.

"All right, baby. You just tell me whatever you need."

She didn't know what she needed, though. A cuddle? A shot of brandy? Some Xanax?

Raid's phone beeped, and she jumped.

"Whoa, darlin'. Is this too much for you?" He gave her a worried look.

"No. I can do this . . . we need to know."

"I can talk to Jake without you."

"Won't he want to hear it from me?"

"Eventually, yes. But he could look into this guy without talking to you. I can probably look into it myself."

"No, you shouldn't!"

"My cousin, Regent, will know someone who can do it quietly."

"No, I think we should go to Jake. I should have told him in the first place."

"All right, but if I think you're getting too stressed, I'm pulling the plug on this. Understand?"

She nodded, knowing that was his serious voice.

"Shit," he muttered, glancing down at his phone.

"What is it?" she asked worriedly. She wasn't sure she could handle much more going wrong.

"Mia wants you to come for Sunday lunch."

Why did he make that sound like it was the end of the world?

Oh God, maybe because he doesn't want you there?

"And you don't want me to go?" There was something going on with him. Something she couldn't put her finger on.

His head shot up, and he gave her a fierce look. "Of course I want you to go. Why wouldn't I?"

"I don't know . . . you didn't sound like you wanted to take me."

"It's my family."

"Um, what?"

"They'll all be there. We try to have lunch together every Sunday."

That was so sweet.

She couldn't imagine having such a big family. It had been her and grandma for so long.

"Not all of us can make it all the time, but they'll all be there if they learn you're coming."

"To make sure I'm good enough for you?" Sure, she knew them all. Some better than others. But it was a different thing when she was seeing Raid. Right?

"Fuck, no. If anything, it will be the other way around."

"What?" she asked, confused.

"I don't want them to overwhelm you, baby. They're a lot."

"I've met them all before, you know. And I won't be over-whelmed."

Okay, that might be a lie. There were a lot of them and all of them had big personalities. But it also sounded like fun. A big family lunch together.

He shot her a look.

"I want to go. It will give me something to look forward to."

"I'll take you away on holiday. To the beach. Me, you, the sand and surf. That's something to look forward to. Not lunch with those crazies."

"Aren't you one of the crazies?" she teased.

He snorted. "I guess."

"It will be all right. If you really do want to take me. If you don't feel like we're at that stage and would rather go alone, that's fine too."

He stared at her for so long that she wondered if she had something on her face. She rubbed at her mouth, then her cheeks.

"What are you doing?" he asked.

"Wiping away whatever it is that you're staring at on my face."

"You can't wipe away your beauty."

She paused and gaped at him. Whoa.

Raid Malone. Super smooth talker. Sexy as heck cowboy.

And hers.

For the moment, anyway.

He knows the truth, and hasn't run away.

"And why the fuck wouldn't I want to take you?" he demanded, returning to gruff, blunt Raid. "If I wasn't there with you, I'd be here with you. Or anywhere. With. You."

Holy. Heck.

Even when he sounded kind of irritated, he was still sweet.

"You want to be with me?"

"I want to be with you, darlin'. I don't want to be anywhere else but with you. I'm your guardian. I'm your man. I'm your fucking everything."

Trust him to tell her that he was her everything rather than wait for her to tell him that.

"I'm not going anywhere, Hannah."

"I want to be normal," she blurted out.

He frowned and opened his mouth.

"I want to be able to give you everything that you deserve. Someone who doesn't wake up in the middle of the night, unable to breathe and clawing at her neck. Someone you don't have to protect all the time. Someone who you can touch without worrying that they'll freak out. I want to give you all of that."

"Baby, you already give me everything. Just by trusting me. Wanting me. Everything else can wait."

But she didn't know if she wanted to wait. She wanted him in her bed and not just to stop her from having a nightmare.

She wanted to play with him. To see what he liked. To have him finally take her over his knee and spank her. Perhaps order her to her knees so she could suck him off.

She wanted to tell Raid she loved him and that she wanted to spend her life with him.

However, she didn't know how to say that. Any of it.

And now wasn't exactly the time.

"Okay," she agreed.

"You haven't eaten anything," he pointed to her still full plate.

Shoot.

"I don't think I can," she said. "My stomach is all in knots. I might be sick."

She knew he'd make her, though. Maybe she could convince him that coffee was a good substitute for actual food.

"All right, darlin'," he said, shocking her.

That wasn't like Raid. He was always trying to get her to eat more.

But maybe it was because of what she was about to do.

That had to be it.

An hour later, she finished telling Jake everything and silence fell through the room.

She squeezed Raid's hand as she waited for Jake to speak. He got up, his face calm. But there was something there . . . something that was leaking out into the room.

Something dark.

"Excuse me a moment." He walked out the door, and she turned to look at Raid, who appeared grim.

Then she heard a shout and the sound of a bang. She jumped and got to her feet. But Raid tugged on her hand, not letting her go.

"Raid! That had to be Jake. Do you think he's all right?"

"He's fine."

"I should go find him and check. What if he tripped up over something?"

"He didn't trip. He's just getting rid of some feelings."

"Huh? Feelings?"

"About what you just told him," he explained gently. "Sit down, baby."

She sat, feeling stunned. "But Jake doesn't get upset about things. He's always so calm."

"Hmm. Most of the time, I guess."

"He sees a lot in his job. What I told him . . . that wouldn't upset him."

"Why wouldn't it upset him? It happened to you, Hannah. Someone he's known a long time. Who he admires. Who he was in charge of."

Shit. "This isn't his fault."

"I know, darlin'," he reassured her. "Jake might not feel the same way."

"Jake doesn't feel the same way."

She turned in her chair as Jake strode back in, looking angry. Grim. Instead of going to sit behind the desk, he stood in front of her, leaning back on the edge of his desk.

"You should have told me, Hannah."

"Jake," Raid said warningly, stiffening beside her.

Jake held up his hand. "No. I should have known. What if this asshole had come back? What if he's not finished with you? I know you thought if you told me that he'd hurt you, but Hannah, I would've taken care of you."

There was a note of brokenness in his voice she'd never heard before.

"I'm all right, Jake."

He shook his head. "You're not. You're not you. You've been pushing everyone away, keeping yourself safe behind a wall of ice. I knew something had happened. I should have pressed you."

"Jake, I wouldn't have told you," she said gently. "I couldn't. I didn't feel safe. Not until . . . not until Raid helped me feel secure enough."

Raid squeezed her hand while Jake nodded. "We need to find out if that guy who was arrested is Steven London. I'll need a description of him. I'll start looking into this other guy, get as much information as I can."

"You'll do it quietly?" she asked. "You won't tell anyone?"

"Not my place to tell anyone, sweetheart." Jake turned to Raid. "You'll keep her safe in the meantime?"

"Of course I will." Raid sounded slightly insulted, but Jake didn't appear worried. "I'm going to drop her at work, then pick her up after. And she won't be going anywhere while she's at work. Will you, Hannah?"

Whoa. That tone told her that she'd better do as she was told. Luckily, she agreed, so she nodded.

"Good," Jake replied, his face growing soft. "Hannah, thank you for telling me. We've all been worried about you and we're here for you. No matter what."

That was really sweet, and she had to blink back some tears as she nodded and followed Raid out.

Thank God that part was over. She felt like a weight had lifted from her. Maybe now, things could find some semblance of normal.

Maybe everything would be all right.

30

There was something wrong with Raid.

Ever since she'd told him everything, he'd been slightly off.

What if he doesn't want you anymore?

But he'd told her that he still wanted her. Nor had he walked away. And he was still being affectionate. He still touched her. It was just . . . different.

Softer. More careful. Like she was delicate.

As if she might break.

The thing was, she couldn't blame him. There had been times she felt like she might break.

But he'd started to build her up . . . she felt stronger just from being around him. And in a very short time. Imagine how she'd feel after a month? Six months? A year? And she wanted more. More of those kisses, those touches. Just more.

Maybe she was imagining things, though.

These were crazy times, after all.

They'd been on two dates already and he'd spent the last three nights in her bed. Yep, he'd taken her out on their second date after picking her up from work yesterday. To the movies in Freestown. And for ice cream after.

Then he'd spent last night in her bed again, holding her tight and keeping the nightmares at bay.

No nightmare could penetrate the safety of his arms.

Now it was Saturday morning, and she was still in her pajamas, nursing a cup of coffee.

"Want to go to the diner for breakfast?" he asked.

"Sure. What do you want to do today?" She had the day off work today.

"How do you feel about horseback riding?" he asked.

She stared at him, wide-eyed.

"Or we don't have to if you're not into that."

"Are you kidding me? I would love that!"

"Yeah?" Amusement filled his face.

"Oh my God! Yes! I haven't been riding since I was a kid and I went to Missy Sue's birthday. Missy Sue didn't like me. I'm pretty sure her mom made her invite me, but I didn't care because she had pony rides. Can we go now?"

He started laughing as she jumped to her feet eagerly. He eyed her. "I don't think I've ever seen you this excited about something, darlin'. Not even when I kiss you."

"Oh," she said breathlessly. "That's a different kind of excitement, but definitely exciting."

"Good to know. These horses are going to be a bit bigger than a pony, though."

"I like them big."

Whoa. Had she just said that? And it was kind of cheesy. But he let out another deep laugh, and she grinned with pleasure.

She loved making him laugh.

Suddenly, he stopped and stared at her.

"What? What is it? Have I got stuff on my face this time?"

Reaching over, he tugged her hands away from her face.

"There's nothing on there, baby. It's just . . . you were smiling. Like you were happy."

Oh.

She guessed she hadn't smiled much lately. If at all?

"It's a good thing, darlin'. I like seeing you smile. Knowing that you're happy."

"I like it too. I didn't think I'd ever be happy again. That I'd ever have this." She waved her hand between them.

How long until he wanted more than she was giving him, though?

For once, the thought didn't spread fear through her. In fact, she was thinking that with Raid, she might be too turned on to be scared.

"Have you got some clothes suitable for horse riding?" he asked.

Shit. Did she?

"I think I have some old jeans and a T-shirt."

"All right, you get dressed. We'll go to the diner and then out to the ranch. If you want . . . you could pack a bag? Stay a night at the ranch?"

Whoa.

Did she want that?

It was completely out of her comfort zone. But it made sense when they were having lunch there the next day.

"We can kick Tanner out for the night if it makes you feel better."

"We can't kick Tanner out of his own home," she protested.

"Sure, we can. I'll put a sock on the door. It's the universal sign for fuck off."

"He'll . . . he'll think we're having sex."

Raid just grinned.

He was terrible. She shook her head at him.

"I'd like to stay," she said shyly.

"Good. Go pack, baby. Get dressed."

Hannah managed to find her old jeans. She had just gotten dressed and put her hair up when there was a knock on the door. That was weird. Who'd be here this early on a Saturday morning?

She moved toward the door, but before she could get there, Raid had stepped in front of her.

"Let me answer the door."

He seemed so serious that she nodded.

Turning, he opened the door. "Jake?"

"Hey, sorry for coming so early, but is it okay if we come in?"

We?

She peered around Raid's shoulders to see Jake standing there. Two huge men stood behind him. One had to stand back on the stairs since there wasn't enough room for all of them on the landing.

Both of them had big builds and dark hair and eyes.

They had a familiar feel to them. Like she'd seen them before.

"Who are these guys?" Raid demanded.

Jeez. Didn't he have any manners?

"Morning, Jake," she said as she stepped around Raid. "Come in."

As she went to step forward, Raid put an arm out. "Stay behind me."

"But Raid, it's just Jake."

"With two guys who I don't fucking know. Stay back."

Whoa. Just when she thought she'd seen all sides of Raid Malone, he showed her another one.

And this one was protective and bossy as heck.

And also sexy as hell.

But she couldn't let him see that. He already had an enormous ego. So she frowned up at him. "Jake wouldn't bring anyone here who would hurt me."

"Damn right, I wouldn't," Jake grumbled. "You want to stand down?"

"Not really," Raid snapped. "Not until you explain who the fuck these guys are."

She looked to the ceiling, searching for some patience.

"I'm FBI Agent Eli Jones," the one closest to Jake said. He had shorter hair than the other guy.

"And I'm FBI Agent Kellan Jones."

She'd heard those names before. And with that last name . . .

"You're Duncan's brothers, right?" she asked.

"That's right," Kellan said, watching her carefully. Almost as though he was worried about her. But that was weird when he'd never met her.

"Did you come back for a nice family visit?" she asked, even though she knew they hadn't.

Because if they'd come back to visit Duncan, then they wouldn't be here at the door to her apartment.

"Can we come in?" Jake watched her worriedly. Like he thought she might shatter at any moment.

Why did everyone think that? She was sick of those looks. Like people thought she would shatter.

Maybe it's because you're constantly on the edge of shattering.

Well, she didn't want to be like that anymore.

"Yes," she replied. "Would you like coffee?"

"They don't need coffee," Raid said as the three men stood in her tiny apartment, making it seem even smaller.

"Raid, that's rude. These are Duncan's brothers."

"Pretty sure that's not why they're here, darlin'."

Yeah, she'd already figured that out.

"We should still be polite. It's hospitable to offer coffee."

"If they want coffee, they can go to the diner and get it."

"We're fine, sweetheart," Jake told her. "Maybe you'd like to sit."

Uh-oh.

Things were never good when someone told you to sit before talking to you.

"Only if all of you do."

They all nodded and grabbed chairs from the dining table. Oh, that probably wasn't a good idea. She hoped the chairs didn't collapse under their weight.

She sat on the sofa with Raid, pressing herself close to him as the three men arranged their chairs across from her.

"What about a cookie?" she asked. "Do you want cookies? Or pancakes? We were on our way out for breakfast. Maybe we should all go get breakfast before we have a chat. Raid can't go long without eating. I'm not sure what happens if he does, but I have a feeling it's something Hulk-like."

Raid turned to look down at her. "Hannah, it's going to be okay."

Huh?

"Whatever they have to tell us, it's going to be all right."

Shit.

"I'm not nervous."

She was such a liar.

"Hannah," Jake said, leaning forward and making his chair creak dangerously. "I did some research into Michael Atwater, the conman who was arrested in Alabama."

She nodded. "Did he . . . does he look like the description I gave you of Steven?"

"Yeah, sweetheart. He does. In fact, we're pretty sure that they're the same person."

"We?" Raid said, eyeing Duncan's brothers. "How do you two come into this?"

"While I was doing some research into this guy, I saw that

the FBI was in charge of his case," Jake explained. "And that I knew the names of the two agents in charge."

"Why would the FBI be in charge of his case?" she asked.

"Because you're not his first victim," Eli said in a soft voice. "In fact, we think you're probably victim number nine."

"What?" she asked as she placed her hand over Raid's. He flipped it over, squeezing her hand with his. "There were eight other women he did this to?"

"That we know of. There could be more," Kellan said.

Shit. She felt like she was going to be ill. Why hadn't she reported him? If she had, she might have been able to stop this. To prevent him from doing this to any more women.

"We didn't catch on to him until about victim number six. We've been trying to track him ever since. He's good at hiding himself online, though. In the beginning, he used normal online dating services. Then, at around victim number five, he changed to using sites that focus on BDSM relationships."

"Why?" Raid asked.

"Unknown so far," Eli said grimly. "We actually know really little about this guy. Because none of his victims are able or willing to talk."

What?

"Did he threaten them as well?" Raid asked.

Both of Duncan's brothers stiffened. Then Kellan turned to her. "He threatened you?"

"I . . . yes." She glanced at Jake.

Jake shook his head. "When I saw these guys were heading the investigation, I contacted them to tell them that one of my people might have been a victim. I haven't told them much else. Michael has dark hair and is clean -haven. But that is easily changed. His approximate height and weight are the same, as well as his eye color. Same MO. In Alabama, he met his victim using an online dating service for those involved in the lifestyle."

"My fault," she whispered.

"It's not," Raid told her firmly. "This is all on him."

"But if I'd reported him, it could have stopped him from doing this to someone else."

"Listen to me." Kellan leaned forward. "Yes, you should have reported him. That would have made our job easier."

She sucked in a breath, trying to fight back tears.

Raid jumped to his feet. "What the actual fuck?"

"Kellan, for fuck's sake. There's a time to be blunt and a time to go easy," Eli said.

"You didn't let me finish," Kellan said. "That would have been better. But that doesn't make any of this your fault. This is all on that bastard, Atwater, or whatever the fuck his name is."

"You don't even know who he really is?" Raid asked. "Don't you have him in custody?"

The two of them shared a look.

Oh no, she didn't like that look.

"We do . . . but there's a problem," Kellan said. "Maybe you could tell us everything that happened, don't leave anything out. Then we'll tell you what is happening with our con man."

She sucked in a breath, squeezing Raid's hand. Suddenly, she realized she was probably holding on too tight and tried to release his hand.

But he just held on.

This had been hard enough to tell to Raid and Jake . . . but these two were strangers. And she wasn't even sure she liked them. Eli seemed nice. But Kellan was kind of blunt.

"You're safe with us, Hannah," Kellan said. "I know that I come across as an asshole, but our job is to protect you. All we want are the facts so we can get this guy. Can you tell us that?"

Hannah nodded. She would try. She started with meeting Steven, then went through everything that happened with the money, and how he'd disappeared. But she left out the part about him attacking her.

"This sounds pretty similar to our latest victim," Eli said. "She sold her house to give him the money. But she called the real estate agent about something before she sent through the money and the real estate agent told her that she had no clue what she was talking about."

"And that's how you caught him," she said.

"She told a friend what was going on, and her friend convinced her to go to the police. We were called in and we got her to call him and delay by telling him she was having trouble getting the money transferred. We looked into the bank account he'd given her, and then we set up a meeting between them so we could grab him."

"That's good," she said. "So now he's under arrest."

They stared at each other again. "He's been denied bail based on the fact that he's a flight risk. But the fact is that our case relied heavily on the witness. His victim," Kellan told her.

"Right," Hannah drawled. "What are you saying?"

"Two days ago, our witness recanted her statement," Eli told her. "She said that she made it all up."

"Why . . . why would she do that?" she asked.

"Was she threatened?" Raid asked.

"That's what we think," Eli said. "We're trying to get her to tell us, but she's not speaking. His lawyer is demanding his release. The thing is . . . this guy is a ghost. There's no history for Michael Atwater. And we've run the name you gave us, but there's nothing there either. The bank account he gave our witness was a dead end. Another fake identity. We don't have the money. We have no witnesses. Without that . . ."

"There's no crime," Raid said grimly. "You have to let him go."

"That's why we need you to make an official statement,

Hannah," Kellan told her. "We need you to step forward now and come and do a formal identification."

"See . . . see him again?" Her heart raced. "I don't think I can do that. He's going to be mad."

"What happens when he gets mad, Hannah?" Eli asked. "Is there a reason why you never told Jake what happened? Why you've only come forward now? You said he threatened you?"

She nodded. This part was going to be so much harder to talk about. Raid lifted her, settling her on his lap with his arms around her.

Lending her his strength.

It was exactly what she needed. She snuggled in and told them everything that had happened.

When she was finished, Kellan stood up and walked out of the apartment, closing the door behind him.

She gave Eli a surprised look.

"This case isn't the worst we've ever worked. We've chased a serial killer, kidnappers, among other criminals. But still, this one . . . it feels like he's always been five steps ahead of us. Women would start to lay complaints and then pull back, changing their minds. There would be no one to track, no pattern, no way of knowing where he would strike. And these physical threats seem to be something he does to silence his victims. But the question is . . . how did he get to his latest victim when he's in jail?"

"Did he get someone else to threaten her?" Raid asked.

"That seems the only explanation. But no one has ever mentioned an accomplice."

"I don't know anyone it could be," she said. "I never met his friends or work colleagues. That should have been another red flag. I was so stupid."

"Don't beat yourself up over this," Eli told her as Kellan returned. "This guy is slick. He's smart. He's been hiding his tracks really well. We have been monitoring all the BDSM dating sites we can find, and we still can't seem to pick his signature up. There's no link to the money. And the witnesses all go quiet."

"What about the real estate agents?" Raid asked. "They've seen him, right?"

"There's not much they can testify to, other than showing him around the house," Eli said.

"So all you've really got is . . . me?" she asked faintly.

Eli nodded. "We've tried to get the other women we believe were his victims to talk, but they're even more close mouthed. Maybe you'd consider talking to her?"

"I don't know. I suppose I could." If anyone would understand what she'd been through, it was this other woman.

Was she strong enough for all of this, though?

"We can do an identification with photos," Eli said. "But we will need a formal statement. However, it would be good if you'd be willing to come to Alabama to meet the other victim."

She didn't really want to leave Haven, though.

"Did anyone see the bruises after he attacked you?" Kellan asked.

"No, I don't think so. But I, uh, I took photos," she told him.

"Good," Eli said. "That's something, at least. We'll speak to the real estate agent and get a positive identification from her if she remembers him. See if we can pick up any fingerprints from where he pretended to live, although I don't hold out much hope of that."

She couldn't really breathe. Was she doing this? Going to go up against Steven when he'd warned her what would happen if she went to the police?

"Hannah won't be going to Alabama unless it's totally necessary," Raid said firmly. "We can do a video call with the other victim."

"The FBI will protect her." Kellan frowned.

"Like you protected this other woman?" Raid asked. "Nope. We can protect her better here since you guys fell down on the job."

Both agents frowned while she leaned against Raid. "Raid, I don't think you're supposed to criticize FBI agents."

"Baby, if they think I'm leaving your protection to them, they're fucking nuts."

Even Jake was nodding, which surprised her. She thought he'd agree with Kellan and Eli.

"You think I should stay here, Jake?" she asked.

"I think we can protect you better here if this asshole sends someone to intimidate you."

She shivered, remembering the feel of his hand around her throat. She didn't understand who would be working with him. But someone had to be. However, whoever this person was, he didn't seem as scary to her as Steven was. Maybe that was stupid of her, though.

"We'll protect her identity as much as we possibly can," Eli said.

"Right, but her name will come out eventually," Raid said. "You know it and I know it. Here, I'll be with her all the time. I'll protect her."

The two FBI agents looked at each other. To her surprise, it was Kellan who nodded. "I'd want to do the same if she was mine. We'll sort everything out. This asshole needs to be stopped. This is a good thing you're doing, Hannah. And brave."

"I'm scared." She didn't want them to think she was braver than she was. She was terrified.

"We'll nail this asshole. And put him away for a long time," Eli reassured her. "Your statement will help us keep him locked up. We're still chasing the money and looking into where he was setting up his next victim. It seems that he would start setting up one victim before he'd finished with the one before her."

Asshole.

Thank God she'd gotten tested for STDs after he'd left. Who knew what he could have given her?

Part of her still felt so scared that Steven would find out that she'd talked to the FBI. And find a way to hurt her.

He's locked away. He can't harm you.

However, he somehow got to this other woman. This stranger she was supposed to talk to . . . to convince to open up about what happened to her.

Rats.

"Will you come to the station with us now?" Eli asked her.

She looked at Raid.

"We'll meet you there in an hour," he told them.

Both of the agents stood and left. Eli gave her a wink as he walked past. He was the charmer of the two.

She just wished she could have met them under different circumstances.

One where she wasn't scared out of her mind.

31

Raid waited until Duncan's brothers had left to turn to Jake. "I don't like this."

Jake nodded. "I know, neither do I."

Hannah glanced between them both. "What do you mean? What don't you like?"

"He's got to be working with someone," Raid said. "And he sent them to intimidate his last victim."

And they had no idea who this asshole was. Would Hannah be safe until they found this person?

He'd just have to make sure she was.

"You're going to move out to the ranch with me," Raid stated. "We'll pack your stuff up and go straight there after you make your statement."

"What?" Hannah asked, looking at him in surprise.

"I can protect you better there." He'd need to tell all of his brothers. But no one got onto their ranch without one of them knowing.

Jake frowned. "She might be better in town. There are more people here to keep an eye on her."

"And I've got to work," she stated.

"No more work," Raid decreed. "You're taking a leave of absence."

"I can't do that. I need the money."

"What you need is to be protected," Raid said fiercely. "And that's what is going to happen."

Her mouth dropped open. "Raid, I can't just move out to the ranch."

"You are. End of story." He wasn't going to hear any arguments.

Jake looked between them both. "Hannah, if you want to stay in town, you can move in with me and Molly."

Raid shot him a look. Did he really just say that?

"You can leave now," Raid told Jake.

"Raid," Hannah said. "You're being rude."

"Jake. We'll see you at the station."

Jake narrowed his gaze at him, then moved to Hannah. "Sweetheart, you have choices here. All right? If you don't want to move in with Raid, you can stay with me."

"She'll be with me." Raid wrapped an arm around her and drew her back against his front. No fucking way she was staying with anyone else.

Jake gave him a knowing look, then nodded and left.

"Raid," Hannah said as he took her hand and led her to the bedroom.

"Where are your suitcases?"

"Under the bed. But Raid–"

He kneeled down and drew them out. "Start packing."

"Raid–"

"I'll get your bathroom stuff."

"Raid!" Suddenly, she jumped at him and he let go of the bag he'd been holding to catch her.

"Hannah, what the fuck? You could have hurt yourself."

"Raid, I need you to take a moment and talk to me. Please."

He could feel her shaking in his arms. Fuck. What was he doing? He was so fucking upset with himself and worried about her safety that he was failing to help her work through this.

Picking her up, he carried her to the bed and sat with her on his lap.

"Baby." He pressed his lips to her forehead, then tilted her head back. "You don't need to be scared."

"I know."

"What?"

"I mean, I am scared, but I also feel safe. Steven is behind bars. And while he might have an accomplice who might try to threaten me, I'm not alone this time. I have you."

"That's right. You have me. I'm going to protect you."

She cupped his face with her hand. "I know you will. But I don't think I need to move to the ranch or give up my job."

He narrowed his eyes. "Are you mine?"

She swallowed heavily.

"Hannah? Are you mine?"

"Mostly."

He reared back. "Mostly?"

"Well, we haven't . . . we haven't taken things further."

"Further?" he asked.

"Yeah, further. You know, beyond kissing."

"Because you need time. And that's fine."

"What if I don't need more time? What if . . . what if I want more now?"

Shock filled him. "You want me to make love to you?"

She sucked in a breath. "Yes. I think so."

"I'd rather wait until you were sure."

"But how do I know that? I don't know how I'm supposed to know it unless we try. I can't believe I'm having this conversation." She pressed her hands to her cheeks. "Can we just ignore that?"

"No, baby. I don't think we can." He had a sudden thought. "You know I've only been holding back because I wanted to give you time, right? Not because I don't want you. Because fuck . . . I do."

"Are you sure?" she asked shyly.

Fuck. He hated that she thought he didn't want her. Bending his face to hers, he kissed her. It started off light, but as soon as she opened her mouth, he deepened the kiss.

Deciding to move things a step further, he cupped her breast, lightly twisting her nipple with his finger and thumb.

She moaned, arching up.

Christ. She turned to fire in his arms. And he loved it.

But he still wasn't certain she was ready for this. If she needed release, he could give her that. He'd have to be sure to go slow and not do anything that might trigger her. The last thing she needed was for him to be too rough or dominant with her.

"Please, Raid. Please."

This wasn't the time. It really wasn't. But there was a desperation in her eyes that called to him, telling him that he needed to help her.

"It's okay. You don't need to beg."

"I need to take my mind off everything else. Please."

Christ. He loved hearing her beg. They didn't have time for much, but there was something he could do. He moved his hand under her top and cupped her breast, playing with her nipple as he kissed her again.

She was moving around on his lap, and he removed his hand, drawing back his lips.

Hannah frowned at him.

"Stay still," he ordered.

Her eyes widened. Fuck. Hadn't he just told himself to go slow and gentle? Now he was ordering her to stay still.

But to his surprise, a look of peace entered her face. She wasn't scared or upset. She appeared happy.

"Yes, Sir."

Fuck.

"Raid. Just Raid, baby." He wasn't sure he liked being called Sir. Although his dick definitely disagreed.

She licked her lips. They were wet and pink. And he had to kiss her again. But first . . .

"I'm going to undo your jeans. If there is anything you don't like, you say your safeword. What is it?"

"Peach."

He knew that before playing they should go through her limits. But he wasn't playing with her. This was just a bit of relief.

So he undid her jeans and, with her help, pushed them down her ass. She was wearing a pair of lacy pink panties.

"Fuck. Baby. These are sexy."

"You like them?"

"Uh, yeah."

"Because I've got more like that. In fact . . . I've got some really sexy underwear."

"Why the fuck haven't we talked about your underwear before now?" he growled.

"We were taking things slow."

Fuck slow. He wanted a fucking fashion parade. Then he wanted her tied to his bed while he feasted on her.

Shit . . . pull on the reins, man.

This was Hannah. She was attacked. She was abused by that asshole. Not just physically, but emotionally and mentally for months.

You cannot push her too far, too fast.

But he could do this. He ran his finger over her clit. She arched, her hips going back.

"Be still, Hannah."

He tried to keep his voice soft. But a rough edge entered it. The command was clear, and she stopped moving.

"That's my g–" Fuck. He stopped himself in time.

She grew tense. "You can say it."

"I shouldn't have said that we could take those words back. I didn't know the full truth."

She bit her lip, looking conflicted. "But I like that you were helping me do that. I want . . . I want to be your good girl, Raid."

"Baby, that's the thing. You always have been."

"I love that."

He did too.

"But I'd love it even more if you could call me your good girl. I want to hear it from you. Please. Can we still take those words back?"

Fuck. Didn't she know that he'd do anything for her?

"Of course we can, darlin'. You're my good girl, Hannah. Now, be my good girl and stay nice and still for me." He pressed a finger under her panties, going slow so she could stop him if she needed to.

But all she did was whimper and close her eyes.

Shock filled him as he found her soaking wet. Christ, she really needed this.

"Have I been neglecting you, baby? Hmm?"

"Noooo."

He brushed his finger over her clit, and she let out a low groan.

"You sure you're not lying to me? Because that's going to get you some punishment."

A shudder worked through her. Shit. She liked that idea, didn't she?

"I'd have to put you over my knee and spank you if you were lying to me." He hoped that wasn't too much.

But she let out another cry.

"Of course I might have to do that considering that you've been in need and you haven't bothered to tell me. That was very naughty, wasn't it?"

Another flick of his finger and she came.

Holy. Shit.

He'd barely touched her. But it seemed she'd really been in need. And his words and touch had driven her over the edge. He drew her finger from her pussy and put it in his mouth.

"Delicious."

She was staring up at him with awe on her face. "I . . . that . . . I don't think I've ever come that quick." There was a flush of embarrassment on her face.

"Baby, far as I'm concerned, that was a fucking compliment. And it also told me I need to be paying more attention to all your needs."

She buried her face in his chest. "Is everything going to be all right?"

"Of course it is. I'm going to keep you safe, Hannah."

She nodded.

He drew her head back. "Tell me you know that."

"I know it. But Raid, I can't not work."

"It's not safe, Hannah. You're mine. And you know that means I protect you. And when you're in danger, I expect you to do as I tell you."

Was this too much for her?

"I don't have enough money to pay my bills if I'm not working."

The shame in her voice was his undoing. Why the hell hadn't he realized that was why she was so concerned? He knew what that asshole had done to her.

"You don't need to worry about money, Hannah."

"I've done nothing but worry about money for a while now."

"And that's now over for you. Being mine isn't just about me protecting you or fucking you. I take care of you in all ways. That includes financially."

She shook her head. "I can't let you do that."

Go easy. Explain patiently.

"Are you mine?"

"I feel like we just had this conversation."

"We did, right before I had my finger in your pussy, making you come."

"Raid! Sheesh." She was red, but her eyes also glittered with pleasure.

"Are you mine?"

"I feel like you think that me saying yes to that means that I'll agree with everything you say."

"Now she gets it," he muttered.

"Raid!"

"You're not letting me do anything, baby. This is what is happening. You're mine. I take care of you. Including when it comes to money. Until you can go back to work, I'll cover all your bills."

"You can't do that."

"Course I can. I have plenty of money and barely any expenses. I can easily take care of you."

And he wanted to. He realized it would make him feel good to look after her.

"But that's your money—"

"I'm going to stop you right now," he said firmly. "If this keeps moving forward, and I'm telling you that's what I want, so it will keep moving forward, then everything is ours. Not mine. Not yours. Ours. You understand me?"

·   ·   ·

NOT REALLY.

How had she ever gotten so lucky to catch Raid Malone's attention? She'd known it would be wonderful. But she hadn't realized how much better it would be than she had imagined.

"If things were reversed, you'd give me whatever I needed, right?" he asked her.

"So you're saying if things were reversed, you'd let me pay your bills?"

"Fuck, no. But I want you to think I would, so you stop arguing with me."

Lord help her. How did she get such a bossy man?

Although part of her was a bit relieved. Because he'd been acting a kind of strange the last few days. But this was pure Raid.

"I wasn't arguing," she said. "I don't argue. I'm actually very easygoing and I get along with everyone."

He gave her a look of disbelief.

"I am! In high school, I was given the citizenship award. Because I always get on with everyone and never make waves."

"Yeah? When am I going to get to meet that Hannah?"

"Rude," she muttered.

"You're going to let me do this. And you're going to listen to me when it comes to your protection, got it?"

Since she really didn't want to be attacked again, then yes.

"Yes."

"I'm sorry, baby." He ran his hand over her head.

"Why are you sorry?" She couldn't think of a single reason he should be. If anything, she should apologize for turning his life upside down. Another thought occurred to her. "We can't go to the ranch!"

"Why not?"

"Because of your family! It could put them in danger."

He snorted. "You think my family can't go up against some asshole and annihilate him? Baby, this is what we live for."

There was no denying that, but . . .

"Alec has kids now. West has one on the way." Beau and Maddox didn't live on the ranch, but they were still close by. "I can't put kids in danger."

His face hardened. "They won't be. I'd never put my nephews or my brothers' women in danger."

"But–"

"This guy won't get close to you or them."

"I don't know, Raid."

"I'll call Alec. He can decide, all right?"

"All right," she grudgingly agreed.

"This is my fault."

"What?" she asked, staring up at him. How could any of this be his fault?

"I'm the one who pushed you to tell Jake what happened. If we hadn't gone to him . . ."

"Then they probably would have to let Steven go," she said. "And I'd never have any peace because what's to say he wouldn't come back for me? No. You were right to get me to do this."

He hugged her tight, kissing the top of her head. And she knew it would be all right.

32

Hannah was exhausted.

Completely done in.

By the time she'd finished packing some stuff up, Raid had called Alec, who'd told him to get her ass to the ranch pronto. Apparently, those were his exact words.

Hannah had misgivings still, but she didn't intend to disobey Alec Malone.

They'd spent three hours at the police station, giving her statement and doing a photo identification of Steven.

Or whatever the hell his name was.

Eli and Kellan had seemed happy when they'd left, so she guessed that was good. They also said that they'd arrange a video call with Steven's last victim.

Now they were pulling up outside the main house and Hannah felt so drained that she wasn't sure how she would get through the rest of the day.

"You need to eat. And to have a nap," Raid said to her as he parked his truck around the back of the house.

"Yeah."

"No argument?" he asked with surprise.

"I told you, I never argue. Raid, do you think ... I mean ..."

"What is it, baby?"

"Can we stay at the bunkhouse?"

He gave her a curious look.

"I just want to sleep in your space with you. Not in a guest room. Is that rude?"

She knew Mia and liked her. But still, it felt strange to stay in her house.

"Darlin', I wasn't going to let you stay anywhere that I wasn't. But we can stay in the bunkhouse. I'll text Alec." He got out his phone.

"Oh God, it's rude, isn't it? No, it's so rude. He's opening up his house. I'm just being silly."

"Hannah, look at me."

She glanced over at him.

"I'd rather stay in the bunkhouse. I'd feel more comfortable there."

"Yeah?"

"Yep. That way, I can get you to make more of those sexy noises."

"Raid!" She gaped at him.

"What? I was talking about when I rub your back." He winked at her.

Oh, sure he was.

He sent the text and then drove them closer to the bunkhouse. His phone beeped as he parked.

"Alec said that's fine. The bunkhouse has as much security as the house. He wants to talk to us as soon as you're settled though."

She still felt like she was disrupting everyone's life, which she hated.

Raid came around and opened her door, then he lifted her

down. Opening the back, he drew out two suitcases. She reached in to grab the duffel bag and follow him in. He'd made her pack a lot of stuff. Then again, no one knew how long she'd be staying.

Raid turned to look at her. "Put that down right now."

She gave him a startled look. "What?"

"You don't carry your own bags, remember?"

"But Raid, I'm only carrying it inside. Otherwise, you'll have to make two trips."

He opened his mouth, then grimaced. "Please put it down."

Please? Had he really said please?

"Did you just say please?" Tanner asked.

She glanced up to see Tanner standing on the bunkhouse porch, gaping down at Raid.

"Yes, I did. So what?" he grumbled.

What was wrong with him? She put the bag down, though. He nodded and then walked in. Tanner came down and grabbed the bag she'd dropped.

"What's up with him?" he asked.

"I don't know. Something changed since I . . . well . . ." Since she'd told him what happened.

She thought whatever it was had blown over. Until now.

He said please. And he didn't threaten to punish me or add to my tally.

What is going on?

"Since he learned what happened with your ex?" Tanner asked.

She gave him a shocked look.

"I don't know the details, Hannah. But it's clear to everyone that something bad happened."

"Right," she whispered.

"Everyone cares about you. Come on, let's go in before he gets grouchy, or should I say, grouchier."

She followed Tanner into what was obviously a common area with a long corridor leading off it. It had a sofa, a TV, an old dining table, and a small kitchenette with a large fridge.

It looked comfortable and worn.

"Tanner, I need you to stay at the main house for a while," Raid said, coming out of a room down the long corridor.

"What?" Tanner asked.

"We need privacy, and Hannah will feel more comfortable if you're not here."

"Raid!" she protested. She turned to Tanner. She couldn't believe Raid had just done that. "Tanner, you don't have to move out. I'll go stay at the house. Alone."

"That's not happening," Raid told her.

"That's all right. I'm happy to move," Tanner said, looking amused.

"You really don't have to. Raid is just being, well . . ."

"Rude? Abrupt? Grouchy?" Tanner said.

"He hasn't eaten all day," she blurted out.

Tanner's eyes widened. "Jesus, it's a wonder he's still standing. I haven't seen him go more than three hours at a time without eating before." He peered at his brother closer. "Pretty sure you're fading away."

"Fuck off."

"Raid! What is wrong with you?" she asked, bewildered.

"Tanner. Leave. I need to find something for Hannah to eat and then we're talking to Alec before she naps."

She was blushing by the end of his explanation. Jeez, did he have to tell Tanner that she was going to need a nap?

But Tanner just nodded and went into what she assumed was his room while Raid started moving around the kitchen.

"Raid, you don't need to kick Tanner out," she said.

"Baby, I do not want my brother listening to those sexy noises you make."

Yikes.

She guessed she didn't, either.

He eyed her worriedly, then ran a finger under her eyes. "You're tired. Sit down. I'll make you a sandwich and then you can rest while I talk to Alec."

"I think I need to be there, too." She had the feeling that if she wasn't, they might make decisions on their own that affected her.

She waited for Raid to argue, however he didn't say anything.

Stranger and stranger.

33

Alec Malone was an intimidating man.

Handsome. Intense. Dominant.

The only thing that made him more relatable was the baby mat on the floor with toys strewn around it.

Alec was also a family man who clearly adored his wife and child. He'd come to every check-up that Seb had at the clinic. Always doting on Mia and their son.

Which is how she could sit across from him and tell him what a fool she'd been.

When she'd finished going through it all, Raid took over and explained about this morning.

Alec sat back and looked thoughtful, tapping his fingers on his desk. "The fact that he's in a federal prison makes things more difficult."

What did that mean?

She looked from him to Raid who was sitting beside her. "Makes what more difficult?"

"Getting to him for a chat," Alec explained, his gaze cold.

"You want to talk to him?" she asked.

"Yeah. There are a few things we need to know. Like who he really is and how he got his last victim to recant. Although, hopefully, when you talk to her, she'll tell you so we can help her. I'll make some phone calls, see what I can do. The sooner we find out more information, the better we can protect you."

"This isn't . . . this isn't your problem, though."

Alec raised his eyebrows. "I thought you were with Raid."

"I . . . I am. But still . . . I don't want to cause issues."

"Raid wouldn't bring you here if he wasn't serious about you. You're his. That means you're ours. And I always look after family."

Shoot. She was going to cry.

"Raid, I don't want her alone at any time. Even on the ranch. If you're not with her, she's here at the house. And you make sure either I'm here, or Tanner is."

Raid nodded. "Agreed."

"Are you sure this isn't too much?" She wrung her hands together, and Raid reached over to grab her hands, drawing them apart before he squeezed one.

"Baby, we've talked about this. You're not a burden. Or a hassle. Understand?"

"Raid is right, Hannah," Alec said firmly.

She nodded, feeling shaky and tired.

"Hannah, can you do me a favor? Mia is in the kitchen; can you ask her to make a fresh pot of coffee?" Alec asked.

Hannah nodded. "Sure. I can do that." She'd do anything for these guys. Plus, she really wanted out of there. She jumped to her feet, but Raid tugged on her hand.

She stilled and looked down at him.

"Give me a kiss when you leave the room."

With hot cheeks, she glanced at Alec, but he was doing something on his phone. So she leaned down to kiss Raid.

"So bossy."

"You love it when I'm bossy."

She did. She was used to bossy Raid. Understood him. It was when he was holding back that she got nervous.

Raid told her where to go, and she barely stopped herself from running out of the room.

ALEC WAITED until the door shut behind her before turning to Raid. "I'm going to call Regent and see if he can help get someone to this guy."

Raid nodded. "Yeah, he owes me."

"But federal prison is more difficult and we don't want to do anything to alert him that Hannah is talking to the Feds."

"How are things between the two of you?" Alec asked.

"I'm taking it slow. I mean . . . we haven't been together that long." Christ, had it only been a week since she'd fainted at the clinic?

It felt like much longer.

Alec nodded. "Probably smart. But make sure she knows you're serious."

"She does. She just has moments of doubt. Did you know her mom dumped her with her grandma because her new husband didn't like having a kid around?"

"Fuck. No."

"Hannah is worried that one day I'll get sick of her. She'll soon learn that I'm completely serious."

Alec nodded. "Has she talked to you about ever returning to Saxon's? About her needs as a sub?"

He narrowed his gaze. "A bit. This asshole took her to a club once and humiliated her. Didn't honor her boundaries. He held her down and choked her. She said that once, he left her tied up, and she had no idea when he was coming back. She was there for over an hour."

"Motherfucker."

"Yeah. So she's nervous about playing again. But I think she needs it. She needs to take back that part of herself. Even if she doesn't want to play like she did before, she likes it when I take charge."

"And you're going to give her that?"

"Yeah. I am. I'm going to talk to Saxon about classes." That would make the other man happy. He'd texted Raid several times since he'd seen him the other day, checking on Hannah.

"Good," Alec said. "I'm glad you brought her here. We'll take care of her."

"Damn right. No one fucks with the Malones."

HANNAH WAS MAKING faces at Seb when Raid strolled into the kitchen.

"Time for a nap." He grabbed her hand.

"Hi Raid, nice to see you. How are you doing? Oh, good, me too," Mia said with a grin.

"Sorry." Raid sent Mia a sheepish grin. Walking over to her, he kissed the top of her head. "How are you doing?"

"Good. I baked you some cookies."

"I love you, Mia. Are you sure you don't want to dump the old guy and marry me."

"Raid! What about Hannah?"

"What? We'll be in one of those poly relationships, like Maddox, Beau, and Scarlett. You'd be okay with that, right, Hannah?" He put his hand to the side of his mouth and whispered loudly. "Mia can bake. And cook."

Hannah found herself smiling at their banter. "Sure, I wouldn't mind a sister-wife."

"There. Done. Mia, you're dumping Alec and marrying me."

"You'd think I might have something to say about this?" Mia asked.

"Mia, are you saying you don't want Hannah? That's really rude."

Mia rolled her eyes, but she was grinning. "You're an idiot. Here, take these cookies. And go take Hannah for that nap. She looks exhausted."

Drat. She must look terrible.

Raid took her hand again. "Come on, darlin'."

She waved to Mia and Seb before leading her outside. They walked back to the bunkhouse hand in hand.

"Should I ask how Alec would be able to get someone to talk to Steven?"

He shot her a look. "Probably best you don't."

"That's what I thought." She leaned into him.

"You feeling all right, baby? No dizziness?"

"No, I'm good. Just . . . tired. Or my body is. I don't think my mind will be able to shut off enough to let me nap."

"You need to try." He led her inside and into his bedroom.

Raid had an enormous bed. It took up most of the room. But it looked so inviting.

"Here, baby. Put this on and use the bathroom." He handed her an old T-shirt. She thought about telling him that she had pajamas. But the T-shirt was soft and worn from use. And it was his.

So she moved to his attached bathroom and stripped before putting it on.

When she returned to the bedroom, he had pulled the curtains, and the bed was ready. She climbed in and he tucked the covers around her before kissing her forehead.

"Want me to stay here until you drop off?"

"You're not napping with me?" she asked.

"No. I have some things to do."

Shoot. Well, she couldn't ask him to put off what he had to do. She was already disrupting him enough.

"You go do what you have to. I'll probably be asleep in five minutes."

34

She was not asleep in five minutes.

In fact, half an hour later, she was still tossing and turning. This was pointless. There were other things she could be doing.

Shoot! She had to let Doc know she wouldn't be able to work for a while. Getting up, she looked around for her handbag.

Rats. She must have left it in Raid's truck. She slid her feet into some flip-flops and made her way out into the common area.

Raid must have sensed her because he looked up from his phone and turned as she walked in, giving her a concerned look. "What's wrong, baby? Can't you sleep?"

She shook her head. "No. I don't think I can sleep anymore without you."

Shoot. She hadn't actually meant to say that, to show her vulnerable side. But the look on his face was worth opening up for.

"Come here," he said huskily, holding out a hand.

She moved toward him without thinking, and he gathered her onto his lap.

"Did I interrupt you?" she asked.

"No, precious girl. You could never be an interruption."

She sighed happily, settling into him.

"I'm sorry."

"What for?" she asked in surprise.

"I should have stayed with you. I thought you were so tired that you'd just drop off. You should have called out for me."

"You can't drop everything you have going on for me." She looked up at him.

"Baby, clue in," he said gruffly. "That's exactly what I can do. What I will do."

Darn it.

"Don't make me cry."

"How does that make you cry?" he asked.

"Happy tears."

"No happy tears," he ordered. "No sad tears either."

She rolled her eyes.

"Sassy."

"Is that going on my tally?" she asked.

He rubbed the back of his neck with his hand. "No, I thought we'd forget about the tally."

"Oh." Disappointment filled her. It had been a long time since she'd been spanked. Maybe . . . maybe she missed it.

Was she considering that she might want to play again?

She wasn't sure. But the disappointment she'd just felt when Raid said he wanted to get rid of the tally and how he'd backed off with his bossy protectiveness, made her think that she might miss it.

"I was going to get my phone. I need to call Doc and let him know I won't be coming in to work for a while. Are you sure I won't be all right at the clinic?"

"I'm sure, and I've already called him."

"What? Raid, you shouldn't have done that!"

"Why not?"

She huffed and tried to get off his lap. "Because that's my job and should have done it! Now, let me up."

"Nope."

"Raid!"

"I want you to stay here until you're not mad anymore."

"Well, that could take a while." When she turned to glare at him, he was grinning.

"What?"

"You never argue, huh? You always keep the peace?"

Shoot. She bit her lip.

"Don't do that," he soothed, pulling her lip free. "Do I look like I'm upset about any of that?"

Nope. He looked amused.

"You just bring it out of me," she grumbled. "I'm not like this with anyone else."

"Good. I like that."

Yeah. She did too.

"Why don't we go lie on the bed and watch a movie?" he suggested.

"Have you got popcorn?"

"Pretty sure it's illegal to watch a movie without eating popcorn, so yeah." He stood and set her down.

"Oh, but I do want my phone," she said. "I think it's still in the truck."

"I'll get it. You grab the popcorn and put it in the microwave."

She got to work and then poured the popcorn into a big bowl before grabbing them some sodas.

Raid returned with her handbag, and she searched through for her phone as he carried the stuff into the bedroom.

Her eyes widened as she saw several texts from her friends, Jenna. Heck, even from Aspen and Saxon.

"Yikes."

"What's wrong?" Raid asked, looking up at her as she walked into the bedroom. He was already sitting on the bed with the remote in his hand.

"Everyone is messaging me, wondering what's going on, why I've moved in with you. How do they all know?"

"I told them."

"What?" she asked, sitting down.

"I called Doc and told him. Said he could tell Jenna. Then I figured you'd want your friends to know. So I texted Brye."

"Brye?"

"I didn't have Mel's number."

"Raid! Did you think I might have wanted to tell them myself?"

"You were napping. Or I thought you were."

"But . . . but . . ."

"Baby, it's done now. You don't have to worry about it."

She didn't? "They're all worried about how sudden this is."

"Tell them to mind their own business."

"You know that's not how things work."

He grinned. "Tell them I'm a Malone. When we want something, we go after it and we don't mess around."

She thought about that for a moment, then shrugged. "That actually works for me." She sent a group text.

"Good. Now, come here."

She snuggled in against Raid's chest. The movie was filled with gunfire and car races, mingled with some hot sex scenes. She found herself shifting around restlessly at one point.

When it ended, Raid turned to her. "You feel like going to sleep yet?"

"No."

His eyes twinkled. "Do you feel like having me eat you out to get your mind to slow enough so you can sleep?"

Holy heck.

Did he really just make that offer?

"I . . . that could help."

"Yeah? You think that would help?"

She nodded.

"Are you going to sit on my face?"

Eek. Seriously?

"I can't do that."

He nodded. "We have to work our way up to that. Got it."

No, no, no. There was no working their way up to that. Right?

"I like anal," she blurted out.

Holy. Crap.

Her eyes went wide.

His eyes went wide.

She moved away from him. "I cannot believe I just said that. What is wrong with me? I won't sit on your face so you can eat me out, but hey, feel free to stick your dick in my ass."

More shocked silence.

"Have I killed you?"

All of a sudden, he threw his head back and started laughing. She wasn't sure she liked that. But then she thought about what she'd said.

It was pretty funny.

"I'm such a dork."

"You're a lot of things, baby. You're cute and you're funny, but you're not a dork. Though apparently, you like anal."

Dear Lord.

Kill her now.

"How about we work our way up to that, yeah?"

Well . . . she wasn't sure about that. She felt like she'd been lusting after Raid Malone for a long time. This morning had just been a taste, and while she maybe wasn't ready for the entire she-bang, Hannah thought she wanted some more of what she'd had this morning.

Okay, so maybe they did have to work their way up to anal.

"Come here," he ordered.

She shook her head.

To her surprise, instead of bossing her around again, he slid over to her and pulled her onto his lap.

"Baby, we'll get there. No rush."

She nodded. She guessed not. "Does that mean no eating me out?"

"Oh no, we're doing that. Unless . . . have you got any triggers around that?"

"Oh no, Steven never gave me oral sex. He demanded it all the time. In fact, that's why he punished me once. Because I wouldn't go down on him. But I had a sore throat, because I was getting a cold. He didn't talk to me all day and then sent a message saying he was going to the club without me."

"Fucking bastard."

"Yeah. I really like giving blow jobs, don't get me wrong. It's just I don't want to be ordered to give them when I feel like crap."

"We need to stop talking about Steven now," he said in a low voice.

She stared up at him. "Probably a good idea. We should talk about something nicer."

"Like you sitting back with your legs spread and raised, and me eating you out?"

Yikes.

"Um, I, uh . . . I could give you a blow job!"

She didn't know why she was suddenly so nervous. Wasn't this what she wanted?

"Baby."

"Yeah?"

"Stop thinking so much."

"That's easier said than done. Sometimes I can't shut it off."

"Is that what happened this afternoon when you were meant to be napping?"

"Um, yeah. I can't seem to turn my brain off."

"All right. Well, let's see if I can." And he kissed her.

Holy. Heck.

The man could kiss. Immediately, her mind went to mush. Her body heated. She grabbed hold of him, wanting more. His hand drifted up her thigh, moving slowly. She knew he was giving her a chance to pull back.

To say no.

But that wasn't happening.

By the time he cupped her pussy with his hand, she was squirming, needing more.

Who knew that Raid could be such a tease?

He drew his mouth away from hers.

"Please," she begged.

"What do you want, baby?"

"Please. I need . . . I need . . ."

"What do you need? Be a good girl and tell me."

She tensed slightly, but only for a second. Because at that moment, his finger brushed her clit, and she gasped, her hips thrusting up.

"I need to come!"

"And how do you want to come? With my finger on your clit? Or my tongue?"

Lord. Help. Her.

What had she done to deserve this? Whatever she had . . . she was glad that she did.

35

"Tell me, Hannah," he urged.

"Tongue. Please."

"What a good girl you are to tell me what you want. Now, I want you to get into position. Panties off. Sitting up, lean against the headboard. Legs spread wide and up."

She was grateful that he was taking charge. Slipping off her panties, she got into position. Although she couldn't bring herself to spread her legs.

Maybe she should have showered.

Perhaps there was a reason Steven hadn't wanted to go down on her.

Oh God. What if this was an awful experience for Raid?

"Hannah, breathe. Whoa. Just breathe. Look at me. Everything is all right. Just keep breathing."

"Shit. Rats. Sorry."

"Hey, there's nothing to be sorry about. If you're not ready, that's fine. You only have to say so, baby. I'm not going to force you to do anything you're not ready to do."

"But I am ready!" she cried. "I hate that he's taken this from me. I hate it!"

"Darlin', he hasn't taken anything. It's just hidden for a while. Buried deep. But we're going to uncover it. I promise." He drew her onto his lap.

"I started thinking."

"That was your first mistake."

She snorted. "No, Steven was my first mistake."

He tightened his hold on her. "Baby, that wasn't your fault. He's done this before."

And then he went on to do it to someone else.

"What were you thinking?" he asked.

"What if you don't like it?"

"What?" He moved back slightly so he could stare down at her. "What do you mean, what if I don't like it?"

"What if you don't like doing *that* to me? You might not. I might . . . I might taste terrible."

"Fuck, baby! That's what you were worried about?"

"Um. Yeah."

"Then let me put your mind at ease right now. Remember how I worked your clit with my finger this morning and you fell apart in my arms?"

"Kind of hard to forget."

"Well, did you forget how I brought my finger to my mouth to lick off your arousal?"

Shoot. She had actually forgotten that.

"And it was delicious. *You* are delicious. Now, get back into position. I want another taste."

A shiver ran through her as she moved. This time, she spread her legs as ordered, and the look of satisfaction on his face made her feel amazing.

Gooey and powerful at the same time.

She was letting Steven get to her, and she was sick of having him in her head. Messing with her life.

"Baby, stop thinking."

"Sorry," she whispered. "I was just thinking I'm sick of Steven being in my head."

"Well, another place he doesn't belong is in our bed."

Our bed.

She liked the sound of that.

"I like that."

"Me too, baby. And what I'd like just as much is to eat you out in this bed. To hear you make those sexy cries *in this bed*."

"When you give me a back massage?" she asked.

He shook his head, grinning. "Nope." Then he proceeded to kiss his way up her leg to her pussy. He placed a kiss at the top of her slit, and she moaned.

"You're such a tease," she told him.

"You love it."

"I don't! I think I want a man that gets straight to it."

"You don't want a man who goes straight to it."

Urgh. It was annoying that he could read her mind so easily. She also kind of loved it. What could she say? She was a contradiction.

"Raid. Please."

"I love it when you beg."

He must have really loved it. Because he set about making her beg for the next ten minutes. He played with her. His tongue flicked her clit before sliding lower to play with her entrance.

Staring down at the dark head between her legs, she could hardly believe this was her life. Raid Malone was eating her out. While she sat on his bed. Wearing his T-shirt.

She'd noticed that he hadn't tried to remove it. Did he not want to see what was underneath?

Stop it, Hannah!

Don't ruin this moment.

Raid must have decided he was done teasing, because he moved his tongue back to her clit and flicked it until she screamed as she came. It was the orgasm to end all orgasms.

The one that would never be beaten. She was sure of it.

As she came back down, she was aware of him shifting her. Spooning her from behind as she lay on her side. But she didn't care what he did to her right then.

She was in happy-happy land.

The place where bad things could not penetrate. Not that being held by Raid was ever a bad thing.

"You okay, baby?" He was holding her tight as though he thought she might float away.

"Uh-uh."

"You kind of went somewhere else for a while, didn't you?"

"Happy-happy land," she said in a dreamy voice.

"Yeah? What's that?"

"Best place in the world." She wished she could stay there, but she was feeling the drop already. Her mind was becoming clearer. The endorphins were fading.

She'd never reached happy-happy land except at Saxon's with a few Doms she'd played with. Never once with Steven, that was for sure.

As she came down, she started trembling slightly. Fuck. Sub-drop. It wasn't a huge drop. She'd only really been skating the edge of subspace. But it was enough to make her feel shaky.

"Hannah?"

"I need the bathroom," she said, trying to break free.

"Hannah, stay still."

Panic clawed at her as the feeling of being trapped hit her. *This is Raid. This is Raid.*

"Please loosen your hold."

Something in her voice must have clued him in because his arms loosened immediately as he swore quietly.

Hannah immediately rolled to the side of the bed.

"Hannah, stop."

There was such command in his voice that she froze, sitting at the edge of the bed.

"I don't want to trap you to me and scare you. Although I hope like hell that you realize I would never hurt you."

"I do. I'm sorry." Shoot. Had she hurt him?

"Don't say sorry. Not for anything he's done. I'm moving in behind you. I won't hold you tight, but I need to touch you."

"I need the bathroom."

"No, you don't."

"You know, being bossy isn't a nice trait to have."

"You love it."

Grr. His mind-reading abilities were very annoying.

Then he sat behind her, his legs surrounding hers, his arms lightly around her.

And she remembered that those annoying traits were also the best part of him. Because he seemed to know just what she needed without her asking.

"What's going on? What just happened?"

"Sub-drop."

He tensed. "I sent you into subspace?"

She hunched over, embarrassed. He had no experience of this. What if he thought her weird?

"Stop thinking," he growled at her.

"Do you think I'm weird? It's never happened like that before. Not from just an orgasm. Urgh, I mean, not without being at the club . . . I was just on the edge of subspace so it's not much of a drop. I could deal with it if you let me go."

"Let you go?" he boomed. "Like fuck. Baby, if you think for one minute that you have to deal with anything on your own, you need to think again. But especially when I'm the cause. You need your butt . . . fuck," his voice softened suddenly.

She had no idea what had stopped him from threatening to spank her.

"Fuck, sorry."

She blinked. What was going on with him?

"Um, Raid . . ."

"What do you need from me?" he asked.

"What?"

"I hate that I don't know this shit. I'll have to remedy that quickly."

"You don't have to do that. I'm fine," she said quickly.

"Hannah, you just went into sub-drop and I didn't realize."

"Yes, but it probably won't happen again because I don't intend to play anymore. I'm not a sub."

"Baby, you're still a sub. And that happened without us even trying. Whether or not you enter a club again, it could happen again, right?"

Crap.

"You're mine, Hannah. All of you. Which means I've got to know how to take care of you in all ways. I'll sort this out. It's not something you need to worry about."

But it was something else on his plate when it was overflowing.

"I'm sorry I'm such a hassle." Rats. Now she was feeling the effects of the drop again. She sniffled.

"Don't you dare," he grumbled. "I just ate my woman out for the first time in my bed, so don't you dare cry after."

"Happy tears?"

"Not even happy tears."

"I hate to tell you, but even you can't stop me from crying. When a girl has to cry, a girl has to cry."

"I don't like it," he grumbled.

Exhaustion was hitting her hard. So was guilt. "I ruined it."

"What?"

"What just happened? I should have been flying high. I should be returning the favor. And instead, I ruined it by acting weird. Who goes into subspace from an orgasm? Although it was a great orgasm. I don't think that orgasm can ever be beaten."

"Challenge accepted."

"What? That wasn't a challenge."

"Sure it was." He lifted her around so she was straddling his lap, facing him.

Darn, he was strong.

"You're not weird. I like that you had such a strong reaction. Because that means I'm reaching you."

"Reaching me?"

"I'm getting below the layers, Hannah. I know you put them there to protect yourself. But slowly, we're getting there. We'll get the real Hannah back bit by bit."

"What if she's changed? What if she's not entirely like the old-Hannah?"

"Then I'll like her even more than the old-Hannah."

But could he love her? Yeah, she wasn't going to ask that. Now that she'd stopped freaking, she was feeling guilty for doing all the taking.

"You know . . . I've been selfish . . . I could . . ." she trailed off as she slid to the floor, kneeling in front of him. She reached up to place her hand on his thigh.

His face filled with heat. "As much as I like that idea, darlin', that's not happening right now."

"Why not? Don't you . . . don't you want me to do that?"

Oh God. Now she was humiliated for a different reason. Would it never end?

She stood. But before she could leave, he took hold of her hips and lifted her onto his lap.

"Let me go."

"Nope."

"It's annoying how you keep lifting me around."

"Baby, every time you say annoying, I know you actually mean pleasing."

Pleasing? Who said that? And, no, she did not.

Liar.

"You didn't do this before," she said.

"Because before, you were scared of my touch. You flinched away from me. Now, you like it."

Damn him. He had an answer for everything.

"And whatever reason you're concocting in your head for why I don't want you to go down on me right now, it's bullshit, and you need to stop."

"How do you know?"

"Because I know you. And the reason I don't want you to do that is because *he* expected it. He made you dislike it. All he did was take from you. And now you've got a man who wants to give."

Dear Lord.

"How did I get so lucky?" She cupped the side of his face.

"I ask myself that every day since you let me in."

"I don't think you're him, Raid. I know that sometimes I get caught in my head and I panic. But I know you're not like him. You don't have to do all the giving."

"Tough. I'm going to." He brushed her hair back off her face. "Now, we're going to lie down and have a nap together. That sound good?"

It sounded about perfect.

36

Raid woke up the following morning on his own.

Something he decided he didn't like.

And he was going to let her know that. Getting up, he walked out of the bedroom to the kitchen. There, he found her wearing his T-shirt, standing at the kitchen stove.

She was flipping pancakes and humming to herself.

She looked happy.

Fuck. This image would be burned into his brain for eternity. His woman, standing in his kitchen and wearing his T-shirt with her hair up on her head, humming with happiness.

"Baby, what are you doing?"

She let out a small cry.

Fuck. It worried him that she didn't notice what was going on around her.

"How did you sneak up on me?" she asked, her hand pressed to her chest.

"I wasn't trying to be quiet."

She let out a breath. "I was just in the zone."

"I like that you're in the zone. That you feel safe enough to go into the zone." He moved over to her, wrapping himself around her back. "But I don't like waking up to an empty bed."

"Oh. I wanted to make you breakfast in bed. But now you're not in bed."

Breakfast in bed?

He couldn't remember anyone ever making him breakfast in bed.

"That's sweet of you, darlin'." He turned her, cupping her cheek. "But I'd rather you woke me up first, okay?"

"All right. I just wanted to do something nice for you. You do so much for me."

He kissed her lightly. "I like doing things for you. Some things more than others."

"Like back massages?" she asked, her eyes dancing.

He laughed. "Yeah, darlin'. Like back massages. Now, you going to flip those pancakes before they burn?"

"Eek!"

THE MALONES WERE CRAZY. Loud and boisterous. Smiling and laughing and joking. They spoke over each other. They didn't really have table manners.

And they treated their women like Queens.

"You get used to it after a while."

She glanced to her right, where Clem smiled at her. She didn't know the other woman that well, but what she did know, she liked.

She also knew Clem was almost as crazy as the Malones, so she fit right in.

Also . . . Clem had come to dinner with a lamb. Apparently, it was one of the neighbors lambs who'd been rejected by its mama. So Clem was its new mama.

That's what she'd said, anyway.

See? Crazy.

"You do?"

"Yep. The best idea is to just relax and have fun. Go with it. These Malone men, they all get what they want in the end. Don't fight it."

"Right. Good advice."

"And if you feel like you want to throttle them, just have a Baileys. It always calms me down."

There was a baaing noise, and she glanced over in shock to find the lamb standing at the large window in the dining room.

"Quiet, Lamb Chop," Clem called out. "Mama's eating."

"Lamb Chop?" Hannah asked in a strangled voice.

"That's his name."

"Jesus, he's noisy," Butch said. "Does he ever shut up?"

"When he's eating or when he's close to Clem," Jaret said. "He managed to get into the house yesterday. I woke up to a lamb staring right at me."

"He just likes you." Clem patted Jaret's shoulder.

"He looks at me like he's working out how to murder me and take my place."

"Hmm, I can see that," Clem replied with a nod.

"West, will you put me down!"

"No."

Hannah glanced over at the doorway to find West carrying a hugely pregnant Flick.

Hannah stood. "Oh no, is she all right? What happened? Do I need to call Jenna?"

Was she in labor? Had she fallen and hurt herself? What was going on?

"I'm fine," Flick said with disgruntlement as West set her down on a chair that Maddox had hastily pulled back. He and Beau had sandwiched their boys in between them. They were old enough to sit up in high chairs now. So cute. And the noise and chaos didn't seem to bother them at all.

"West just won't let me walk anywhere. Anywhere! It was bad enough when it was just the stairs. Now, it's everywhere! I'm pregnant, not injured."

"I don't want you to fall," West said gruffly. "You could hurt yourself."

Damn.

"That's so sweet," Hannah said.

Everyone turned to stare at her. Oops. Should she not have said anything?

"Well, heck," Flick said. "I guess it is. I still think you're going to put your back out, though."

Every man in the room frowned at her.

"You're not heavy. Stop talking like that," West told her. "You're carrying our baby."

"Yep, and if it's anything like West, that baby is going to have a bowling ball for a head," Beau said cheerfully.

Flick gaped at him. "Why would you say that? I've got to give birth to this baby!"

West scowled and stepped toward Beau, who jumped up and grabbed one of his baby boys. "Don't kill me! You can't kill me while I'm carrying your nephew."

"Oh my God!"

Hannah turned to see Scarlett standing with a plate of bread rolls, which she set on the table. "Beau Malone! What have I told you about using your sons as a human shield!"

Holy. Heck.

"But West is going to kill me!" Beau yelled.

Scarlett narrowed her gaze. "What did you do?"

"He told me my baby is going to have a bowling ball head. I'm going to have to push out a bowling ball head baby!" Flick cried.

Was this even happening?

She turned with wide eyes to Clem, who was grinning as she sat back in her chair. "See what I mean?" Clem sent her a wink.

Dear Lord.

"Beau, you didn't!" Scarlett breathed out in horror.

"I'm sorry, Flick! I didn't mean it," Beau said, looking repentant as he put his son down. "I was having West on. I didn't mean to upset you. He won't have a bowling ball head. He's going to be all you. Sweet, gorgeous, with a tiny head."

"Are you saying my head is tiny?" Flick asked.

"I'm going to go help with lunch!" Beau ran off.

Lara and Butch followed him. Lara giggling, and Butch shaking his head.

Flick sat back with a satisfied smile. "That was fun."

Wait. Had she done that on purpose?

West shot her a look, but to Hannah's surprise, he didn't scold her. Instead, he sat next to her, wrapping an arm around her shoulders, and talked to her quietly.

Mia, Lara, and Butch entered, setting trays of food down on the table.

"Oh, can I help?" she asked, standing. Shoot. She should have already offered.

"I'm not allowed to help anymore," Clem said. "Last time, I dropped a bowl of potatoes. On my foot. They were really good potatoes too. I miss those potatoes."

Umm.

"Nearly done," Mia told her with a smile.

Raid helped her sit back down and put his hand on her thigh, squeezing. When she looked at him, he winked.

Beau came in with some more food and a contrite look on his face. They all sat, and the men started filling their women's plates.

Wow. That was just another sign of how these men doted on

their women. They made sure the women and children were fed first.

Raid did the same for her as the food came around. When they all settled in to eat, she glanced down at her plate, noticing Raid hadn't put much on it.

That was surprising, since he seemed to be constantly trying to feed her. But she guessed he was learning that she didn't have a huge appetite.

"Mia, this all looks delicious," she told the other woman.

"Then why don't you have more on your plate?" West asked.

Um. Huh.

"Raid, put more food on her plate," West added with a frown.

"Hannah doesn't eat much," Raid explained.

"There're no seconds around here," Lara said with a smile. "You might want to get more in now."

"Oh, this is fine for me. Really, I don't need much."

Everyone stared at her, then their gazes moved to Raid.

"You need more," West said bossily.

"West, leave her alone," Flick said, shifting around in her chair, clearly uncomfortable.

Actually, she didn't look great if Hannah was honest. She was kind of pale and she'd just grimaced.

Could be heartburn.

Could be something else.

Hannah suddenly realized everyone was quiet and staring at her. The women with concern. The men with . . . something else. Something intense.

"You want some more potatoes?" Clem asked. "I can share some of mine."

Hannah glanced down at the mound of potatoes on Clem's plate and her lips twitched. "Thank you, but no. I don't eat much nowadays."

Everyone grew more tense.

"What is it? Is something wrong?" she asked.

"You need to do something about that," Alec said, staring at Raid.

"Everything is fine. Leave it alone. All of you," Raid replied firmly.

"You feeling all right, brother?" Beau asked.

"I was feeling better before you all started interfering," Raid grumbled.

Suddenly, she didn't feel like eating much at all. Not only had Hannah thought it was strange that Raid wasn't reacting to her lack of appetite, she now got the feeling that everyone thought it was odd too.

He was handling her with kid gloves. Why hadn't she realized that before? Oh, he had moments of pure bossiness. But he often seemed to rein himself in.

Was he worried about scaring her?

"Ow!" Flick let out a low groan.

Hannah's gaze went to her, and she stood. "Flick?"

"Flick? What is it? What's wrong?" West jumped to his feet, his chair crashing on the floor. "What is it?"

"It's all right. I'm just . . . I think I'm in labor."

"How long have you had pains for?" Hannah asked, coming around to the other side of the table where Flick was trying to stand while West had a hand on her shoulder, keeping her down.

"Um, about four hours."

"What?" West roared. "Why didn't you tell me?"

"Because I didn't want you to freak out."

"I'm not going to freak out! Why would I freak out? Fuck, we need to go to the hospital. Now. Where're my keys?" West stormed off, and they all stared at the door in shock.

"Yeah, that's what I was trying to avoid," Flick muttered.

"Do you know how far apart the contractions are?" Hannah asked.

Flick grimaced. "Um, they're become about three minutes apart in the last half hour. Before then, much further apart."

"All right, we can probably head to the hospital," Hannah said calmly with a smile. "As soon as someone finds West, that is."

"Let's head out anyway," Alec said, coming over and lifting Flick into his arms.

"I can walk," Flick protested.

"And have West have a shit fit when he comes back?" Raid asked dryly. "I don't think so."

They all walked out to find West in the truck with it running. He stared over at them, then his mouth dropped open and he jumped out of the vehicle. His limp was more pronounced when he ran. He grabbed for Flick. "Give her to me."

"I got her, brother," Alec replied. "Get back in the truck. In the back, though. You're not driving. I am."

West looked set to argue, but Flick let out a low moan.

"I'll come behind you as soon as I can," Mia called out.

"We all will," Butch yelled.

"I want Hannah. Hannah, will you come in the truck?" Flick asked.

Hannah stared at her in shock. But what could she say? "Of course."

Raid turned her to him, cupping the side of her face as Alec got Flick situated in the back with West. "You okay?"

"I'll be fine."

"See you there." He grinned. "Another Malone. Yee-hah!"

HANNAH SAT on the uncomfortable chair in the waiting room of the hospital. "I can't believe that just happened."

Raid placed his arm around her shoulders. "Thanks for taking care of her on the way here, baby."

"Of course. Although I mostly tried to keep West calm. He was . . . um, urgh . . ."

Raid chuckled. "Very unlike West?"

"Something like that."

"Don't worry, I'm not crazy like the rest of them. I won't freak out when you go into labor."

She sucked in a breath. Holy. Heck.

"That's if you want kids? We haven't had that talk yet."

She looked around the waiting room. All the Malones were here. They'd gotten a babysitter for the kids. And now Mia and West were back with Flick while they all waited.

It wasn't really the place for this talk. But . . .

"I want kids."

She did. Desperately.

"A lot of them. I don't want . . . I don't want a child of mine feeling lonely like I did."

"Baby." That was all he said. But that one word said a lot.

"Have you thought about having kids?" she asked.

"You're mine, darlin'. You're going to stay mine. So yeah, the thought of a gorgeous little girl with your eyes and smile has crossed my mind."

Damn. She was so freaking lucky.

"Does that freak you out?" There was a note of concern in his voice.

Those kid gloves again. She needed a way of showing him that she wasn't breakable. So she looked up at him.

"I like it."

He grinned. "Me too."

They all looked up as the door opened and Mia stepped in, looking stunned.

"What is it? Is Flick all right?" Alec asked urgently, striding over to his wife.

"She's fine. They're both fine. That was so quick." Mia seemed to shake herself together. "West is coming soon with the baby."

"Flick's had the baby already?" Maddox demanded.

Mia nodded.

"She's had the baby," Raid whispered.

She stared up at him with a smile. His eyes softened.

Then West walked into the waiting room. If Mia looked stunned . . . West looked like he'd been knocked over by a train, then brought back to life by a miracle.

And that miracle was in his arms. Everyone stood and crowded closer, but not too close.

"I'd like you all to meet Mitchell Alec Malone. Or Mitch."

Mitch Malone.

Perfect.

"I'm WIRED and exhausted at the same time," Hannah complained as they lay in bed that night. She was wearing his T-shirt again and a pair of panties. She was confiscating this T-shirt for herself.

After they'd all left the hospital, they'd stopped at Dirty Delights for drinks and food. She'd been a bit nervous about that. Mixing with lots of people wasn't her favorite thing anymore. But she should have known that it would be different with the Malones. They seemed to sense how she felt, and made sure to keep her surrounded.

Not to mention that Raid never left her side.

She rolled into him, her hand on his bare chest. As usual, he was wearing pajama bottoms to bed, which looked sexy as hell on him. Probably because he had a gorgeous body with a broad chest and thick arms.

Leaning up on one elbow, she bent in to kiss him. He didn't let her take the lead for long. But she didn't mind him taking over.

"I know what could help me sleep," she whispered.

Him. Fucking her.

"Yeah, you ready to sit on my face yet, darlin'?"

"That's not what I meant!"

But also, maybe.

He must have sensed her agreement because he cupped her ass, squeezing it before he rolled her onto her back and slid off her panties. "You're ready to sit on my face. Do you want to keep the T-shirt on?"

"I, um ... do you want me to?"

He froze. "What? Why wouldn't I?"

"You haven't tried to take it off before now," she whispered. "I thought that maybe ..."

The bathroom light he'd left on for her gave off enough light to see his face, and she saw him close his eyes. "Fuck, baby. It's not that I don't want to see you naked."

"It's not?"

"Christ, fuck, no!" He opened his eyes and gave her a firm look. "He tried to make you get naked when you didn't want to. I didn't want you to feel vulnerable."

He was such a good guy.

But also ...

"I'm a bit nervous to show you my body. I'm different than I was before. And maybe not right now, but soon ..."

"Soon works for me, baby."

She let out a deep breath as he lay on his back. "Now come here and sit on my face."

Which is just what she did.

And she discovered that the most amazing orgasm she'd ever had could be beaten.

And beaten spectacularly.

It wasn't until she was on the cusp of sleep that she realized he'd distracted her from her ultimate goal.

Getting him inside her.

Rats.

37

"Damn, West and Flick made one beautiful baby," Clem commented from where she was sitting on the kitchen counter in Mia's kitchen.

Mia was finishing up a batch of brownies, and Hannah was keeping her company since Raid was out working on the ranch. Alec was in his office.

Clem had popped over for a visit and to gush over photos of little Mitch.

"They sure did," Hannah said.

"Wonder who's gonna pop one out next. My bet is Scarlett. I mean, she does have two men. She's twice as likely to get pregnant, right?" Clem said.

"I think they're going to wait a while," Mia said with a grin. "Maybe it will be you."

"Good Lord, no. I have enough trouble keeping the babies I've got under control."

As if he'd heard and understood her, Lamb Chop appeared in the doorway that led to the mudroom and started making noise.

"Jeez, Lamb Chop, don't let Alec catch you in here or you really will be a lamb chop." Clem got down and shooed the lamb outside.

Mia refilled their coffee mugs and sat across from Hannah at the table in the middle of the big kitchen.

"You doing okay?" Mia asked.

"Sure, why wouldn't I be?"

"You've been through a lot, Hannah. And then you moved in with Raid after a few days of being with him. People are concerned."

"It was more than a few days." Well, not exactly. It depended when you started counting. "And I'm good . . . sort of."

Drat. Why did she add that last bit?

"I swear, lambs are demanding." Clem walked in and plopped down in a free chair. "What's wrong? Why do the two of you look like your lamb ran away with Mary?"

Um. What?

"You can tell us anything, Hannah," Mia said softly. "If it's about what happened with your ex or what's going on with Raid. We'll listen and it won't go beyond this room."

"Malone women's creed." Clem nodded. "Even if your last name isn't Malone, if you're seriously involved with one of them, you are a Malone."

"So I'm learning. It's just . . . did Alec tell you? What happened to me?"

"Not the details," Mia told her. "But I guess it was something bad? He said that something to do with your ex has put you in danger."

"That asshole," Clem said. "What'd he do?"

She decided to take the plunge and tell them all of it. When she finished, Mia had tears in her eyes and Clem looked murderous.

"Oh, Hannah, honey. I'm so sorry." Mia reached over and squeezed her hand.

"Someone better kill that bastard before I get to him," Clem added.

"Is there anything we can do?" Mia asked. "Raid is being careful with you, right?"

"Um, yeah. The thing is, that's the problem."

Mia and Clem shared a look.

"He's being a bit too careful. After I told him everything about Steven . . . well, he's been handling me with kid gloves for the most part. Sometimes, he forgets and the real Raid pops through, bossy and protective. But he's being so careful with me."

Mia looked confused. "Isn't that a good thing?"

"You want more," Clem mused with a nod. "Is he getting you all riled up and then not giving you the good stuff?"

"Umm."

"Because if he's anything like Jaret, he knows how to give the good stuff."

Yikes.

"Alec does too." Mia looked dreamy. Then she shook her head. "But it's understandable why Raid is holding back."

"I know. And I think it's sweet. It's not that we haven't done some things. It's just, he thinks he has to do all the giving. And when I try to take things further or give to him, he distracts me with some more of the good stuff."

Clem nodded, looking like she understood. "Got ya."

"I just . . . I've told him I trust him and I do. But there have been times when I've forgotten where I am or who I'm with and reacted badly."

"I'm sure Raid understands," Mia said.

"He does. But I think he believes I'm not strong. That I'm too weak for anything, and I want to show him I'm ready for more.

I'm not sure now. He hasn't even threatened to punish me since I told him everything that happened with Steven."

"Whoa, no spankings?" Clem asked. "That's just crazy talk."

"Do you want that, though?" Mia asked. "It would be understandable if you didn't."

"I just want to feel normal again."

"It's okay to have a new normal," Clem told her.

"I guess so. And I don't think I want to go back to everything that old-Hannah was into. Or at least that will be a longer process. But I don't have any triggers associated with being spanked. I like when he takes charge."

"Raid isn't a Dom, though, right?" Clem asked.

"Not that I know," Mia said. "Although he can be as bossy as the rest of them."

"Okay, so the issue is that Raid is treating you like you're fragile and you want to show him that you won't break if he gets bossy with you or throws you over his knee or fucks you against a wall, right?" Clem asked.

"I guess." Yikes.

"Have you got any rules?" Clem asked.

"Uh, yes."

"Then break one. He'll have to punish you. Seal broken."

"Break a rule? On purpose?" That idea was so foreign to her. She was a good girl.

Whoa. Had she managed to think that without cringing?

"Alec would be so mad if I did that," Mia said.

"Exactly." Clem nodded. "Problem solved."

"I don't think I can do that," Hannah told her.

"Really? Hmm. Let me think of something else . . ." Clem tapped her chin. "I've got nothing."

"What about some sexy lingerie? Candles? It might put him in the mood?" Mia suggested.

Hannah blushed. But the idea had merit. "Maybe that might work."

"Well, remember to report back. We want details," Clem said just as they heard Lamb Chop making noise outside. "Gotta go. A mama's job is never done. Coming Lamb Chop!"

Mia and Hannah looked at each other and giggled.

RAID'S PHONE beeped where it sat on the nightstand and she grabbed it, intending to take it to him in the bathroom.

It was two days after Flick had given birth, and she was due home the day after tomorrow. Hannah couldn't wait for baby cuddles. Also, helping with the baby would give her something to do. She was feeling rather lazy since she wasn't able to work.

She hadn't attempted her plan to get Raid in the 'mood' so to speak. She still wasn't sure how to prove to him that she was strong enough to take everything he had to offer.

Maybe tonight. Although she kind of needed him to go out for a while so she could set everything up.

As she walked to the bathroom, she glanced at his phone. She knew she shouldn't have, but it was accidental.

Sort of.

Saxon's name was there. Along with a message.

SEE you at class tonight. 8 p.m.

WHAT CLASS?

Dummy, there's only one sort of class that Saxon holds.

But why would Raid be going to them? Did he want to enter

the lifestyle? He definitely had some dominant tendencies. Did he . . . did he want to play at the club?

Shit.

Was he doing this for her?

Of course he is.

That was so darn sweet.

He was such a good guy. Why wouldn't he tell her, though?

As she heard the shower turn off, she moved back to the bed, putting the phone down where it had been as she lay back on the bed.

"What do you want for dinner?" she asked as he walked into the bedroom.

In just a pair of boxers. Yum.

"Anything is fine, baby."

They'd started eating here in the bunkhouse. She liked it being just the two of them. Mia had stocked the small kitchen for her since she couldn't go grocery shopping without one of the Malone men with her.

He picked up his phone and frowned. "I've got to go out in about an hour. Can we get something quick?"

"Sure. Where are you going?"

"I just want to meet with a friend."

Hmm. Now he was lying. That should earn him a punishment. Although she could hardly tell him that she'd read his message.

"Um. Okay."

Raid zeroed his gaze in on her. "Are you all right? Would you rather I stayed with you?"

"Oh no. It's fine."

"You sure, darlin'? You've been acting a bit strange these past few days."

Right, because she'd been plotting with the other Malone women to get him to fuck her. And maybe some other things . . .

Actually, that gave her another idea.

"I'll be fine. I'm going to laze in bed and watch a movie."

He frowned. "I want Tanner to come sit with you."

"No! I mean, um . . . I'll go over to the house. I don't want to put anyone out."

He eyed her strangely. Then he sat on the side of the bed. Whoa. How did he not have fat rolls when he sat? It was unnatural.

"Are you worried about tomorrow?"

"Tomorrow?" she echoed.

"Your phone call with Rosa."

Rosa was Steven's other victim who had come forward. The one who had recanted her statement. Somehow, Eli and Kellan had convinced her to talk to Hannah via video chat. They still had no idea how Steven had gotten to her. And they were hoping Hannah could find out.

So, no pressure.

They were also planning on releasing some information to the press soon, and Steven's lawyer was pushing for more information about her.

It wouldn't take long until it all came out.

Eli had called yesterday and told her that their tech guys were close to tracking down where her money had gone. Which would help the case a lot.

And maybe get her some of her money back. Eventually. Perhaps.

What it wouldn't do was let her buy back her grandma's house. She hadn't been to look at it yet. She didn't think she could stand to see someone else living in it.

Their tech guys had also retrieved all the digital conversations between her and Steven through the dating website. Which was kind of embarrassing and made her feel ick if she thought about it for too long.

The people who ran the website were horrified about what happened, and were looking into their vetting system.

"Um, I'm trying not to think about it."

"I can stay if you want."

She shook her head. "No. Honestly, I'm fine. Really."

Raid gave her a skeptical look, but then nodded. "All right, let's eat. Then I'll take you over."

"Are you sure about this, hon?" Mia asked as they walked into the bunkhouse. Tanner was behind them.

"I'm sure." She leaned into Mia. "Just keep Tanner out of the bedroom."

"You bet."

As soon as they got inside the bunkhouse, Hannah let out a fake- yawn. "I'm going to get ready for bed. Mia, you want to come with me?"

"Sure. Girl stuff," Mia said to Tanner.

Tanner eyed them but shrugged and settled on the couch. Soon, he had a game on the TV.

Perfect.

Hannah raced into the bedroom and grabbed the lingerie she'd hidden at the back of the closet. Mia pulled out a long, thin velvet rope she'd somehow stuffed down her shirt.

"Don't ask," Mia told her. "You get ready, and I'll secure this to the headboard."

Hannah nodded. She showered, moisturized, and then slid on one of her sexy pieces of lingerie. She loved this one. It was white and lacy. Revealing even while it covered everything. Sort of. Her boobs practically fell out of the corset top while the bit between her legs had an open crotch.

She put on her robe and walked out. Mia had pulled the covers of the bed down and secured the middle of the rope to the headboard. Then she'd fashioned two cuffs.

"Right, put your hands in the cuffs and then tighten them

with this piece of the rope. You should hopefully be able to do it with your hands in place. Although they won't be that tight."

Nerves jangled in her stomach. "Got it."

"Are you sure about this, Hannah?" Mia asked worriedly.

She hugged Mia tight. "I am. Thanks."

"Don't put the cuffs on until you know Raid is here. I'll call through when he gets here. And I'll keep Tanner out of here."

"You're the best. Thanks, Mia."

She knew that Raid wouldn't be long since he'd texted Tanner just before they'd come out here, letting him know that he was on his way back.

Still, it was the longest five minutes or so of her life until she heard a truck park. Then Mia called out a loud greeting to Raid.

Hannah put her hands in the loops before grabbing the ends, tugging them to tighten them. As soon as she felt the rope tighten, the panic began to hit.

You got this. You've done this heaps of times before.

There was silence as the others left. Then heavy footfalls. The bedside lamp was on, but she still felt that moment of panic. That thought that it was him.

Shit. Shit.

"Hannah! What the fuck!"

38

"U m, surprise." Hannah was aiming for sultry, but she thought it might have come across more like panicky.

"What the hell? Who did this?" Raid demanded.

"What?"

"Did Tanner do this? Why the fuck would he tie you up?" He stormed over to her, taking in her bound hands.

"Raid! Tanner didn't do this. I did this!"

"You?" He reared back.

"Yes! Me!"

"What? Why?"

"B-because you're taking l-lessons with Saxon! And because I want you to know I'm not f-fragile! And I want more than to just take. I want sex. I don't want you to forget the tally! I want the tally. I want the spankings. And the bossiness. You telling me when to sleep, and trying to feed me, and not tip-toeing around. That's not you!"

He just stared at her for a long moment. "You did this to yourself."

"Y-yes."

"For me? To show that you're not fragile. And you don't want me to treat you like you are?"

"I mean . . . sometimes I might be. Like tomorrow, after I speak to Rosa, I might feel like falling apart. Then I might need you to handle me with care. But I don't need you to change who you are. You've . . . there have been several t-times you've held back. Or changed what you were g-going to say. I know it and so do you."

You're all right. Don't panic.

You're fine.

You can do this.

"I know that you don't want to s-scare me. Or to remind me of him. But I know who you are. I trust you. Things are going to come up. Maybe when I don't expect it. But I can't help that. And I've spent so long in stasis. Too scared to move forward. Too busy trying to protect myself. I don't want to do that anymore. We're taking back parts that I lost. Like my body. Like my choice. My choice to give you my body."

He was staring down at her. His eyes moved over her.

"How did you know where I was?"

Crap.

"Um. Why were you having lessons with Saxon?" she asked.

"Hannah," he said warningly.

"I'm sorry! I saw your text from Saxon. Why didn't you tell me what you were doing?"

"You saw my text from him. Hmm. So you were peeking when you shouldn't be. That was naughty."

A shiver ran through her at him calling her naughty. And it chased away some of the nerves. Unfortunately, they started coming back as he moved toward her.

He started stripping.

"I'm sorry," she whispered.

"I think that deserves punishment, don't you? Although I don't think I'll add that to your tally."

"You won't?"

"Nope. I think I'm going to give you that punishment right now."

Uh-oh.

"Why didn't you tell me, though?" she asked. "You lied when I asked where you were going."

"I didn't tell you because I didn't want you to react in a crazy way."

Oh.

"Like, say, doing something like this." By now he was down to his boxers.

And Lord . . . his body . . . it was delicious.

"And I didn't know how I was going to like it," he added. "Whether it would be for me."

"And?"

"Oh, it's for me." He moved to the bottom of the bed and pressed her legs apart. "Which is good, because I'd do anything for you."

"Just don't change. I like you who you are."

I love you how you are.

She was too nervous to say the words.

He licked up her thigh. "Spread your legs."

Pushing her legs apart, she tried to keep her mind in the here and now.

This is Raid.

Raid cares about you.

"Damn. This is convenient, isn't it?" He'd found the slit in her panties and he ran his tongue along her slick lips.

She moaned, trying to move. That's when she was reminded of the bonds on her wrists.

Shoot. She froze.

Relax. This is Raid.

"Hannah?"

"Yes?"

"You okay?" he asked.

"I'm fine."

"What's your safeword?" he asked.

"Peach."

"And where are you at? Green, yellow, or red?"

"Green," she lied.

She was definitely at yellow. On her way to red.

He slid his hand along her side to cup her breast. Oh God, that felt good. Then he drew the cup of her lingerie down so he could suck on her nipple.

Shoot. Even better. A deep groan escaped. It felt like she could feel the tug of his lips on her clit.

"You're so beautiful. Such a good girl. But next time we do this, I want you naked. Easy access."

Next time . . . crap.

Raid. This is Raid.

"Hannah? Where are you at?"

"Green."

"Good. Tell me your triggers," he urged.

"Um. Uh." Crap. She couldn't think. "No name-calling. No blood. No disfigurement. No humiliation. No extreme pain. I don't like canes or whips."

"Good girl."

Nope. Fuck. No. Her breath froze in her lungs.

It's Raid. We're taking those words back.

He brushed his fingers along her chest to her other breast, freeing it. Then he leaned over her, straddling her legs. And his mouth sucked on her other nipple.

Fuck! She couldn't breathe.

"Hannah, where are you?" he asked sharply.

"G-g-green."

"Fuck. No, you're not. Peach." His hands were working at the ties around her wrist before he'd even finished speaking.

What was he doing? Why had he said her safeword?

"Raid? What are you doing?" she asked.

As soon as her hands were freed, she felt better. Like she could breathe easier. Which was stupid.

Raid rubbed at the marks on her wrist. "Being tied up is now a hard limit unless you want to work on it, and then we'll find a way to work up to where you don't keep freezing on me."

"I'm sorry."

"Oh no, you don't need to be sorry about that part." He grasped her chin.

"There's something I have to be sorry about?"

"Yep. And we'll get to your punishment as soon as you stop shaking." Raid sat back against the headboard and drew her onto his lap, holding her firmly.

In his arms, she felt safe.

"Um, I'm sorry about reading your text," she said hastily. She wasn't sure about being punished when he sounded as stern as he did right now.

"Yes, although that's only part of what you have to be sorry about," he informed her.

Only part? Eek.

"What else?"

"When I asked you what color you were, what did you say?"

Oh. Hell.

"Green."

"And what color were you?" he asked in that same dark voice.

Shoot.

"Yellow, bordering on red."

"You do not lie to me. And you especially do not lie when we are playing. Do you understand me? I might be a beginner at this, but I know that consent is key. So is communication. So you do not lie."

Shit. Fuck.

"You're really mad."

He sucked in a breath, let it out slowly. "Do you know why I'm angry?"

"Because I lied."

"And those lies put you in jeopardy. What if I hadn't realized you were lying? What if I'd kept going and pushed you into a panic attack? Do you realize how damaging that could have been for both of us?"

"I'm so sorry, Raid." She stuck her face into his chest, fighting back tears. He hated when she cried. And she'd already caused enough issues tonight.

"I don't like that, darlin'." He ran his hand up and down her back.

Crap. Those tears were coming. "I just wanted to be normal again. To show you that I wasn't weak."

"Fuck, baby. I don't think you're weak. You're the strongest person I know."

She shook her head. "I'm not. I have panic attacks and nightmares. I was a coward who wouldn't tell anyone what happened. All I did was hide from everyone."

"You survived as best you could," he told her fiercely. "You don't think someone else would have just given up? You didn't. Instead, you came back to the place where you knew you were safe. You got a job, a place to live, and you kept going. That is brave. That is beautiful. Understand me?" He cupped her face in his hands.

"I understand." And for the first time, she might almost believe it.

He kissed her hard. "Good. Now, go get ready for bed."

"Wait. Aren't you . . . aren't you going to punish me?"

He shook his head. "I am, but not tonight. I think you've been through enough." He tried to lift her off his lap, but she clung on. "Hannah?"

"I need you to punish me tonight."

"Hannah–"

"I can't wait until tomorrow or whenever. The guilt will eat me up. I know I did the wrong thing. I know I deserve this. Please, Raid."

FUCK.

Could he do this? Well, yeah. She wouldn't be the first woman he'd spanked.

But this was different. This wasn't a fun, sexy spanking.

And this was Hannah.

She was a million times more important than any of those other women. And she'd been through so much trauma. He didn't want to do anything to add to that.

"I don't know, Hannah."

It was her turn to grab his chin, surprising him. "Raid, sometimes you have to trust that I do know what I need. I know I'm not good at taking care of myself–"

"Finally, she admits it," he muttered.

"But I do know I need this. Now. Or it will eat away at me."

He studied her face. She seemed determined. But she was also wrong. She was delicate. And he did have to be mindful of her. However, he didn't want her to stay awake all night thinking about this and worrying.

He put her on her feet. This time, she let him. But there was a look of despondency on her face. Then he turned her to the bathroom and slapped her ass. She jumped.

"Go do anything you need to do to get ready for bed. Then I

want you back here with no panties. You're getting twenty over my knee."

She sucked in a breath and looked over her shoulder at him. The look on her face . . . it was filled with such happiness and love that it shook him.

"Thank you."

Christ. This girl. She constantly surprised him.

39

Hannah stepped out of the bathroom, dressed in just Raid's T-shirt, feeling shy and filled with trepidation. She stilled and took in Raid. He was sitting at the side of the bed, wearing just his boxers. He widened his legs and crooked a finger at her.

"Come here, Hannah."

She walked over to him and he drew her between his legs, his hands on her ass, massaging it. "You good, baby?"

Damn.

Such a good man.

"Yes, Raid."

"Are you going to be my good girl and take your spanking?"

There was no panic.

Just warmth. And a bit of nerves.

"Yes, Raid."

"I love the way you say my name. What's your safeword?" he asked.

"Peach."

He gave her a stern look. "The main reason you earned this

spanking is because you didn't use your safeword when you needed to. Can I trust you to use it if you need to during your spanking?"

Shoot.

She hadn't realized it . . . but what she'd done had affected his trust in her.

"I promise. I won't do that again." He grunted, then lifted her, setting her back away from him.

What was he doing? To her surprise, he stood and, taking her hand, then led her to another bedroom.

"Raid?" He wouldn't make her sleep in here tonight, would he?

"I don't want to give you a punishment spanking in our bedroom. That's a safe space for you."

He was such a good man.

"And this room has a mirror."

She looked at the big mirror affixed to the wall and the chair he'd placed in front of it. The chair was from the dining table in the common area and had no sides. It wasn't facing the mirror but sat side-on.

He sat on it, facing the wall, and patted his lap. "Over you come."

It was then that she understood. If necessary, he could use the mirror to check on her. Moving more slowly, she climbed over his lap with his help. His thighs were hard and warm against her tummy.

She sucked in a breath as he raised the bottom of her T-shirt up over her bottom.

"Easy, darlin'. Look at me in the mirror."

She raised her head and stared at him. He studied her for a long moment, then he nodded. "You'll do."

She would? What did that mean?

Then a spank landed on her ass with a suddenness that

shocked her. And wow. That hurt!

Every other spanking she'd had, there had been a warm-up. Not this spanking. Raid started as he meant to go on.

Hard and fast.

By the time he got to ten, she was breathing heavily, her feet kicking and tears welling. Her ass felt like it was on fire.

"Look at me," he said sternly.

She raised her face up so she could see him in the mirror. There was concern on his face. "Where are you at?"

"Green."

More silence as he studied her. She understood that she'd done this. But then he nodded, and she sagged in relief. She wanted this spanking over and done with.

He continued her spanking. A sob broke free as she tried desperately not to move too much. She deserved this. She'd put his trust in her in jeopardy.

But as much as it was about punishment, it was also cathartic. It felt like it was helping exorcise Steven. His hold on her was definitely cracking.

Raid thought she was strong enough for this. And she wanted to be. By the time he finished, she was sobbing, and he rubbed her back before turning her so she was straddling his lap. Then he stood and held her cradled to his chest as he carried her back to their room.

He lay on his back with her on top of him and continued rubbing her back, crooning to her quietly as she cried. When she was all dried up, Hannah slumped on his chest, exhausted.

"Thank you."

He froze under her. "Why are you thanking me? I just spanked you."

"That's why I said thank you. Because you always give me what I need, Raid. You always look out for me. And every day, you help me be stronger, to want to live, and that there are good men out there. Because you're the very best man I know."

"Baby, fuck."

Hannah leaned up and kissed him. Long, slow, and sweet.

Then she snuggled back down on his chest and drifted off to sleep. It was the best sleep of her life. Held tight in her man's arms.

40

I t was sore to sit.

She shot a look at Raid as she sat in Alec's office chair while he set up the computer for her.

Raid just raised his eyebrows. "Everything all right, darlin'?"

"The seat is a bit hard."

"The chair is fine," Alec said. "I'm guessing you're having trouble sitting because you got your ass spanked last night. And I'm also guessing it has something to do with why my wife smuggled some velvet rope out to the bunkhouse in her bra."

She gaped at Alec. "Is there anything you don't know?"

He grinned at her. "No. And you should remember that."

Oh, she would.

"There, you're all set up. The call should come through in five minutes." Alec squeezed her shoulder lightly. "Good luck, sweetheart."

"Thanks."

Raid came over and crouched next to her. "You want me to stay, darlin'?"

"Actually, I think it will be easier to do this on my own."

"All right. Just remember that I think you're incredibly brave and I'm so proud of you." He kissed the top of her head.

"Thanks." Her stomach settled. It seemed like he knew just what she needed to hear. With a deep breath, she settled in to wait.

RAID WAS LEANING against the wall outside the office when Hannah emerged an hour later. She felt shaky and exhausted.

But she also felt lighter.

Rosa had been wary of her to begin with. But that was to be expected. And Hannah had known what she had to do. She had to open up first. Be honest and vulnerable.

So she'd told Rosa what happened to her with Steven. By the end, the other woman was no long standoffish or cold anymore. She'd been in tears. Then Rosa told Hannah what had happened to her. And it was so similar, it had tears sliding down Hannah's cheeks.

Unfortunately, Rosa didn't have many people around her, supporting her.

Certainly not a whole town like Hannah did.

"Have you been there the whole time?" she asked Raid, pausing in the doorway.

"Yep." He opened his arms. "Come here, baby."

She practically threw herself at him and he lifted her into his arms, holding her tight as he walked out of the house and over to the bunkhouse. She let him carry her without complaint as she wasn't sure she could walk at this stage.

"You're trembling. Fuck. Was it too much?"

"No. No, I just . . . I'm so lucky to have you. I have so many people who care about me. She's got no one, Raid. And she's so scared."

"Baby."

"I told her to come here."

"What?" he asked as he sat on their bed. He kicked off his boots and scooted them both up so he was leaning against the headboard.

"I told her that in Haven we take care of each other. That she might have to follow some rules, but that she'd be safe. I don't know if she will come here, but I hope she does."

"My baby." He kissed her head lightly. "Always looking out for everyone else."

Lately, it didn't feel that way. It felt like everyone had to take care of her. It was nice to do something for someone else for a change.

"She told me what happened to her. And I did the same."

"Was that hard?" he asked.

"It was actually harder to hear about what happened to her. And after all that, after she's brave enough to report him, he sends someone to threaten her."

"Did she tell you who?"

"She didn't see his face. They wore a mask. But she said it felt like it was Steven who was threatening her. Like he was there in the room. He told her that if she didn't recant, he'd come back and make sure that she could never talk again. That every time she peed, she'd hurt. And that she'd never take another man in her pussy again." A wave of anger came over her. "That mother-fucking bastard! I hate him! I hate him so fucking much!"

He didn't try to quiet her as she started to rant.

"How dare he ruin her life? How dare he do that to her? Who does he think he is? And for what . . . money? So not only does he ruin her sense of safety, her self-esteem, her trust in people, but he takes everything she has?"

She heaved for breath.

"He did it to you as well, darlin'," he said gently, running his hand over her hair.

"Yes, but I've got you. And you're making all the bad stuff go away. I know I'm safe with you. I know you'll take care of me when I can't do it myself. You won't let me disappear."

"Christ, baby. No. I won't ever let you disappear."

"That's what I was trying to do. I realized it as I looked at her. I wanted to just fade away. To have no one see me again. But you saw me."

Raid turned her so she straddled his legs and then cupped her face between his hands. She stared up into his gorgeous face.

"I'll always see you, Hannah."

She nodded, sniffling.

"No crying. I don't like it."

She grinned. "I know."

"God, your smile. It's a fucking gift. What can I do to make this better, baby?"

Hannah knew she should tell him that he was making it better just by holding her. But she wanted something more. Needed it.

"I want you to make love to me. Will you do that?" she asked.

She braced herself for him to question whether she was ready. For him to tell her no.

But a slow, sexy smile came over his face. "All right, my precious girl. I think I can do that."

"You think?" she teased to hide her sudden nerves.

"I misspoke. I know." His hand brushed over her hair. "I've been working all morning, though, so I'm tired. That means you're gonna have to do most of the work."

"What?" she asked in a choked voice.

"You up for that?"

Um. Yep. She thought so.

He shifted them around so he was on his back and she was kneeling, straddling his hips.

Good Lord.

This was happening. She had Raid Malone right where she wanted him.

Yum.

Nerves filled her as she stared down at him.

"Darlin', I hate to tell you, but if you want this, then you're gonna have to move."

Right.

Hannah, you big dork. Move.

She started by opening each button on his shirt until she revealed his magnificent chest. Then she explored, using her tongue, her lips, and her fingers. She moved over every inch of his firm chest. Licking his nipples, kissing his neck and collarbone, running her tongue over his abs.

"Fuck, baby. Fuck."

She tugged at his shirt. "Off."

Scooting back, she watched him sit up and remove his shirt before he lay back down. Then her fingers went to his belt buckle. They trembled slightly, but when he didn't move, she felt the courage to undo the belt and take off his pants and boxers.

He helped her so it wasn't long until he was lying naked on the bed.

"Holy heck." Her gaze ate him up.

"Like what you see, darlin'?"

She licked her lips. "Yep."

"You going to touch me, then?"

"Yep." She didn't move, and his lips twitched.

"Sometime this century?"

Hannah glared at him. "Maybe I want to torture you since I'm sitting here with a sore ass."

His eyes darkened. "You deserved that spanking, and you know it. We've also got to work through your tally. I'm thinking five spanks each morning and night for a week ought to do it."

"Raid!"

"What?"

"You can't do that."

"Why not? I think it will have the added bonus of reminding you to behave."

She huffed. "I'm a good girl."

His eyes went so warm and liquid that she thought she might drown in them. Then she realized what she'd said without flinching.

"You sure are. Come kiss me."

Leaning in, she kissed him. Then she moved down his body. All the way down to his cock. Moving to his side, she bent in and wrapped her hand around the base of him while she took the head into her mouth.

He ran his hand over her head. "You don't have to, baby."

"I know. But I want to." And she took him deep into her mouth.

Lord. So. Good.

She loved hearing the noises he made, knowing that it was giving him pleasure. She'd always felt forced to do this with Steven. With Raid, it was completely different.

To her shock, he grabbed her under the arms and she had to let go of him or risk hurting him. He rolled her so she was on her back and he was kneeling next to her.

"What is it? Did I do something wrong?" she asked.

"Fuck no, baby. That was good. So fucking good that I was about to come."

"That was the idea."

"Another time. This time, I want to be in you."

Damn. She wanted that, too.

Leaning in, he kissed her before laying back. "Strip off and come sit on my face."

"I thought I was in charge," she grumbled half-heartedly as she started stripping.

"Now, where would you get a fool idea like that?"

She held her breath as she stood there in front of him, naked.

His gaze darkened as he watched her. "Fucking beautiful. Most gorgeous girl I've ever seen in my life. Come here."

She went to him, straddling his stomach as he drew her in for a kiss. His hand was at the back of her head as he held her there, kissing her, while his other hand ran down her back, squeezing her ass.

"I need to taste you."

She climbed over his face, grabbing hold of the headboard. It was still a slightly disconcerting position to be in, and she worried she'd accidentally smother him. But he was strong enough to shift her if he needed to.

And, oh Lord, the feel of him in this position . . . amazing.

The man had some talent. He clasped hold of her hips with his hands as he ran his tongue along her pussy, burying it deep inside her before flicking her clit.

Then he moved his tongue back to her entrance.

The man had skills. Her breathing grew faster, and she fought the urge to ride his face. His tongue moved to her clit once more, and she moaned with pleasure.

She was so close. So freaking close when he drew her away.

"Raid, no!"

"I want you to come around my dick," he told her.

Evidence of her arousal was coating his lips. Leaning down, she didn't think, she just licked him clean.

"Fuck, baby. If you don't get my dick inside you soon, I'm going to come embarrassingly fast."

She better get to work, then.

"You're still okay with not using protection?"

She loved that he was checking in with her, even though they'd discussed this.

"We're both clean and I'm on the Pill," she told him. "So yes."

She slid down his body and grasped hold of his cock before guiding it into her. There was no trepidation, no hesitation.

Part of it was the fact that he was letting her guide things. Part of it was because she knew this was Raid.

They both let out low groans when he was deep inside her.

"Move, baby."

God. Yes.

That's what she needed to do.

She started sliding up and down his dick. But it was obviously too slow for Raid.

"Faster, baby. Harder."

She moved as fast as she could. "I can't. I need help!"

He grabbed hold of her hips, guiding her movements as she put her hands on his chest.

"Please, Raid. Please."

"Take us there, baby. You feel so fucking good. Such a good fucking girl for me. My girl. Take. Us. There. Come. Now!"

She cried out as she pulsed around him, her orgasm rushing through her. She floated, her heavy breathing almost drowned out by her heavy breathing.

Gathered up in his arms, she was rolled to her side. She buried her face in his chest as she tried to calm her breathing. To find her way back into her body.

"Good, baby?"

"Better than that," she murmured. "So much better."

"Yeah. Let's see if we can beat that."

And then they did. With her on all fours and him behind her. In the shower while getting cleaned up.

Then, later on that night.

It just kept getting better and better.

41

Raid drew his ringing phone out of his pocket and glanced at it.

Eli.

Shit. He needed to take this. He glanced at Tanner, then nodded to where Hannah and her girls were having a girl's night.

Tanner nodded back. His brother would watch her.

Over two weeks had passed since Hannah spoke to Rosa. And since she'd jumped his bones. That's what he liked to tease her had happened, even though he'd jumped hers right back.

Since then, things had been amazing. She'd had a couple of flashbacks that they'd worked through. Things that she hadn't realized would trigger her had reared up, but they dealt with them as they came. And he'd been to a few more classes with Saxon.

The one problem with their bliss was that she still wasn't completely safe. Not with Steven's accomplice still out there.

And his girl was getting impatient. She didn't like staying on the ranch all the time. Which was part of the reason they were here tonight. She needed a change of scene and to see her girls.

He stepped into a quieter part of Dirty Delights and answered the call.

"Jones, what do you have for me?" he asked.

"We got him."

He sucked in a breath. "What? How?"

"We found the accomplice. Steven gave him up as a show of goodwill."

That was good news.

Why didn't that feel like good news?

"He just gave him up? After all this time? Why?" Raid asked.

"Rosa couldn't give us much. She never saw the guy's face. But more women have come forward since the press release. Oh, and it might have something to do with him moving gingerly for the last couple of days. But you wouldn't know anything about that, right?" Eli asked dryly.

He didn't. Mainly because Alec kept him in the dark. Raid didn't like it, but he understood. Eli and Kellan weren't likely to question Alec. And this meant that Raid wasn't lying when he said he didn't know anything.

Not that he really had a problem with lying.

But it made things cleaner.

"Nope. I don't."

"That's what I thought you'd say. Anyway, you can tell Hannah that she's safe now."

"That will make her happy." It also meant that they could start moving on with their lives. He didn't like her living in a bunkhouse. She deserved far better than that.

And he was making moves to give her that. He needed some more time, though.

Hopefully, it was what she wanted.

"Thanks for letting me know."

"Later," Eli said.

He turned and started walking back to the main room, needing to get back to his girl.

"Raid."

He turned toward where someone was calling his name. He saw Saxon walking toward him.

"I didn't think this was your usual place," he commented.

"I had a meeting with Devon. Is Hannah with you?" Saxon asked.

"Yep, she's out in the bar."

"Is she being watched?"

"Of course she is." As if he'd leave her alone. Even without this threat, he wouldn't do that.

"Good. When are you bringing her to the club?"

"I don't think she's ready for that yet."

"Neither of you has to play. But you can come in. See everyone. They're still worried about her."

He nodded. "I'll talk to her."

"I'm going to go say hello."

Raid stepped back into the main room and watched Saxon approach his girl. He didn't touch her, but it was evident he was concerned. And when she smiled that wide smile at him, Saxon's shoulders visibly relaxed.

Everyone might be worried about his girl, but they didn't have to.

Because nothing was allowed to happen to her.

42

Hannah was trembling as she stepped into Saxon's club.

"You're shaking. We're leaving," Raid said abruptly.

Shaking her head, she looked up at him with a smile. "I'm fine. This place . . . it's a good thing coming back here. It was always a safe place for me. I want that back. Although now my safe place is with you."

He drew her close and kissed her.

She was dressed more conservatively than she usually did at the club. She wore a black dress with a sweetheart neckline that was tight over her breasts, then it flowed out. It ended just above her knees, and all she wore underneath was a pair of lacy black panties.

Her hair was back in a sleek ponytail and she had some killer eye make-up on. She still wore her coat. She wouldn't take that off until she felt more comfortable.

As they walked through the bar, a few people waved to them, but she was too nervous to do much more than nod.

The bouncer let them through with a nod. Hannah stood for a moment, looking around and taking everything in. This was so familiar that it almost felt like coming home.

But there was still a jangle of nerves in her stomach. She moved closer to Raid, and he took hold of her hand.

"You okay, darlin'?"

"Yes. No. I'm not sure. You won't leave me, will you?"

"Never. Even if you have to go to the bathroom, I'll be right outside."

"Right. Right."

"We won't do anything that you don't want to. If all you want to do is walk around and watch, that's fine. We're here for you."

"You don't want to be here?"

He turned her, placing his hand under her chin. "I want to be wherever you are, to give you whatever you need. But I'm not being entirely selfless. I also want to see this place in action. However, baby, if you can never do anything while we're at the club, that's fine with me too. Okay?"

"Okay."

"Hannah. Raid."

She turned to see Saxon approach. His gaze was watchful as he studied her.

"Master Saxon," she greeted him.

Raid stiffened slightly, but didn't say anything.

"You've come to play or watch?" Saxon asked.

"Just watch for the moment," Raid said.

"Good. If you need me for anything, send one of the monitors to get me. If it gets too much, Hannah, just say Red or your safeword and we'll get you out of here."

"I have Hannah. I'll look after her," Raid said firmly.

Saxon nodded. "Good. Then I'm guessing you don't need a club collar."

Club collars let people know those submissives were under Saxon's care and protection.

"Um, no. Actually . . ." She reached for the buttons of her coat and Raid helped her draw it off.

Underneath, she wore the most beautiful collar. Raid had given it to her before they'd come tonight. It was rose gold with soft leather at the back and a chain at the front that had a delicate, hollow heart dangling from it. The outside of the heart had little diamonds embedded in it.

Saxon drew in a breath, then looked at Raid. "You collared her?"

"Yep."

"You haven't even played together yet."

"So? I want everyone to know she's mine. And this collar shows she's under my protection here, right?"

"Right." Saxon nodded. "And you're happy, Hannah?"

"Happier than I can ever remember being."

Raid sucked in a breath. But it was the truth. She was so happy. It had been a week since Eli called to tell them that Steven's accomplice had been caught. The relief she'd felt had almost made her dizzy.

For some reason, Raid was still feeling a bit protective and didn't want her off the ranch alone yet.

But she was going to work on that. She needed to get back to work.

And back to your apartment?

Okay, that part she didn't want to think about too much. She didn't want to go back to the loneliness of her apartment. Even if she felt a bit stuck on the ranch, she liked being surrounded by all the Malones.

But she especially liked being with Raid.

Worry about that later.

One thing at a time. Right now, she had to concentrate on

being here in the club again. She was here with Raid. She was wearing his collar. That had to mean something.

Right?

"Allow me." Saxon took her coat. "I'll check it for you. I'm glad you're back, Hannah. We missed you."

Wow. That was . . . wow.

"Hannah? You okay?"

"Um, yeah. I just didn't expect him to say that," she told him.

"He cares about you. He was worried."

"Seems there was a lot of that going around." She chewed on her lower lip.

Raid freed her lip and tugged her close. "You had to do what you had to do to take care of yourself. But now you have me to take care of you. So you can get pieces of you back. Don't feel bad about any of that."

Lord.

So sweet.

~

RAID KNEW SHE WAS NERVOUS.

She was also turned on.

They were standing by a station. A man was secured in a cage. He was on all fours and another man was standing outside the cage, feeding a large anal plug into his ass.

The sub had a chastity cage around his cock and balls.

Ouch.

Raid could only imagine his discomfort as the Dom pressed the plug deep inside him.

"You like this, baby?" he asked, pulling her in front of him.

They had spent the last two hours walking around the playroom. Plenty of people had stopped to talk to them. Partly curious, but mostly wanting to check on Hannah.

Now, they were on their own and he wanted to see where her head was at.

"I used to love being in the cage. Feeling on display and kind of helpless." She paused for a moment. "I'm not sure I could do that again."

"Maybe you'd like to try something else." He brushed a finger over her nipple and found it was hard. He pressed his mouth to her bare neck. "Is there something you want to do?"

"I don't want to be bound or blindfolded or gagged."

They'd discussed all of this, so he already knew it. "I know, precious girl. But you don't have to be bound to have fun."

He ran his hand down her stomach and drew up her dress, cupping her mound.

"Are you wet?"

"Raid! You can't ask me that!"

Smack!

He slapped a hand down on the side of her thigh.

"I can, and I expect you to answer me."

She whimpered. "Yes."

"I think you need a good girl spanking."

Another noise of need.

"Don't you?"

"No."

"Are you lying to me, naughty girl? Oh, unless you don't want a good girl spanking. You want a bad girl one?"

She tensed. She knew that a bad girl spanking meant she wouldn't get to come. They'd done some soft play after the last couple of weeks. And both of them enjoyed it. She liked letting go, giving control to him.

And he fucking got off on being in charge.

She'd already had both good girl and bad girl spankings, and he knew which she preferred.

"I'm a good girl. I want the good girl one."

"Do you want it here or at home?" he asked.

She glanced around. "I want to try having it here . . . but if I can't . . . if I say my safeword, then . . ."

"Then I'll be proud of you for doing what you need to do, baby."

He spotted an open spanking bench and led her over. The monitor, who was watching another scene, glanced over at them.

"Hannah, you good?" the person asked.

"I'm good, thanks, Master Jed," Hannah replied.

Raid stiffened.

She glanced up at him. "You don't like me calling other men, Master, do you?"

"No. I don't."

"It doesn't mean anything. I mean, it's respectful, but it's not because I think of them as my Master."

He let out a deep breath at her nervousness. He had to let this go.

"I guess it's just like you hearing me call other women, darlin'."

"Oh. But you don't want me to call you Master, do you?"

"Nah. I'm not into that. I like to hear my name on your lips. It's all right, darlin'. I'll get used to it."

"We don't have to keep coming here. It's nice to come visit. But I like it being just the two of us more."

He drew her to him and kissed her. "I like that too. You want to go home?"

"No. Not this time. We're here and I feel like I need to do this."

"My brave girl. All right. Take your panties off and get over the spanking bench."

Once she was straddling the spanking bench with her knees and elbows bent so she could rest her forearms and shins on the wooden slats, he moved in behind her.

They hadn't brought any toys with them, which was unfortunate.

Then Saxon appeared out of nowhere with a black bag. "I got this for you. A gift for taking care of Hannah. All new. All yours and hers."

Raid just nodded, unzipping the bag.

"What is it?" Hannah asked, turning so she could see.

"Did I say you could move, darlin'?" he asked in a low voice.

"No." Her eyes grew wide. But there was no fear in them.

"Then move back around before you get a naughty girl spanking."

She squeaked, then moved.

He grinned. Oh yeah, this was definitely fun.

He drew out a wand vibrator. Perfect. And it was all charged up and everything.

Saxon was actually an okay guy.

Next, he drew out a plug and some lube. They'd been experimenting with anal play and his girl went off when he touched her ass.

So this should be fun.

Moving to her, he drew her hips back so her pussy and ass hung off the end of the spanking bench.

He put the wand, plug and lube down on a small table before he drew her dress up her back, revealing her naked ass and pussy.

He ran his hand over her ass. Then he gave it a sharp spank.

He counted up to five before pausing to rub the heat in. He moved his hand to her pussy, running his finger along her slit. Yep, she was soaked.

Five more spanks. More rubbing. Then he played with her clit before pushing his fingers into her pussy.

God.

"How are you doing, darlin'?"

"Green, Raid."

"Good girl. You're being such a good girl for me." He waited for her reaction. But if anything, those words seemed to turn her on more.

Perfect.

He grabbed the wand and turned it on. Then he slid it into the slot to hold it in place before situating her so the wand was vibrating against her clit.

"Ohhhh."

"That's it, baby. Let me hear all those delicious noises." He smacked his hand on her ass two more times.

Then he massaged her bottom lightly.

He carried this on for several more spanks until her cries grew stronger. Then he quickly turned off the wand and grabbed the plug, covering it with lube.

He also coated two of his fingers before parting her bottom cheeks.

"Where are you, baby?"

"Green, Raid."

Good. There was no stress in her voice. He slid a finger over her back hole and she shivered in pleasure.

Then he pressed his finger inside her. A low moan of pleasure escaped from her as he pushed it in and out of her ass.

Then he added a second finger.

"Oh. Ohhh. Please," she begged.

"Good girl. That's it. Let me hear all those noises." He pumped his fingers into her while he used his other hand to play with her clit. When he thought she was ready, he drew them back and grabbed the plug.

"Get ready, darlin'. Breathe in. Now out. Perfect." He slid the plug inside her.

"Please, please, Raid."

"What do you need, precious girl?" he asked

"I need you. Please."

"Do you want me to fuck you? Here?" He was down for that if she was.

"Yes. Oh yes, please!"

Christ. He undid his pants, pulling them and his boxers down enough to free his dick. And then he was sliding inside her.

God. Had anything ever felt as right as her?

He didn't think so. Raid pulled out and thrust forward, taking them both higher and higher. He didn't care that people might be watching. All he cared about was her.

"Where are you at, darlin'?"

"Green. Raid, please!"

"Hush, I'm going to give you what you need. Baby, I want you to come with me." His finger went to her clit. "Come with me now."

He heard her cry out before he felt her pulsing around his dick. And it soon had him flying over the edge as he slumped over her.

Fuck. Him.

Magical.

"So perfect for me," he murmured to her as he slid out and did up his pants. Then he drew the plug from her bottom. Someone appeared with a washcloth. He didn't even see who to thank them. He was too busy cleaning up his girl, then wiping his hands before he picked her up in his arms.

She stared up at him with a soft smile, her eyes dazed. Looking so damn beautiful.

And his. All his.

43

Hannah was still riding those happy endorphins as they stepped out of the club and walked toward Raid's truck.

Wow. That had gone so much better than she'd expected. She wasn't even sure why she'd been so worried.

Raid made everything better. And he was always there for her.

No matter what.

Suddenly, he came to a stop and then shoved her behind him.

"Raid? What are you doing?"

"Uh-uh, don't try to protect her now. All that's going to get you is dead." A crazy laugh filled the night.

What. The. Hell.

Dead? What was happening?

"Hannah, Hannah, Hannah, I just knew it would be you to talk to the cops. You were just too dumb to heed a warning, weren't you? And now you and your cowboy boyfriend are gonna have to pay."

Wait. Shit. Hannah sucked in a breath. That voice. She knew that voice.

It was him.

Steven.

But it couldn't be. He was in prison. She stepped around to Raid's side. "Steven?"

"Stay back, Hannah," Raid ordered, pushing her behind him again.

She peered around him, studying Steven under the security lights in the parking lot.

Oh God! He had a gun! Why did he have a gun? Nausea bubbled in her stomach as she realized that the gun was aimed right at Raid.

"Raid," she said with a whimper.

Her entire body started to shake. She wasn't made for this sort of excitement.

"It's going to be okay, baby."

"Oh, it's really not," Steven said with another creepy laugh.

"Steven, what are you doing? How did you get out of jail?" she asked.

"Fuck. Clue in, Hannah. You are such a moron. A sweet piece, I'll admit. I wished he'd given me more of a go with you, but he's always so cautious. Unless he needs me, of course."

She stared at the man standing a few feet in front of them, holding a gun that was pointed at Raid.

This couldn't be happening.

It was Steven. And yet . . . what was he talking about?

"Who are you?" Raid asked.

What did he mean? This was Steven.

Not-Steven grinned. "I'm Ellis. Ellis Watson."

Wait. Who? How did he look just like Steven? Shit. She really didn't think it was a good thing that he was telling them his name.

Clue in, Hannah! He has a gun! He likely intends to use it.

"I don't understand," she said. "You look just like Steven."

She was so confused.

And scared.

This asshole had a gun on Raid. He could shoot him. She had to protect him, but how?

Ellis rolled his eyes. "You really aren't that smart, are you?"

Wow. What a jerk.

"Identical twins?" Raid guessed.

What? Holy hell. How had she not guessed that?

"Your guy is smarter than you," Ellis said. "Although not so smart that he didn't realize you were still in danger."

"You're the real accomplice, aren't you?" Raid asked. "The one who threatened Rosa. Who was that other person your brother led us to?"

Ellis smiled. "We had to find someone who'd take the fall to keep the radar off me. Amazing what people will do when they're desperate for money." His smile turned to a scowl as he looked at her. "You went to the fucking cops, Hannah. Didn't I warn you that you'd pay if you did that?"

"How . . . how did you know I spoke to the police?" she asked.

"We pay our lawyer well. Very well. He was informed that a new victim had come forward. I guessed that it was you, but Steven likes facts before he acts. But our lawyer managed to discover your name. The FBI has so many leaks that it's laughable."

"Wait . . . you just said that *you* warned me?" She swallowed back bile, her hand going unconsciously to her throat. "That was you? Not Steven."

"Yep. Me. Not Jared. That's his name, not Steven. My brother doesn't like roughing up his marks. He prefers the wooing side. I come in when things get heavy. Like when we needed to warn you off from talking to the cops or when you needed a punish-ment for embarrassing him at that club."

He grinned evilly.

"That was . . . that was you?" She was going to vomit. How had she not known the difference between him and Steven?

"God, getting to touch you was so fucking satisfying. Unfor-tunately, when I had to warn you off talking, I couldn't take my time. I was on a time crunch."

"I'm going to be sick." She started to gag.

"Easy, baby." Raid took a step back, pushing at her to move away.

"Don't move!" Ellis yelled.

"You're not going to get away with this. Someone will figure out what happened," Raid warned.

Ellis scoffed. "No one knows about me. I'm completely off the radar. She didn't even know which brother was fucking her!"

Oh God.

Keep it together, Hannah.

You have this. You can deal.

"How did you find Hannah?" Raid asked. "How did you know we were here tonight?"

"Pfft. Like that's so difficult. She told Jared where she lived and what she did. I figured I'd start there. And I found a really helpful colleague of yours, Hannah. A tall, tanned blonde with big tits who was only all too eager to tell me that you were currently living on his ranch with him."

What? Oh God. There was only one person he could be talking about. Simone.

That. Bitch.

"I've been watching and waiting for my moment. And tonight, it's finally come. Once you're gone, so is the case against Jared. The FBI will have no legal reason to hold him."

He raised his gun at Raid, who tensed.

Oh shit. Oh hell.

"Why are you doing this?" she cried. "What did I ever do to you or your brother? Why do you target innocent women for money and then threaten them to get them to stay quiet?"

He just smiled. It was Steven's smile. She'd once thought that smile was handsome.

Now, it just looked like pure evil.

"Because we grew up with nothing. And when we were old enough to do something about it, we figured out a way. I'm a fucking genius on a computer and excellent at intimidation. Jared, he's good at getting people to believe him, love him, and do what he wants. We're amazing at what we do. And we've amassed a fucking fortune. And as soon as Jared gets out of prison, we're going to go somewhere warm and live it up."

Her breath shuddered in and out of her lungs, and she pressed her hand to Raid's back.

"I'm so sorry, Raid. I'm so sorry."

"Hush, baby," he told her gently. How was he not freaking out?

"Time to say goodbye!" Ellis cried.

"Do not shoot! Drop it!" someone yelled.

She cried out as Raid shoved her to the ground, covering her with his body. There was the sound of multiple gunshots, and she screamed again, certain that he was going to hit Raid. She wriggled, trying to get out from under him.

Noo!

He'd been shot, and she'd never even told him that she loved him!

She needed to help him.

"Calm, baby," Raid urged. "Wait for the all-clear."

She froze. What?

"Are you hit? Raid! Please, are you hit?" She gasped for

breath. Why couldn't she breathe? Tears flooded her eyes as she shook with tremors.

"I'm fine, baby. I promise. Everything is all right. Just calm down and wait for a moment. Then I'll look after you."

She didn't need him to look after her. She needed him to not be shot!

"All-clear," a voice called out. Wait. Was that Saxon? What was he doing here?

Then Raid suddenly moved. Standing, he leaned down and picked her up. Her legs could hardly hold her up and she nearly collapsed to the ground.

But she managed the strength to stay on her feet. Turning, she sobbed hysterically as she ran her hands over him. "Are you hurt? Did he shoot you? Where is the blood?"

"Baby, baby, I'm fine." He grasped hold of her hands. "I told you. He didn't hit me."

"I heard g-gunshots." How had he missed shooting Raid?

"That would be me."

She glanced over to see Saxon standing over the prone body of Ellis. "S-saxon? What? How?"

Saxon gave her an assessing look. "You're all right, Hannah."

She wasn't sure that she was. Raid wrapped an arm around her and she leaned into him.

"It's okay, baby. It's over. He's not going to hurt you."

"I was worried about you!"

"Or me," he soothed. "How did you know we needed help?" Raid directed this question to Saxon.

"My security guy caught sight of this asshole hanging around the parking lot. He called to tell me and that's when you stepped outside and he pulled a gun on you both. I quickly grabbed my gun, then I came out and snuck around behind him, then signaled to Raid."

"What? You knew he was there?" she asked Raid. She hadn't seen him at all.

There was the sound of sirens in the distance. Saxon or his security guy must have called the cops.

"Yep." Raid squeezed her with his arm. "Baby, stop shaking. You're all right."

All right? She wasn't all right. She was upset and, she was kind of mad!

"Why didn't you tell me? I was freaking out thinking he'd shot you!" She turned to him and pummelled her fists against his chest.

"Baby, calm down."

"Don't tell me to calm down! He could have killed you. Oh my God. I can't believe this! Steven, whose real name is Jared, had a twin brother who has been watching and waiting for his moment to kill me! And Simone, that bitch, told him where I was staying!"

She almost missed the way the air around her grew heavier. Glancing up, she saw the fury on Raid's face. Then she looked at Saxon as Jake pulled up with one of his deputies.

Saxon looked like pure ice. Holy. Heck.

"Yes, she did," Raid said. "It's time Simone learned what happens when you betray someone in Haven."

Shit. It was going to suck to be Simone. But she didn't have it in her to care.

All the fight left her as she leaned into Raid's chest, sobbing. He wrapped his arms around her.

"You know I don't like you crying."

"I'm going to cry and don't try to stop me," she told him.

He sighed long and loud. "I'll allow it this once."

Damn right, he would.

∾

RAID CARRIED her into the bunkhouse. She was so exhausted she didn't even think about protesting.

This had been one hell of a night. From going to the club, to getting a good girl spanking and having one heck of an orgasm, to being confronted by an armed man and thinking he'd shot Raid, then spending hours explaining everything to the cops.

Eli and Kellan had flown in the moment that Jake had called them. And once they'd arrived, she and Raid had gone through it all again.

Now it was hours past dawn and neither of them had slept.

"Come on, precious girl. Let's get you into bed."

"I'm so tired," she moaned. "But I don't know if I can sleep. My brain keeps going over everything. What will Jake do about Simone?" What she did was kind of a breach of privacy, but not really, since pretty much everyone in town knew she was staying the ranch.

The only thing was, no one else would have told Ellis anything.

"Jake is going to talk to Doc about getting rid of her."

"It might not be that easy." She couldn't imagine going back to work with Simone there.

"Jake's also going to spread the word about what she did. The whole town will get behind, making her time here in Haven very difficult. And I have a few ideas on how to make the rest of her life far less fun, too."

"Raid," she said warningly as he set her down on her feet by the side of the bed.

He placed his hands on her cheeks. "You're not going to talk me out of this, Hannah. She messed with you. She had no idea who that asshole was, but she told him where you were staying."

"Maybe it was innocent . . . he could have told her anything."

"So she should have called you to tell you that he was asking about you. She had access to your number. Or she could have told Doc or Jenna. Did she ever call and tell you that someone was asking about you?"

She swallowed heavily. "No."

"No, because she likely sensed something bad was going to happen. Or she just didn't care. Either way, that is not someone we want working in Haven. Or someone I want around you. Understand me?"

"Yes."

"Now, you're going to get into bed and not think about any of this."

She hoped she could do that. But she was certain the nightmares were coming.

Ellis had been taken to the hospital. Saxon had shot him in the shoulder, but he'd hit his head when he'd fallen, which is why he'd been unconscious.

Raid stripped her off and then put his T-shirt on her before he helped her climb into bed. Then he took his clothes off and got in next to her.

A shudder worked its way through her. The room was spinning because she was so tired. But all she could think about was how close she'd come to losing him.

"I thought you were going to die." She climbed on top of him, her breasts pressed to his chest. "I thought you had been shot and all . . . all I could think about was that I haven't told you that I love you."

"Baby–" he said softly.

But she wasn't going to let him interrupt. She had to get this out.

"I love you, Raid Malone. I want to spend my life with you. And I don't want to move back into my apartment."

"Baby–"

"I don't want to spend any nights apart from you. I don't care if it's too soon or whatever. I just want you. So, there it is. I love you."

"Baby, I don't want to spend any nights apart from you, either. And you definitely won't be moving back into your apartment. Because I love you as well."

"Really?"

"Really," he said firmly.

"I think I'm going to cry."

"No, you're not."

"I am."

He rolled them so she was on her back and he was lying on his side next to her. Then he cupped the side of her face. "You won't. I love you. And I want to spend the rest of my life with you."

"I like that."

"Yeah, baby. Me too."

EPILOGUE

"**D**o you like that, baby? Do you enjoy watching him make her come?"

They were standing in the shadows of Saxon's. Ahead of them, a sub was tied up with her arms above her head and her legs spread. She was lying on her back on a bench while her Dom held a violet wand between her legs, and they could all hear her cries of pleasure as he brought her to orgasm.

"What do you need, precious girl?" Raid stood behind her, with one arm securing her back to his front. He had her leg up on a stool that was to her side and slightly in front of her.

And with his other hand, he was toying with her clit.

Two months had passed since Ellis held them at gunpoint.

She hadn't thought she'd ever be able to or want to return to Saxon's. But with Raid's support, she'd decided that she needed to tackle this fear.

Or it would eat her alive.

"Please, please," she begged.

"Please, what?" he asked.

"Make me come."

She wasn't going to lie as they'd pulled into the parking lot of Saxon's, her stomach had been a mess. Every time she looked around the parking lot, she remembered what had happened two months ago when Ellis had tried to kill them.

He'd recovered from the gunshot, and thankfully Saxon hadn't gotten into any trouble, considering the whole thing had been caught on camera.

Now that they had some names, the Feds were able to do some more research into Jared and Ellis. Apparently, they'd grown up off-grid with a crazy uncle who'd kept them up in the mountains of Colorado in a ramshackle cabin.

It had obviously damaged them. Jared had come clean about a lot of things once his brother was arrested. Ellis, on the other hand, was under psychiatric observation. He seemed to take pleasure in hurting others.

She'd definitely experienced that.

She'd had her share of nightmares since that night. But most of them had been about Raid getting shot and dying rather than what Ellis had revealed.

Both men would be going away for a long time and that went a long way to helping her sleep easy at night.

That, and having Raid beside her at night.

Simone had basically been run out of town. No one would even speak to her. People would turn their backs when they saw her coming.

Simone had had a lot of trouble in Freestown, too. Hannah was pretty sure that Raid and his brothers had something to do with that. About two weeks ago, she'd moved across the country.

Good riddance.

After Simone quit, Hannah went back to work. Although Raid wasn't really that happy about her driving so much. She was thinking about finding another part-time job too. They needed to get out of the bunkhouse and into their own place.

And she knew Tanner wanted to move out of the main house.

"You want to come?" Raid asked as he toyed with her clit.

"Please, please!"

"I'm not sure you're desperate enough."

Her breathing increased. They were standing in a dark corner. Someone would need to get close to see them. But that was a possibility.

And that turned her on.

"Please, Raid. I need to come. Please."

"That's my good girl. Begging so nicely for me. Come for me. Now!"

He flicked her clit hard, and she soared. She bit down on her lip to stop herself from crying out.

Suddenly, she was turned and her lip was freed before his mouth dropped to hers. Then he was kissing her.

And oh Lord. That was sooo good.

He held her tight. And he kissed her for a long time. Until she drifted down from her high. Hannah pressed her face into his chest and tried to even out her breathing.

"You good, my precious girl?"

"I'm good," she whispered. "I'd be even better if you let me go down on you."

He drew her back and stared down at her, studying her. She looked back at him, letting him see her eagerness.

A smile tilted up the ends of his lips. "Go for it, baby."

She didn't need any more encouragement. Dropping to her knees, she quickly undid his jeans and yanked them down over his ass. His boxers followed the same path.

And then his dick was in her mouth.

And it was heaven.

Lord, it was more than heaven. It was everything she'd ever

wanted and more. She slid him into her mouth, sucking vigorously before pulling back.

Up and down.

She grasped the root of his dick, holding it firmly as she licked her way around the head.

So. Darn. Good.

"Christ, baby. I'm not far. Get ready."

She didn't need to get ready. This was something she was always prepared for. When he exploded, she drank him down, licked him clean, and then let him pull her up so he could kiss her hard.

Perfect.

~

"READY?" Raid asked.

They were standing by the door to the parking lot of Saxon's. It was time to leave. She wanted to go home and have her man fuck her brains out.

And she wanted to conquer this fear she had.

Nothing will happen.

Ellis and Jared are behind bars.

You're safe. Raid is safe.

He wrapped his hand around hers and squeezed. "Baby?"

"I'm ready."

For some reason, he drew out his phone and sent off a text. Maybe to Saxon, who had been watching her closely most of the night.

"My brave girl. Let's go." He opened the door and then led her outside.

Hannah sucked in a breath. She had this. She totally had this.

Raid had parked close to the entrance, so they didn't have far to go. She placed her free hand on her tummy.

She wasn't going to be sick.

To her surprise, several people started climbing out of cars around them. She stared in shock as she saw all of his brothers there. And most of their women. Then she saw Saxon and Aspen. Renard. Jake and Molly. Doc. Jenna and Curt. Carlie, Josie, Melody and Brye. Duncan. Even Kellan and Eli, who were apparently back to spend time with their brother.

"What are they all doing here?" she asked quietly.

"They're here to support you, baby. They knew we were coming tonight and that this part would be hard for you. I texted them thirty minutes ago to let them know we were close to leaving. And again, just now."

"They're all here . . . for me?" Tears filled her eyes. "That's so sweet."

He turned to her once they got to his truck and cupped her chin with his hand, tilting her head back.

"You're the sweet one, Hannah. And they just want to show you how much you mean to them."

Totally. Perfect.

"Do I really need to be blindfolded for this?" Hannah asked.

"Yep," Raid replied.

Hannah was sitting in the passenger seat of his truck. He'd tied a blindfold around her eyes before they'd even left the ranch.

Apparently, he had a surprise for her. It was two days after she'd gone back to Saxon's. The next day, she'd felt so much lighter. As though a weight had been lifted from her shoulders.

"Right, we're here. Stay where you are and I'll come around and get you."

Where were they?

She waited impatiently as he opened her door and undid her belt before lifting her down. Then he took her hand. "This way."

Hannah trusted him to guide her as he walked her forward.

"Stop here." He moved behind her and removed the blindfold.

Blinking, she stared in shock at the house in front of them. It was a wooden house with the main body painted a dark blue-gray. The wrap-around porch and trim were all an off-white.

"Why did you bring me here?" she asked.

The cul-de-sac the house sat on was perfect for raising children. Wide with big trees. All the houses were on large lots. At Halloween, they even had a street party.

But she didn't understand why they were there. Then she saw the for sale sign in the front yard. Only it had a sold sticker over it.

Shit. She hadn't even realized it was for sale. Not that she could afford it. The Feds were trying to get her money back for her, but that would take a while.

"It's been sold again? To who?" she asked, turning to Raid.

"To me."

She gaped at him, her mouth dropping open. "You?"

"Yep."

"You bought Grandma's house?"

"I bought our house, baby. For us to live in."

No, he didn't.

Then he dropped to one knee and pulled a ring box from his jeans pocket.

"What . . . what . . ." She couldn't make her mouth work properly.

"I love you, Hannah Megan McLeod. And I want to spend

the rest of my life taking care of you, spanking you, giving you back massages, and bossing you around. And I want to raise our family in *this* house. The house that was made for us. Marry. Me."

It wasn't exactly a question. But she didn't need it to be. Instead, she said the only thing she could.

"Yes! Yes, I'll marry you, Raid Malone."

He quickly slid the ring onto her finger and then, standing, he swept her into his arms and twirled her until she laughed.

It wasn't so long ago that she thought she'd never laugh again. And now . . . her life was so filled with joy that it was bursting out of her.

This . . . this was perfect.

Printed in Great Britain
by Amazon

44928973R10229